Acclaim for The Bowsinger

The "Bowsinger" grabbed me with the opening chapter and never let me go. This moving and inspirational adventure, filled with elves and dragons and an evil mage unfolds in a richly developed world of magic, climaxing in a battle between good and evil. Underneath the thrilling story, a melody of grace and divine majesty will give every reader comfort for their souls as Aralyn, the bowsinger, receives affirmation from the one true deity, "I am with you.".

—Bruce Hennigan, author of The Chronicles of Jonathon Steel

The Bowsinger invites the reader on a journey into a creative world. The themes of forgiveness and forsaking bitterness are encouraging and needed.

—Katherine Briggs, author of The Threshold Duology

The opening of the novel The Bowsinger pierced my imagination, and I couldn't put the book down. My curiosity held firm as I read about a young lady, Aralyn, and all the risks she faced as life threw battle after battle into her path. Elves, dragons, and kingdoms in realms among good and evil make this mysterious epic fantasy captivating. I highly recommend this novel for all who enjoy adventure and mystical enchantment.

—Wanda Bush, author of the novel Seat 4F

Eileen Copeland's debut fantasy has what fans of the genre love–elves, dragons, magic, and a Chosen One. Aralyn's search for belonging will strike a familiar note with readers, and her discovery of love and hope in the midst of darkness and tragedy proves that good triumphs in the end.

—Kim Vandel, award-winning author of Into the Fire

The Bowsinger

Cover design by: Getcovers.com

Printed in the United States of America

ISBN 979-8-9861595-2-2

ISBN 979-8-9861595-3-9 (ebook)

This is a work of fiction. Names, characters, places, and incidents are products of the author's imagination or are used fictitiously. Any similarity to actual people, organizations, and/or events is purely coincidental.

Dedication

To my husband Mike, for your loving support and encouragement in my writing journey

Chapter 1

The smell of burning flesh robbed Aralyn of breath. Flames rose from the village below. Voices she knew cried out. And then grew strangely quiet. Aralyn let go of the wild boar she had killed and sprinted toward home. Smoke filled her vision and lined her mouth with ash and grit.

The attackers had come again, Rogues from various regions who had no allegiance to king or country. More cries slammed against her ears. A spear landed near her feet, its tip buried in the dirt.

Aralyn struggled for air, her eyes watering. She kept moving, and the curtain of smoke thinned to a haze.

Done with their looting and killing in the village, the Rogues fanned out to prey upon the outlying farms—including her home if she didn't stop them. Her feet flew soundlessly, and she drew near their farm. She crouched in the dry grasses, knowing she could only stay hidden for so long.

A warrior, naked from the waist up, pinned Mother down. A second man stood over them—laughing.

No.

A flash of crimson crossed her vision. She needed to move before the anger chased away all logic. Her mother was under attack. And where was her sister, Terrwynn?

Aralyn rose out of the grasses, but neither man saw her. Her vision narrowed to the scene before her. The surrounding cries faded, and she heard none of the screams or hisses of fire. Time slowed. Her hand moved without her thoughts attached and nocked the broad-blade arrow. She pulled the tension to its full draw and sang to her bow. The arrow found the laughing man's unprotected throat, and her bow answered, thrumming in her hand. The sound affirmed her kill. Before he fell, Aralyn launched another arrow. It landed in the ribs of her mother's attacker.

Mother grunted as she pushed her attacker's body off her. Aralyn needed to go to her, but there must be more of them.

She ducked down again as another Rogue strode out of her house, Terrwynn thrown over his shoulder. He tossed her to the ground and took a bite of a potato he must have stolen from their pantry. Terrwynn rose to her feet, eyeing the huge man before her.

What was she doing? Run, Terrwynn! But her sister's gaze seemed to freeze the man in place.

Aralyn stood. The Rogue glanced up in time to see Aralyn aim her bow, and the arrow protruded from his eye. Terrwynn watched as Aralyn ran to him. He reached for the arrow as blood flowed from the wound and gurgled in his throat. He uttered his last words. "A girl."

"Yes," Aralyn replied in his language. "A girl." She watched as his look of surprise and horror passed with him into death.

Aralyn jogged to where her mother lay exhausted. Blood from the Rogue's wounds soaked her clothing. Bruises and cuts marked her face, thighs, and exposed belly. She had fought hard.

Terrwynn watched them, her head held high, and remained where she was.

"Go inside." Aralyn waved toward the door.

Terrwynn lifted her head higher but then did as Aralyn said.

Something was odd about the look on Terrwynn's face. Her eyes held a confident, superior air. Not frightened like the weak and trembling girl she had been for over a year.

The bodies nearby drew Aralyn's attention as she prepared to take her mother inside. A morbid gaze on their tattoos confirmed these two Rogues were from the region of Gehallia. Mother groaned, and Aralyn spun back to her. She crouched to lift her, but footsteps approached, and she readied her bow.

"Aralyn." The man's voice was gentle, but she didn't recognize the figure backlit by the sun.

When he moved closer, she let the tension out of her bow and cried out with relief. Re'ah. The olive-skinned man with silver-streaked hair was a teacher of Elyon and a healer who frequented their village. His gaze met hers, and he said, "It is all right. They are gone. The Rangers and some Dwarves are chasing them down."

Aralyn pointed to her mother, and Re'ah was by her side in a moment. He knelt beside her. "Deirdre, it is me. Re'ah. No need to be afraid." And he wrapped his cloak around her.

Aralyn should have thought of that. *I could have given up my cloak for my mother's modesty.*

Re'ah swung her mother up in his arms and took her inside the one-room house they called home.

Aralyn wanted to follow him, to make sure Mother was all right. But Re'ah was here to care for her, and Aralyn wanted the bodies gone. How long would it take for them to stink with the warmth and humidity? Probably less than a day.

The creak of wheels caused Aralyn to look up. Men not fifty yards away struggled with oxcarts piled high. With what, she wasn't sure. The stench hit her first—blood and death mingled. As they neared, she jogged to the people she recognized as neighbors. Bodies of men and women in warrior garb lay strewn over the carts, most Gehallion, but Montravian Rogues had joined them as evidenced by their tartan battle skirts.

"Are your families all right?" Aralyn asked.

Only two of the dozen or so men nodded. Most bowed their heads.

"My wife …" said one with a gash on his lips and a swollen and bruised face. "M-my sons … are …" He stared into the distance, a look of shock in his wide eyes. "My daughter, May. They took her." He shuddered. "What will they do with her?"

It was Sanders. Aralyn had at one time been friends with May.

She, Mother, and Terrwynn had been fortunate.

"But we did some killin' too." One farmer held a crude plowshare in muscular arms, and a satisfied grin crossed his face.

"Yes, we did." A bitter laugh came from a wiry, short man with narrow eyes. He had a prominent lump on his head.

"Will you help me?" She knew they would.

"Of course, Aralyn," a middle-aged man with a graying beard said. "What do you need?"

"Bodies …" She choked on her words. "We could use your help with the bodies of Rogues."

Her hands shook. She hoped they didn't notice.

"Your family?" Sanders asked.

"Fine. They're fine." She spoke a half-truth, but at least they were alive. Mother injured, yet alive.

Two men took a cart to where Aralyn directed.

"Who killed these?" One man asked.

"I did." Aralyn's voice wavered.

The two men exchanged glances, and one raised an eyebrow.

The shock wore off as she looked over the bodies once more, and she knelt on the ground, her stomach in full rebellion. She heaved and felt her gut empty. The men ignored her as they pulled bodies toward the carts. Re'ah was by her side. He knelt with her and murmured words she didn't understand, but somehow, they comforted her.

She wiped her mouth and stood. "I'm all right, Re'ah. Go tend to Mother and Terrwynn."

"If you are sure."

"Yes." Aralyn watched him walk away and secretly wished he had stayed with her.

The men tossed a body into the cart, piling it on top of another. The slap of flesh on flesh ... more odors of blood and human waste filled her nostrils and wound their way to her gut.

Aralyn noticed a young man standing by himself, staring at a body. She approached him. "What is it, Brannon?"

"This one—I've met him in battle. He sliced off my finger and killed my sister. This is Bek."

The name meant nothing.

"While I am glad he's dead, if you killed him,"—his face paled—"you have made enemies."

She moved closer. In this dead man's face, she saw something—an eerie look into the future. Powerful enemies. Swords and spears wielded with precision, the whispers of dark magic. And coming after her, as well as Terrwynn and Mother. The vision broke when two men picked up the body.

As though a hand gripped her throat, Aralyn choked. Bek. She had stared into the face of an enemy who, even though he was dead, still posed a threat. Just as Brannon said.

***

Aralyn's eyes adjusted to the dim light of their home. Hand-drawn portraits and a desk were on the opposite wall. She and Terrwynns's simple bed—a feather-filled mattress—was rolled up in a corner. Wattle and daube filled the cracks between timbers. The doors on front and back allowed a breeze through, although not enough to remove the lingering stench of battle. A small wooden table with three chairs sat in the center where they normally ate. Re'ah sat in one of the chairs, poring over some ancient writings.

"Have you seen Terrwynn?" She asked him.

"She went outside. I assumed to take care of her personal business. I thought I would wait to make sure she returned safely. Lot'fe is coming soon."

Aralyn's mouth turned up at this last information. Lot'fe was the village herbalist, a woman from the country of Drestani. She and her husband had made their home in Sathria long ago.

"Have you checked on Mother?"

"I helped clean off some of the blood, but thought I should do no more. She is not bleeding—it is blood from her attacker."

Aralyn went to her mother and, through the discolored, torn curtain surrounding her bed, Mother slept still wrapped in Re'ah's cloak. "Should I try to wake her?"

"No, let her sleep."

"You'll stay until Terrwynn returns?"

He didn't chide her for asking a question he had already answered, but said, "Yes. I will stay with you."

He knew. He knew she didn't want to be alone with no one but her sleeping mother. Aralyn paced in the limited space of the house. Past a desk with its hidden compartments. Shelves next to and above the desk contained food—what Mother called their pantry. In a cubby hole, was a rolled-up document. Curious, Aralyn reached for it but pulled back. Whatever it was could wait. "I'm going to find Terrwynn."

Re'ah nodded. "Be careful, child."

Aralyn searched everywhere she thought Terrwynn might be, calling for her.

"Non-dragons seldom think to look up." Words from a dragon whom she had known years ago in the land of the Elves.

Aralyn did as the dragon advised and gazed into tangled limbs and a hazy sky.

There.

Near the top of a tree, her sister balanced on a thick branch where few non-dragons would ever think to look. Aralyn watched transfixed. Terrwynn lifted one foot and spread her arms. She leaped to another tree with barely a sound. What was she doing? She needed to stop this nonsense and come inside.

"Terrwynn!" Aralyn called again. "Come down."

Her sister's gaze fell on Aralyn. She swung down, easily moving from branch to branch.

Aralyn couldn't believe it. "What were you doing?" Why was she even asking? Terrwynn would give her no answer. She motioned for the younger girl to go inside. Her heart still pounded from the danger she had faced today, not convinced the enemies were entirely gone.

Terrwynn drew herself up and lifted her chin, giving Aralyn a look a queen would give a peasant. But in the next moment, her shoulders drooped, and she strode past Aralyn into the house.

Aralyn followed and entered their home. A memory of a majestic dwelling with paintings, tapestries, and running water struck her, and her Elven blood cried out for her home in Eyndor. But years ago, because of her mother's powerful talent, the Council had forced them out. Instead of seeing Mother's abilities as an advantage for the land, they saw it as a threat. No one could be stronger than the chief male Council member. Dierdre was female, a strike against her, and she could control both air and fire, a dangerous combination in their minds. What if she used her abilities to control all of Eyndor?

So they subjected her to a horrendous ritual called a *tra'nmeh* in which they removed her talent or magic. They told Aralyn to watch and learn, a *nanio,* a little one, barely past her first decade.

Mother knelt in the dirt before grim faces, arms twisting in agony. Aralyn still heard her Mother's screams. She grew numb as she remembered.

A motion from the front door drew Aralyn out of the memory.

Lot'fe had arrived. The village herbalist, a tall woman with a long, narrow face and a turban upon her head, sat on the bed with her now awake mother.

Terrwynn sank onto a huge square pillow, and Re'ah sang to her—a song passed down from the ancients. Terrwynn leaned against him, moving her lips in an attempt to join in. She spread her skirts, and Cat, their one-time mouser-turned-spoiled pet, crawled into her lap.

Mother cried out, and Aralyn jumped. "I need a bath." Her fists beat on the bed. Lot'fe tried to quiet her, speaking in her strong Destrani accent.

"I'll take care of it," Aralyn said.

A lull in Re'ah's melody, and Aralyn told Terrwynn, "I'm going to get something for Mother to bathe in."

Terrwynn only gave Aralyn a brief nod.

Aralyn couldn't blame Terrwynn for only acknowledging her on occasion. After all, Aralyn had failed Terrwynn before. Failed her entire family. And now Terrwynn could barely speak.

But it was in the past.

No, it wasn't. The effects were still there, cruel webs tightening their grip every day.

Aralyn didn't know how she would manage her task, but she would make sure Mother got a bath. She built a fire outside. Easy enough. After she had the blaze going, she ran to the stables where they had once kept horses, found the largest barrel she could manage, and headed to the house, struggling to see around the hefty burden. The wood splintered as the barrel slipped, and Aralyn knew her hands would be bleeding. Dragging it proved to be an even slower process.

Aralyn glimpsed Re'ah standing outside with his head bowed, perhaps praying to Elyon. At times Re'ah's mind touched Aralyn's in a whisper to let her know he was coming. She'd not sensed his approach today, her attention focused on fighting off the Rogues.

Re'ah must have seen her struggling, and he ran to help.

By the time she returned to the fire, it hissed against the logs, sap popping and giving off a pungent aroma. She pulled the barrel inside with Re'ah's help. Mother wanted her privacy, no doubt. Aralyn swallowed hard, trying not to think about what her mother had gone through. She grabbed a pot, intending to run back outside when Re'ah spoke.

"Slow down, child. Let me see about these cuts," He took the pot from her and set it down. Took both her hands in his.

Aralyn tapped her foot, glancing at the doorway while he pulled out splinters, placed cloth on her hands. As soon as he finished, she snatched up the pot and jogged outside. She dipped it into the barrel of rainwater they collected from the roof and placed it over the fire.

Through the open back door, she heard Lot'fe murmuring to her mother and her mother's retort.

"It doesn't matter. He almost ... and look ... look at this." She pointed to the bruises and cuts. "He did more than touch me. He beat me. Cut me with his already bloody knife. I need a bath."

"Aralyn is getting it, Deirdre." Lot'fe assured her.

Aralyn, disturbed by Mother's words, ignored the salty perspiration dripping down her cheeks and neck.

Re'ah placed a hand on Aralyn's back. "I have to leave, but I will be in the village if you need me."

Aralyn attempted a genuine smile.

Re'ah's hand dropped, concern written on his face. But he left. He had to.

Mother insisted the water for her bath be hot, so hot that Aralyn was afraid it would scald her. But she warmed pot after pot of it.

She and Lot'fe helped Mother into the makeshift tub, and Aralyn noticed the dirt, clay, and blood still clinging to her.

"More. I need more," was all Mother would say as she scrubbed.

Aralyn and Lot'fe helped Deirdre slip into a gown and back into her bed.

Aralyn backed away to allow Lot'fe to work—administering more herbs and rubbing oils on Mother's feet.

Terrwynn slept, lying half on, half off the bed. How could her sister sleep after what had happened? Perhaps Re'ah's songs did this. Aralyn squatted and brushed back a strand of silver-streaked hair from Terrwynn's face—so different from her own dark hair. Terrwynn's chin quivered, long dark eyelashes fluttering. Her skin was such a lovely shade of brown, again so different from Aralyn's, whose complexion remained pale no matter how much time she spent in the sun. Probably due to their different fathers. Born to Elven parents, Aralyn was aware of the differences between her and the people of the village and surrounding farms. Daniel, her stepfather and Terrwynn's father, was human, but he was gone now because of Aralyn's neglect, her failure.

Just as her father was. And Aralyn could not remember how. She had tried asking Mother, but only received a vague answer. "He was killed," or "He was careless."

A few moments of silence passed, and Lot'fe motioned Aralyn to come outside with her.

"Aralyn, the man who attacked your mother tried to force himself on her, but I could tell he hadn't. However, your mother is suffering considerable distress. He beat her into submission, but he died before he..."

I know, Aralyn wanted to say. *I killed him.*

"It will take time for her to heal."

Mother still had nightmares from Aralyn's foolish actions a year ago. And fresh injuries, fresh emotional upheaval would only compound that. But at least they were alive.

Lot'fe's eyes were gentle. "I will be back if you need me."

Aralyn nodded and met the herbalist's concerned gaze. She stepped inside, leaving the door open.

Aralyn wanted to say something to comfort Mother but wasn't sure what. She could at least sit by her. As she approached the bed, Mother barely moved. Her eyes were closed. Aralyn sat on the edge of the bed and watched Mother's face.

"I wish he were here." Mother's eyes opened, and her gaze was upon Aralyn. "But you know that, don't you?"

Aralyn blinked.

Her stepfather. Mother seldom grieved over him except with bitterness. The words stung.

I wish he were here. Words Aralyn said to herself every day. Even though she'd saved Mother's and Terrwynn's lives just moments ago, it wasn't enough. And Aralyn wondered if it ever would be.

Chapter 2

The bodies of Rogues lay in the flames all night, and the odor of cooked flesh haunted Aralyn's dreams. The smell faded by the time she woke, but the memories didn't.

Mother, who was already up, paced and swept the same spot on the dirt floor over and over again. "I need my sewing things," she demanded.

"Of course, Mother. Have you eaten?"

Mother only glared. "I'll eat when I'm ready."

Mother surely remembered where her needle, thread, and scissors were and didn't expect her daughter to fetch them for her, but she did so anyway.

Aralyn picked up her bow, even though it was too late to hunt. She'd done enough killing for a while, but leaving the bow in a corner didn't feel right. She slung her quiver over her shoulder.

Aralyn trudged toward Enemy Tears Hill, where her neighbors had gone to burn the Rogues' bodies. She intended to see that the bodies were in ashes, but the smell of them grew as she approached. Two bowshots away, she sat on the sun-scorched grass. Humidity hung thick in the dawn breeze, and sweat clung to Aralyn's brow. "I hate those men." She sighed, laid her bow down, and her head fell to her knees.

Re'ah had returned, and his shadow fell over her. "Yes. I understand."

"I know better than to hate, but right now I hate them." The truth of the words had a savory taste. She lifted her head, attention on the smoke persisting in the distance.

Re'ah sat, and his gaze followed hers. "You are honest, and I value that in you."

He did?

"They"—he jerked his chin toward the distant hill—"are not easy to love."

Aralyn sighed. "I need to run to the village after I dig up my weaver plants."

"Be careful," Re'ah warned her again. "Some areas escaped the attack, but there is still a lot of damage. Entire structures have fallen, and there may be a few fires smoldering that will be difficult to see until you are upon them."

"I will—I will be careful."

"And Aralyn, try to forgive."

His eyes gentle, Aralyn read the reproving message. Forgiveness would be difficult, but best for her. Aralyn still did not understand that. Re'ah taught that forgiving freed the one who clung to anger and bitterness. Well, hating them certainly served no purpose. Or did it? Perhaps the determined loathing would help ready her for their next attack.

Aralyn's shoulders sagged. She would need to think on his words. "Perhaps I can one day." She stood in thought. "I suppose...it does no good to hate the dead."

"No, it does not." His voice was tender, but just as resolute as her anger.

They stood, and Re'ah surveyed the distant hills. He nodded in their direction, and Aralyn glanced over her shoulder, her eyes wandering over their outline.

"What, Re'ah?"

"You will find adventure one day." He paused. "Out there. A much better adventure than any you have had."

What was he saying?

Re'ah hugged her, almost squeezing the air out of her lungs. She couldn't help but laugh. Aralyn bid him goodbye and trekked toward the forest.

One hundred yards in, the ground grew steeper, and Aralyn had to climb hand over hand. Her patch of valuable plants, her weavers, peeked through the palm fronds where she kept them hidden. Fortunately, they thrived in the sparse light.

Aralyn dug up at least two dozen before she lost count, cut dead leaves back, and pulled stubborn weeds. By the time she was done, the morning sun indicated it was almost noon, and she galloped down the slope toward the village. The River Hochness, which was no longer much of a river, lay before her. Most people in the village longed for the days when the ships came up the Hochness to deliver, sell, and trade goods in Sathria. Aralyn had heard them bemoaning their isolation and poor economy. But she was secretly glad. The river mocked her memories even in its depleted state. She jogged past rundown docks where fishermen's lines dipped into the water. The smell of fresh fish, combined with fish too long dead, wafted through the air.

Ahead of her, labor bosses shouted.

"Get your backs into it."

"Tote them bricks over here." An exasperated sputter. "No! Here! Not over there."

"*Idita.*" A demeaning name for common laborers.

They placed stone upon stone, building a sturdy wall to replace the mounds of dirt that had never been much protection. A wagon full of metal spikes sat in the middle of the activity.

Off farther in a clear, flat field, men practiced with swords, knives, and bows and arrows. Aralyn watched them line up, some in the uniforms of soldiers and guards, others in everyday work clothes. The guards, as well as civilians, became more diligent after a Rogue attack.

As she approached the practice grounds, she saw young boys who could not have been older than Terrwynn and others even younger. These tended to wounds that men and older boys accumulated while practicing with swords and knives. Aralyn knew from watching them practice that the more seasoned men wasted no time with the inexperienced, letting them know firsthand what would happen if they let their guard down.

Daniel, her stepfather, should be here. He could train the men with a blade and bow and arrow. Aralyn bit her lip and rubbed her arms. A chill ran through her. *Oh, Daniel ... I am so sorry.*

As Aralyn drew closer to Sathria, the nightmare began anew. Bodies still lay in the street as men worked to uncover and clear them from the smoking remains of homes.

As usual, she heard the cries of children. Several little ones followed her and tried to dig into her pockets, hoping she had something for them. They always did this. She shoved their hands away and picked up her pace, following the narrow, cobbled streets to narrower dirt roads. A half-starved stray dog, the same one that had been here for years, approached her, wagging his tail. She squatted, and he sniffed her hand. "Well, my friend, it looks like you survived."

He scratched his ears, his neck, and his belly with his back leg. Probably fleas. Poor thing. She wished she at least had a bone to give him.

Another street over, children played or worked with their mothers by their doorstep. Some had little in the way of clothing. Aralyn's family at least had clothes to cover them. Not everyone could afford the luxury of modesty.

As she jogged past, the air grew clearer, and she came to a place clear of the evidence of the Rogue attacks. Lotfe's business still stood. She found the open door to the herbalist's shop and stepped onto a wooden floor.

Instead of Lot'fe, her husband appeared from the back. Aralyn smiled as the man looked her over. Something about Siaon disturbed Aralyn. His cool gray eyes didn't smile when he did, and his turban seemed to hide something, and not just part of his dress.

She swallowed and spoke first. "Hello, Siaon."

"Aralyn, it is good to see you as always." His oily voice slid over her.

"Is Lot'fe here?"

"Yes, of course." He retreated to the back room, calling his wife's name.

When Lot'fe appeared, Siaon was not with her. Aralyn would shed no tears over that. Lot'fe came to the counter, where she sold herbs and made mixtures of oils and plants designed to heal. "How are you, little one?"

Even though Aralyn was taller than the herbalist, Lot'fe insisted on calling her "little one." Usually, that made Aralyn smile. But not today.

"Very well, Lot'fe." Her throat tightened even as she said it. Aralyn reached into her pockets and pulled out the plants she had dug up.

"Ah, you have weavers." A smile, like a rare gem in sunlight, lit Lot'fe's narrow, brown face. "And how is your mother doing?"

Along with her throat, Aralyn's belly tightened. "She was up today. Asked for her sewing things. But she still won't eat."

Lot'fe nodded. "It is difficult for her." The compassion in her eyes spoke more clearly than her words. "And how are you?"

Hadn't she just asked that? "I'm well."

Lot'fe's gaze bored into Aralyn. "You are not well, little one."

Why did she do this? Tears threatened, and Lot'fe came around the counter.

"You know it is all right to cry."

Not for her. Maybe for others, but not her. Aralyn wiped at her face, felt a loose thread of her sleeve rake across an eye. "I don't wish to speak of this. It's over."

"I see." Lot'fe took Aralyn's hand in her calloused one. Aralyn let it remain, but she didn't need Lot'fe's comfort. She needed to sell the weavers and return to her family. The lump was choking her now, and she couldn't form words to object.

"You, little one, often think what you see in others is all there is to know." *What?*

"But," Lot'fe continued, "we all have a history, and sometimes we understand better than you might think. Sometimes we—I have experienced some of the things you did yesterday."

Perhaps Lot'fe had once killed men, too. But she couldn't imagine the kindhearted herbalist as a warrior.

"Lot'fe, I didn't ..." Aralyn's nose was running freely.

"I'll pay you for those weavers. Give me a moment." She went to the back of her store.

Aralyn paced, her bow bouncing in the loose circle she formed with her thumb and forefinger. Through the herbalist's open door, she saw Re'ah on the street, kneeling before a crying child. He gathered the child in his arms. Perhaps she could follow his example and be kinder to the children, but they deliberately annoyed her.

Arguing erupted from the back, and Aralyn swung around, straining to hear. It was Lot'fe and Siaon, but both were speaking in Drestani, their native tongue. The voices grew quieter, and Lot'fe appeared, a locked box in hand, chin lifted. Her expression revealed nothing. Siaon's was right behind her, a scowl upon his face. He opened his mouth, but no sound came out. Shaking his head, he glanced from Lot'fe to Aralyn and went back to whatever he was doing.

Lot'fe unlocked the box, took coins from it, and counted out her payment. "Here you are." She lifted the bag and handed it to Aralyn.

The coin bag felt heavier than usual. "Thank you." Something was amiss. Lot'fe knew the value of herbs and plants, and Aralyn never had to haggle with her. But she must have given Aralyn extra money today. "This is too much, Lot'fe."

Lot'fe shook her head. "I always pay a fair price, don't I?" She didn't wait for an answer. "Be sure to bring me more soon, and perhaps some seeds? Your plants are of the best quality. I wish I knew your secret."

"Yes, I'll be glad to bring more, and if I ever leave Sathria, perhaps I'll tell you."

"Then I hope I wait a long time for that secret." Lot'fe bowed her head in farewell.

Aralyn bit her lip. Her dreams of doing that very thing—leaving Sathria—had been snatched away for good. She would never be able to leave Mother and Terrwynn now. Even though Re'ah had hinted at such.

Outside, the stomp of horse hooves in the dirt caught her attention. She moved to the door, and her eyes widened. A long line of horses paraded down the street carrying riders dressed in colors ranging from forest green to powdery pink. Their cloaks shimmered in the early afternoon sun, as did their dark satin hair—much like her own—although some heads were covered by warm brown, fiery red, or bright golden hair. A few had hair streaked with gray. Many carried weapons of knives and swords, and yes, there were archers among them. Their longbows lay across their laps. She would love to get a closer look at them.

Pack animals and wagons carried waterskins, food, and other staples. By their pale complexions, silver-flecked eyes, and long hair of various colors, she knew these were Elves from Eyndor or perhaps Woods Elves. Where were they going? And why were they traveling through Sathria?

"They are fascinating." Lot'fe stood next to her.

Aralyn didn't take her gaze from the Elves. "Oh. Yes, they are." Did Lot'fe know that Aralyn belonged with them?

As they disappeared up the street, Aralyn swung back to Lot'fe. She bowed her head to the herbalist. "I must go. I'm curious as to why they are here."

"Yes, I would like to know too." Lot'fe patted Aralyn's arm. "Go, little one."

At Lot'fe's dismissal, she jogged to catch up and noticed the very air felt different.

Home.

Her true home. Eyndor. It was not a forgotten place but something she needed as much as food. A male Elf, who had to be close to seven feet tall, spoke with the magistrate. There was an exchange of some kind. Money perhaps. The magistrate was coming out ahead on this one, Aralyn was sure.

An Elf glanced her way from atop his horse. He spoke to his female companion and nodded toward Aralyn. The female turned, and a smile spread across her face. She whispered something to the male and chattered until he held up his hand. The Elves came to a stop and dismounted. A few of them pulled items from their saddlebags, and others unloaded pack horses.

Voices prattled. Feet shuffled. Curious children and adults eyed the newcomers.

Food! They had food and water! Aralyn blinked as the Elves somehow kept the villagers from mobbing them. Aralyn had not even thought about sharing what little they had. It had never occurred to her. But the Elves had come. Hungry adults, but especially children, grabbed the food and waterskins offered.

She watched as a few male Elves made their way up the street into the more damaged parts of the village.

The children gathered on the steps to Lot'fe's and other businesses, wolfed down dried meat, and drank huge gulps of water. One pair of Elves had set up a tent and table to the side and were selling their goods. How odd. It seemed they were exploiting the situation. They took silver coins from some of the more prosperous merchants in exchange for various lengths of fine cloth. Some would always have an abundance, Aralyn supposed, while others starved before them.

Aralyn approached the male and female Elf who had acted so peculiarly when they saw her. The woman's face could barely contain its grin as Aralyn approached, and she realized they had a small table set up as well.

"You came here to sell jewelry?" Aralyn eyed them with less enthusiasm now.

The woman brushed back hair the color of almonds. Her eyes danced. "We know most cannot afford these." She waved a hand over the jewels. "But we manage to sell a few. And we have some that are not very expensive. My name is Elnala. May I ask yours?"

Aralyn met her gaze, not sure she wanted to give this stranger any information about herself, but decided to trust them with her name. "I'm Aralyn. Do you mind if I look?"

Elnala glanced at the man with her. She had probably already decided Aralyn was one of those too poor to afford their merchandise.

"Not at all," the man, who had a decidedly prominent chin and nose, said. "I am Orandon." He bowed his head to her, and long, blond hair swung forward.

After a moment, Aralyn saw a small trinket that drew her. It was impractical, but ... "How much is this?"

"Three coppers."

So they had a few things she might be able to buy. The money in the bag was not hers, but she had done her part to earn it. Aralyn hesitated, and Elnala frowned. "We know of the Rogues' attack. We hoped we could be here in time ..." Tears sprang to the woman's eyes. "Don't buy unless you can spare the coin."

Aralyn opened her coin purse. There had to be at least fifty coppers. Yes, Lot'fe had been generous, and Mother wouldn't know how many weavers she had sold, but ... no, it wasn't right. Her wants, the family's needs ... she always knew which came first. She lifted her chin. "You are right. I cannot spare even that much."

"Well, perhaps ..." The man cleared his throat and whispered something to his companion.

Elnala's eager grin spread across her face. She pulled out a wooden box much like a miniature bureau and plucked a shiny object from it. "Give me your hand, Aralyn."

Aralyn wasn't that naive. "No." She shook her head. "Let me see what you have first."

Elnala's gaze remained steady. "I need you to trust me."

And for some reason, Aralyn knew she could trust Elnala. She held her hand out with eyes shut, opening them when she felt a smooth, cool object in her palm.

"It's beautiful." A gem the size of a small throwing stone lay before her, begging Aralyn to hold it close. It reminded her of the dragon she once knew—crimson, many-faceted, shimmering in the light. The one who had told her to look up from time to time. Drehensil. That was his name, and yet it was more than a name. It seemed like a power known only to a few. Her fingers wrapped around the gem.

Recollections of his dry humor and wise words flooded her, and she longed for his presence. Where was he now? She could not remember. Had he even told her or anyone where he had gone? So many memories played around the fringes of her mind. Teasing her. But this she knew; Drehensil was gone now, unlikely to return to her. She grasped the gem once more.

An unwelcome thought, and with it a chill, a vision of the night sky. Long ago it had swallowed Drehensil as he carried something...or someone precious from her. What exactly was she remembering? And why wasn't it clearer? But without Drehensil, she knew something dear to her was missing.

"Aralyn." Orandon roused her from the memories. "Will you take this?"

"No, I cannot. I have no money." She placed the gem on the table.

"We won't take money for it." And Elnala placed it back in Aralyn's palm, then curled her fingers around it. She exchanged a look with Orandon.

Aralyn held it for a moment, feeling the warmth that now emanated from it. Pride demanded she not take this without paying. "I have to give you something."

Elnala clasped Aralyn's closed hand. "It will be our secret. And as for payment, if you ever come to Eyndor, you will have to come sing for me."

The longing grew as her memories and dreams wound around each other in an intimate dance.

"And for my wife and me as well." The man smiled now.

Aralyn frowned. "You're not husband and wife?"

The man chuckled, and Elnala burst into musical laughter. "Oh, my no! Orandon is my father. But you can still come sing for us? Soon?"

Soon? How could she leave for Elven lands anytime soon? But the words pulled at her heart. They needed her. "But why? Why do you appear in Sathria now and ask me for this favor?" Shadows settled on Orandon's face, and he seemed to age ten years. "We need your singing in Eyndor, although many don't realize what is at stake. The land itself longs for it."

Elnala wore the same solemn expression.

"I will remember your words, although I have no idea when I will arrive in Elven lands. But I have every intention of coming." Aralyn said the words as if her journey to their borders had already begun.

"By the way," Orandon said, "Be sure to hold the gem close. It will help you find something dear to you, but use it only in the ways it reveals."

What was he saying? Just as she was about to question him, someone called her name, and she cringed.

"Aralyn?" It was the magistrate—the new magistrate. He often confronted the young women in his jurisdiction and asked questions that were none of his concern. Aralyn had not spoken with him yet, so maybe she could ignore him and pretend she didn't know anyone named Aralyn.

But he moved closer. "Aralyn? Correct?" Magistrate Affort's smile displayed wide gaps between his teeth. His complexion was a pasty white, his head balding, and he wore clothes of pale yellow. Shorter than Aralyn, the man strained his neck to meet Aralyn eye to eye.

Aralyn's shoulders sagged. "Yes, sir."

He glanced at the Elves. "Come. Walk with me." He had to look up to meet her gaze.

She trudged along beside him, feeling trapped. When he stopped, he asked, "Are you still living at home with your mother?" Affort's voice reminded her of grit-filled hinges.

"Yes." Aralyn looked past him, longing to escape.

"Are you not of age?" His breath smelled like he'd had rotten eggs and pig's tongue for breakfast. "I would think you were." That lingering appraisal again.

"I am." She tried to avoid his gaze.

He frowned and pulled out a roll of papers. "Let me see. No one has claimed you yet?"

Aralyn's heart pounded. No, they hadn't, and they'd better not. She'd seen too many girls dragged off to wed an old man and then die in childbirth with no one to mourn for them because the husband was too busy celebrating his new son or infuriated because he had a daughter to raise alone.

The magistrate glanced up. "Well, have they? I see no record ... oh, wait ... Eldersmith. Uh, let's see." He frowned. "Hmph." The magistrate muttered a few words and shuffled his papers again. "Ah."

What did he mean by "ah?"

"Looks like everything is in order." Affort patted the edges of his papers, gave her a nod, and excused himself.

Strange. Glad to get away so easily, Aralyn let out a sigh of relief. But too soon. He stopped, spoke to her over his shoulder. "You need to think about your future, Aralyn." Affort pivoted so he was facing her again, a glint in his eye that Aralyn didn't like. But if she showed disrespect or said anything in rebuttal, it would mean time in the stocks or worse. "A healthy man with a good trade would likely give you healthy children. I don't see why that's so hard for you. Your mother seems to think...Well, I don't understand either of you." His lips puckered as though he'd tasted something sour. "Just consider my words."

Aralyn bit her tongue as he tucked his papers away, saluted her, and headed down the street. What made him think every woman wanted a man or children? Just the thought of a marriage to someone she barely knew, let alone pregnant and bearing a child, was not something she wanted to consider. Not now. And why would the magistrate address her about such so soon after the attack? He should be more concerned about the devastation in their village.

Wait. Affort had said a name. "Eldersmith."

Aralyn closed her eyes. No. Surely, he didn't want her. Eldersmith owned the butcher shop. Technically, he was above her station as a businessman with a respectable trade. She pictured him with his large face, small eyes, and beefy hands. And the thought of those hands on her churned her stomach. He had claimed her? Perhaps he had a decent position, but he was also cruel. She'd seen him use fists on a child who had stumbled in front of him. The time he had thrown a knife at a stray cat, he had nicked its back leg. It had taken Aralyn a long time to stop the bleeding.

Aralyn noted the angle of the shadows, surprised at how much of the day was gone. She had only two other purchases to make. She jogged to the next shop, made her purchases, and continued to the road out of the village. Ahead of her, the slurred singing of men reached her ears. Once again, the thought of the recent attacks made her wonder how they could drink themselves silly while people gathered their dead from the streets. She was about to turn away when a pull on her wrist forced her to stop. Eldersmith swung her around to face him.

"Hold up there, girl."

Aralyn narrowed her eyes. "Let go."

"Of course, my beloved." He dropped her arm and bowed.

"I am not your beloved. I am not your anything." Aralyn caught a whiff of alcohol and sour sweat.

"Ho, now! You're not?" He scratched his chin, causing his beard to wriggle like a rat caught in the mud.

Aralyn barely managed to swallow a laugh.

"Well, you will be soon. Haven't you heard?"

Aralyn fisted her hands. "Leave me be. I won't be your woman or wife or mate or—"

"Oh yes, you will. I know what your mam's been doing, and it won't work." His mouth was on her ear as he murmured, "I will have you."

Aralyn suppressed a shudder. "Let go of me if you don't want an arrow up your nose."

"Ha! And you plan to do this how?" He pulled her closer, trapping her in a vise-like grip. "You will not threaten me."

Aralyn pulled her hands to her chest and twisted away from him. Eldersmith swore and reached for her again. His hand grabbed air as Aralyn took off.

"The best defense in a fight" — Her instructor had said long ago—"run."

And Aralyn ran.

***

She was past the wall, past the shouts of guards training, when a half-drunk voice called out. "Aralyn!"

Oh no! She didn't have to glance back. It was Eldersmith, and he was on horseback. Aralyn didn't stop but churned her legs faster.

A footpath to the forest. He would not follow her into these woods with their strange echoes and shadows that formed from nothing. If only she could get there in time. The hoofbeats grew louder. Aralyn's legs pushed harder. Almost to the footpath. The horse was upon her. A hand reached down and snatched at her cloak. Her breath came in gasps. She drew an arrow from her quiver, placed it in the hand that held her bow. Eldersmith seized a handful of her cloak. With a quick motion, she loosened it, let it fall to the ground along with her quiver. Eldersmith had slowed her enough that he was able to slide off his horse and grab her from behind. He wrapped his arms firmly about her. Despite her awkward position, she wouldn't let him do whatever he had come to do. Apparently, he hadn't thought about her bow. All she had to do was make him loosen his hold, and she could twist away and ready her bow.

"I intend to have you for my own." He whispered in her ear, and the stench of his breath washed over her. "I can wait until after the wedding. I'm a decent man after all."

"You're drunk," Aralyn said, stating the obvious and struggling against his hold on her.

"True, but you're not getting away from me until I have the marriage agreement."

Bile rising in her throat, Aralyn relaxed in his arms. "All right."

"What? All right? That was a quick change of heart." He tightened his grip.

"What do you have in mind?" Aralyn was surprised at how easily the flirting ruse came to her.

He still held her tightly. "I know what you're doing. Give me that arrow. And the bow."

Perfect.

"You're going to have to let go of me."

"Don't try anything."

As soon as he loosed her, Aralyn spun around and had the bow aimed at his chest. His hands went up.

So...he wasn't too drunk to understand when he was in mortal danger.

Eldersmith grunted. He backed away from her and mounted. "You'll soon be mine, Aralyn, and I'll make sure you are stripped of your weapons before the wedding night." He laughed and looked her up and down.

Aralyn had her bow in hand, an still arrow trained on him. And he dared to lean towards her. "I will—"

An arrow flew over his shoulder. She snatched one from the ground and had another one nocked, ready to shoot.

"What did you do? Maybe you don't care about me, but you coulda hit my horse."

Aralyn shook her head. "No. I never miss. That was a warning." She squared her jaw. "And don't you try to strip me of anything. Ever." Her gaze traveled down the shaft of the arrow and landed on his face.

A low growl came from his throat, and his upper lip twitched. The next thing Aralyn knew, dust from the road flew into her face. She watched him go, retrieved the arrow, gathered her cloak, her quiver, and the arrows she had spilled. Turning to the footpath, she took several deep breaths and headed to the woods.

A few yards in, she came to a halt. "Elyon," she prayed from the shelter of the trees. She wanted to cry out to the goddess of Sathria, to the gods of the sky-haven—to anyone who would listen—but Re'ah's reminder to trust Elyon kept their names off her lips. "Elyon," she repeated. "I need to get away from this village. I know my family needs me, but if I must marry, I don't want Eldersmith or any of the other men of this village." Besides that, as a wife, she couldn't continue to care for a mother and sister, especially if she had children of her own. She did not want to consider what had to precede that event. And with Eldersmith.

It would never happen. Never. She didn't know what she had to do, but she would not marry him.

Chapter 3

Aralyn trotted to the door of her home, slowed to what Mother would consider a proper stride, and stepped inside.

Terrwynn gazed at Aralyn from her spot beneath the window where she petted Cat, a light in her eyes that had not been there in a long while.

"You certainly took your time." Mother's words cut through the air.

"Yes ... I ..." She didn't want to tell Mother about the time spent with the magistrate or talking with the Elves. Or Eldersmith. "I got copper for the weavers."

Mother, in her rocking chair, was sewing—a steady, rhythmic motion. Push, pull. Over and over.

"How much? And did you get tea and sugar?" Mother's gaze did not leave the pieces of leather she stitched.

"About fifty coppers, and yes, I did." She grasped the dragon gem in her pocket, remembering what Elnala had said. Aralyn produced the tea and sugar and placed them on the shelf.

"About fifty? Did you count it?"

No, she hadn't had a chance. "I will." She dumped the coins onto the table and counted. Deducting what she had paid for tea and sugar, Lot'fe had given her precisely fifty coppers. So forty-four remained. She told her mother, pulled the ledger out from a drawer, and wrote it down. Aralyn tucked the money away in the false back of the drawer.

"Are you all right, Mother?"

Her bruises had turned a deep purple, and the cuts looked better.

No answer.

Aralyn tried again. "Are you taking the herbs Lot'fe gave you?"

Mother placed her sewing in her lap and stared at her elder daughter. "Yes, I am doing as Lot'fe and Re'ah told me, Aralyn." She stopped rocking, and the look Mother gave Aralyn made her freeze in place.

"I'm just aski—"

Mother held up her hand. "You think what happened makes me weak."

Aralyn lifted her chin. "No, Mother, I don't think anything akin to that." Aralyn's hands became unsteady again. The terror at seeing her mother attacked washed over her. Aralyn knew Mother was no weak woman.

Mother stood, put her sewing down, and paced just as she had last night. "You have no idea ... none!"

"Mother." Aralyn gripped the gem once more and squeezed it. A flash of the dragon's image came to her.

Deirdre muttered something Aralyn couldn't hear except for curse words that Aralyn was sure were aimed at her.

Aralyn turned to Terrwynn and took a few steps toward her. It was unfair for Terrwynn to have to listen to this.

Terrwynn rose and motioned Aralyn out of the way. That look again—one of command and self-assurance. She made a cutting motion and stood between them. Mother stopped pacing and stared. Terrwynn worked her mouth as if to speak, but only a guttural noise escaped. She pointed to her picture on the wall. Then to something Aralyn had noticed a few weeks ago. Yes, she knew her portrait was gone. And knew the reason why. Mother could no longer stand to look at it. But now Terrwynn was trying to tell her something else.

Terrwynn pointed at Aralyn and back to the empty place on the wall, back to Aralyn.

She got it.

Aralyn's heart went from unsteady to a race. The huge knot in her throat traveled to her heart. She grabbed at her chest and swung around to her mother. "So I'm going away?"

Mother sat. Picked up her sewing again. Push. Pull. Slower but still steady. "Yes, you are to marry."

"Eldersmith. Why didn't you tell me about him?" She'd known this day was coming. And she had dared to hope Mother would make a match with a good man. But Eldersmith was not a good man.

Mother's brow furrowed. "How did you know ...?" Deirdre shook her head. "No, not him."

Aralyn felt her shoulders relax, but she couldn't let the tension go entirely—not until she knew who the man was. Mother rose again, and for a moment, Aralyn was afraid she was going into another rant. Instead, she paced to a cubbyhole in the far wall, pulled out the roll of parchment Aralyn had seen earlier, and tossed it on the table. A sketch fell out, and Aralyn picked it up. It was the face of a man with hair well past his shoulders. He had no beard, his sky-blue eyes were almost perfectly round, and his ears had small, colorful markings on the upper edge.

"This is the contract we drew up with Brone of Maizehollow."

Aralyn's heart sank. The city of Maizehollow was days away. Leagues and leagues away. But he wasn't one of the men of the village—at least she had that. And she had just prayed for Elyon to help her escape, to get away. At the same time, she wanted to remain close to Mother and Terrwynn.

"He is quite wealthy and will provide well for you." Mother spoke as if the words wearied her.

Aralyn glanced up at the wall. "Is that where my sketch went? You sent it to him?"

"Yes." A curt answer. "I hope it gives him an idea of what you're like."

Not just "what you look like." But "what you're like." *All right ... just keep breathing.*

Aralyn looked back at the picture in her hand. He was certainly handsome, but she knew that meant nothing in a lasting relationship.

"His mother was an Elf, and his father was ... human," Mother said, continuing to sew. "Your children should be strong and healthy, even if they won't be pure Elves like you. They may even outlive you."

"He's part Elf." Aralyn frowned. "But Elves—they normally don't mix with other races." She knew her mother had married a human after her dad died, but memories of vicious words washed over her, a raging sea pounding, pounding. The Council trying to rid Elven lands of the non-pures. Her friends, among them.

Aralyn glimpsed anger and sadness and bitterness on Mother's face, but then it was gone. "Sometimes they do, Aralyn," she said, her voice void of emotion.

"But, if he's rich, why does he want me?"

"He knows our family. He knows ..." Mother's voice faded. Again.

"He knows what?" Aralyn's voice lifted, molded like red clay by forces beyond her control. A short time ago, she had taken control of her destiny and that of her family. Had it just been yesterday that she had killed three Rogues, pulled arrows from her enemies' bodies, and watched men take those bodies to burn? She had saved Mother's and Terrwynn's lives. But now tradition demanded she let someone provide for her. But why would he do that? He wanted Aralyn for some other reason, and Mother wanted ... what?

Aralyn gripped the edge of the table as a terrible thought occurred to her. "How much is he paying you, Mother?"

Mother shook her head. "That's got nothing to do with it. He's—"

"Nothing to do with it? You don't care that you're selling your daughter?" No, she probably didn't.

"I'm not selling you!" Mother closed her eyes and pinched her fingers against the bridge of her nose. When she spoke again, her voice was almost too soft to hear. "You will marry him, Aralyn. Why is this so difficult? Don't you realize how fortunate we are to be free? We've not been taken as slaves by Rogues or other scoundrels. Forced to mate with one of them. You won't have to marry a villager and stay h-here." Aralyn read the fear in Mother's eyes. "I don't think you appreciate any of that. You don't remember the Gehallion and Destrani mages coming with their spells and their swords and their..." Mother's gaze drifted and stared past Aralyn.

Yes, Aralyn knew. So many in Eyndor had disappeared unexplainably. Warriors. Innocents. Children who had been her friends. The memory crashed upon her.

"No, I suppose you were too young...you were just a small child, a *nanio*." Mother shook her head. "I can explain no more. *Ontena may nona*."

Mother spoke, not in the Common tongue, but Aralyn translated from Elvish easily. *It matters not*. The attacks Mother spoke of, she could barely remember them. But when the flashes of memory came, her heart pounded with fury and fear.

Mother waved her hand to dismiss her older daughter. Aralyn had plenty more to say and still wanted to argue. Instead, she nodded. "All right, Mother. I will do as you say. I will marry this man."

Without another word, Mother placed a pen in Aralyn's hand and pushed the contract toward her daughter. "Sign it."

Aralyn bent to do so. Stopped. "I would like to read it first." But she had already decided, remembering her vow to do anything to avoid marrying Eldersmith.

Mother lifted her eyebrows. She nodded. "Of course."

Its simplicity surprised Aralyn.

I, Brone of Maizehollow, will take Aralyn of Sathria to be my wife. I will cherish her and care for her, and together we will bring new blood into the world. I understand this contract is legally binding in all the Land of Lahilla.I reserve the right to withdraw from this contract before the binding ceremony only under the most grievous of circumstances.

At the bottom were Brone's own words.

Aralyn, I pray you will become my loving and faithful wife. I will be a good husband to you, and I will give you my genuine love, just as I trust you will be respectful toward me, fulfilling all the duties of a grateful wife.

Brone.

He didn't know her. How could he say he would love her? Maybe she was young enough. Humans preferred younger women, and Brone was half-human.

Aralyn stared at his picture. Something stirred in her. Brone. "He's a friend ... was a friend of our family?"

"So you remember him."

They had lived close to his family years ago. Hadn't he been kind to her? The memories grew faint, and she grasped for them, willing them to stay.

Aralyn didn't want to leave Mother and Terrwynn, but maybe if she did this one thing, Mother could be proud of her again, especially if Aralyn bore a child. Waiting for and marrying for love—well, that would likely never happen. It wasn't a perfect solution, but better than she had hoped for. Untangling her feelings about marriage and bearing children was a challenge

Aralyn did not want to think about. But that would come as she and Brone got to know each other. She hoped.

Aralyn would be out of her mother's sight, with Brone providing for them from his deep pockets. Even so, he couldn't protect them like she could. What if the Rogues returned? What if their own soldiers came, demanding quarter or ensuring the payment of taxes?

There was one thing she could do. "I will hunt tomorrow. I will help build up your meat stores." And she could replant the vegetable garden, show Terrwynn how to harvest and manage it. She would even show her the secret patch of weavers.

"No. There is no need. We will be fine." Mother chewed on her lip.

"I wish to help feed my family before I leave."

Mother put a hand to her forehead, rubbing it, and a dead look returned to her eyes. "There is no need," she repeated and continued to stare at her oldest daughter. Silent. Not unlike Terrwynn.

Aralyn looked away. Perhaps she should go outside and find her little sister. Ease her worries. Perhaps the blues and greens, and even the dust from the ground, could soothe her. She gave her Mother one more glance as the walls closed in. Aralyn grasped the door's latch, and it creaked open. She wrestled with the hope of freedom from this place and her uneasy feelings of her family's future. And her own.

***

The stream flowed and gurgled, a quiet song emanating from its current. At least that was what it sounded like to Aralyn, but ashes also floated down from Enemy Tears Hill. Pieces of Rogue? She hoped so. Hoped they were but mere ashes on the wind, skirting the village where they had done so much damage.

She found a place where the water formed a calm pool and knelt. She pondered the Elves who had reacted so strongly to her. They desired her songs, but there was something else they wanted. Aralyn pictured the trees of Eyndor, majestic trees with huge trunks her arms could not encircle. It took several sets of arms to do that. She remembered those children with round eyes, singing and laughing with joy, the prominent ears with strange markings. Like she'd seen in Brone's picture and like those on her own. Her connection with the land of Eyndor grew, enveloping her. Brone—he perhaps would return with her to the land of the Elves. If they ever let non-pures back in. This had to be part of Elyon's plan. Her husband and she leaving human lands and living in Eyndor.

Aralyn stared across the meadow and into the woods. In the distance, she caught movement. Terrwynn? Again, she was out here, exploring with no one to watch her. But hadn't she done that at Terrwynn's age?

Aralyn stood and quietly drew closer. Terrwynn had a rabbit in her arms. It whined in a way that always made Aralyn cringe, even though she hunted them. The broken shaft of an arrow was buried in its side. But it wasn't one of her arrows. Terrwynn stroked the rabbit's head. Spoke to it, and the whining stopped. Aralyn continued to approach and ducked into some shrubs as Terrwynn looked up.

Terrwynn whispered to the rabbit, and its ears twitched. She pulled gently on the shaft of the arrow.

If you are trying to save it, Terrwynn. That will only make it bleed out.

Seeing Terrwynn's gentle care of the rabbit, she knew her sister didn't want that. Before she could stand, Terrwynn had the arrow in hand, but there was no blood. None. And the rabbit bounded into the forest.

***

Aralyn wanted to question her mother about the behavior she'd seen in her little sister—Terrwynn's gaze forcing a Gehallion Rogue to freeze in place. Terrwynn balancing in the trees. Terrwynn whispering to a wild rabbit and healing it. Maybe the most obvious answer was her Elven heritage. Aralyn had never seen this behavior before and wondered if Mother knew.

Instead, Aralyn asked her about the wedding or binding, as they called it in Maizehollow. She approached the fire where Mother cooked, and crouched next to her.

Mother glanced at Aralyn, but said nothing.

"Is there any way I can be married here?" she asked. She wanted her mother and Terrwynn to be there.

Mother shook her head. "No, that is not the way it's done."

"Perhaps you and Terrwynn could come to Maizehollow?" It seemed such a reasonable request.

"No. We don't have the supplies or the horses to travel that far. Here. Take this." Mother handed the wooden spoon she was stirring with to Aralyn and stood.

Aralyn took it, surprised that Mother was allowing her to cook, and peered into the pot. They were having rabbit stew. Great. After watching Terrwynn heal one, she wondered if her sister would eat.

"Mother, I want you to know something. I still remember those who died in the plagues, but so much is missing."

Mother's feet shuffled in the dirt, and she sighed, taking a seat on a stump opposite her daughter. She stared into the distance. To the north, the direction of Elven lands.

"You were so...hurt. Your feelings..." And for a moment, Mother's gaze landed on Aralyn and flooded with compassion, but then her lips pursed. All concern disappeared. "I would forget too. If I could. Maybe you're lucky."

Aralyn stirred the pot. Maybe she should let it burn in the same way her mother's words scorched her. But no, this was nourishment for her and her family. She was not going to ruin it deliberately.

Even as she remembered the tragedies of Eyndor, her Elvish roots drew her to the land and to the Elves. She had seen them up close today, and hadn't her heart stirred with longing? Perhaps she did need to go back, maybe even visit the two she had met today and sing for them as she had promised. But there was something else they wanted. More than a song. The girl—Elnala—wouldn't have been so excited to see her if she were just another Elf who could sing.

The three of them sat down to eat. Terrwynn had no problem diving into her food. Aralyn watched her, and a chuckle nearly escaped.

As she stifled the laugh, she grew troubled. How had Terrwynn learned to climb trees and heal animals without Aralyn knowing?

Mother straightened, her gaze piercing. "What is wrong, Aralyn?"

"N-nothing, Mother."

"Something is bothering you." She glanced at Terrwynn. "I can tell you are upset about something."

Mother "knew things" that Aralyn would often rather keep to herself, feelings and thoughts that were nothing to others, yet caused anguish in her. To Aralyn's surprise, instead of insisting on an answer, Mother's next words were of a practical nature. "We need to see about getting material for new clothing. He'll be here within the month."

Aralyn blinked. "Brone?"

"No, of course not. He's sending an escort. A good man. A Peacekeeper."

An escort. And he was a Peacekeeper? What did that mean?

At Aralyn's puzzled look, Mother said. "He helps the magistrate enforce the law in his region, but more often travels and does as the king assigns. He's an honorable man and holds to the same standards as our guards. No need to worry about his ability to behave virtuously."

Aralyn was not concerned about that. She just didn't want to be on the trail for days with someone she didn't know.

But then, she really did not know Brone. Aralyn swallowed the last of her food, cleaned the dishes, and pulled Brone's sketch from the cubby hole. She gave her future husband's sketch a half smile, calm enveloping her. She traced the line of his jaw and sighed. This new phase of her life intrigued her.

Chapter 4

Aralyn ran into the forest before dawn. A rabbit trembled in the brush. She took aim and the arrow burrowed into its side. But when she picked it up, the face was that of a Rogue, snarling at her. The next one was the same. She kept shooting and gathering the "Rogue rabbits" until their faces changed. Changed to Terrwynn's. She dropped them and ran home screaming.

Aralyn tossed, woke sweating, and checked to make sure Terrwynn was still there. Yes, she was fine. Terrwynn slept soundly.

Another nightmare. It was because of the killing she'd done. Aralyn knew she was being punished for it.

I was protecting my home! But was Elyon angry? From what Re'ah said, the answer was no. Elyon understood. He was merciful and forgave when she asked. But what about the other gods? Did they hold grudges for the bad things she had done? *Elyon, if you want me to believe in you, don't ever put me in a place where I will have to kill someone.* At the same time, she had threatened Eldersmith yesterday. Without hesitation. Aralyn felt sick.

How did people ever get used to the killing? The lust for human, Elven, and Dwarfish blood never ended from what she had seen. It also solved nothing. Battles and border disputes came and went. The fighting would die down, only for more to start, or for another attack to come from Rogues. Aralyn wanted peace, but that would probably never be. Re'ah even said so. A peaceful man but with dire warnings of the failures of Elyon's creations, at least those with the intelligence to wage war.

Over the next two weeks, while Aralyn's nightmares continued, she often heard Mother up, also unable to sleep. Aralyn noticed the worn look, the bags under Mother's eyes. Mother stayed busy during the day. She stitched a new tunic and warmer undergarments for Aralyn and packed a thick blanket. Dried meats, a few carrots, and turnips went into her pack as well.

Terrwynn dropped some colorful stones into Aralyn's hands. Aralyn ran her fingers over them and admired the bright hues, their smoothness, their warmth. "Thank you, Terrwynn." She wanted to ask her sister where she found them but knew she would get no response. At least Terrwynn didn't hate her and perhaps would miss her.

That night, Mother slept. Aralyn did not. And now she couldn't stop the memories that filled her head. Memories of Brone. His smile, his laughter, how he used to tease her and make her laugh. From that same world, more memories of happier, richer times flooded her—times when they wanted for nothing. Mother held her hand, walking along the waters of a clear stream, brilliant with light. Then came the day when she heard Mother weeping. Aralyn waited outside their home on a rusty iron bench as mourners visited. She kept silent. While friends wailed, she refused to cry. But was this a memory of her father or her stepfather? Two men whom she had loved as her da were gone.

With silent footsteps, Aralyn made her way to the door and stepped outside. She pulled the gem to her chest, and yet another memory came to life. A Grand Dragon Drehensil had fought as an ally to the Elves, a rider upon his back.

She gripped the stone tighter and could sense him. He was near. He was searching for something or someone. Maybe, just maybe, it was her he sought. It began to rain, and the patter against the ground and the parchment-covered window was soothing. She loved the feel of rain upon her, loved to let it soak her skin. This meant, of course, she would have to strip down before she went in and hang her clothes to dry.

She turned her face skyward, and gentle moisture fell upon it. The silhouette of treetops touched the darkened sky, and light from the moon peeked through the rain-soaked clouds.

Was that Drehensil's voice? She wasn't sure. And off in the distance, just below the treetops, three silhouettes pirouetted in the rain. The dragon lizards were here. They loved the rain, and they also loved Drehensil. The trio was often his companions in travel. Perhaps he was not far behind.

Drehensil—her dragon. No. He belonged to someone else. Or did he belong to anyone? She remembered clearly that dragons didn't take anyone as master. She listened for his voice or an impression of his thoughts.

And she saw him. The Grand Dragon rose over the dragon lizards and hovered, his wings spread to their full width.

Drehensil was here.

She sprinted toward him, but after a few strides, she halted. The last time she saw him, something went very wrong. She said words in anger, in a horrible rage. A chasm of darkness spread around that memory, making it impossible to reach. She closed her eyes and stretched out her arms to him, willing the dragon to come to her. She also knew Drehensil had to be careful, for many people feared the dragons. She looked out over the darkened village—no light except for the few stars and the moon. No one in Sathria would be up for hours.

"*I am here, Aralyn. Worry not.*"

She could hear him? Yes, somewhere in the past, he had spoken to her mind as he did now.

A downdraft from Drehensil's wings swept over her, and Aralyn shivered in her now-soaked clothing. He landed not ten feet from her and folded his wings.

"*The last time we spoke, you told me—*"

"To leave me." The memory came swiftly. "So why did you come, Drehensil?"

"*To give you direction. You are anxious about what is coming, are you not?*"

"Yes. But why are you asking this? I hurt you with those words. I was angry and ..."

"*Angry, yes. And sad. Horribly sad.*"

"I don't remember why." The memory remained out of reach. Did it have to do with her father? Aralyn took a step toward Drehensil. Another. He didn't move. He appeared to welcome her approach but made no move toward her. At his side, she reached out to stroke his flank. With all four legs on the ground, his back arched above her, taller than her house, taller than many of the buildings in the village. His neck dipped toward her. Scales covered his head, neck, and flank, but their crimson color was impossible to discern in the dim light.

Aralyn's hand moved to the soft skin surrounding his nostrils—the only place not covered by scales. She touched her fingertips to bare skin. Too late to pull back, emotions not hers churned—a raging sea. It was the dragon's sadness and loneliness and, yes, his horror. Those emotions were embracing her, rolling her in a tight grip, like a water dragon with its prey. Aralyn snatched her hand away, but his grief brought her to her knees. She covered her face, unable to escape his heartbreak.

"*You understand now.*" His neck wrapped around her.

Yes, she had told him to leave. Not asked, but demanded it—and he had acquiesced to her wishes. That much she understood, but could she ever comprehend more? Dragons' emotions could fill a human heart to the breaking point.

"I will speak no more of my grief. Not now," Drehensil replied. *"It is better for you that way."*

She sensed his inner turmoil fading, and his emotional hold on her lessened until it became nothing. Aralyn leaned against him, enjoying the rain as the dragon lizards fluttered above.

The rain slowed, and the smaller dragons ceased their dance. Confusion passed over their faces, and they looked at Aralyn as if asking her where the rain had gone. When Aralyn shrugged, one of them, Aletha, bobbed her head and leaped onto Drehensil's back. Aletha's scales were the color of midnight, and without the white star on her forehead, it would have been almost impossible to see her. Those dark scales made her unique among the smaller dragons.

Vandel flew to the top of Aralyn's head and bent her limber body to peer into Aralyn's eyes. Her favorite of the two females, Vandel, was the color of chestnuts with a few spots of royal blue punctuating her legs and flanks.

The third landed on Aralyn's shoulder and pulled on a strand of hair. "Oh, stop it, Elouard." He withdrew with such an innocent expression—as if he didn't realize what he had done—and Aralyn had to laugh. Elouard had not yet shed his juvenile colors of sea green with a tint of orange around his eyes and nostrils. The two of them were much smaller than a Grand Dragon, but soon grew heavy on Aralyn. At the same time, she wanted them close.

Aletha bobbed her head at the other two while she made a series of clicks. She stepped across Drehensil's back with a flap of her wings. The other two mimicked her, tapping small claws on Aralyn's head and shoulder. The three of them were probably communicating a joke to one another. Aralyn let Elouard creep down her arm to her wrist, and she scratched behind his tiny ears. Vandel leaned into Aralyn's face and made a sound much like a purring cat. Aralyn laughed as the small dragon begged for attention.

"You needed me for something, did you not?" Drehensil asked, interrupting their antics.

Aralyn was so overwhelmed by seeing the foursome she had almost forgotten.

"Drehensil." Aralyn pondered her next words.

Elouard and Vandel swooped to the ground, stirring insects from the grass.

She took a step closer to Drehensil. "I am sorry for causing you sadness."

His head swung toward her, his huge eyes eddying with a storm, gray and flashing with brilliant white.

"I don't know why I told you to leave me. I wish I could always have you nearby."

Drehensil lifted his head above the trees. His neck and side quivered. When he brought his head back to meet her gaze, his eyes were calmer. *"That is not"*—Drehensil tightened his jaw— *"the only reason I grieve, and that is not why you wanted me to come—to issue an apology."*

No, that was true. "But why are you grieving? Can you not tell me?"

"I said I would speak of it no more." His eyes now churned with bright orange and scarlet that shone in the darkness.

"And I don't wish to cause you more pain." Aralyn pinched her lips together. "Drehensil, an escort is coming for me. He is taking me to be wed."

"Go with him. Do not fear. You have made a promise, and so has your mother." Drehensil's answer was immediate and direct, just what she had expected. *"I will not help you to run from this."*

"No, that would be wrong." Aye, she knew running never solved anything, but if Drehensil had advised her to find a way out, she would have done so. If he wanted, she would let him take her wherever he wished.

"You know I cannot take you anywhere unless you are my rider."

Was he reading her every thought? She leaned against him. "Drehensil." Her hand ran over the crusty scales on his side. He needed a good scrubbing. The idle thought fled as memories returned of long conversations with this Grand Dragon. During those relaxing times, he had taught her customs, history, and lore of dragons, and also how to care for one, feeding and cleaning, but a small part of it.

The dragon frowned. *"Aralyn, I will tell you this—I must keep searching until I discover where my rider fell and claim that ground for him."*

That must be the reason for his grief. "Will I see you again?"

He closed his eyes. *"I will try, my Aralyn."* He placed his cheek against hers and made a purring noise similar to Vandel's but deeper and more calming.

He was about to leave, and she couldn't stop him. They were all leaving her. Why was this so hard?

The three dragon lizards hovered around her, their way of bidding her goodbye. Drehensil dipped his head, and his eyes became a calm pool of indigo. She swallowed hard and strode back to the house. She stripped down to her undergarments and placed her clothes on a peg outside the door. When she crept back in, Mother was up, watching the door.

Did she know Drehensil was about?

"They think they need you," she said.

"Who, Mother?"

"The Elves. They think they need you in Eyndor. For the approaching era, they think your presence can save them from ruin. Don't listen to them, Aralyn. There is nothing but death there."

Chapter 5

A pounding upon the door rattled the latch, and Aralyn opened it. A young boy with flaming hair and a smattering of freckles reported to her. "The escort—he's less than a day away."

Aralyn nodded and reached into her pocket for a coin, but the boy was shaking his head. "Master Gillis paid me already."

"Gillis?"

"Yes, that's his name. The escort who's coming for you, miss."

"Very well, thank you for the message. And for your honesty." Aralyn stepped inside.

Mother again was sewing, finishing a pair of gloves for Aralyn. Where did she get the money for the material? What they sold in weavers and vegetables was not nearly enough. She needed to look at the ledger more closely.

Aralyn jumped when arms wrapped around her waist from behind.

Terrwynn? Aralyn pivoted on the balls of her feet and reached down to return the hug just as Terrwynn pulled back.

"He will ... love you." Terrwynn's voice was rough and sounded like a man's. Placing a hand on her throat, she stared past Aralyn and returned to her own world. That was the most Terrwynn had said in over a year, and Aralyn's decision gelled into place. She would make the most of this marriage. If Terrwynn had faced who knew what horrors, then Aralyn could face whatever was coming and honor the promise she and her mother had made.

She took the sketch of Brone from its place and rubbed her thumb over his chin, his cheeks. She could see where the artist had tried to capture the same silver flecks in his eyes that she had seen in her own. His kind expression. A small smile on his face. Aralyn hoped he would earn the respect he desired from her.

***

The beat of a horse's hooves approached the next day. She knew it would be him—the escort. But when the knock came, and she swung open the door, it surprised her to find Re'ah. Mother and Terrwynn had gone to pick berries, and Re'ah motioned for her to come outside.

Before he could speak, a pang clutched Aralyn's chest. "I won't see you again, will I?"

Re'ah had ridden hard to get here. With sweat on his brow, he grabbed his knees, and his head bobbed.

What did that mean?

Re'ah stood. "Yes, you will see me. I often go to Maizehollow and the surrounding regions, and even into Montravia."

"You'll come visit me?" Aralyn blinked, relieved and surprised.

The warmth of his hands on hers was reassuring. "Yes, Aralyn. I will."

A long gaze into those eyes that crinkled at the corners and seemed to see into her soul confirmed that he would still sense when she needed him.

Aralyn's shoulders relaxed, and the tension in her jaw lessened. Still, she perspired as the humid air formed a moist blanket over her.

Another horse approached, and Aralyn lifted her head. She steadied herself against Re'ah. The rider had a firm grip on the reins, and while she couldn't see the details of his face, she sensed his unflinching determination to complete his task. This had to be him.

"Aralyn, don't fret, child. You will find what you need on this journey."

Anger and hope battled together. "Re'ah, you've never lied to me. But how can you know I will find I need?" Anger seemed to be winning. "And what is it I need?"

"Child, please trust Elyon. He will not fail you."

The rider drew closer. She could see his dark bearded face now, a few light scars evident, and a prominent nose that seemed to be carved from stone, an odd cleft running its length. Another scar?

His horse came to a stop, and Aralyn could tell the man was dressed for a cooler climate. He wore a long-sleeved woolen tunic, leather jerkin, and leather boots. He had a band on his sleeve with two symbols that Aralyn couldn't make out.

The man's face was grim but lit up when he saw Re'ah.

"Greetings, Gillis." Re'ah let go of Aralyn and turned to the rider.

So Gillis knew Re'ah. Was he then also a believer in Elyon?

Gillis dismounted, and he grabbed Re'ah's forearm in greeting. "'Tis good to see you."

Aralyn didn't recognize his accent, but she liked it. After a brief exchange with Re'ah and thumps on the back, the stranger glanced at Aralyn. "Are you the one who's coming with me?"

Aralyn swallowed and managed a nod.

"Are you ready to go?"

No. She wasn't. Mother and Terrwynn should be back.

"Well, are you?" Gillis cocked his head.

"I ... I need—"

"Where's yer horse?"

"Taxes. We paid for ta—"

"All right, we can ride together for now." He let out a long sigh and scratched his forehead under his headband.

She'd never seen a man wear a headband like that. Curious. "Let me get my things." Once inside, she grabbed her pack and her bow and quiver. She stood in the middle of the floor and turned in place, taking in her home. What memories would she take with her?

"Aralyn." It was Gillis. He stood in the doorway. "Ye can't take those." Gillis nodded at her bow and arrows. Re'ah leaned toward him and whispered.

Gillis grunted, and his gaze landed on Aralyn, studying her. "All right. Bring them. Where's the contract?"

Aralyn reached into the cubbyhole and placed it in her pack.

Gillis had already mounted when she stepped outside. "All right. Now,"—he raised an eyebrow— "you ready to go?"

Aralyn didn't want to leave without saying goodbye to Mother and Terrwynn. "Would you like something to eat?"

"Lass, I'm mounted already. Let's go."

"Surely you'd like to refresh your waterskin."

"It's full."

Aralyn glanced at Re'ah, who pulled her to him in a hug. "It will be fine," he murmured. "You will be safe with Gillis." He held her at arms length and his gaze brought her comfort.

Aralyn frowned. "I only wanted to see my family before leaving."

"I know."

"But they're not here." She dropped her pack. "They deliberately left. They knew. Mother knew he was coming today."

"Now, how could she have known?"

Aralyn couldn't answer, but Mother was like that. She sensed things just like she often sensed Aralyn's thoughts and feelings.

"Don't mean to interrupt you, Re'ah, but I need to take the lass."

Aralyn hoped the escort wouldn't always be so impatient.

Re'ah's hand was firm upon her, strengthening her. He was always strong in moments when her courage failed. She took a last look at the forest beyond her home, the path to the village, and the secret way to her weaver garden—this place where she never lost track of the days between hardships. But she would go without a fuss, without complaint, and without tears. She couldn't imagine shaming her mother by doing any of those things, and above all, she refused to break the contract.

This was another leg of her journey. It could be an adventure.

Adventure.

The word seemed to mock her now. She remembered what Drehensil had said. *Go with the one they send.*

"Yes, we need to leave." Aralyn's voice was fresh with determination. She noticed Gillis had a sword on his horse's side and several daggers on his belt. He was well-equipped to fight off any danger they might face. She had to admire that.

Aralyn approached the horse's left side, and Gillis pulled her up behind him as if she were made of feathers.

Re'ah tied the pack onto the horse and handed Aralyn her bow. She had to place it over her shoulder, as there was no room to lay it across her lap. If there was danger, she would never get it readied in time.

"You need to hold on, lass."

Aralyn wrapped her arms around Gillis' waist and noticed the earthy smell of him, mingling with his leather clothing. The horse galloped forward, and she remembered the powerful feeling of riding horseback. She turned back to watch Re'ah fade in the distance. He gave a long wave.

Gillis took off toward the river, and Aralyn heard Terrwynn's cries. Without meaning to, Aralyn searched for her in the muddy waters. But the cries weren't coming from the river. Loosening her grip on Gillis, she swiveled around and saw Terrwynn, not floundering in the river, but running toward her on solid ground. Terrwynn grabbed at her throat. Made a mewling sound that chilled Aralyn, unlike the cries she had just imagined.

"Stop!" Aralyn commanded.

But Gillis kept going.

"Please. Stop." Yelling in his ear now.

He slowed the horse to a walk, and his eyes bored into hers. Then his face softened as he saw Terrwynn nearing, trying her best to make her voice heard.

"Let me say goodbye to my sister." She wasn't asking. The horse hadn't quite come to a stop when she leaped down, escaping Gillis' attempt to help her.

Terrwynn almost tackled her. "Aralyn." Again in that deep, rough voice. "I'm ... sorry."

What did she have to be sorry for? Aralyn hugged her close and caught the smell of the forest and honeysuckle. "I don't want to let go of you. Ever." She kissed the top of Terrwynn's head. Aralyn took a deep breath and bent towards her sister. "Listen, I must leave. But I'll come back." Aralyn had no idea how she would fulfill that promise.

"Aralyn ... don't ... worry." Terrwynn coughed and spat phlegm.

They held each other a moment longer, and Aralyn stroked the smaller girl's head and whispered words she hoped would bring comfort. Terrwynn had made it in time to see her off. But Mother, Mother was nowhere in sight. Only the empty hills gazed back.

She remounted and scanned the sky, hoping to sight Drehensil. But there was no sign of him. Just graying clouds, one wind sculpting them, another pushing them to the south. The horse bolted forward, and she grabbed Gillis' waist again. Aralyn didn't know how long Terrwynn watched. She turned her cheek to Gillis' back, squeezed her eyes shut, and swallowed her tears.

***

Aralyn rode in silence as the horse galloped over a path embedded with rocks. Already, the landscape looked different from home. More rocky and fewer of the trees she was used to seeing. How long would they keep up this pace?

They finally slowed when the trees grew thick and almost blocked their way. Aralyn wondered why Gillis seemed in such a rush. Surely the horse would be foaming at the mouth and unfit for riding later in the day. The ceremony wasn't for another week, and it would only take a few days to get to Maizehollow.

They stopped by a stream, and Gillis helped her down. Aralyn took her bow from her shoulder and grasped it in her left hand. The horse drank while Gillis waded out to deeper water, where he topped off their waterskins.

Aralyn patted the horse's neck and stroked his mane. "Why do you ride him so hard? Aren't you afraid he'll grow overly tired?"

Gillis didn't even look her way. "I ride him hard because he's meant to be ridden hard. His name is Restless for a reason. He's been bred for this very purpose." He turned toward her and raised an eyebrow. "Not getting a sore rump already, are you?"

No, she wasn't, but knew she would if he didn't slow down, especially over the more rugged terrain. "I'm fine."

"Well, I suggest you walk around a bit while we're stopped. We've got a ways to go before nightfall." He waded back to the bank. "You're traveling quite a distance to marry, aren't you, lass?"

"It wasn't my choice, but I go willingly."

"Well, lass, Brone's a good man."

He kept calling her *lass*. That meant female or girl or something like that. Aralyn took a drink from the waterskin he handed her. The water was refreshing and cool upon her throat. "You're friends with him?"

"Aye, good friends. I'm his companion." He took a few swallows of his water as the horse took deep gulps from the pond.

His companion. The man who stood with the groom. She knew the term. "Except for leaving my family behind, I'm glad to go."

Gillis turned his gaze on her. "Aye, it's hard to leave family. I know that much." She heard the compassion in his voice and a tinge of sorrow.

"Hopefully I'll see them again." Aralyn forced herself to be positive. "I know Brone and I have met before. I was a good bit younger than he and his friends, but he was always kind to me."

Gillis ran a hand through his hair and adjusted his headband. "Good to hear."

Tiny leaves from unfamiliar trees lay at her feet, and she swept her foot over them. "Just what did Re'ah say to you that made you decide I could keep my bow?"

"Said you were quite capable with it, and you might come in handy." Gillis' brow furrowed. "You're not the girl who killed twenty of those Rogues, are you?"

"No, I only killed three." She wondered what girl in or around Sathria could have killed twenty. Aralyn blinked. Wait. That was what they had said about *her*?

"Only three, eh?" Gillis chuckled. He checked the cinch around Restless's girth and took some oats out of his pack to feed him. "Well, these stories do get blown out of proportion. I'm sorry that you had to kill at all." Again, there was compassion and the same sadness he had expressed a moment before. Maybe there was more to this man than impatience and his abrupt manner bordering on rudeness.

The sickening feeling of seeing men fall at her hand came over her. "One of them I killed was Bek. He's brother to—"

"Mal'ev." Gillis peered over his horse as he adjusted straps and checked the horse's bridle, his eyebrows raised. "I know who he is. That is not good, but I'm sure Mal'ev doesn't realize you're the one or where you are. He may not even know his brother is dead. And the Rangers have indicated the road is safe up ahead. Next village, I'll check again. Mal'ev, he's trapped in his own city right now, so he shouldn't be a problem."

"He's trapped?"

"Not exactly trapped, but he can only use his power there. It's a good thing, too." Gillis glanced at the sky, shading his eyes against the sun. "We need to move on if we're to get you a horse."

They mounted, and Aralyn grabbed hold of him as the horse moved forward, taking her closer to her destiny.

Chapter 6

Gillis felt he knew the young woman better now, but he still didn't know what it would be like traveling with her. They were only a few hours into their journey. So far, he'd heard no complaints, and she displayed concern—albeit misplaced—for his horse. Gillis noted how tightly Aralyn held on to him, not the least embarrassed, it seemed, to have her arms around him. That was good, as he truly didn't feel like picking her up off the ground when they got to steeper ground.

It was late morning when they came to the village where Gillis planned to get her a horse. The streets were muddy from recent rain, roofs still dripping. It would cost good money to rent a horse, but Brone had given him an allowance for every contingency. He planned to take advantage of that, knowing they could move faster if both of them had a mount. She'd indicated her family had horses at one time. He hoped she hadn't forgotten how to ride.

They arrived at the stables where his friend Lemmon, who was an Elf, had horses for lease. He called himself Lem to blend in with the humans. His full name, when mispronounced, sounded like a type of fruit humans often enjoyed in their drinks.

A beardless man like most Elves, Lem greeted Gillis with an extended hand, but Gillis was having none of that. He gave Lem a hug and a hearty thump to his back.

"This is Aralyn," Gillis said. "I need a horse for her. Just to rent for a few days until we get to Maizehollow. I'll have it brought back to you by someone reliable. I promise that."

"No need to promise. Your word is good here." Lem bowed his head to acknowledge Aralyn, and she nodded in return.

At least she didn't complain about the smells of the horses or manure. She didn't even wrinkle her nose, and she lingered over the first horse Lem indicated they could rent.

Gillis looked the horse over. "What do you think?"

"Me?" she asked.

"Aye, you're the one who's going to be riding her."

"I'm not sure. I'd like to see the others."

"Over here." Lem led the way to a large corral where he had at least a dozen horses.

A red mare with a star on her forehead caught Aralyn's attention. "That one." She pointed.

Lem opened the gate and led her into the corral while Gillis watched, leaning against the top rail of the fence.

"Ah, she is spirited, Aralyn, but doesn't have a bit of meanness." Lem waited as Gillis and Aralyn continued their appraisal.

Aralyn smoothed her hands down its left flank and legs and scratched the horse's forehead.

Lem patted the horse's neck. "Her name's Monpomme."

Gillis chuckled. "Good name. What are you thinking, lass?"

"I like her. I think we're a good match."

A good match? She said it with such confidence. He'd also seen the gentle touch of her hand on the horse, and confidence was a good thing when riding. "All right, we'll take her."

Gillis was discussing the charges with Lemmon when Aralyn spoke up. "I have copper of my own. How much is the payment?"

Lem opened his mouth, but Gillis held up his hand. "No. You'll not be paying for it. Brone is taking care of all expenses."

"I know he has money, but Brone should realize he isn't the only one with copper or...whatever the color of his money is." Aralyn raised her chin.

Gillis agreed to a compromise. "I'll rent the horse, and you can rent the bridle and saddle. How's that?"

"No." Her hands were on her hips. "I don't need those."

Gillis threw a saddle on Monpomme's back without a word. The mare did not object. Aralyn's eyebrows come down. "All right, I can agree to the saddle."

As if she had a bloody choice.

When he started to put the bit and bridle on the horse, she tried to stop him. "I said I would agree to the saddle. She shouldn't have to wear all that."

"And how do you think you'll steer her?"

"I know how to use my knees and the mane to get a horse to go where I want."

He heard Lem stifle a laugh.

Aralyn glanced at Lem. "I think bridles, and especially bits, are cruel."

"Well, this horse isn't used to doing things your way." Gillis' gaze met hers once more. "When we get farther down the trail, you'll be glad you don't have to steer with your knees. How long's it been since you rode a horse?"

"Two years." There went that bloody chin again. "But I haven't forgotten a thing."

Lem hid a smile, but at least he kept his mouth shut.

"I'm sure you haven't. Nevertheless, this is the way it will go. Bit and bridle."

"Fine, then. Brone will pay for them." She tightened the strings on her coin purse. Gillis muttered words he hadn't said in ages.

Lem's laughter wasn't so easily ignored this time.

***

After Gillis spoke with a Ranger in the village, who assured them the way was safe, they took the road toward the outskirts of the village. He noticed Aralyn eyeing the shops where they sold jewelry and other trinkets, material, thread, and looms for weaving. Did she fancy such things? He doubted it, but there was another matter he needed to address.

"I want you to understand, Aralyn." His voice was low, almost guttural.

Her head snapped toward him.

"While we're on the trail, ye'll listen to me. Ye'll follow my instructions. That includes how a horse is outfitted. If I am to keep ye safe, ye have to do what I say." He was aware his accent had grown stronger, and he had reverted to his old manner of speech. That always happened when he was emotional. Not a good sign.

"You seem to know a lot of people. Do you expect all of them to do as you say?"

She wouldn't let it drop. He didn't want to take the bait, but Aralyn needed to understand. He pulled Restless to a halt, and she followed suit, looking at him curiously. He grabbed Monpomme's bridle. Aralyn glanced at his hand, surprise and indignation on her face as her eyes met his. He had her attention.

"I'm a Peacekeeper for this region. So yes, people listen to me, and I expect no less from ye while ye're in me charge."

"Am I not allowed to make any of my own decisions?"

His fist grew tighter around Monpomme's bridle. "My duty is to get you to Brone safely." Gillis let go of the bridle and released the tension in his arms and neck.

The fairer sex could be so aggravating, and yes, Aralyn was one of the prettier ones. His thoughts turned to those in Maizehollow. He couldn't make sense of their giggles and long lashes—long lashes they batted at him. Gillis had to admit he understood this Aralyn of Sathria a little better. She had a mind of her own and certainly had no intention of batting her eyelashes at him. Seemed a fair trade, he supposed. Still, he would be glad to get her to Brone. Let her give him the headaches.

After a moment in which her gaze turned forward, she asked, "Can we go?" She took off without waiting for a response.

"Of course," he replied as if he were still in charge.

The ground grew muddier as they rode into the desperately poor areas of town. The stench of sewage overcame the scent of flowers growing wild in the fields and by the roadside. Gillis noted the tremor in his hand as the cries of children and infants overwhelmed him. He had to convince himself the memories were just that—memories. They couldn't hurt him anymore. All he had to do was force them from his thoughts. Think of something else.

His mind snapped to Aralyn. Perhaps she would be a good mate for his friend. Yes, she was pretty, and he found thoughts of her more pleasant than the past, even though she was stubborn as a blind mule. Still. Perhaps Brone would find comfort in her.

They left the village behind, and Gillis' lungs cleared. Gradually, the ground became drier, and they could move more rapidly. The hills he loved lay ahead, hills whose view still took his breath and often refreshed his haunted mind.

***

The incline was steep, but Aralyn stayed upon her horse even when it was difficult to get the horses through the trees and around huge boulders. She did indeed know how to ride. They couldn't avoid the branches that reached out for them, leaving scratches or stinging them with thorns. They reached the top of a ridge. The trail was clearer here, almost as wide as the main road. They rode for a couple of hours when Aralyn broke the silence. He noted the gentle concern in her voice.

"Gillis, will I ... somehow endanger Brone? Or Maizehollow?

He shook his head. "You, Brone, and his family should be safe."

"His family?"

"Yes, he has a family." He raised an eyebrow at her. "Did no one tell you?"

"I really know nothing." Her eyes grew wary.

"He has a son by a previous wife. She passed away, and Brone's sister lives with them—helps in the boy's care."

"So I'll be a stepmother right away." With a blink and a small shake of her head, she grew silent. She asked nothing about how old the boy was or his name. Nothing.

The ground sloped upward again, but not as steeply as before. With Aralyn in front of him, they reached a plateau where shades of gold and orange stretched out below. He pulled on Restless's reins and rested his eyes on the peaceful valley. The piney scent of the trees wrapped around him.

Aralyn apparently didn't notice he had stopped, and she rode ahead. That was fine as long as she didn't get too far ahead. He called out to caution her, and she slowed her horse. She asked him something, but he didn't hear, for at that same moment the sky whispered to him, and he looked up. He caught a glimpse of something he had not seen in a long time. The downward stroke of a dragon wing.

Chapter 7

Aralyn touched the dragon stone in her pocket and smiled as she remembered the two Elves who gave it to her. Gillis called out to her, and she realized the trees hid her from him. He wanted her in his sight, she was sure, so she stopped.

She gasped when an enormous shadow fell over her. A thump on the ground and the folding of leathery wings caused her to turn forward. Drehensil. He had come. But why so soon?

His head lowered in a greeting. Aralyn made a clicking sound and urged Monpomme forward.

"You're here," she whispered.

"Do not leave Gillis' side." Drehensil's mind speech was firm but gentle.

She knew his words were for her protection, and coming from the dragon, the admonition was not unwelcome. He had always watched out for her. Hadn't he? He called her "my Aralyn," as if she somehow belonged to him. She could not imagine calling him "my Drehensil." Her mouth turned up at the thought. Her father...something about her father and this dragon...Another memory fled.

"Dangerous times come. For now, be safe with your escort. I am pleased you go with him."

Gillis halted when he saw the dragon, and Drehensil's head eased upward.

"Get back, Aralyn!" He urged his horse to her side and drew his sword.

"It's all right, Gillis. We know each other. He's safe."

"Tell him to put his sword away. I am no danger to either of you or the animals upon which you ride."

Aralyn was about to relay the message when Gillis sheathed the blade. "Look, Dragon, I'm not touching it." He held up empty hands.

So Gillis heard the dragon as well, and Aralyn found she was glad, but she wondered how he knew dragons. He must know others if he was not surprised by Drehensil's mind speech. Most humans wanted nothing to do with them. As far as she knew, only Elves had dealings with dragons, let alone heard them speak.

Drehensil lowered his head. *"My name is Drehensil. Please address me as such."*

Gillis nodded. "I have a healthy respect for dragons, but don't threaten me or my charge."

"That is fair, Gillis of Maizehollow. But as I said, I am no danger to any of you." Drehensil's eyes swirled with the colors of fire. *"You are brave indeed. Your king should be proud."*

Gillis scoffed. "I'm not sure if it's bravery, but I will inspect anything I feel is a danger to the ones I'm sworn to protect."

"That would include my Aralyn, would it not?"

Gillis raised an eyebrow. "Yes, dra—Drehensil. I will protect her with my life."

He would protect her with his life? No. No one would do that for her.

"I am glad you watch out for my Aralyn, Gillis of Maizehollow. She means much to me as well." The dragon's head swung to Aralyn. *"I must leave again. But I sense my wanderings will be over soon. I long to take you with me, but cannot. Not now."*

Aralyn dismounted and ran to Drehensil's side. She wrapped her arms around him as far as his thick neck would allow, and he circled her in a dragon embrace. She lay her face against his smooth scales.

"You must go, my Aralyn."

Aralyn stepped back, and as she did, the dragon lizards swooped toward her. Vandel landed on her shoulder, while Aletha hovered before her. The sunlight danced across Aletha's midnight scales. Elouard seemed tired, and his head drooped as he landed on Drehensil's back.

Gillis nodded to the trio. "Interesting names you have."

They had told him their names? "You can hear them?"

"Aye. That I can."

"I hear Drehensil, but not them." Aralyn frowned. That did not seem right.

"They tell some interesting tales, lass. Had several around when I was much younger."

Drehensil called Aralyn back to his side. *"I am searching, but I keep my eyes on you as well."* He wound his neck around her in a fierce embrace. *"I needed another hug."* His voice was gentle, almost meek.

Aralyn chuckled. As if he had to explain himself. How had she survived so long without him? To humans, her relationship with dragons would be considered foolish.

They released each other, and Aralyn swallowed hard, not knowing when she would see them again.

***

"Just how do you know these dragons?" Gillis asked. " Not everyone is familiar with, let alone friends with them."

"I wish I could remember more, but I've known Drehensil since I was a child, as far back as my memory goes. Seems the dragon lizards came along later. They were tiny when I first met them."

The horses trotted on as the shadows grew longer.

"I think we should try to find an inn," Gillis said as dusk approached.

Aralyn didn't know if she liked that idea or not. She'd never stayed in one but knew she would not enjoy sharing space with an untold number of people. "If I find a decent place to camp, could we sleep there instead?"

"Of course."

Aralyn stayed close to Gillis, but as the sun moved toward the horizon, she urged Monpomme a short distance ahead. She peered through the trees and spotted a clearing with a stream splashing nearby. "I think I've found a good place." She led Monpomme to the swift-moving water and tried to relax. As Aralyn listened to Monpomme's gulps, she thought about her stepfather's words from years ago.

"Horse comes before you, Aralyn. Remember that. No matter how tired you are. You take care of that animal before you eat or drink or even think about cleaning yourself up."

It seemed like silly advice—almost common sense—but she was sure many people never learned how to treat a horse. As tired as she felt, it was good to have that reminder.

Gillis approached her, leading Restless. "I'm glad you suggested this."

"I'd rather not stay in an inn. Too many people, and we'd probably have to sleep on the floor anyway."

"Aye, and a dirt floor at that."

Aralyn led Monpomme back to the clearing, tied her to a tree, and gathered some kindling and firewood. She had the fire going when Gillis returned with Restless. He carried an armload of firewood.

"You've got it started already?" He gave her a small smile and a nod of approval. Dropping the firewood, he squatted next to her. "I plan to make some coffee. I can fix us something to eat if you like."

"I've got my provisions for tonight." Gillis needn't worry about her. "Would you like some of mine?"

Gillis shook his head and put the water for the coffee on to boil. "No, lass. I've plenty and enough to share."

"I'll eat my own, thank you."

Gillis grunted, sat, and leaned back against a tree. He really didn't feel up to cooking, but coffee was a must.

They were silent as Aralyn pulled food from her pack and asked Elyon for a blessing over herself and the food. The fire popped, and an owl hooted in the distance. She looked up when Gillis rose to get his coffee. He was eyeing her. "Look, Aralyn. I don't have any objection to you taking care of yourself as long as you let me help a bit when you need it."

Aralyn's brow furrowed. She bit her lip, but her tongue worked loose and took off on its own. "Yes, but Brone wants you to feed me. Doesn't want me to spend one copper of my money or use any of my provisions. Does he want you to tuck me in at night?"

Gillis blinked. "Tuck you in?"

"Yes, you know, make sure I have my blanket wrapped—"

"I know what it means." He sipped his coffee. When his gaze lit upon her, it was with a mixture of irritation and amusement. "I'm not concerned with how well you take care of yourself when you're not my responsibility. But right now, I'm to get you to Brone in one piece and not half-starved. I've a job to do. That's all."

Just as Aralyn had taken care of Mother and Terrwynn at home. It had been her job. Her responsibility. The tension left her shoulders. "I understand, Gillis."

"Go ahead with what you brought." Gillis gave her a nod.

Aralyn pulled out a turnip and a small strip of dried meat—pork and mostly fat.

She noticed Gillis had a fistful of Elvish bread, and her mouth watered.

He must have noticed her watching him. "Would you like some?" He held out a large portion of the bread to her.

"No, I have pl—" She changed her mind. "Yes, Gillis. I would love some." She reached for the generous piece he offered. The bread was fluffy and tasted of honey. She closed her eyes to savor it. "Did you make this, or did one of the Elves?"

"A friend of mine made it."

She chewed, but that was barely necessary. It almost dissolved in her mouth. "Gillis, are you part Elf? You know Elves ... like Lem. And Brone is part Elf." Aralyn didn't like the cloud that flashed across Gillis' face.

Gillis considered the question a little too long. "Brone has chosen me as your escort and his companion for his binding because we have been friends for almost two decades. We have gone through some hard times—similar tragedies—and we understand each other."

There was something Gillis wasn't saying. He had evaded her question. She let it go and studied him for a moment. Despite his scars, in this light, there was a certain gentleness to his countenance.

Aralyn reached into her pack and took Brone's picture out. She'd almost forgotten about it. "Gillis, is this a good likeness of him?"

"Who?"

"Brone." Who else would she be speaking of? She extended the sketch to him.

Gillis looked it over and scoffed. "I don't know, lass. It's ... well, for starters, his nose is a good bit longer. And his eyes ... one of them is usually staring straight at you, and the other—"

"Are you saying he's cross-eyed?"

"Of course not. It's more like one eye just seems to do as it pleases." He made a motion, pointing up and all around. "And his ears stick out more than that. Much larger, too." He handed the sketch back to her.

Aralyn frowned and considered the picture again. Why would someone draw this so inaccurately? And why did she remember Brone so diff—wait. She put the sketch down. "So you think he's ugly?"

"Didn't say that." Gillis emptied his coffee cup with one last swig.

"Well, I remember something of him, and he looked nothing like you describe. This is more like what I remember." She waved the sketch at Gillis. "A little older certainly, but he never had big ears or a long nose or an eye that does this." She imitated Gillis' motions.

Gillis chuckled. "But for a moment you believed me."

Aralyn folded her arms. "This is what I remember, Gillis. Not only was he handsome, but he used to defend me when I would talk about the dreams I had of adventure and fighting for humans and Elves alike. I remember others laughing and even threatening me if I didn't shut up."

Gillis nodded.

"Now's when you should be laughing." Aralyn waited for his guffaw.

"No, no. I know what you're saying. Nothing wrong with a little adventure."

"It all sounds so silly. I thought I could sing for great audiences, maybe even the leaders of the Elves and the human kings."

"I know that many people—especially the Elves—put a lot of value in songs."

"They must. Two I met in the village invited me to Elven lands to sing for them. I thought it was odd." She gazed at the picture again. "Is he truly nice? He'll be good to me, won't he?" Aralyn needed to hear him say it. Needed to hear more about this man who would be her husband soon.

"Yes, I believe he will. He's been a good friend. He cares for his animals, which I think says a lot about a man—or woman." He glanced Aralyn's way, and she took it as a compliment.

"Thank you, Gillis," she said softly. "And by the way, if he's kind, I don't care what he looks like."

"Oh no, of course not. I've met many people who didn't care about their spouse's appearance." Sarcasm. He was good at it. "But I did enjoy that look you had for a moment."

"Half a minute at most." Aralyn sat, picture still in hand.

The fire snapped. The air was still, and in the distance, owls hooted.

"I think it's time to put the picture away. You can gaze at it tomorrow."

He was teasing her, and Aralyn found she enjoyed their easy banter. Just how long had she been staring at Brone's likeness? She shrugged and tucked the sketch into her pack.

"Gillis, what did you mean when you said Monpomme is a good name?" She spread out her bedroll.

"It means 'my apple,' as in the apple of my eye. It's from the ancient writings, meaning someone very precious in Elyon's eyes."

Aralyn wasn't sure what to say to that. "Oh. Well. She's been a good horse, so I suppose that makes her precious to me." Aralyn crawled under the woolen covers that she was glad her mother had insisted on. "Good night, Gillis."

He bid her good night as well, still stirring the fire. She watched for a moment and wondered if he would sleep. And even though he was miles away, Drehensil's call of grief invaded her thoughts. He was mourning again. And the cry was not just in her mind but in her heart as well.

***

They attached themselves to her legs, and Aralyn struggled, but the monstrous creatures clung to her, sucking on her skin. She woke, her face covered in sweat. This was no dream. Their fleshy bodies wriggling on her. This was real. She threw her blankets off. The creatures were still there. Cream-colored blobs thick upon her feet and calves. Gully lizards.

No, no, no.

Restless neighed and pulled on his rope—his warning cry. Gillis awoke and was on his feet.

She managed a small "H-help."

"What is it?" Gillis rose and rushed to her side.

"Look at my legs, my feet." Her voice was tiny. "I need your help. Please."

Gillis stared at her legs where she pointed, and his brow furrowed.

"Please," Aralyn begged again.

Gillis shook his head and crouched next to her. Aralyn watched as Gillis plucked the finger-long lizards from her feet and calves. The suckers on their legs gave them such a tight grip that Aralyn was afraid tiny pieces of them might remain behind. She closed her eyes, shuddered, and let Gillis do his work. Didn't even try to help. She hated the things.

"Any more?" he asked.

"No," she squeaked. "I don't think so." Aralyn opened her eyes and met Gillis' gaze.

"You're all right now?" His voice held a hint of humor.

The gulley lizards scampered off into the woods. A few of them, confused, ran toward the fire. "Yes, I'm fine. Now."

A smile played on Gillis' lips. And that smile became a chuckle. And the chuckle became a belly laugh. He was laughing at her terror. Earlier, he had been concerned about her safety, and now he was laughing at this?

"You ..." Gillis gasped. "You ... should have ..." He was still laughing. "... seen yourself. Absolutely ..."

"It's not funny, Gillis. They're horrid. They feel awful."

He grew serious as if he were truly considering her lament. But it was a brief moment, and he was laughing again—laughing so hard, she had to admit, "I guess it is kind of silly."

"*Kind of* silly?" Gillis roared and slapped his thigh. His laughter finally quieted enough that he could speak. "You can talk to a dragon, make friends with a bloody dragon, yet you're afraid of those ... what did you call them? Horrid creatures? Ha!" He held up his thumb and forefinger to demonstrate how small they were.

Aralyn's mouth twitched. Now that he put it like that, she had to agree, and a chuckle rose in her throat, joining his laughter.

Finally, Gillis' mirth faded. "Aralyn, I would never make light of the situation if you were in any real danger. But this ... you have to admit"—he leaned toward her—"is bloody hilarious." His chuckle faded. "You know, I'm glad you can laugh at yourself."

"My father always taught me to never take myself too seriously."

"Sounds like a wise man. And I must say, it's been a long time since I've enjoyed a good laugh with a friend." His eyes still held a hint of humor.

Aralyn tilted her head. "Is that what we are? Friends?"

"Yes, I would hope so. You'll soon be my best friend's wife, so I'd like to think that's what we are." He stood. "Now sleep well, my friend. The creatures won't return."

"How can you be sure?"

He shrugged. "I told them not to."

Aralyn didn't know whether or not to believe him. She lay back down and watched Gillis retreat to his bedroll.

A friend. She liked the idea of being friends with this man.

Chapter 8

The sky was clear and the sun poured over them, but Aralyn pulled her cloak tighter, the air growing chillier as they rode.

"Why is it getting cold? It's just past noon."

"Aye. We're getting to a higher altitude."

"Altitude?"

"Elevation—when the land gets higher."

"I would think that would make it warmer."

Gillis chuckled. "No, that's not how it works. You may tire more easily, too."

"Is there some reason for that?"

"I think there's less air. It's thinner—or something like that."

They settled on rocky ground that night, where they would be well hidden. The horses, she noticed, seemed alert to danger. Just that day, Restless had stopped dead in his tracks when a poisonous snake crossed their path.

In the warmth beneath her cloak and blanket, Aralyn fell asleep quickly. She wasn't sure how long she had slept before she woke to a strange buzzing in her ears. Something or somebody was trying to communicate with her. Was it Drehensil?

No, this was different. Instead of a gentle or mournful thought, it felt as though fingers pressed on her brain, kneading her mind like bread. Fear and pain gripped her. She grasped her head and tried to make those fingers loosen their grip. It did no good. *Breathe in. Breathe out.* After a few moments, she felt calmer and lay back down.

Aralyn felt at home now with a roof over her head and a straw bed beneath her. How strange. Hadn't she left with an escort? This must be a dream. She blinked, tried pinching herself, and wiggled her toes. She was awake, wasn't she? And at home? She closed her eyes and opened them. The walls, the ceiling, the packed dirt floor—all of it was real. But Terrwynn was gone, and Mother was not in her bed either.

She could tell by the lack of light from their one small window that the sun was not yet above the horizon, but it would soon be dawn, and she had to find food. With her bow in hand and full quiver on her back, Aralyn ran into the dark morning, grasses slapping against her bare thighs. She'd taken her skirts off to better move through the forest. Mother would never approve. But Mother was nowhere in sight.

She drew closer to the forest, and the sun still hovered below the horizon. A few stars hung in the sky, and wolves howled. Wolves? She came to a halt. Something wasn't right. Aralyn shrugged. She had to hunt. As she entered the forest, the trees grew thick and blocked what little light was available. Eyes glowed from the blackness around her. Low growls emitted from the trees, threatening her. Aralyn hesitated.

Perhaps she should go back. There was no sense in risking her life. Something in the back of her mind screamed a warning, and she nocked an arrow. Crouched low. A set of glowing eyes moved, and the animal ran to her left. The creature snarled as she released the arrow.

Aralyn stood over her prey and knelt by it, a gray rabbit with nose twitching, showing teeth, and snarling. Rabbits didn't do that, even if it was not a clean kill, but she never failed to kill an animal with a first shot. What was wrong with her?

Aralyn picked up the rabbit, avoiding its teeth, and took the head in one hand and legs in the other. In one motion, she pulled and gave a twist. She looked up at the sky. Stars shone between the branches of trees. This couldn't be right. The sun was rising when she left, or perhaps the sun wasn't following its regular path today. For some reason, that seemed logical.

Aralyn picked up the dead rabbit. As she walked, the scenery changed. Scrub brush, palm trees, and vines changed to pines and firs. The sky grew lighter. Again. She blinked and saw a man in the path facing her. Gillis. He had come after all.

Gillis strode toward her. "What in the flames are ye doing?"

Aralyn looked at the rabbit in her hand. The bloody arrow. "I ... I went hunting? I didn't mean—"

"I can see you've been hunting. Do you realize what you've done?"

Aralyn gaped at him.

"You've been hunting in the king's woods."

"I didn't mean to. I didn't even mean to leave ... I just—"

"You didn't mean to. How in this world can you go hunting without meaning to?" He didn't wait for an answer.

That was good because Aralyn didn't have one.

"Do you realize what could happen?"

Aralyn knew he was fighting for control. "I could be arrested?"

"Oh yes, you could be arrested! I'm thinking I could be arrested as well. Even if I take you in." Gillis stroked his beard and stared at the ground. He looked towards the forest, brow furrowed.

Aralyn swallowed. "You would do that?"

His gaze swung back to her. "You broke the law, and I'm a Peacekeeper."

"Gillis, I thought ... I know you won't believe me—"

"Try me, Aralyn."

"I thought I was dreaming, but I wasn't. It was too real. Something happened to me. I would never ..." Aralyn gave him a pleading look. "Something was in my mind, Gillis. It's like it forced me."

Gillis took her by the shoulders and examined her face. He took his time, and Aralyn squirmed.

"Be still." All the blame and anger had left his voice. He focused on her eyes for what seemed longer than necessary, but when he spoke, it was with calmness. "You've been meddled with."

"Meddled with? What do you mean?"

"Your mind's been drawn out, used by someone, turned against you. Those are the best terms I can think of."

"But who, Gillis?"

"I would suspect Mal'ev, but I'm thinking he's not powerful enough. Not now."

"Someone got into my ... my thoughts?" She knew Drehensil could do that, but he would never manipulate her.

"Something like that. Mages are capable of such if the person isn't trained to stave off the attacks. They can make you think you're somewhere else or even someone else."

"I thought I was at home."

"By all rights, I should take you in, but I can't let you be punished for this. It would be unfair. I don't know who's the magistrate or lord here. Too many variables." Gillis drew himself up.

"Maybe we should just leave. I know what they'll do to me. I've seen it."

Hoofbeats approached, and Aralyn could see the crest on the horse—a series of red half-circles interspersed with stars that indicated his position. The same emblem was on the man's chest. A lord's man, representative of the nearby lord and the king. This was not good.

Aralyn dropped the rabbit and tried to control her heartbeat as he approached.

"Just stay here." Gillis strode toward the man.

The horse's step slowed to a gentle clip, and the lord's man greeted them. "Good morning. What is your business in the king's woods?"

Aralyn tried not to stare.

"We're just passing through. I'm escorting Aralyn of Sathria to her betrothed."

The man eyed them. "All right, and what is your name, sir?"

"I am Gillis of Maizehollow."

"So all you're doing is passing through?"

Gillis nodded. "Yes, 'tis."

He nodded. "All right then. Be on your way in peace."

Aralyn sighed with relief, but she must have caught the man's eye.

He leaned toward her, and a look of curiosity crossed his face. "Perhaps I should inspect your camp. Make sure everything is in order." He dismounted and walked to the exact spot where Aralyn had dropped the rabbit. "And what is this?" He pointed to her kill and gave them both an icy stare, gaze moving from one to the other.

Aralyn still held the arrow. There was no way to hide it now. She didn't even try. "I killed it."

"You did? On your way to your wedding, and you decide to go hunting?"

"She's lying, of course," Gillis said. "I killed it. Thought I would surprise the lady with a bit of rabbit meat for breakfast. I take full responsibility—"

"No. You won't," Aralyn cut in. "I'm the one who killed it. I didn't ..." There was no way to explain what had happened.

"What? You didn't ... know? That is no excuse," the lord's man interjected.

Aralyn's chin lifted. "I realize that."

The lord's man raised his eyebrows. "I'm glad to hear it." He picked up the rabbit. "Evidence." His feet crunched against the rocks as he stepped before Gillis. "You should know ..." Something on Gillis' arm caught his eye. "You're a Peacekeeper?"

"Yes." Gillis' voice rang steady. "Yes, I am a Peacekeeper."

The lord's man nodded. "So one of you has lied to me, a representative of the king. You will have to come with me. Both of you. The lord will determine your punishment. And I will take that." He pointed at Aralyn's bow. She instinctively snatched it back.

"Give that to me, miss."

Aralyn stood rigid.

"Give it to him, Aralyn." Gillis' voice held a warning.

Aralyn swallowed. Everything in her objected as she handed it to him.

"And your arrows, including that bloody one in your hand."

Again, Aralyn turned them over. The king's representative hung her bow and quiver on the side of his horse and placed the bloody arrow in a leather bag, probably used for gathering such evidence.

The lord's man pulled out two lengths of rope. "I hope you won't think of resisting." His eyes darted between them again. "Even if you did, I am not an easy person to defeat. Any other weapons?"

Aralyn reached for the hunting knife at her waist and held it out. Gillis gave him his sword and the belt of daggers as well.

The lord's man tied their wrists, tethered their horses to his, and helped them mount, still not an easy task. It was only a short distance to the lord's manse, and they followed him in. Columns of Delorean-style towered over them, serpents carved into the sides, odd-shaped flowers at the top. The cold passed through Aralyn's thin boots as they walked over red and black tiled floors. Velvet tapestries lined the walls, muffling the footfalls of the men's boots. The lord's man led them through a wide open doorway. Royal colors decorated them—banners of red, white, and purple.

"Lord N'elde—"

"What is it, Aih'len?" The lord frowned from behind a polished desk of Drestani wood, papers piled high. He glanced up.

Aih'len stretched his hand to indicate Gillis and Aralyn, gave his version of what had happened, and showed Lord N'elde the evidence.

The lord stood and waved his arm at the rabbit. "All right, get that out of here. I've seen enough."

"Yes, milord."

Lord N'elde's head swung to Aralyn and Gillis.

Aralyn's skin crawled as she recognized him. He had been in Sathria at one time, advising the magistrate, and his advice had not been good. When he found people breaking the pettiest of laws, he suggested thrashing or having a horse drag them through the village. Now, here she was standing before him after hunting in the king's woods.

Lord N'elde looked her escort over. "Gillis?"

"Lord N'elde." Gillis bowed his head.

"Oh come, Gillis, that's no way to treat a friend." Lord N'elde slipped around his desk and strode toward Gillis.

They knew each other?

The lord stretched his arm to Gillis. His hands still tied, Gillis made no effort to return the greeting.

"Untie him. Untie them both." Lord N'elde gestured to a guard.

Aralyn's hands swung loose, and she rubbed her wrists.

"You know." Lord N'elde cleared his throat. "I have to do something. If word got out that you did not receive punishment, the woods would soon be filled with poachers, and people would say I'm getting soft. Especially the king."

"The king is a good man, a merciful one." Gillis' eyes glinted with anger.

Aralyn knew the lord wasn't listening. He sat down at his pile of papers and drummed his fingers on the one clean area of his desk. His critical eye raked over them. "What made you decide, Gillis, as a peacemaker, to hunt in the king's woods?"

"The lass was hungry, and I suspect, milord ..." He appeared to choke on that last word.

"It was me." Aralyn stepped forward. "He's try—"

The lord tilted his head at her. "Did I address you?"

Aralyn bowed her head. "No, milord."

But Aralyn had his attention now, and his hard gaze landed on her. "What were you about to say?"

"I ... I didn't know I was in the king's woods."

"I see." Lord N'elde scratched his chin. "Well, you know ignorance is no excuse."

How many times had she heard that?

"Don't listen to her. I was the one. She fancies me and wishes to take the blame." Gillis raised his voice.

Aralyn's chin dropped. "No! That's not true. Gillis, you can't—"

"All right!" The lord stood. "Enough! I see what's going on." He gestured toward Aralyn. "She had the bow. She was found with the bloodied arrow in her possession. I judge from her reaction that she does not fancy you."

Gillis tried again. "But I suspect an outside force was at—"

"I said 'enough.'" A cold determination marked the lord's voice. "I shall have her thrashed, a good salting when she comes to, and perhaps a night in the dungeon."

Aralyn swayed. Lord N'elde's voice droned on, but she no longer heard him. Had he said twenty? Twenty lashings? That was half the usual number but...no, please. What had she done?

"She's a young woman, milord." Gillis was arguing for her. "She's on her way to her betrothed. Let me take her punishment."

Lord N'elde narrowed his eyes and seemed to consider. He shook his head. "No, you perhaps are just as guilty as she." He tapped fingers on his desk. "But like our king, I will show mercy in this. I will keep the weapons she used, but will only punish her with fifteen lashings and without the flagellum."

No flagellum. Good. But would there be barbs? The nasty hooks that tore into a person's flesh did severe damage. Always.

"I can take some of those if I am guilty too," Gillis offered again.

"No, it is a merciful sentence." Aralyn couldn't believe she'd said that. Compared to his more extreme punishments, this was indeed merciful. But still ...

Lord N'elde's head came up at Aralyn's words, and he gave her the barest of nods. "You see, Gillis, she realizes she has done wrong. Since she is so forthright, I will not place her in the dungeon but release her to you. But she will still receive the lashings."

Gillis clenched his fists, took a step toward the lord, and shouted, "I appeal to the ki—"

Aralyn shuddered as a guard hit Gillis on the head with the hilt of his sword. Gillis fell to the floor unconscious. Aralyn cried out and stepped toward the fallen figure. Someone grabbed her arms. "Let me go!" She struggled, knew she shouldn't, but she couldn't leave Gillis like that. She kicked at the guard, and he grabbed her ankles, lifting her feet off the ground while the other held her arms. They carried her out.

She stopped fighting as they brought her into an expansive sand yard. The place smelled of dung and old blood, urine, sweat ... all the smells that came with an abused human body. She tried not to gag as they dropped her and rolled her onto her stomach. A guard placed a foot on her back. "Don't move."

Another guard called out for two whips and some rope.

Two whips?

They forced her to her feet, stripped her of her cloak and tunic, and wound a rope around her waist, securing her to a pole. Another man had her wrists and pulled them above her head, tying them to the top of the pole.

Her stomach dropped as reality set in. By now, a large crowd had gathered to watch. Expectant faces, hungry for punishment that didn't involve them, appeared above a nearby wall. A young boy sat atop his father's shoulders.

Two guards brought Gillis out, bound and gagged, a rag stuffed in his mouth. His brow furrowed over moist eyes. There was nothing more he could do for her, but at least she wouldn't scream. Would not scream.

And she kept her word until the whip snapped and the first lash fell.

**

Aralyn's face imprinted the sand, and she shook to the point of convulsing. Gillis knelt next to her. Her tunic and cloak were nearby, but he didn't reach for them. Soldiers and guards had trampled them, and they were too much of a mess to bother with. Done with her, the soldiers had thrown her to the side. Of course, they had others to bring in for "justice." He heard the screams of a young boy. Gillis forced himself to ignore it. He had to get Aralyn to their horses, and she needed water. Too much blood for one girl to lose. He wrapped her in his cloak. He wanted to know if she was conscious and spoke gently. "Aralyn, can ye hear me? Can ye walk a'tall?" Aralyn moaned and clung to him as he brought her to her feet. Her head dropped, and her knees gave way.

"No, I guess not." He gathered her in his arms while trying his best to shield her modesty and avoid pressing on her wounds.

A narrow, covered passageway led him to a smaller and better-smelling courtyard. He wasn't sure where to go, but knew he was headed in the right general direction. Meanwhile, his head still pounded from the strike on it.

Lord N'elde appeared with their horses. He shifted from one foot to the other. "I ... I didn't realize, Gillis. And I forgot about you ... Peacekeepers and Rangers ..."

Gillis felt as though flames lit his eyes. "Ye forgot what? That I have the ear of the king?" Gillis heard his old manner of speech come forth, but it didn't betray half the anger he felt. Even with the horses loaded with generous provisions and his sword in its rightful place, he was unmoved.

Lord N'elde froze. "And, and...I didn't realize it is Brone of Maizehollow she is to wed."

Gillis raised an eyebrow. He knew Brone? How? Perhaps they had business dealings. He didn't ask. Didn't matter.

The lord continued, "Tell him that, will you? That I didn't know? I would never harm his bride."

"I think I shall let ye sit on that one. Like you said, ignorance is no excuse."

"Perhaps she should see a healer before she leaves." He stepped forward. "There are good ones on the estate."

Gillis fumed. He needed to get away from this place, but Aralyn had needs.

"Clean clothes for the lass and blankets," Gillis said. "Bandages. Lots of them."

"Of course." Lord N'elde snapped his fingers, and a passing servant set off to find the healer. "I'll help you put her on her horse, naturally."

Had the man always been such an idiot? "She'll be riding with me. Ye'll not touch her."

"Very well, Gillis." The lord spun on his heel and departed.

Aralyn roused, murmuring, groaning. She was bleeding through his cloak.

A rather matronly-looking woman arrived with bandages and Windsor oil. Well, they had one thing right. Windsor oil was the best thing for this type of wound. A young girl came behind the older woman with a bundle of clothes, including a warm cloak.

"Let's lay her down on the bench." The short woman had amazing strength, and she took Aralyn from him. "I'm a healer. My name is Manya."

They washed out the wounds, and Gillis could see where skin and muscle were torn on her right side, on both shoulder blades, and down the middle of her back. One cut wrapped around her neck, and one left a mark on her breast. Gillis wanted to pound his fists on the lictor's face. Both of them. He hadn't counted the number of lashings but knew it had to be more than fifteen. After all, they were training the younger lictor, and his marks were not as deep. Gillis flinched as he remembered. They had dragged him into the yard where they were about to punish his charge. His charge whom he should have been able to protect. The sound of the whip and her screams had made his head pound harder, but that was not the worst of it. The complete helplessness he felt at having to watch and listen—that was *his* punishment.

He and the kind-eyed healer placed oil on the wounds, which immediately produced a change. Some of the wounds closed, and the bleeding slowed. They cut away pieces of Aralyn's skin, and Gillis debated whether any of the deep cuts needed stitches. He decided to wait to see what the Windsor oil did. Manya helped Gillis place thick bandages across her back. She and the younger girl dressed Aralyn so that the tunic they provided opened in the back. They even had a warm cloak for her. At one point, Aralyn opened her eyes and mumbled. She was semiconscious now. That would help in getting her on his horse, but the pain he read in her expression made him wish she were unconscious. She shook from head to toe, her breathing erratic.

"You've got blood in your hair, sir," the younger girl said. "You're bleeding."

"Let me see." Manya was standing on her tiptoes to get a look.

Gillis waved her off.

"Oh no, you don't. You've got to take care of the girl. You'll let me take care of you. How did this happen?"

"Guard knocked me out for speaking up for the lass." Gillis winced as she pressed on the wound. She snipped hair, cleaned the wound, and smeared ointment on it that first stung and then soothed.

With the healer's help, he managed to position Aralyn on his horse, leaning her over Restless's neck. The horse remained still as if he knew what they needed. Aralyn was aware enough to hold on to Restless's neck.

Manya's brow puckered as she held Aralyn in place. Gillis mounted with her in front, pulled her close. He hoped he could find a place to camp and quickly. Perhaps he should take the lord up on his offer to stay.

No.

He could only imagine more violence coming from that plan, and he would likely be the instigator of it. He urged Restless forward, hoping never again to see this place. Monpomme trotted beside him and nudged Aralyn's hand. It almost made Gillis smile. Almost.

It occurred to him they'd had little to eat this day, and yet he was not even hungry. After traveling about half a league, Gillis knew he had to stop. Aralyn was moaning, and her head drooped forward, hair drenched in sweat. At least the shaking had subsided. He found a stream not far from the track they traveled. Getting her off the horse by himself would not be easy.

He reached behind him, worked a blanket loose, and threw it on the ground. He laid her down on Restless's neck and managed to keep one hand on her back while he slipped from the saddle. While Aralyn clung to Restless, he lay out the blanket.

When he lifted her from his horse, she moaned and opened her eyes. "Gillis."

"I'm here, lass."

"Good." She lifted her hand and patted his.

As he worked to place her in a comfortable position, Aralyn whimpered.

"I know, lass. I know. I wish it coulda been me." He meant it, and he hoped the words brought her a bit of comfort.

Gillis took out his bag and found cloves, root of salnik, and a few drops of mint oil. He took the ingredients, made a paste of them, and placed the mixture on her tongue. She didn't need to swallow for it to take effect, though she tried. He missed the hoofbeats approaching, missed the sound of leather creaking until the man squatted next to him and spoke. "How is she?"

Gillis shook his head. "Not good, Re'ah. I'm glad to see you. How did you find us?"

"I heard the betrothed of Brone of Maizehollow and a Peacekeeper were in trouble with the law. I knew you had to be near the lord's manse."

Gillis raised his eyebrows. Word traveled quickly in this land. "I need to look at her wounds again. I used some Windsor oil on her."

"Yes, it will not hurt to check."

Gillis sighed deeply. Self-recrimination took its bead on him. And it had him.

The bandages were bloody but not soaked. It still wouldn't hurt to change them as Re'ah had taught him. Fortunately, Lord N'elde's healer had made sure he had plenty. Re'ah washed off the excess blood, and Gillis readied the bandages. He could better see where they might need to stitch. Even though he had seen many men wounded from battle, he lifted his eyes to heaven, willing away the thoughts of what this would do to her.

Re'ah took charge. "Start some coffee, and bring me some fresh water."

"Aye." Gillis got the thread and needle for Re'ah. He grabbed their waterskins, filled them, and gathered wood. He soon had the fire going and put water on to boil.

Gillis returned to Re'ah's side, and they worked on the cuts that the Windsor oil couldn't heal. It still felt unnatural to pierce a human's skin with a needle, even though he'd lost count of the number of times he'd done this, but never on a young woman.

"I think that's the best we can do," Re'ah said. "Let me see if I can get her to drink some water. Then I will join you in downing some of that coffee."

"Sounds good." Although his stomach still felt queasy.

Aralyn drank and barely whimpered.

When Re'ah returned to the fire with their coffee, Gillis commented, "It'll be a good three days before she's able to ride any distance."

"More than likely. It might be good to find shelter."

"Aye, fewer flies." Gillis glanced at the sky and noted gathering clouds. "I wish we'd made it to Crel. I know there's a decent inn there where we could put her in a room."

Re'ah sipped his coffee. "There is a deserted cabin about a mile up the road and off the main trail. We could move her there. It is close enough to Crel that I can go into the village for more provisions."

"All right, we'll do that." Gillis closed his eyes, praying for Aralyn. How could he have let this happen?

Re'ah placed his hand on Gillis' back. "She will make it even though she has lost a good deal of blood. We should take turns watching her tonight."

"Of course." Gillis choked down some of the Elven bread. He couldn't eat anything else—even the dried fruit Re'ah offered him.

Gillis rose with a grunt and went to Aralyn's side. He squatted next to her and placed a hand on her damp head. When he touched her, the memories of what had happened came rushing back. He reviewed each step of this mishap, wondering what he could have done differently. He shook his head. If this was the work of Mal'ev, that could only mean more danger awaited them. Mal'ev was relentless and enjoyed manipulating those he considered enemies.

Chapter 9

The pain wound through her as a vicious snake in her veins, trying to crawl outward. She called for her mother. For Lot'fe. But they would never hear her pitiful calls. Screams from within her made it to her throat but only came out as a strangled moan. She heard men nearby, their voices familiar. Every so often, one of them came closer or knelt beside her.

"Here, lass, can you swallow? Just a little." It was Gillis, the escort.

"I know. You want your mother, but I am here, Aralyn." Re'ah's voice was filled with such concern that it scared her.

Someone held her hand, smoothed her hair, and placed something cool on her brow.

She must have slept for when she came to, pain seared through her again. A small room with four wooden walls surrounded her, a door in one. She lay on her stomach, the smell of blood and medicine heavy in the air. Mixed in with that was the aroma of fragrant oils. The mattress beneath her must have been down-filled, but it did nothing to soothe her.

A shadow fell across her face.

"Are you with us?" It was Re'ah.

"I hurt." Her voice was a tiny squeak, and the first thing it did was complain.

Re'ah's presence was a comfort, but she wanted more than comfort. She wanted relief. He assured her he would take care of the pain right away, and he mixed ingredients in a small porcelain mortar.

"Here." He placed a minty substance on her tongue. "Leave it in your mouth, and let it go down slowly."

Aralyn did as told and waited for the pain to abate. "Water, please." It would be awkward trying to drink while lying on her stomach.

Re'ah brought her a cup with a hollow reed extending from it. She sucked on the reed, and water trickled into her mouth. The pain was gone. "Mmm." She drank and drank.

"Easy, slow down." Re'ah placed a hand on her head. "You have not had anything in your stomach for a while."

"Please don't make me eat."

"I will not, but I do need to look at your back."

Aralyn nodded. She knew this would be painful, but it couldn't be worse than what she'd already been through, and Re'ah was a practiced healer. Even so, Aralyn felt every pull on the bandages as he removed them.

"Not bad, Aralyn. You're healing. This wound,"—he glanced at her— "it does not look good. Infection is setting in, perhaps. Let me get something for that." He returned with a tiny vial. "This might sting."

And it did. The smell of lavender mixed with an unfamiliar scent wafted toward her. She pulled on the mattress, scrunching it in her hand, and bit her lip to keep from crying out.

"I am sorry." Re'ah's gentle voice settled upon her.

"Please do what you need to. I have to be ready for my wedding." But would she ever be ready for it?

"Where is Gillis?" Aralyn realized he was not in sight. "And where are we?"

"Gillis stayed up with you last night. He is nearby, sleeping. He feels very responsible for what happened."

"It was me. And ... he tried. He tried to take the blame ..." Her voice grew weaker. "He tried to take my punishment."

Re'ah smiled. "That sounds like Gillis."

"And they knocked him out, Re'ah."

"Yes, I saw the lump on his head."

"He's all right, though?" The concern she felt tugged in her chest.

"Yes, he is."

"I'm glad." Aralyn sighed. "I'll have scars, won't I?"

"I am afraid so."

She could handle scars. But Brone ... what about his reaction? "How far are we from Maizehollow?"

"At least a day. We sent word to Brone to let him know of our delay."

A horrible taste came to her mouth. "My stomach..." She didn't finish and heaved.

Re'ah placed a hand on her shoulder as nausea swept over her. "Here." He offered the cup of water again. "Now slowly."

She let the cold water linger before swallowing.

"Keep that down, and I'll see about getting you more. Perhaps some tea with honey."

Tea sounded wonderful. She stirred and felt the pull of muscles against wounds, her skin trying to open, and she couldn't help but weep. "I'm sorry for my tears."

Re'ah's hands rested on her arm. "Child, it is fine. I imagine I would weep too. I have seen grown men wail from lesser wounds."

Despite the pain, that made Aralyn smile.

***

How long had she been asleep this time? She pushed herself up and turned on her side, surprised at how little pain she felt. Her stomach rumbled.

There must have been a stove in their shack. The smells of cooking were too strong to be coming from outside. She turned her gaze toward the back wall and spotted the stove and Gillis standing before it.

He swung around as Aralyn placed her feet on the floor. "Ah, lass, you're up!" He sounded elated.

"How long?"

"How long have we been here, you mean?" He sighed. "Two days and two nights. You've been sleeping most of that time."

How many days had passed since her punishment? Did the lost days matter? At least they'd sent word ahead.

"Where's Re'ah?"

"He went into Crel to get supplies." Gillis stirred something on the stove.

"Could I have something to eat?"

"You're hungry?" Gillis' face lit up.

"Yes, I am." Her stomach growled in agreement.

"Well, I've got just the thing for that." He pulled whatever he was cooking off the stove.

Aralyn attempted to stand.

"No need for you to get up, lass."

"Gillis, I need to go outside."

"Ah." A look of understanding came over his face.

"Unless you have a pot somewhere." She glanced around the room.

"I'm afraid not. So it'll be outside." He wiped his hands on a small rag and came to her side.

Aralyn used the bed to push herself up. Unexpected dizziness made her sway, and she reached for something to steady herself, but Gillis had already placed his hands on her waist. She leaned against him and grabbed his arm.

"Take it easy. No need to rush things," he murmured.

"That's what you think."

Gillis' mouth tugged upward, and he led her to the door. He took her to a secluded spot and turned his back. She hiked up the thin skirt they had put on her, wondering for the first time who had provided it for her. She felt skin pulling against her injuries again as she bent. The sound of water hitting the earth brought relief. She tried to rise and instead fell backward. "I need some help."

Thoroughly embarrassing.

"I've got you, lass." From behind, Gillis placed her underarms in the crook of his elbows and lifted Aralyn to her feet. She had to let him help with her undergarments as well. But at least he didn't say anything.

"Thank you," she said in a low voice.

"Don't mention it."

"I won't ... don't worry."

Gillis' chuckle was a pleasant sound.

***

"Re'ah and I both think you're ready to ride. What do you say?"

"I believe I am, Gillis." Aralyn managed a smile. Her injuries still caused shooting pain through her back, but surely, she could ride at least for a while. Her old skirts smelled clean, and she was glad to have them back. One of the men must have washed them out for her. The tunic was gone and she had a new cloak in place of the old one.

"Re'ah is getting the horses ready. We'll be taking it slowly, lass. And anytime you need to, we can stop, or you can ride with me or Re'ah."

Slow sounded good, but she was anxious to see her groom. She thought about Brone's son—the boy whose name she did not even know. Perhaps she would learn to care for, or even love him. Perhaps she could help ease the heartache he surely felt after losing his mother, just as she had felt after losing her father and stepfather. Something in her longed for that connection, although she'd always found children, other than her sister, rather annoying.

When Aralyn and Gillis came out, Re'ah was putting Monpomme's bridle on. "You ready, Aralyn?"

Aralyn nodded.

"Are you sure you do not want to ride with me?" Re'ah offered.

"No, I'd like to make a go of it on my own. But I could use some help mounting."

Re'ah cupped his hands, she stepped into them, and threw her other leg over Monpomme's back. Restless was eager to pick up the pace and kept straining at his bridle, lifting his forelegs to break into a trot, but Gillis restrained him.

"Gillis, what is the name of Brone's son?" Aralyn asked as they started down the trail.

"Charles. He's my godson." Gillis' note of pride was hard to miss.

"And he'll be my stepson. If something happened to Brone, you and I could end up raising him togeth ..." Why had she said that? "I didn't mean ..."

"Not to worry. You and Brone are destined to be happy together for a long while. I know it."

"Will he be upset with my injuries?"

"I'm sure he will be, especially considering the circumstances."

Aralyn shook her head. "I mean...the way I'll look...my back like it is."

"I doubt it, lass." Gillis paused, and Aralyn read compassion laced with anger in his gaze. "No, I'd be more concerned about Lord N'elde."

"Brone won't do anything foolish, will he?"

"In retribution? He could, but I doubt he will. He'll be busy being a newlywed." He gave her a wink.

The heat in her face rose. But how would she be with him? Would she even be able to? Aralyn wished she had a woman to talk to, and for some reason, her thoughts turned to Elnala.

Re'ah, riding behind them, spurred his horse forward. "I found this when I cleaned up your skirts." He held out the dragon stone.

Aralyn gasped. He had found it! How could she have forgotten? "Thank you, Re'ah."

He dropped it in her hand, and she tucked it in a pocket.

Despite the slow pace and the short distance they traveled, Aralyn was exhausted that night. At one point, she woke, eyes wide open. Had she dreamed? She couldn't remember, but something wasn't right. Gillis slept nearby, and Re'ah was up, pacing and looking out into the forest. He must have heard Aralyn stirring, for he swung around, and his gaze landed on her. "Are you all right, Aralyn?"

"I'm fine."

Re'ah cocked his head. "I believe something is bothering you."

Aralyn didn't bother to argue. He would know if she were lying. He came to her side and sat down. "What is it?"

"It must have been a dream—about Brone and his son—they were in trouble."

"I see." He leaned back, looking up at the stars. "Gillis told me about the attack on your mind. How some outside force manipulated you into thinking you were at home and that you needed to hunt."

"Yes, that's what he thought."

Re'ah nodded. "Aralyn, this dream may have had nothing to do with what I believe is an attack from Mal'ev, but it occurs to me you need help in staving off his manipulation. Next time it happens, think of a wall. Imagine building a fortress against those attacks. You have the ability, but you need more training than I can give you."

"I shall try, Re'ah. But if you can't train me, who can?"

Re'ah glanced at a softly snoring Gillis and lowered his voice. "An Elf. One with the proper talents."

Aralyn's thoughts turned to the two who had given her the dragon stone and then to her betrothed. "Perhaps Brone could help? He's part Elf."

Re'ah pinched his lips together as shadows leaped over his face from the firelight. "I am not sure, Aralyn. But you need to get back to sleep."

Aralyn bid him good night and crawled back into her bedroll.

"Yes, my Aralyn. Rest."

***

Aralyn approached Re'ah while he cooked breakfast the next day. He told her to sit while he finished. She did so, watching him turn biscuits and stir eggs.

"Good morning. Re'ah. Aralyn." Gillis greeted them with a yawn.

Re'ah handed him a cup of coffee.

"Ah, good man."

Breakfast tasted better than usual. Re'ah fixed Aralyn some tea made from an unfamiliar leaf, and she felt much refreshed.

As they rode, Aralyn tried not to complain about the pain and pulling she still felt. Her wounds were healing nicely, according to both Re'ah and Gillis, but their complete healing would take some time.

Re'ah again came beside her. He seemed to know she was not all right. "I will tell Gillis to stop."

Aralyn shook her head. "No, I want to keep going."

But Re'ah insisted, and Gillis nodded, giving Aralyn a concerned glance. She wanted them both to quit fussing over her, but she still needed their help. More of her pride fled, and in its place, a soft humility blanketed her as Gillis helped her dismount.

"Why don't you ride with me?" Gillis suggested as they prepared to leave.

Aralyn frowned, but she agreed that might be best.

They remounted with her in front of Gillis.

"Lean back against me," he said, placing a hand on her waist.

All the irritation he had exhibited before was gone from his voice. It seemed he only wanted to care for her.

Aralyn was amazed at how much better she felt with his support. But after a moment, she grew uneasy. They were too close. No, that wasn't it. On the first part of their journey, she had held onto him. This was no different. Or was it? The disquiet melded with a strange feeling, something gentle and new, as wisps of his breath ran through her hair. His smell of forest and leather caught her in its grip. More than just a desire for comfort, the emotion went deeper.

She tried to sit up straighter to avoid the disquieting feelings, but before long her strength gave out, and she fell back against him, once again enveloped in his warmth.

Chapter 10

Re'ah bid them goodbye at the branch off to King's City. As always, it was difficult to see him go. But King's City was less than half a day from Maizehollow, so they would surely see him soon. Maybe he could even make it for the binding.

Her strength returning, Aralyn told Gillis, "I'd like to ride Monpomme. I think I'll be fine."

"All right. If you think you can. We don't have much farther to go."

As they approached Maizehollow, the outlying farms came into view—two- and three-story houses—with acres of land around each. Familiar smells of manure and freshly cut hay hit Aralyn's nostrils.

"Do you hear that?" Gillis asked.

A gruff humanlike voice traveled through the trees that lined the roadside. "What is that?"

"It's the Renora birds."

"What are Ren—"

"Listen." Gillis put a finger to his lips.

Aralyn gasped as she realized why this was a phenomenon. The birds greeted Gillis by name. Bright plumage, the color of ripe grapes, made them stand out from their surroundings.

The birds twittered as if consulting one another and called out with a tentative "Arah ... Arl ... Then excitedly, "Aralyn, Aralyn, greetings, greetings."

She chuckled despite her discomfort from the long ride.

"I had to help them with your name a bit, lass, but they've got it now and won't forget."

Aralyn cocked her head. The birds had learned her name, and Gillis had somehow taught them? As they rode past, the flock continued to call out to Aralyn and Gillis, blending their names into a song.

The walls around Maizehollow reached higher than any Aralyn had ever seen. The stone structures punctuated by murder holes made Sathria's defenses look pitiful indeed. Iron gates gave the city a sense of foreboding. But her groom waited inside those gates, and after all these years, she would again see the one who had promised to love her.

From just outside the gates, a group of riders charged their way. The men brandished swords and shouted warnings.

Plagues. That was Aralyn's first thought. Inside the broad defenses, people were dying. "Gillis?"

He ignored her, pulling on his reins to halt Restless. Aralyn followed suit, and Gillis placed a hand on the hilt of his sword.

The riders stopped about two horse lengths from them. "What is your business here?" one shouted.

"I bring Aralyn, intended of Brone of Maizehollow." Gillis' brow furrowed.

"Intended of ... Brone?" The man gave him a curt nod. "I see. You're Gillis, aren't you? The Peacekeeper?"

"Aye."

The leader gave the other men a signal to sheath their swords, and he did likewise. "I'm afraid I have bad news then. No one is allowed into the city, nor will they be for the foreseeable future."

"What do you mean?" Aralyn cried as the thought of plagues ravaging the city clutched her.

Gillis signaled for her to be quiet. "Why? Is it sickness?"

"No, but people have died." The guard's voice was harsh, but Aralyn read the pity in his eyes. "And I'd like to speak with you in private, sir."

"Stay here," Gillis told her. There was no debate over Gillis' command. He followed the man over a grassy field, about half a bowshot away. Their voices were just low enough that Aralyn could not hear. She waited, keenly aware of the four other riders eyeing her. Her gaze went to each of them in turn, and they shifted in their saddles.

"What's going on?" she asked.

Only one looked at her. "We cannot say, miss." He pointed toward Gillis and the apparent leader of the group. "They will have to tell you."

Aralyn focused on Gillis and the man he spoke with. She could see mouths moving but heard only indistinct murmurs until Gillis spoke with clear alarm.

"What do ye mean? He's....no." Gillis placed a palm on his forehead.

The other man jutted his chin in Aralyn's direction. She caught a few of his words. "... bind ... you realize."

Gillis was shaking his head. His face unreadable, he met Aralyn's gaze and rode back to her side. "You're coming with me. Like the man said, we can't go into the city. They've got it locked down." His eyes were full when he lifted them to her. "Brone's been killed." His jaw worked. "And everyone on his estate."

No. This couldn't be happening! Her betrothed was dead?

She spoke past the lump rooted in her throat. "How, Gillis?"

"Not sure exactly. Rogues or perhaps assassins. Not sure..." His head was down, staring at the pommel on his saddle. When he lifted his eyes to her, they were dark with rage and sorrow. "All of them. All in Brone's household are dead. Including his servants ... the whole lot of them."

"Gillis? All of them? The boy?"

"Yes, little Charles." Gillis' face turned to the sky. "Elyon, he was only six."

"I have to go home then. Mother will be—"

"No, Aralyn. Yer not listening. Ye'll be coming with me. Did you not hear what he said about ..." He rubbed his chin.

"I only heard a few words." Aralyn knew her voice was rising, and demanded. "What is it?"

"Never mind. Ye have to come with me."

Aralyn didn't like the finality of those words.

The leader and three of the guards headed back toward the gates. Another one stayed with them.

What was going on?

Gillis was in shock no doubt, just as she was, but she wanted to know everything. "Why must I come with you?"

"I'm to keep you safe, remember? To do that, you have to...I must..." He cleared his throat. "Just follow me, lass."

So he wanted her to keep her mouth shut and ride? No. She wouldn't do that.

Gillis took off, but Aralyn held Monpomme back. With fire in his eyes, Gillis turned back. "Are ye crazed, lass? Come with me."

"Tell me what is going on. If Brone is dead, I will return to Sathria."

"Ye can't go back to yer Mother. It won't be safe, and it's understood you have to stay here...with me."

Stay with him? What exactly did that mean? "But—"

"Aralyn, come. I can explain more later."

Aralyn followed him, and the guard with the salt-and-pepper beard stayed with them.

"He's coming too, Aralyn. For your and my protection," Gillis explained.

"But—"

"They'll send a priest later, Gillis. Maybe in a few days," the guard said. "They've had their hands full with last rites and comforting almost the entire city. Brone was well-loved."

A priest. What did they need a priest for? Perhaps to counsel, to pray with them?

They rode hard to the north and east, outside the walls of the city. The hills grew steeper, and Aralyn's back grew stiffer. Needles of pain shot through it, but she kept up as Gillis led the way.

The path leveled, and they rode through trees that formed a tunnel and arched overhead, like a rabbit trail but large enough for horses and people. The trees blocked the sunlight for a few hundred yards. Finally, a clearing lay ahead. A wooden house stood in the middle of a fenced yard, outbuildings nearby. Gillis dismounted and opened the gate. He led them to the stables and watering trough. To the guard, he said, "Make yourself at home. I'll see that ye're fed."

"No need." The guard shook his head. "Got my rations. Be better if I stay by the gate after the horses are put up."

"Come with me, Aralyn." Gillis' voice was that of a disgruntled commander.

"I need to take care of Monp—"

"I'll see to the horses, Miss Aralyn," the guard said.

"And Hermes is here, sir. He'll help," Gillis added.

They dismounted, and Gillis took Aralyn by the elbow and led her to the front of the house.

"I'll answer your questions the best I can." He looked skyward to where the sun was leaving streaks of orange and red.

"What is it?"

The hard line of his jaw let her know this was more bad news.

"You didn't hear, so I will tell you." His throat worked. "You and I ... we're to be bound." The gaze that had held her in place dropped to the ground.

Aralyn shook her head. "What? No. I won't marry you." She'd just lost Brone and had not yet wept for him.

"Aralyn, I'm not asking." His voice was a monotone. Emotionless.

"You're telling me? You're forcing me?" This had to be a mistake. A joke.

"No!" His voice exploded, and Aralyn felt as though a thousand shards of glass shot through her. Gillis reached for the side of the house, hands trembling.

Aralyn waited, her throat swelling.

Gillis lifted his eyes to the heavens once more, and his voice was gentler as he spoke. "Ye've got to understand. Traditions around here are deeply entrenched. When a groom dies before he can consummate the marriage, the companion is expected to take over that ... 'duty.'"

Aralyn shook her head. Backed away from Gillis. "And you're his companion. They can't make us do ... that ..."

"I'm afraid they can." Gillis' face became a mask.

"But it's tradition, right? Not a law."

"Doesn't matter, Aralyn." He closed his eyes. "You and I, by Maizehollow tradition, must marry. There's little difference in the two—we abide by them both here or suffer the consequences."

And what could the worst of those consequences be?

"Aralyn, if you're thinking there's some way to get out of this ... there isn't. They'll put us before a priest, and it will be a legal marriage or binding. They will follow us to our bed chamber and..."

"Make certain ..." Aralyn finished for him. "We're together."

"Depends on a number of things. Usually, with people of my rank, they enter, make sure we're in bed, and give their blessing."

"But they could stay and ... and watch?" Aralyn felt the color drain from her face.

Gillis shook his head. "Not likely with someone of my rank. Not that—"

"I heard the guard say a priest was coming?"

"Yes. In a few days, perhaps. What was the date of your wedding?"

"Date? The sixth day after the first full moon of the Cold. I think. Does it matter?"

Gillis shook his head. "No. They probably rescheduled when they got the message about our delay."

"So at this point, it doesn't matter? Just as long as we're bound."

Gillis ran a thick hand through his hair. "It matters. The sooner the better, the way they see it. But, Aralyn, I need ye to—"

A commotion in the front interrupted Gillis.

A sword drawn. Loud voices.

"Who are you, man?" the guard demanded.

"I must see them!"

Gillis' hands dropped to his side. "Re'ah!" He ran to the gate where the noise had erupted, Aralyn trying to keep up. "Guard, let him in. It's all right."

Re'ah was breathing hard. "I rode as fast as I could. Where is Aralyn? Is she all right?"

"Yes, Re'ah. I'm right here." Aralyn made her way past the men, and a look of pure joy came over Re'ah's face.

"Aralyn. I heard about Brone ... his family."

Mute, she gazed into his face. He was concerned she had been killed, too. Perhaps that was the reason Brone and his family were dead. Because of her. Maybe this was the Rogues' revenge. Her travel schedule had changed. The flogging. It may have saved her life. But they—Brone and his family—were supposed to be safe too.

"Gillis, Aralyn. I am sorry for the loss of your friend, and Aralyn ... your intended. The child ..." Tears sprang to Re'ah's eyes. "An innocent." His voice trailed off.

"They were all innocent." The guard sheathed his sword. "Brone never hurt anyone. Didn't deserve this." His gaze landed on Aralyn. "Your intended was a good man, miss."

No one said a word for a moment.

"I heard the priest was coming," Re'ah said.

"We'll be bound in a few days, perhaps sooner," Gillis answered.

Re'ah nodded. He pulled Aralyn into his arms, but this time she found little comfort, not even a hint of calming or assurance of normalcy.

"Aralyn, Deonella's made coffee, I'm sure." Gillis touched her shoulder. "Not sure what we have in the way of tea, but maybe she can put some on. Why don't you ask her for something to eat?"

Eat? How could she possibly eat?

Gillis walked her back to the house, opened the front door, and released Aralyn's arm.

"Kitchen's through there." He pointed. "Aralyn ... I'm sorry. I didn't want—"

"This way?" Aralyn cut in, pointing.

"Aye." He closed the door behind her.

Aralyn glanced down as she stepped inside. A wooden floor. Sturdy, swept clean. She would have danced on it if it weren't for the news she had just received. Aralyn walked through what she was sure had to be a living room. Several wooden chairs covered by golden cloth and flowery pillows gave it a decidedly feminine touch. A tapestry hung above a cushioned bench with padded arms. She opened the door that led into the kitchen. A small wooden table was to her left, and to her right, a slender woman with a pale, heart-shaped face.

"Hello, miss. I'm Deonella. Sounds like there's been some trouble?" Deonella raised an eyebrow. "I assume you're the one Gillis served as escort to?"

"Yes," Aralyn replied. "I'm Aralyn. Brone ... my intended has been killed. And his family. His servants." She felt numb as she said it.

Deonella swung around so her back was to Aralyn. She was cooking some type of meat, and it smelled wonderful.

Aralyn took in the up-to-date kitchen. "You have a stove and a water pump." Why did that even matter right now?

"Sit, miss, and I'll serve you." Deonella motioned to the table.

"We can't even go into the city." Aralyn's throat felt like splinters were erupting in it. "And I am to marry Gillis, so I'll be staying here ... I suppose. Until we're bound?" Her thoughts fractured, and she felt sure of nothing.

Deonella placed chopped meat and gravy on a plate and poured Aralyn some coffee. "Aye, you'll stay here, but not in his bedroom. There are extra rooms upstairs." Was that a hint of resentment in her youthful voice?

Aralyn sipped the coffee. It was bitter, but it warmed her insides. She didn't think to ask about tea. "Did you know Brone?" Aralyn picked up a fork.

"Not that well, but yes, I knew him. I knew his servants better, although they were a little too toffee-tossed for me. But I suppose I shouldn't speak ill of them now." Her voice grew softer at her next words. "And I knew little Charles."

Aralyn noted tears on the woman's face. If Deonella wanted comfort, Aralyn had none to give. She stared at her plate. The meat had the aroma of all the spices Aralyn loved, and she scooped a tiny forkful into her mouth. The taste was as good as she had anticipated, but she almost gagged on that one bite. "Deonella ... would you excuse me?"

"Perhaps you'd like to clean up a bit?"

Aralyn's head came up. "Yes, I would."

A room to the side of the kitchen provided her with privacy, and a large bowl of warm water refreshed her. Deonella had Aralyn put her head under the pump to wash out her hair.

"I've got a clean dress for you. Been in the closet for a while and might be a bit musty, but I think Laella was close enough to your size."

Aralyn didn't care. She was just glad she didn't have to put dusty clothes back on. The dress was on the small side—too short around the hem and sleeves. "Who did you say this belongs to?"

"It belonged to Master Gillis' first wife."

His first wife?

"Yes, miss, he was married before. She is...gone."

Aralyn shifted her feet. "He won't mind me wearing it?"

"I don't think so. If he does ... well, I shall speak with him."

It bothered her, though. "What happened to her?"

"Died tragically. You'll have to ask Master Gillis if you want to know more."

Aralyn nodded. "I need some air. If you will excuse me."

"Of course. Tell those men they need to come eat. I saw them out in the back."

Aralyn slipped out the back door and shivered in the chilly night, her hair still damp. Re'ah and Gillis stood near a fence beyond an overgrown vegetable garden. They were so caught up in conversation, they didn't see her approach. Re'ah had a hand on Gillis's shoulder, and both of them bowed their heads. They were praying. Their heads lifted, followed by a soft "amen," and Gillis wiped his eyes. Aralyn was about to step forward when he spoke. She froze when she heard her name and bits of the conversation.

"Aralyn is quite ... but, I thought about ... guild for her ... learn a trade, but ... nice to have a woman to warm my bed ... my-my duty as a husband ..."

Aralyn backed away from the two men, who still did not see her. What was Gillis saying? Give her up to a guild? That didn't make sense. That it would be nice to have a woman to warm his bed? She had to think, but first, she would go to the stables. Perhaps Monpomme would be a comfort to her.

When she entered, an older man was there. Must be Hermes. Was that his name? Instead of introducing herself, Aralyn turned to the back gate. At one time, it would have opened to the forest. But the latch was rusted in place, and vines entangled it. She pulled them loose and forced the latch. The gate swung open on creaky hinges. Stepping out into the forest, she felt calmer. Surely her thoughts would slow.

The night grew cooler and the stars brighter. Aralyn took off down a narrow path that ended in briars. What was she doing? Her muscles spasmed where the whip had injured them, and she shuddered at Gillis' words. Her emotions from the past two weeks churned together—excitement at leaving Sathria, her beating—which might leave her scarred and muscles damaged—her loss of Brone and the stepchild she would have learned to care for, her hope for a better future for her mother and Terrwynn.

All of that—gone.

Perhaps she should leave this place and never return. She could survive—set traps, make a new bow. Her plans came together. But what about Mother and Terrwynn? What would become of them? Running from problems never solved them. Hadn't Drehensil taught her that? Several minutes of quiet and rationality settled on her. She decided to return, confident that Gillis and she could work this out. Aralyn gazed through the darkened forest toward Gillis' home. Her home. She headed back with a new resolve. That was when she heard the cries of dragon lizards.

Chapter 11

Dragon lizards. Perhaps caught in a hunter's trap. Trapping dragon lizards for their hides was an illegal and cruel business, and Aralyn felt a surge of rage. Torn between returning to Gillis and the potential danger of helping dragon lizards, she only hesitated a moment before she took a running leap over the stream in the direction of their cries.

Aralyn kept a lookout for hunters' traps in the trees. She saw none, and Aralyn glanced over her shoulder toward the house, hesitating. The cries were louder and sounded like Aletha's, Elouard's, and Vandel's. Was it them? Aralyn took off at a run, ducking under tree limbs, letting the voices lead her. Off in the distance, she saw lights. Movement in the shadows. She drew closer. A few more yards and she would be able to see what exactly was going on.

The dragon lizards seemed to know that she approached, and their cries became more frantic.

Then silence.

Aralyn's pulse raced, not only from the run but from their cries and the worry that the sudden quiet brought. But she could see more clearly now.

Dozens of tents occupied a clearing about a bow's shot away. She could make out a man who sat by one of the fires, sharpening his weapons, his chest bare. She slowed her pace and ducked behind a tree.

There appeared to be no guards, but she had to be sure, so she waited. In less than a minute, she spotted two men moving around the perimeter of the camp. She watched long enough to detect a pattern in their patrol.

Many in the camp were Gehallions. Standing off to one side was a group of men and women from Drestani. She thought of running back to let Gillis and the guard know. Enlist their help. But she was afraid of what would happen to the dragon lizards. Maybe they weren't in any danger, but their cries seemed to indicate otherwise. The deepening shadows would help hide her movements, but she estimated her chances of rescuing the three on her own were slim. Still, she had to try. Her mind made up, she pulled the new cloak around her and the cowl over her head.

Aralyn ran to a nearby tree that was closer to the camp. Waited a beat. Ran to the next. A guard appeared off schedule. He must have seen something. She froze as if a spiral-nose snake threatened her. His eyes searched the trees and grasses, and he stared at the spot where she stood. But he never focused on her. He scratched his head and continued his rounds. She'd managed to escape his notice. The thought did not slow the pounding of her heart.

Aralyn crept toward the camp. About twenty feet from one of the tents, Aralyn heard the low clicking and soft cries of the dragon lizards. Aralyn scrambled to a clump of bushes. They were tall enough that she barely had to crouch inside the shrubbery. She made sure no one approached the tent from either direction, knowing she would have to risk leaving her cover.

Both hands slippery with sweat, she wiped them on the dress Deonella had lent her. Darting from the bushes, she stepped in front of the tent where the dragon lizards' cries came from and pulled back the flap. She had to crouch low to enter. Only a small lamp lit the tent, and Aralyn allowed her eyes to adjust. All three dragon lizards were in a cage, chained together and unattended. This didn't make sense. Dragon lizards were valuable. People did not leave them unguarded.

All of them perked up when they saw her. Elouard attempted to move his head, but the chains held him down. Aletha regarded her expectantly, and Vandel made a happy clicking sound despite the weight around her neck. But Aralyn had no idea how to get them loose. She had nothing to cut through the chains and heavy lock that bound them. How could anyone do this to those precious creatures? Aralyn wanted to weep at the sight, but she bit back her tears.

Something stirred in the pocket where she kept the gem the Elves had given her. When she pulled it out, it shifted. Wings flapped, sending a shower of lights. A tiny dragon stood in her hands, the same color as the gem.

Without prompting, the dragon smoothed back its wings and crawled into the lock's opening. All but its tail was inside. The tail flicked, and the lock opened. The chains fell loose, and Aralyn's mouth dropped. The dragon backed out of the lock and flew into her pocket. The dragon lizards gathered around the door, pecking at the latch.

"Stop playing. Let me unhook it."

All three obediently ducked their heads, watching her open the cage door.

Once out of the cage, Vandel twirled, her tail swinging about. Elouard flew straight for the flap Aralyn had come through, Aletha close behind.

They were all clear of the tent, but they had to find their way safely to the forest. Vandel opened her mouth as if she wanted to say something, and she huffed out a one-word command: "R-r ... ru..!"

Aralyn didn't understand her.

"Rrrun!" Vandel repeated. "Rrrun. Rrrrrrun. Rrrrrrun."

"But I need to see you to safety."

Vandel batted her wings at Aralyn and nipped her arm. Aralyn jerked away and caught sight of a soldier wrapped in a passionate embrace with a half-dressed woman. Aralyn guessed he was the one assigned to guard the dragon lizards and was shirking his duties. But he must have heard them, for he pulled back and caught sight of Aralyn. He shoved the woman away and drew his sword.

The dragon lizards dove at him. Hovered, nipped, and batted at his face. He called for help as the woman squealed, and before she knew it, another guard had grabbed her from behind, placed heavy arms around her, and shouted in Common. "Look what I have!"

Idiot. She lowered her mouth to his bare, sweaty arm and bit. Hard. The man swore, grabbed the wound she had inflicted, and Aralyn was free. Just as Vandel had ordered her, she ran, hating herself for leaving the dragon lizards behind. Above, she heard branches creaking, breaking. Leaves showered upon her. A downward gust followed, and a powerful force yanked at her shoulders, the agony causing her to cry out.

She rose in the air.

Drehensil.

He had come for her.

A thick-browed man grabbed for her ankle but missed as Drehensil lifted her. The soldier's eyes grew wide when he realized what was pulling her upward. "Dragon!"

"I know you are hurting. I am sorry." Drehensil adjusted his grip, and the claws of one foot were around her as a secure cage.

The wind chilled her as Drehensil climbed into the sky. *"You rescued the dragon lizards."*

Knowing he would not hear her over the winds, she attempted mind speech for the first time. *"But did they get away?"*

Something in her thoughts sounded like a chuckle. *"Indeed, they ride above you on my back. I will leave you here in the forest. The guard at your home will not be happy with my presence. Prepare to jump. I will not land."* The dragon began his descent. His claws opened, and she tumbled to the ground.

Aralyn landed on her stomach with the wind knocked out of her. She gasped, and air gradually made its way back into her lungs. When she rose to her feet, she realized she was still in the forest, inside a small clearing. Aralyn was a good distance from Gillis' home and close enough to the camp for her sharp hearing to pick up the enemy voices. She crouched and watched them, listening for anything she could understand.

The men and women were crying out in a confused mixture of Gehallion, Destrani, and Common. A dragon had come for them, some shouted, for taking the "baby dragons." Others were ready to pursue and fight the beast. In the middle of the commotion, a man in dark robes came forward.

"Enough!" he shouted in Common, with a heavy accent. She knew that voice and crawled into the shrubs.

"We will go after those dragon lizards. We will find them, and the girl, too. Bring her back alive. Is that simple enough for everyone? Mal'ev has plans for her." The light from one of the fires flashed over his face. The cheekbones, the eyes, his turban.

Siaon? Her friend Lot'fe's husband. She blinked. It was him. Her dislike of the man made an easy jump to hatred. Lot'fe joined her husband, and Aralyn couldn't suppress a gasp. Siaon and Lot'fe were both in league with Mal'ev? They spoke in low murmurs, and Aralyn heard nothing.

Another voice joined their conversation. It came out of Siaon's mouth, raspy and yet powerful. It echoed across the forest. "Siaon, get her back. Your wife set the trap, and it did not work. Burn her! The girl escaped!" A roughly bearded face grew from Siaon's head. "Instead of trapping her, you released her along with my dragon lizards!"

Lot'fe stepped toward the Mal'ev apparition, no trace of fear in her voice. "Yes, I captured them and set the trap. Yes, they all escaped, but the girl did come for them. I know where her vulnerabilities lie and can keep you informed as to how to use them."

As Aralyn considered their words, she was certain they spoke of her.

Siaon's voice returned. "We will recapture them. You have my sincerest apologies for this travesty, mage Mal'ev. And a good thrashing will teach my wife a lesson. Burning—perhaps later. Her death should come at a time when we have extracted all the information we need from her."

Mal'ev. The mage she had heard so much about. He had possession of Siaon's body somehow? She averted her eyes, afraid she would be ill. When her stomach settled, her gaze traveled back to the camp.

"See that you do." An entire body, in the form of an apparition, came forth, linked to Siaon by a wisp of darkness. "Or I promise there will be retribution, my good servant. You have until morning to bring her to me." The apparition disappeared, sucked back into Siaon's body. Siaon convulsed, and he dropped to the dirt. He raised his head, shook it, placed one foot then the other underneath him, and struggled to rise.

Lot'fe's gaze swept the grasses and shrubs around Aralyn, and even though she was hidden, Lot'fe found her.

Siaon noticed Lot'fe's distant look and grabbed her by the shoulders. Aralyn couldn't tell if Lot'fe replied or not, but Siaon swung around and tried to focus on what his wife had seen. His eyes never landed on Aralyn, but he came to the correct conclusion.

"She's still out there!" He shouted and gestured to a soldier. Siaon spoke in Gehallion and pointed to where his wife's gaze had landed. Siaon was giving Lot'fe orders again. He swung his arm in Aralyn's direction. Lot'fe nodded, then bowed to her husband. From that exchange, Aralyn could draw only one conclusion—a force of unknown numbers was coming for her. And Lot'fe would be with them.

Aralyn ran. She could handle Siaon's betrayal, although it still tasted bitter. But Lot'fe? *Please, Elyon. Gods of the sky-haven.* She prayed mindlessly. Hadn't Lot'fe hinted that she had fought in battles the last time they spoke? Her one-time friend was a warrior and had killed before.

**

Gillis asked Deonella if she had seen Aralyn.

"Yes, but I sent her out to fetch you and Re'ah."

"We never saw her."

Deonella lifted her hands from the dishwater and turned to him. "Then I have no idea where she is."

Gillis checked upstairs, the barn, and questioned the guard. The guard stood near the front gate and had not seen her.

Perhaps Aralyn had been able to open the overgrown back gate and was now in the forest somewhere. Gillis found her footprints exactly where he had predicted, and the gate was wide open. He followed her steps down a dead-end path to where only a determined rabbit could get through the briars. At the streambed, he found leaves torn and trodden down. On the other side of the stream, smeared footprints deeper in the soil indicated where she must have jumped. Gillis turned to head back.

Re'ah stood by the stable with their horses saddled and ready to go. He handed Restless's reins to him. "Do not worry, we will find her."

Gillis grunted in return, not sure what he would do once they found her. She'd better have a good reason for disappearing.

The men mounted and headed to the stream. Five wolves stood in their path. The leader stepped forward, and Gillis dismounted. He peered into the leader's dark eyes as he had done many times before. He didn't know why he could connect with this wolf, but it was second nature to him now.

Their minds touched. The wolf lifted his head, and he placed a paw on Gillis' foot. Gillis felt the wolf's insistence that the men follow him. This small pack knew the forest, and more importantly, if Aralyn were in danger, they would do whatever it took to rescue her even if it meant their own lives.

They crossed the stream and entered an area where ferns and pine trees grew thick. The wolves scrambled through, and Gillis and Re'ah followed. They led Gillis to a point where he heard a frenzy of activity in the distance, but he could only see pinpoints of light. What in blazes?

Raspy breathing came from nearby.

With a gesture from Gillis, the wolves set off on a run towards a group of armed men. Gillis followed while Re'ah broke off from him. The wolves crouched before the soldiers, growling, teeth bared. The enemies froze. A woman—wearing a commander's band on her arm—hunkered, knife in hand. She didn't stand a chance. The wolves were predators now. Growls turned into threatening snarls.

Gillis didn't wait for the soldiers to draw weapons but gave the command to attack. The wolves lunged forward, forcing teeth into bellies, necks, groins, and faces. Men screamed inhuman sounds, and swords swung in useless arcs. The woman's knife flew from her hand neatly, rapidly. Hit its target. A wolf whimpered but charged and knocked her to the ground, paws on her shoulders. A battle ax carved the air, and another wolf fell. Gillis joined the fray from atop Restless. With a downward thrust to one soldier, followed by a slash across the neck of another, he dispatched two. One wolf continued to wrestle and chew on an arm. Most stood with legs braced until Gillis commanded them to stand down. At the sound of hoofbeats, Gillis turned. Re'ah had Aralyn. The look on Aralyn's face made him think she had never seen such carnage. Re'ah whispered to her and tightened his grip around her waist.

"Aralyn." Relief flooded Gillis, but his fear for her caused anger to follow. He directed Restless to her, settling on something between the two conflicting emotions. "You're hurt. What happened?" He didn't wait for answers but pulled out his medicine bag. "Let me take a look at her, Re'ah."

"I will tend to these others." Re'ah dismounted.

Gillis wanted to tell him not to bother, but Re'ah had his way of seeing things and would help an enemy as easily as a friend. Gillis bandaged Aralyn's wound. It was barely a nick, but she was shaking. He gazed into frightened eyes, and his anger abated.

"What are you doing out here?"

"I came out here ... just needed to..." She gasped, her voice unsteady. "The liz ... dragon lizards ... Drehensil." She swallowed. "And ... and Gehallions and ..."

She wasn't making much sense, but his gaze came up at the mention of Gehallions. "All right, all right. Just be still. You're safe now. That wound will be fine. We'll talk later."

"What about Lot'fe?"

"Someone you knew?"

Aralyn pointed to the woman Re'ah was tending.

"You're sure that's her?"

Re'ah pressed on a wound, trying to stop the flow of blood from the woman's side. The men around her lay dead. One had fled into the forest.

Aralyn dismounted and approached Re'ah, her legs unsteady. Gillis followed.

"No, that's not...Lot'fe." Obvious surprise in her voice. "But she was there." She pointed toward the camp. "With soldiers. Her husband, too. He is working with Mal'ev. Said Mal'ev wanted me." She stared at the camp, and her mouth dropped. "Where are they? Surely they're still here."

Gillis glanced up. The lights—the lamps in the trees and the fires—had disappeared. But how so quickly?

Re'ah's attention was on the woman. "No, come on. Stay with me!" Then, addressing Gillis, "I lost her heartbeat."

Gillis came to his side and squatted down. "Re'ah," he said, knowing the man realized the truth. "She's not breathing." He was aware of Aralyn's gaze on them.

Re'ah sat back on his heels and closed his eyes before he nodded. "You are right. She is gone." He swallowed.

"Did you know her?"

Re'ah shook his head.

"I suppose we could have gotten some information from her," Gillis said, trying to make sense of Re'ah's reaction.

"Aye." Re'ah nodded. "I suppose." He stood, still staring at the woman.

"Let's get you home," Gillis said to Aralyn. "Ride with me."

"I shall stay and bury them," Re'ah said.

"Suit yourself." If it were up to him, he would leave them for the vultures and crows. "You need a shovel?"

"I have one. I'll manage."

Gillis placed Aralyn in front of him. While he wanted to know what she was thinking, his emotions churned, and he couldn't question her right now. If Mal'ev had been here searching for her, it proved Aralyn had made a dangerous enemy.

Chapter 12

The city of Maizehollow required Aralyn and her escort to marry or bind—whatever they called it here—Aralyn had to remind herself as she stared out a glass window. Had yesterday—any of it—been real? Yes, Brone's death, the rescue of the dragon lizards, and Drehensil's presence—it had all happened. She had fallen asleep downstairs and now lay on the cushioned bench.

"The officials in town are lifting the lockdown." Gillis' voice drifted from the kitchen. "The priest will likely come later today."

Aralyn was wide awake now.

"They're coming here?" Deonella asked.

"Yes, they want to keep the curious away, those who would delight to see the woman meant for Brone with his best friend. A binding like this doesn't happen every year."

"Hardly happens at all anymore."

"No, it doesn't." A heavy pause. "And Brone, little Charles, and his household will be buried on his estate tomorrow."

"You'll go to their burial?" Deonella asked.

"I'd like to. I would also like to have seen the type of wounds they had ..." Gillis' voice broke. "Shouldn't even be thinking of that, but I want to know what clues they left, and—much as I would hate it—seeing firsthand would have helped."

"I know, Master Gillis." Deonella's voice wavered. "I know."

Aralyn sat up straighter, still listening.

Gillis' boots sounded on the wooden floor, and he appeared in the living room. He raised his eyebrows. "Ah. You're awake. Just came to check on you. I suppose you'd like to break your fast."

"The ceremony will be today?"

Gillis ran a hand through his hair. "Yes. Today."

Aralyn rose, and she followed Gillis into the kitchen.

Breakfast was cinnamon biscuits made from Elven bread, coffee, and something like mush but with a sweet, nutty flavor. Aralyn had an appetite now, and she ate spoonful after spoonful. The coffee was more bitter than she remembered, and the tension in the room was thick as a woolen blanket.

"I hadn't planned to do laundry." Deonella put her hands on her hips. "But anything you need washed for the ceremony—I can have it clean and dried in plenty of time."

She left the room, and Aralyn heard the clunk of a washbasin from the back of the house and wondered if she and Gillis would have a moment to talk. "Gillis, I want you to know I never intended to go as far as I did, but I heard the dragon lizards crying."

Gillis stopped eating and placed folded hands in front of his face.

"And I had to do something when I heard them."

His gaze told her nothing, but she didn't like the way his eyes pierced hers.

"I am sorry for the trouble I caused. I only wanted to find a quiet place to sort my thoughts. I never meant for all that to happen."

His hands tightened. "I hear your words, but you had no business runnin' off like that." He paused. His voice had a rigid tone that she didn't like, and he continued. "You say you had to do something when you heard the dragon lizards. Why didn't you come back and tell me or the guard?"

That was the question she was afraid of. How would she explain? She bit her lip, trying to plan an answer that would satisfy Gillis. None came.

"Yer answer doesn't matter because I'm thinkin' ye don't have one." He laid his hands on the table. "Other than ye wanted to be the one to rescue them, and nothing else mattered."

That wasn't true, but she doubted anyone else could have saved them. "I didn't want to wait to come get you. I was afraid ..." As soon as the words were out, Aralyn knew she'd said the wrong thing.

"Ye didn't want to wait?" He raised a fist, and Aralyn knew it was about to pound the table. But he stopped an inch above it. His gaze became softer, and he opened his hand to her. Concern filled his voice. "Aralyn, do you understand that Brone and his family met death by violent means? So violent that their bodies are not fit fer viewing?" His eyes filled with sorrow, a sorrow so thick, Aralyn felt it from where she sat. "It may not be my duty to protect you as your escort anymore, but as long as you are in my home, I want to know you will do *your* part to stay safe."

Aralyn's thoughts darted to Brone, Charles, Charles's aunt, and Brone's servants. Their bodies—no one would be able to see them and bid them goodbye? She couldn't process it, and numbness enveloped her.

"We may be forced into this binding, but I still don't want anything to happen to you. Do you understand that?" His commanding demeanor had returned.

Aralyn nodded.

Gillis studied her for a long moment. His voice was quiet now. "You mentioned Mal'ev last night. Did you see him? That shouldn't be. He wouldn't leave his city and desert his powers."

"Not him exactly. It was an apparition." She described the scene with Mal'ev and Siaon in detail, told him about Lot'fe and the Gehallions, and how she had rescued the dragon lizards. She even showed him the dragon stone.

He took the stone from her, rolling it in his hand.

"Two Elves gave it to me and told me to keep it close." She didn't want Gillis to take it from her.

His head came up, and he raised an eyebrow. "Elves gave you this?"

"Yes. They were in Sathria. I couldn't afford anything they were selling, so they gave me this gem."

Gillis' eyebrows lifted further, but he handed the stone back to her. Seeing his expression, she asked, "What is it, Gillis?"

"It's a valuable gem. Seems odd they would give it to you because you couldn't afford anything else. But that's not important now. I'll need to report what you saw last night. I sent a few men in this morning to investigate. But if what you say is true, Mal'ev can, in some form, leave his city and exert his power over others. Maybe that's how he attacked you on the trail—by using Siaon."

"He wants me for something, Gillis. I think Mal'ev wants me alive."

"He wants you alive," Gillis repeated. "Then they are probably not the ones who attacked Brone's family. I'm thinking the ones who killed them wanted you dead, too."

"The Rogues may have. I know they don't usually seek revenge, but if someone killed Brone's family, they could come after us." Aralyn's voice caught.

"That was exactly my concern last night, but whoever killed Brone—they most likely believe they accomplished what they came for. As for Mal'ev's crew, I'm willing to wager the dragon scared them away. But my men will look into it further and see just where they've gone."

"I am truly sorry."

Gillis' lips turned up a bit, and he sat down next to her. "I hear you. I just want you to be all right. You truly frightened me when I couldn't find you, especially with those wounds. How are they?"

"They are a bit uncomfortable at times, but I think they are healing over well."

He took her hand again, laying it on his rough palm and covering it with the other. "I just want you to know—"

"Master Gillis!" Deonella entered the room. "I just heard. The priest will be headed this way in a few hours. You both need to get ready."

***

The priest came as the sun was setting, and Gillis welcomed him. Gillis recognized him as Brother Abe, the man who had helped him bury his first wife. He wore a dark cloak and a pale-yellow tri-cornered hat and held the book of rites in his hand.

Abe raised his shrub-like eyebrows when he entered and greeted Gillis. "Gillis, it is good to see you." The man's slender face contained thin lips that curled up in a bare smile. "And where is your intended?"

Aralyn. His intended. *No*, he wanted to say. This whole binding was *un*intended. "She's upstairs."

"I'm right here, Gillis," Aralyn said as she descended the stairs.

Gillis turned to face her. Her dress was the typical blue of most brides, but unlike others, Aralyn's face was somber. No longing, no love-lit eyes for her groom. He had expected no more.

Deonella and Re'ah entered the room.

Brother Abe greeted them. "They will serve as witnesses?"

"That was the plan," Gillis answered.

"And by the way, Aralyn, you look lovely." The priest's eyes lit up more than Aralyn's.

Aralyn thanked him with a wooden smile. But she did indeed look lovely with her hair up and little pearls hanging from it. The dress she'd said her mother had made fit her well, showed off her figure ... nicely. Embarrassed that he had noticed her curves, Gillis turned his gaze on the priest.

"I'd like to go outside," Aralyn said. "May we?"

Gillis gave a nod, and Aralyn led the way to an old, sturdy oak.

This was all happening too fast. Aralyn was to marry Brone, but Brone was dead, and now Gillis had to marry her as an obligation. It was wrong. Nothing right about it at all.

Re'ah stood by Gillis' side, and Deonella stood with Aralyn.

"Gillis," the priest declared. "You will take Aralyn and be her faithful husband and promise to love, cherish, and care for her, and assure her of children as well."

It was not a question as it had been with Laella, but he answered with the required "I will." It felt like a lie. He couldn't possibly be all those things to Aralyn.

Brother Abe fixed a narrow gaze on Aralyn. "And you, likewise, will be faithful, fulfilling wifely duties, cherishing and respecting your husband, giving him sons and daughters."

Gillis felt her gaze on him. She lifted her chin. "I will."

"Do you have a ring or some token to give her?" Brother Abe asked.

Gillis remembered the ring. He pulled it from his pocket, his fist wrapped around it. It was Laella's. But this was how it had to be.

More meaningless words, a chant in a low monotone. A wave of Brother Abe's hands in a circular motion symbolized a never-ending commitment and a blessing on their marriage. "Turn to each other and join hands. Gillis and Aralyn, you are now bound."

That was it.

"You will now retire to your marriage bed," Brother Abe intoned. "The other priests and I will give our blessing for the consummation of your marriage."

His new wife grew a few shades paler, and he was afraid to touch her, but Gillis took one of her clammy hands in his own. "Let's go."

Chapter 13

As Aralyn lay in the bed, oil lamps flickered and spread shadows at odd angles. The ache and exhaustion swept over her.

Just yesterday, a Grand Dragon had carried her into the sky, she'd rescued three dragon lizards, and she'd discovered that Lot'fe's friendship was untrue at best. And now ... she faced her wedding night.

What went through the mind of a new bride? Surely Gillis would want to fulfill his "duty" as a husband. He had bound himself to tradition and law. And this night was supposed to be for Brone. Even if she hadn't been in love with Brone, she had known and had a crush on him at one time. With Brone, it would have been different. She wouldn't be someone to merely warm his bed. Yes, she did at least like Gillis. Maybe it wouldn't be so bad. And she could lie on her back without much discomfort, at least. It was all so confusing and unfair.

She left the chemise on, as the night was chilly, but even that would have to come off before the priests arrived. Three more were coming for the "blessing."

Gillis entered the room, and heat rose in Aralyn's cheeks. He had respected her on the trail. Would he respect her wishes now—now that they were legally bound? According to what he'd told Re'ah, it seemed unlikely, and she clearly understood the priest's words concerning their obligation to have children and Gillis' part in that. She decided to slip off the chemise. Get it over with.

Gillis' silence was like the booming of a cannon. Just as he rolled toward her and spoke her name, a knock at the door made her jump.

The priests entered. Four of them. All wore smocks and tri-cornered hats. In their hands, they carried smoking lamps filled with incense. Aralyn choked, her memories of smoke from the village pulling her in. Blurred faces. The echoes of swords and spears clashing. Dead bodies in carts. Mother on the ground. Terrwynn ... No! She had to stop this.

Breathe. Think. She wasn't in the village. She was in a bed. She was covered in a soft blanket. She lay next to a man who had cared for her. Helped her to heal. A roof was over her head. She had food in her belly, and Mother and Terrwynn were safe. That was what mattered.

A priest chanted in an ancient language. The consummation blessing. Ridiculous. Sick. But here she was—a part of it. One priest came nearer, still chanting. Her skin crawled, and she pulled the cover to her chin. Her heart pounded as the glow from the lamp swung in an arc. It hissed at her, sending wisps of smoke to her eyes. Aralyn caught a glimpse of Gillis' profile as he stared at the ceiling.

One of the priests addressed Gillis in Common, telling him of his duty to his bride. Another swing of the lamp scared up more unnatural shadows. It kept swinging as the intonations grew higher in pitch, volume, and tempo.

All the lamps stopped at the same moment. All voices cut to silence.

Aralyn's ears rang with it. Two priests broke away, and the other two stood for a moment. A chill came over Aralyn, and Gillis turned to her. He placed a warm hand on her forearm, drew her close, and kissed her temple. She froze. Squeezed her eyes shut. The rustle of robes made her open her eyes. They were gone, and Gillis released her.

They wouldn't stay. Good.

"I am yours, you know. You can do what you wish." Had he heard her? Did he need to hear her? She was his. He was a Peacekeeper and had the utmost respect for the law. He had to respect this responsibility, just as he did his other obligations, and honor the promise they had both made. Her lips pressed together as thoughts of Gillis' body next to hers stuttered across her mind.

Residual smoke from the priests' lamps crept into her mouth and eyes.

Rogues were attacking her, and she had no bow, no arrows, not even a knife. They grabbed her, and she fought, swinging her arms and landing punches on their bellies as they held her. Her fist smacked against a muscled jaw. Her hand stung, and her knuckles became stiff. Had she broken her fingers?

Someone held her arms in a solid brace.

"Aralyn! I'm not going to hurt you!"

No, they certainly wouldn't hurt her.

"Aralyn. Stop it." Hands pressed her arms into the mattress.

Then the voice made its way through her terror. A sob caught in her throat. Gillis' face was above hers, and she struggled against him. "No, Gillis! Please."

"What are ye doin'?"

"Please ... please don't—"

"Listen to me! There's no need for all that. I have no intention of ... anything. I kept trying to tell you before now."

Aralyn swallowed. His words didn't make sense, and yet they did. He didn't want her? She gazed at his scarred face and saw not anger, but confusion and vulnerability. His eyes grew gentler, and she remembered those same eyes, moistened with tears as he stood by helplessly right before her lashing.

"Gillis." An apology would be appropriate, but the words caught in her throat.

He released her.

"I thought I was fighting Rogues. It felt so real, and I had—" Her heart thundered in her ears.

"Aralyn, look at me." He pulled a lamp from the shelf and studied her the same way he had when she had been "meddled with." But this incident was not like that. No fingers kneaded her mind. It was a memory, twisted and haunting. He shook his head. "It's not Mal'ev this time."

"No, this was different." She watched him put the lamp back. "I smelled smoke, and you seemed like an enemy—"

"What?" Gillis turned on his side to face her.

"You were a Rogue, but then it was you, and I know you respect the law, Gillis, and we made a vow to have children, and I thought maybe you wanted to and—"

"Stop right there. You thought I would force myself on you?" Indignation tainted his voice. But so did compassion. "Yes, I bloody well respect the law, but you—you are more important than any law."

She was?

"You will never need to fight me like that. For any reason. I can promise you that much. Do you understand?" He searched her face, rubbing his jaw.

Had she actually struck him?

Aralyn nodded in response to his question, unable to look at him.

"I want to hear you say it."

She nodded harder, trying to shake the words from her throat. "I understand. I won't ever need to fight you."

"Now, are you all right?"

What? Was she all right?

"I didn't hurt you?"

Aralyn shook her head. Although the injured muscles pulled against her scars, he had not hurt her.

"Good. I'll take you to your room unless you'd rather stay. The night is more than a bit chilly, and we could use each other's warmth." He said it in all seriousness and with due respect.

"Yes, I will stay."

"You're sure? I can always sleep on the floor."

"No, Gillis. I trusted you on the trail. I can trust you now."

"Good to hear you say that."

***

Aralyn felt the ache in her muscles worse than the night before. She had tried to fight Gillis off, maybe even hit him, although he hadn't said anything to that effect. Gillis was already at the table, and the smells of breakfast reached her growling stomach. She took the chair across from him.

"Good morning," he said.

"Good morning." She wished it didn't sound so forced. "Re'ah is gone?"

"Aye, he left early." He sipped his coffee.

Aralyn toyed with her food. She didn't know what she had expected, but she didn't like the silence between them. She thought of the laughter they shared on the trail and wished she could make him laugh again—even at her expense. Yet she had some questions, but wasn't sure this was the time. Besides, Deonella was in the room.

"Master Gillis?"

Gillis grunted.

"Would you like some more coffee? More eggs?"

Gillis gave her the half smile so typical of him. "Yes, I'd like some coffee. Nothing else. I guess my appetite doesn't seem to be what it should."

"I see." Deonella gave Aralyn the barest of glances before filling Gillis' cup. Deonella cleared her throat. "You can be sure I know my duties to you."

"Aye, that you do." Gillis didn't look up but took a few bites of a biscuit, one of many Deonella had heaped on his plate.

Aralyn clenched her fists. What was Deonella implying? And had Gillis just agreed with her?

Deonella gazed down at Aralyn again. That look—it was one of triumph. Deonella leaned over and poured Aralyn some coffee. "Unlike some people," she said just loud enough for Aralyn to hear.

"Why are you doing this?" Aralyn said in an equally low voice.

"Whatever do you mean, mistress?" Deonella's voice grew louder as she pulled back in mock amazement. "I was just pouring you a bit of coffee. Oh, is that it? You prefer tea? I've got some glider leaves I occasionally use."

Aralyn relaxed her fists, and she replied with equally false cheeriness, "No, Deonella. That's not necessary. But thank you." She had just turned down tea and said she would settle for this bitter black brew.

Deonella excused herself and left the room.

Aralyn lifted a bite of egg to her mouth, chewed, and swallowed it. She couldn't make herself pick up more, and she grabbed a biscuit. Her eyes dropped. She had to ask him. "Did you really want to send me to a guild?" Aralyn reached for the butter.

"What? No!" Gillis' confused look softened to understanding. "Oh. You heard me speaking to Re'ah."

She nodded and barely tasted the fluffy bread in her mouth.

"Re'ah and I were just talking. Sometimes I say things I don't mean. But Re'ah understands. Seems to know when I need to express my thoughts."

"While you proved yourself to me last night, you also told him you would like to have a woman in your bed?"

"Ah, you heard that too." He sighed.

"I am confused. Are you sure you won't change your mind about ..." She struggled to keep her voice even. What was wrong with her? Why was she asking this? Perhaps she feared him and his superior strength more than she wanted to admit. What if he grew tired of her just lying in the bed with him?

"What did I tell you last night? What were the words I had you repeat to me?" His jaw worked.

No, she hadn't forgotten, but ... he was a man.

He continued. "I only offered to let you stay because it's cold at night. Not only that, I didn't know if they had left someone standing outside the door. They do that sometimes, and I was hoping to offer some comfort after ... what happened with Brone." He swallowed. "Besides, I know you had your heart set on him. He is ... was the handsome one. And do you think I like the idea of taking my best friend's betrothed for myself?"

Aralyn pinched her lips together, and she could no longer look at him.

"Not only that, I failed him, and I failed you when I didn't protect you."

"Failed me? No, Gillis. If anything—"

"I did! I bloody well watched you beaten, your back torn to shreds. Watched as they used you to train another lictor. I'll see to it that nothing like that happens again." He shook his head, apparently trying to rid himself of the memory. "But you've got to listen to me, and yesterday when you left...don't—" His jaw clenched as his gaze met hers. "—ever wander off like that again."

And the words slipped out before she could stop them. "Are you going to hold that over me?"

Gillis' shoulders sagged, and he leaned back in his chair. He picked up his fork, balancing it between his thumb and forefinger. "No." He dug into his food.

Aralyn lifted a bite, but the eggs were cold, and when she took another bite of biscuit, it turned to paste in her mouth.

Gillis rose from the table and took his plate to the sink. The back door opened, but Aralyn didn't hear it close. In a moment, he returned. "Aralyn. There's something else we need to talk about. The attack from Mal'ev—it will probably happen again. Be on guard, and let me know if it does. And I meant what I said last night. You're more important than any law." He stood there a moment, running a hand through his hair. His voice was gentle, but his next words felt brutal. "And you can sleep in your own room tonight. I'll make sure there's a fire to keep you warm."

Chapter 14

"I'm going to meet up with my apprentice today," Gillis told her the next morning. "Two of the Rangers are coming with us. We need to investigate the campsite again—the one where you discovered Mal'ev and his men. There's been no sign of the people who were there. It makes no sense." He scratched his head. "We'll be back before lunch." He gave Aralyn a long look. "You'll stay close by. Don't go wandering off."

She wanted to tell him to stop repeating himself, but decided on something kinder. "All right. Is there anything you'd like me to do today?"

Gillis raised an eyebrow and shook his head. "No. There's nothing I'm needing today."

Nothing he needed from her. She was surprised that the words cut her the way they did.

"Be careful, Master Gillis," Deonella said. "Don't get into a scrape that I have to get you out of." In her mock anger, she shook a wooden spoon at him.

"I wouldn't dream of it, Deonella."

"And I'll keep her in line." Deonella motioned to Aralyn.

Aralyn didn't know if she was kidding or not, and Gillis only nodded.

Both women saw him to the door and watched him ride off.

***

Aralyn longed to have her bow back. She could at least set up targets and practice, and perhaps see how badly the lashing had damaged her muscles. But Lord N'elde had her bow, the weapon that had been part of her life as long as she could remember—something she had used to provide for and to protect her family ... and to kill three men. An invisible wound twisted inside her whenever she remembered the bodies. Justified she may have been, but three were dead because of her. Yet her mother and Terrwynn were alive. That made it all right. She just had to convince herself of that.

Unable to keep still, she wandered out to the stables to see Monpomme. Aralyn fed her a handful of oats, found a brush, and began to groom her coat. The horse's muscles quivered at her attention. The thought of the inevitable squeezed her heart. "I don't know when we'll have to send you back. Probably soon." Aralyn scratched the horse's forehead and wrapped her arms around Monpomme's neck. "You've been good, you know. Sweet and gentle and never complaining." Aralyn smiled at her little joke, and Monpomme tossed her head as if she understood.

As she finished brushing Monpomme, an older man entered the stable. "Hello," she called out and stepped out of Monpomme's stall. "You must be Hermes."

"Yes, that be me." His eyebrows came up. "And you are?"

"Aralyn."

"Of course. Master Gillis' new wife." He barely looked at her. Hermes was much shorter than she, but stout and muscular for someone so aged. He had a small tuft of silver hair on his head and large gray eyes that bulged from their sockets. Hermes grabbed a pitchfork off the wall. "I guess ye know, I take care of these stables and anything else that needs doin' for these horses."

Aralyn patted Monpomme's neck. "I'll take care of Monpomme while she's still here. I don't mind a little mucking either."

"That's fine, but I want my job back when you're done."

"Your job back?"

"Yes, lass I be the one who takes care of these animals, and I don't want anyone tryin' to do it for me. I may be old but, I'm good at what I do. So even if you are the master's wife, perhaps you should think about staying in the kitchen."

Stay in the kitchen? He couldn't be serious.

"You know Hermes, you may be an old man and perhaps your views were fine in your day, but let me assure you, I have no intention of staying in the kitchen. As you said, I am the master's wife so if I wish to—"

She was cut off by Hermes' laughter. He doubled over and slapped his thighs.

Aralyn stared at him.

"Oh, lass, that look you gave me..." He gasped for breath. Still chuckling, he said, "I think we've established that I am old, but I am also a gentleman, and if you, mistress, wish to help care for the horses..." He stopped laughing and regarded her serious expression. "Surely, you didn't think I would speak like that to a lady."

Aralyn lifted her chin. "So as a gentleman, you feel it is all right to enjoy a laugh at someone else's expense."

"Ah." Hermes' eyes danced. "And what did it cost ye?"

"Cost me?"

"Not one copper, did it?" His lopsided grin was somehow enchanting, and Aralyn wanted to laugh with him.

Once again, she was reminded of her father's admonition not to take herself too seriously, and she had to admit that Hermes was right. Someone enjoying a good-natured laugh was not a crime. She bowed her head to the man and smiled. "You have a point. Well-said."

"I think we have an agreement then."

"And what's that?"

"We can work together, and perhaps, since I'm so old—" He chuckled to himself. "—I could use your help. And I promise not to be laughing at ye too much."

"And I promise not to take you so seriously."

"Atta girl." Hermes winked at her and picked up his pitchfork.

"I'm going to take Monpomme for a ride. Is there somewhere Gillis would consider safe?"

Hermes cocked his head. "Anywhere along the crick as long as you don't go too far."

"Thank you, Hermes." The day felt lighter already.

"You know, Aralyn, I'm wishin' the best for you and Master Gillis." He gave her a nod and turned back to his mucking.

The best for them. She sighed, wondering what "the best" could possibly be.

***

After exploring as far as she dared with Monpomme, Aralyn returned and let her loose to join Restless in the front. She wandered into the kitchen, where Deonella sat on a stool drinking tea.

"Gillis will be returning with the Rangers at noon. Maybe we should fix them something," Aralyn suggested.

Deonella sighed. "Since I'm his cook, I probably need to fix them lunch. And you don't need to worry. I know how to take care of my master and his guests."

"And I'd like to learn how." Aralyn put her hands on her hips and reached for a spoon.

Deonella scoffed. "And you expect me to teach you?"

Why not? And what had Aralyn done to deserve this rudeness? She bit her lip. Was this woman joking, as Hermes had? Aralyn plastered on a pleasant expression. "I would appreciate it, Deonella." Then, with a note of authority. "After all, I am the mistress of the household now."

"I see." Deonella's ungentle gaze bored into Aralyn. Another scoff. "Well, there's more than cooking and cleaning that needs to be done since you're his wife. And the mistress." She turned her back. "Not that it's any of my business."

Aralyn walked around so that she was in front of the woman. "What exactly isn't your business?"

"Oh, well, mistress ... I just feel that Master Gillis deserves to be happy."

"Perhaps so, and I would like to ... at least attempt to make it so. And besides, I would like to be happy as well, you know—"

"Oh, of course, you should be happy. And your attempts to make him happy would be believable if you'd give ..." Deonella waved a hand. "Like I said, it's none of my business."

Aralyn's mouth quit working as Deonella's meaning sank in. Just like at breakfast. This woman was referring to their intimacy.

Deonella's eyes flashed. "If you were trying to make him happy, he wouldn't have been so stoic this morning, would he? He would have looked at you and you at him with...something other than what I saw. And he had me ready your room for last night, so you know exactly what I'm talking about."

Aralyn pulled her tongue loose from the roof of her mouth. "As you said, it's not any of your business."

Deonella's eyes narrowed. "Look here, you may want me to teach you how to take over my job, but I'm not going anywhere."

Was she serious? Unlike Hermes, she seemed truly concerned about someone else replacing her.

"Deonella." Aralyn tried again. "I'm not going anywhere either. It looks like I'm here to stay. And I do not want your job." Aralyn had unconsciously lifted the spoon and was wagging it at Deonella. She laid it down and swallowed, waiting for the saucy retort.

But the woman was quiet.

Aralyn didn't know what to say when she heard a humbled voice. "All right."

"All right?" Aralyn repeated.

"Yes, I'll ... I'll teach you what I can."

What had Aralyn said? Well. Fine. She grabbed an apron. "Now show me where the tea is so I can make some." Aralyn paused.

"Tea is fine, but—"

"They'd prefer coffee." Aralyn finished for her.

Deonella waved her hand. "As I said, tea is fine."

Something was distracting her, Aralyn sensed, and she caught Deonella's gaze.

"Are you all right?"

"Aye." A pause. "No. My father is ill. But I will make sure this meal is served right, and I need to do some cleaning."

"Perhaps you should leave early. I can serve the meal, and don't worry about cleaning." Aralyn wondered just how sick her father was, but didn't ask. Deonella didn't seem inclined to offer the information.

They cooked rice at Aralyn's suggestion, and Deonella tried to show Aralyn a simple dish, but as Aralyn stirred the pot, she realized that something was sticking.

"You've got to move it off the fire a bit," Deonella said. "You're going to have bits of blackened mess in there. Now, what about the bread?"

Oh no. She had forgotten about it. Aralyn pulled it out of the oven. It had burned on the bottom. Cooking was her downfall, but she didn't want to tell Deonella that.

The servant sighed. She sliced off the bottom portion of the loaf, but the smell of burned bread remained. Deonella then fished most of the "blackened mess" out of the pot, added the cooked rice, and it was ready to be served. "I guess that will have to do."

"Something smells good." The front door creaked open.

Was he serious? She stuck her head out of the kitchen, and Gillis' eyebrow raised. With him were two men and a boy. Their boots clunked to the table, bringing dirt and mud, and Deonella clucked her tongue.

The boy grabbed a chair and sat. The others remained standing.

"Deonella and I fixed you something to eat." Aralyn beamed.

"Yes," Deonella said. "*We* did."

Aralyn's eyes slid sideways to the servant. "Well, I suppose Deonella deserves most of the credit."

"Oh, nonsense, it was your idea." Deonella gave them all a brilliant smile.

Gillis looked from one woman to the other. "Well, now that's settled,"—he turned to Aralyn—"this is Ranger Evan and Ranger Bart and my apprentice ..."

Just as Gillis was about to introduce him, Aralyn realized the boy's blunders—obviously, serious blunders to Gillis.

"Close your mouth, lad. That's my wife you're ogling. And where's your manners?" He gave the boy's chair a kick, toppling him in the process. He jumped to his feet, face reddened.

Gillis placed a hand on the boy's head. "And this fine gawking lad is my apprentice, Duncan." He motioned to Aralyn. "Gentlemen, and you too, Duncan, this is my wife, Aralyn, and you know Deonella."

Aralyn extended a hand to each of them. Duncan gazed at the proffered hand, and Gillis gave him a shove. "This is where you say hello or give some kind of proper greeting."

"Hello, uh, Ara ... Mrs. Gillis ...um ..." He fumbled for words.

"It's a pleasure to meet you, Duncan."

"Yes, me too." He scratched his head with dirty fingernails.

Aralyn withdrew her hand when he didn't take it.

"Oh, sit down. All of you. Please."

The foursome did so, and Gillis unrolled a map. He spread it on the table, and they murmured in low tones.

Aralyn ran some water into a pot for tea and prepared to serve the meal. Aralyn whispered to Deonella, "Perhaps you should see to your father."

"But, mistress. You need help," Deonella glanced at the men and the young boy.

"Go look in on your father," Aralyn insisted. "I am capable of serving."

Deonella's brow furrowed and then relaxed. "Thank you," she whispered back. She grabbed her hat and was gone.

The men looked up, and Gillis rolled up the map as Aralyn served the meal. Duncan had no problem diving in, but the others were waiting.

"Uh, Duncan, are you forgetting something?" It was Gillis.

Duncan looked around. "Oh. Uh ... I need a...napkin?"

"Try again."

Duncan gave up and shrugged.

The Rangers chuckled, but Gillis did not.

"We need to say a blessing."

"Oh." Duncan wiped his hands on his trousers, and Evan offered a short prayer.

The map out of the way, they continued to discuss the happenings from two days ago between slurps of soup.

The dragon lizards came to mind as they discussed and speculated over the unusual events, but came to no conclusions. Aralyn reached for the dragon stone in her pocket and ran her thumb over its faceted surface. The gem seemed to have a connection to dragons, which made sense. She'd used it to free the dragon lizards, and what about Drehensil? Was there a connection with him, too? He had come to her shortly after she'd received it from the Elves. He also came to her on the trail when she held the stone and when she used it to rescue the dragon lizards. Was that just a coincidence? She didn't think so.

Gillis rose, and Aralyn side-stepped to move out of his way. He dished up more of the food and motioned for Aralyn to take his chair. He laid the plate before her. She blinked at the food. He had served her? His hand brushed her shoulder, and she sat. Feelings of camaraderie and calm coursed through her. But there was something more—a pull toward him, an incredible warmth.

As soon as she finished her meal, Evan unrolled the map again, and Aralyn rose to clear the table.

Gillis' attention turned from his friends to Aralyn. "Lot'fe turned herself in to the authorities last night."

Aralyn dropped her plate into the sink with a clatter. "She did?" So what did that mean? Was she the traitor that Aralyn assumed she was?

Evan's voice interrupted her thoughts. "I just don't understand how they got so close to the outskirts of Maizehollow. We were patrolling and should have caught anything unusual."

"We would have caught them if they had used conventional means. I suspect they have mages," Bart chimed in.

Aralyn stopped as she pumped water into the sink, remembering something from long ago. "Or tunnels."

Gillis stepped closer to her. "What did you say?"

"Tunnels," Aralyn repeated. "What if they found a way to tunnel their way in?"

"That would be nearly impossible." Evan shook his head. "The rocky ground is solid. At least that is what we've been told. Hmm."

"Maybe the rockhounds are wrong." Gillis took a closer look at the map.

"Look at this." Duncan pointed to a spot hidden from Aralyn's sight. He stood and leaned over the table. "Here's Linorum's chasm. I heard there are caves down in there. Lots of them. What if they reach from here to here?" He drew a line with his finger.

Gillis scratched his head. "You could be right, but how would they get down in the chasm to begin with? They'd have to climb in somehow."

"I know!" Duncan's youthful voice could barely contain his enthusiasm. "And think how dangerous it would be. It is pretty dangerous, right?" His face was alive as if he couldn't wait to experience the adventure.

Evan scoffed. "No, it's not dangerous unless you consider poisonous gases and sharp rocks that can impale a man as dangerous. Not risky at all."

"But maybe the caves aren't that far down." Duncan scooted his chair closer to the table and glanced from one man to the other. "What if they used ladders and ropes? I've heard of mountain climbers using picks and ... and ..." He made a hammering motion. "Pitons! That's it."

"Still, they would have had to spend a lot of time exploring those caves." Gillis ran his hand through his hair. "Most caves are easy to get lost in."

The three men looked at Duncan, at Aralyn, and back to Duncan. It seemed they had developed a new respect for the boy. And possibly for Aralyn.

"The other problem is, how would they tunnel up through the rock? How would they know where to tunnel? What if they ended up in the town square?" Bart looked pointedly at Duncan.

Duncan shrugged. "I thought you guys could figure out that part."

"Well, I suppose, if you eliminate the impossible, the improbable begins to make more sense," Aralyn said.

The men stared at her, and Gillis chuckled.

"She's right," Bart said with a nod.

"Still doesn't eliminate mages." Gillis folded his arms, his eyes distant.

Both the Rangers nodded. "No, it doesn't," Evan said. "Siaon is not that powerful, so I doubt he could have accomplished this alone."

"There are other signs that show Mal'ev grows stronger by the day." Bart's brow furrowed.

"And he uses this man Siaon according to Aralyn," Gillis said. He grabbed the map, rolling it back up. "Gentlemen, I suggest we head back out there."

Duncan asked for more tea. Gillis said no and told him to go use the privy, or at least find a tree before they left.

Aralyn's muscles spasmed, and she had to stop herself from crying out. She slipped away from her guests and leaned back on the padded bench in the living room. Gillis would tell her to go to her room and sleep for a bit, but manners dictated that she see her guests off. Besides, she honestly didn't know if she could make it up the stairs. The thick cushions and pillows would make for a comfortable place to nap despite her tall frame. She adjusted the pillows and was about to drift off when her back spasmed again, and she heard voices in the living room.

"Thank you, Aralyn, for a good lunch." Bart gave her a small bow, as did Evan.

Duncan glanced at Gillis. "Thank you, Mrs. Aralyn. I liked the rice."

Gillis nodded his approval.

"Go ahead, you three. I'll be right out." Gillis turned to Aralyn. "You needing something? Some ointment? You look a little pale."

"And perhaps some brandy and honey?" She was teasing him, and Aralyn could tell that she had surprised him.

"Well, we'll see about that." He chuckled and gathered some oils and ointment.

Aralyn removed what clothing she needed to and lay down on her stomach. He rubbed the medicine on her back, neck, and shoulders. His roughened hands were gentle as he massaged it into the muscles.

"There's a mark here that I've not seen before ... hmm." He grunted. "And I see these muscles spasming." He traced a finger along her ribs. "You've done a good bit today. Perhaps too much. You should've gotten Deonella to help you more."

"She did, Gillis." Already she was relaxing, eyes drooping. "But her father was sick, and I sent her home."

"You convinced her to go home, eh?"

"It wasn't easy, but I did, yes."

He pulled the chemise back into place and helped her with the vest. "Then you've conquered one of the great challenges of running a household."

Aralyn sat up and managed a small smile.

"I've got to go, lass." He said with gentle concern in his eyes. "Rest while I'm gone."

"Gillis, I'll rest after you leave, but I'm coming out to say goodbye."

"There's no need."

"Yes, there is. I wouldn't be much of a hostess if I didn't see you off." Aralyn stood.

"You have to argue." Gillis shook his head, but she caught the gentle teasing in his expression.

The other three mounted their horses as Aralyn said her goodbyes and told them how nice it was to have them. The pleasantries her mother had taught her came easily.

Before Gillis had a chance to mount, Duncan gave him a shove toward Aralyn. "This is the part where you say goodbye and give her a proper kiss."

Gillis handed his reins to the boy and stepped toward Aralyn. He hugged her—not a passionate embrace by any means—and placed a light peck on her cheek.

"Ah, come on, Gillis." That was Bart. "Act as if you like her."

Evan joined in the ribbing. "Let's see what you're made of. Give the woman a proper kiss."

"Do you mind?" Gillis whispered.

Aralyn heard him swallow as he leaned against her ear, and she gave him a barely perceptible nod.

He kissed her mouth, not too passionate, but not altogether gentle either. He lingered just long enough for Bart to clear his throat.

Gillis released her abruptly and mounted. "Now, do as I say." He raised an eyebrow at her.

"I will."

As they rode off, the voice of young Duncan carried in the breeze. "I hope if I ever have a wife, she's as pretty as Aralyn."

The sound of manly laughter rang through the forest.

Chapter 15

Hours later, a cry from the gate interrupted Aralyn's rest. It was Duncan. Aralyn rose, opened the front door, and ran to let the men in the gate. Duncan led Restless with Gillis slumped in the saddle. Behind him, the two Rangers rode.

"Aralyn." Duncan gasped. "Gillis is hurt." He sounded more mature than he had a few hours ago, as if something had forced him to grow up in that short time.

Yes, she could see Gillis' injuries.

Both Bart and Evan had barely a scratch, but blood dripped from Gillis' head and soaked the headband he always wore.

Evan and Bart waved off her concern for them, and together the two Rangers carried Gillis inside.

Aralyn took Duncan's arm as he seemed a bit dazed, and she guided him toward the door.

"I can walk by myself," Duncan insisted, to which Aralyn said he would lean on her or she would carry him.

She placed him on a cushioned chair, and he lay his head back, eyes closing.

"I'll find something for bandages," she said.

"I've got that," Evan answered. He pulled some from his pack, and Aralyn grabbed them. Knelt by Gillis' side.

"Another pillow, would you, Bart?" What else?

"I'll get some water heating, Aralyn," Evan replied.

Of course.

Evan headed to the kitchen, and she heard water splashing into a pot. The smell of burning wood and the clunk of metal on the stove let her know the water would be ready soon.

Bart handed her a pillow as she tried to stop some of the bleeding.

"Bart, what happened?"

"We traveled past that camp you spoke of and found another trail. We saw where they had tunneled into the ground. You were right. But as we attempted to enter the tunnel, ruffle birds attacked us. Gillis and Duncan got the worst of it." Evan knelt by Duncan and began bandaging the wounds on his arm and side.

Evan brought her more cloth for bandages as well as a blanket. "The water is heating."

Aralyn pulled at Gillis' torn and bloodied headband.

Evan's boots scuffed the floor. "There's something you need to know."

"This headband probably needs to be cut off," she muttered. "Why does he wear it anyway?"

Bart laid a hand on hers. "Stop a minute."

"Let her see, Bart."

Aralyn pulled back on his headband, unpeeling it from the sticky blood. She stopped, staring at the blood on his headband. It had gold flecks in it, much like her own.

Bart brought the pail of hot water, and she finished washing off his ears. Why had she not noticed before? His ears were marked with tiny symbols that followed the top curve. Again, like her own.

She stood and backed away. "What is this?"

"It's what it looks like, Aralyn," Bart said.

"He's an Elf?"

"Part Elf."

"Why did he keep it a secret from me?"

"Why do you think?"

"I ... don't ..." But she remembered something. "He's *part* Elf?" He hadn't denied it when she'd asked on their journey, but he hadn't confirmed it either.

Bart nodded. "His grandfather was human."

He was not a pure-blooded Elf, and again she thought back to the large droves of Elves leaving the lands, driven away because the Council, one of the ruling bodies in Eyndor, did not consider those of mixed blood true Elves. Something else niggled the back of her mind. They had also blamed them for the sickness that had spread throughout the land.

"Here, take this." Aralyn gave Bart the pail of water that was already a deep red. Aralyn wiped away more of her husband's blood, her own hands covered in it. She put pressure on a large gash and added more bandages. Gillis never stirred, and Aralyn did the only thing she knew to do. She prayed to Elyon, deliberately neglecting the gods of the sky-haven. *Please let him be all right.*

Gillis' dry lips moved, and he moaned. His eyes flew open, filled with terror. His arms flailed, almost hitting her. Aralyn could do nothing to stop him, and Evan grabbed his arms while Aralyn spoke softly to him, not knowing if he could hear. But the flailing stopped, and he slept once more.

"Duncan will be all right." Evan threw a thumb over his shoulder at the boy. Her attention on Gillis, Aralyn forced out a quiet thank you.

Gillis opened his eyes again. "Laella." His voice was soft, almost reverent. His hand brushed Aralyn's face. "We need to keep the cows from climbing in the trees. They're in the way of the ducks." His face grew pale, and fear tinged his voice. "Please don't leave me ..."

Aralyn glanced at Evan. "Why is he talking like this?"

Evan raised an eyebrow. "Perhaps he's delirious. He may have some kind of infection or head injury."

Aralyn felt his face. "He's burning up."

***

"Your father is better?" A strange woman was asking.

"Yes, mistress."

"And you think Gillis has been poisoned?"

A stranger was in Gillis' house. Something was wrong. And he couldn't open his eyes. The voice was not Laella's. What was going on?

But the other voice was more familiar. "Yes, mistress, I've seen this before."

That was Deonella. And she was saying something about a poultice to pull out the poison. But who was she calling mistress?

Gillis felt muscles contract, and pain ripped through him. Horrible pain. But he couldn't cry out. He didn't have the strength.

That strange voice again. "Duncan, are you all right?"

"Yes, Mrs. Aralyn."

Aralyn? Gillis struggled to remember. But the pain came at him like hot coals on bare skin. He remembered dark feathers turning to a myriad of colors, a blur of darker eyes, wings beating against him, and beaks ... no, they were swords piercing him. Birds carrying swords?

Everything faded.

***

Aralyn joined Deonella in the kitchen, where the servant made a mixture of herbs.

"This will be for later when Gillis wakes up." Deonella chopped and stirred. "I wasn't here, but Ranger Bart said you did most of the bandaging and caring for Master Gillis. Looks like you did a decent job of it."

A compliment from Deonella? Aralyn hesitated for a moment. "Thank you. And thank you for returning. You're the one who thought it might be poison, and you knew what to do. You saved my husband's life."

"Ho, I doubt that."

"Well, I do not, so thank you."

She returned to Gillis' side, crossed her ankles, and lowered herself to the floor just inches from where he lay. Aralyn had heard of Elves who tried to hide their true identity from humans for various reasons, such as their magic abilities or a simple desire to fit in outside their homeland. But Gillis keeping his identity from her felt like a betrayal. Unable to think any longer, her eyes grew heavy, and her head dropped forward, landing on the couch next to Gillis.

"Come—let's get you to bed." It was Deonella, placing a gentle hand on Aralyn's arm.

"No, I'll stay right here." She shook herself awake, remembering how Gillis stayed up all night with her after the lashing she had received.

Deonella sighed. "At least get in this chair. I'll get you a pillow and blanket."

"I'll be fine." She was too tired to move.

"You need your rest to be any good to him, you know."

"Mmm-hmm." Aralyn couldn't lift her head. Her hand reached out to Gillis and landed on his chest.

Deonella's footsteps faded. Aralyn opened her eyes for a moment to gaze on Gillis' face. She wondered at the scars she had observed before. Evidence of past conflict? Perhaps something he was proud of fighting and surviving. Aralyn watched the up and down motion of his chest. He breathed more deeply now. In a dream, she kissed his scarred cheek, his forehead, and his limp hand, the skin rough, but soothing against her lips. That was a dream, wasn't it?

***

Gillis' memory returned. She was by his side. Aralyn. His wife. Her head rested near his chest, eyes closed, breathing deep and even. He tried to sit up and moaned louder than he meant to. Aralyn's eyes flew open, fell shut, and opened again.

She raised her head. "Gillis."

"Yes." His voice was a bare whisper.

"You're awake."

"Yes." That seemed to be the only word he could utter.

"I'll get you some water." She rose, stumbled, and reached down to rub her foot.

Had she stayed there all night?

He watched as she limped to the kitchen. Soon, water was against his lips. A fresh rain trickling down his throat. The rain stopped. He grasped Aralyn's free hand. "Thank you."

"Do you remember what happened?"

Gillis nodded. "Ruffle birds. Tore into us."

Aralyn's gaze was steady. "Yes, and you got the worst of it. They must have poisoned you somehow. Thankfully, Deonella recognized the symptoms and knew how to treat them. The birds barely touched Ranger Bart and Ranger Evan, but they hurt little Duncan enough that he required some serious care. He's sleeping. He said something about being an Elf."

Gillis closed his eyes, listening to her voice. Aralyn's voice, he realized, was the one that had come to him in a dream. A voice he had mistaken for Laella's.

"And so are you," she said.

"So am I?"

"An Elf."

"Yes." He had to admit it now. "Part—"

"I know. They told me. I am not going to ask why you kept that from me ... for now. But when you are feeling better, I want an answer."

"Of course." His throat was tender, and the words wavered. "Coffee?"

"I'll make some."

Gillis wanted to say Deonella could do that, but perhaps this was her day off. He must have fallen asleep again, for he woke to the clink of a coffee cup on a saucer. The smell of bacon permeated the air, and he caught sight of fluffy biscuits on a plate. Perhaps he could eat.

"Do you want help to sit up?"

Gillis shook his head. It seemed funny that their roles were reversed. Hurt his pride. Deeply.

But as he tried to sit, his arms gave out. Blast! He tried again. And again. All the while, Aralyn stood by him and waited, plate in hand. He finally looked up. His eyes, he hoped, communicated his need for help after all.

A half smile curved Aralyn's lips.

All right, Aralyn. Just help me. But he didn't say it, couldn't say it.

She put the plate down and hooked her elbows under his arms. With amazing strength and gentleness, she pulled him into a sitting position. "Thank you," he whispered

The coffee was hot and felt good on his throat. The biscuits were steamy, although a little doughy in the middle. He ate a few bites of one and chewed on the bacon. Hmm. Not cooked as crispy as he liked, but it would do. He took it slowly, didn't want his stomach to rebel. It was then that he saw Duncan sprawled out in a chair.

The boy's lips moved, and a pained expression came to his face. "Mama," he called out. "Please."

Aralyn approached the boy and knelt, "I'm not your mama, Duncan, but I'll do what I can."

Duncan's eyes flew open. "Oh. Mrs. Aralyn." He repositioned himself in the chair. "I didn't know ... I thought I was ... you know, at home. Can I have some of that bacon and a biscuit?"

"Of course. Glad you're hungry." She rose and reached for the plate that held plenty for Gillis and Duncan.

Gillis scoffed. "He can get up and take care of himself. He's not that bad off, are you, boy?"

Aralyn withdrew her hand. "Gillis, I don't mind."

"It's all right, Mrs. Aralyn, I can do that." He rose and grabbed a biscuit and three slices of bacon. "I need some water." He glanced at Gillis. "Never mind, I'll get it."

"See? The lad's fine."

Duncan headed to the kitchen.

Aralyn glanced over her shoulder as he left. She approached the couch and glared down at Gillis. "Duncan's been injured too, and he's just a boy. It won't hurt to—"

Gillis lifted his head. He kept his voice low. "I know he's just a lad. But when I'm speaking to him, allow me to do so. I'm teaching him to stand on his own two feet. Just remember, he's *my* apprentice." Pain lanced through his head with that brief effort.

"I see." The disapproval was plain in Aralyn's voice, but she relaxed her stance. "I will let that go. I know you're not feeling well."

Of all the bloody, condescending, prideful, stubborn—he couldn't pursue the thought with his head throbbing. Yes, he, too, would have to let it go for now.

Duncan returned with a cup of water. Gillis hoped Aralyn would keep quiet with his apprentice in the room.

Aralyn stepped away and glanced at Duncan and back at Gillis. Did she see the lad was fine? Gillis released the tension in his shoulders, and the muscles in his face relaxed. His gaze fell on Aralyn. Seemed he couldn't help it. In the morning sun, her dark hair swung from her shoulders, catching traces of light. "How long have I been asleep?"

"Just last night." She leaned forward. "The healer came to check on you both earlier and changed your bandages. I was surprised she knew to do that."

Gillis nibbled on a biscuit and sipped his coffee. His head eased.

"I'm going upstairs." He pulled back the blanket.

"No, you don't. The healer said for you to stay right here until she comes this evening."

Gillis sighed and pulled the covers over his bare chest. He motioned her to his side. "Aralyn, I know I wasn't truthful about who and what I am, but—"

"Seems we both need to work on being more forthright with each other."

"I was hoping it wouldn't matter." He didn't want to tell her, but she deserved to know the truth of the Elves' treatment of him. "I wanted to give up my identity as an Elf. I'm of mixed lineage—part human, and so is Duncan." His voice was giving out. He took another sip of coffee. "But the Elves don't like the mixed among them, and I left when they spoke of driving us from Eyndor and then wouldn't take care of certain injustices." That wasn't the entire truth, but it was enough for now.

Aralyn nodded. "But what injustices, Gillis. Can you tell me?

Gillis' fist tightened. "A certain Elf, a mage, did something that deserved punishment, and neither the Council nor the Elders would bring charges." That was all he wanted to say, and he changed the subject. "And what about you, Aralyn?"

"Me?"

"Your features, your accent. I should have said something sooner, but you speak a bit like someone from the southern regions of Eyndor."

"I thought you knew. I was marrying Brone, after all. I didn't intentionally keep it from you."

"We'll talk more ..." Gillis' voice broke again, and he lay back and closed his eyes.

"Can I get you anything else?" She said gently.

He opened one eye a fraction and touched Aralyn's face. "... beautiful." That was all he could manage before he lost consciousness once more.

Chapter 16

A few days later, Gillis swung his feet to the floor and sat up. A wave of dizziness came over him. He waited for it to pass and stood. Determined to walk to the kitchen, he placed one foot in front of the other and grabbed the door frame. Deonella hummed as she swept, and he entered.

"Good morning."

Deonella raised her eyebrows. "Glad you're up, Master Gillis.

He approached her and held onto the table. "I need to go to town today."

"Are you sure you should?" She set the broom aside and pumped some water into the sink.

"I'll take fresh bandages. I promise."

"See that you do."

"Besides, Restless knows the way home. I know you don't want to have to come pull me out of a ditch." He nudged her with his elbow, and she chuckled.

"Go on now, Master Gillis." She frowned. "And just where is your lovely bride? She doesn't want to keep you company?"

"Aralyn is at the stables helping to care for the horses."

"Hermes doesn't mind?"

"No, Deonella. I think the two of them have reached some sort of agreement. She wants to spend time with Monpomme before we send her back to Lem." Gillis paused. "You know, I wish we could keep her."

Deonella's head came up. "Keep who?"

"Monpomme. For Aralyn."

"Oh." Dishwater swished over a plate in the sink. "Well, why don't you?"

"One of Lem's best horses? It'd cost me more than I could afford."

Deonella swallowed. She seemed torn between two warring desires. "I've got some money, Gillis."

"I can't take your money."

Deonella stopped what she was doing, bowed her head, and squeezed her eyes shut. Her voice trembled when she spoke. "I've no need for it. It was for a dowry." A catch in her voice, she continued, "This is something I've been thinking of for a long time—giving the money to something worthy."

Gillis sensed her hesitation.

"Do you love her, Master Gillis?"

"Aralyn? It was a marriage forced on both of us. I never saw myself getting married again."

"But do you love her?" Her hands in the dishwater lay still.

Gillis shook his head. "I can only love her as a friend. Never as a wife or ... a lover."

"I wish you could. She cares for you, and perhaps she could love you like that."

"I doubt it, but I didn't think you liked her."

"I didn't. I don't ... not much. But ..." Deonella looked at him, tears welling, and one escaped. "Take the money, Gillis. As much as you need."

"Take it?"

"Yes." Deonella's eyes were dry now. "I'm one hundred twenty-eight years old now. I know that's young for an Elf, even someone who is part Elf, but ..." Deonella's throat worked. "No one would want me now."

He touched her cheek where the tear had fallen. "Age makes little difference among Elves. You know that."

"Take the money."

"I'll consider it." But the very idea felt wrong. "You are a selfless woman, Deonella, but I cannot."

"I don't know about the selfless part. Don't let your pride stand in the way of your happiness. And I do want you to be happy, but if I had my way to begin with, she'd be gone."

"You tried your best." Gillis chuckled. He thought of the careless remarks Deonella had made, remarks he had perhaps agreed with?

"Aye." Deonella scrubbed another plate. "That I did."

***

Aralyn wished she had known Gillis was going to town, but he'd said nothing to her. It might have been a pleasant trip. She had left Hermes for only a moment, and when she came back, he told her where Gillis had gone.

"You couldn't stop him?" she asked. "Surely he could have waited a moment for me."

"No, lass. He seemed determined to go without ye."

Aralyn was silent. Why would he do such a thing?

Hermes gave her a sidewise look. "Now, listen, don't ye be thinkin' the worst. Your Gillis is an upright man."

Her Gillis. Aralyn shook her head at that. But yes, he was an upright, moral man, and she felt ashamed for thinking he was less than such. She'd lived too long among the men in Sathria.

When Gillis returned, she was still in the stable. He approached her, holding both hands behind his back. "I have a gift for you." His lips tugged upward. "Close your eyes."

Aralyn looked doubtful but did as he said. She could trust him. Hopefully.

"Put your hands out. Yes, both of them."

Gillis laid the gift across her palms. "Open your eyes."

Her fingers wrapped around smooth wood. No, he couldn't have. Her eyes grew wide as she pulled the gift closer, speechless. He'd bought her a bow? It looked new, the wood polished and the drawstring not worn at all.

"Consider it a gift, a wedding gift. 'Tis customary."

"But, Gillis. I didn't—"

"You had no need to get me anything."

She ran a hand over the wood she recognized as oak, noted the carvings on it, and tested its flexibility. She hated to ask, but ... "Where are the arrows?"

"The quiver and arrows are on Restless. I wanted you to see this first."

"I ... thank you, Gillis." She gave him an awkward one-armed hug, her other hand still clinging to the bow.

He patted her back in return. "Well, I know how much a weapon can mean to someone. You needed this. But I must warn you not to hunt for now."

"For now? You mean I can hunt?"

"Yes, you can. Later, when I'm sure it's safe."

"But these are the king's lands, aren't they?"

Gillis chuckled. "He gives me pretty much free rein here."

Aralyn didn't want to even think about the consequences of her actions from last time.

Gillis must have noticed the change in her expression. "The Rangers, the magistrate, they all know you're my wife. In a few days, it should be no problem. I'll get your arrows."

He had bought her a gift—a bow, and she would be able to use it. A man with the ear of the king told her she could hunt on this land. No guards or whip to worry about.

She followed him to Restless, and Gillis held out the quiver.

She slipped the strap from his hand and asked him to hold her bow while she examined the arrows.

"They might need new fletching," he said.

"But that is easily remedied." Most of the arrowheads needed sharpening, but they were made of sturdy bone. She held an arrow up to her eye, looking down the shaft. She repeated this with each one while Gillis watched, his eyes smiling.

"These are the best, Gillis. I have never seen such a fine bow and such fine arrows." Aralyn shifted the quiver to her shoulder and hugged Gillis once more. "Thank you. Thank you, my husband."

He pulled her close this time, and she relaxed against him.

"And I've got another surprise for you." He released her, and Aralyn's eyebrows went up.

"What is it?"

"Monpomme."

"What do you mean?"

"She's yours."

"Mine?" Aralyn shook her head. She had to be hearing things.

"Yours to keep, lass."

"Did the man at the stables ..."

"No, it's not from Lemmon, but it is a gift."

"From who?"

Gillis pinched his lips together. "I'm obliged not to tell you."

Aralyn leaned her bow and quiver in a corner and ran to Monpomme's stall. She threw her arms around the horse's neck. "Monpomme," she whispered. "You're staying with me." She found Hermes's dancing eyes. "She's staying!"

Hermes chuckled and gave her a wide grin before he went back to mending a bridle. She turned around. Gillis was a few feet behind her.

"In a single day, I've received two of the best gifts ever." The one from her husband allowed her to hunt again, and the other from an unknown person left her speechless. How could she ever thank this person for Monpomme, who was not only her means of transportation but an attentive companion?

Aralyn wondered who could have had the money to buy her such a gift.

***

Gillis only accepted a small portion of Deonella's money but felt even that was too much. He swore he would pay her back. The rest he borrowed from a businessman who had such resources. But he would never tell Aralyn.

He was upstairs, placing new bandages on his wounds, when he heard Aralyn's voice from the front room. "We have company, Gillis."

He joined her at the window and watched as the riders came closer, two of them. They stopped at the gate.

"Hello, the house." The voice belonged to a man with brownish-blond hair falling to his waist. The voice had a familiar ring to it, an Elvish accent much like Aralyn's.

Aralyn gasped. "I know them, Gillis." She touched his elbow. "Elnala and Orandon are their names." She rushed to the door and lifted her foot to step over the threshold.

Gillis barely had time to grab her arm. "You sure you know them?"

"Yes, Gillis. They gave me the dragon stone."

"Let's wait and let them give their greeting." He still held her arm.

The male had a spirited horse who pranced and pawed at the ground. He greeted them in Elvish. "Aralyn and Gillon, we ask permission to enter."

"They wish to enter, but he's not saying your name right." Aralyn grew uneasy and glanced at Gillis.

"Indeed." So she understood some Elvish still.

She blinked, and her gaze met his. "Gillon ... that's your Elvish name? And ... and that's a banner of peace they carry, is it not? Why would they mean us harm?"

He wouldn't answer the first question, but the others made sense. "Yes, it's a banner of peace, and usually, they wouldn't mean any harm, but I'm cautious around any stranger. Part of my training."

"Let's walk out there. It can't hurt, can it?" Her eyes pleaded with him.

He released her, and the tension in his neck and jaw tightened.

Elnala's smile was an eruption of joy. She wore robes of cobalt blue and had the pale skin and powder-blue eyes of the southern reaches of Eyndor.

The male, Orandon, held a strong resemblance to the woman. He spoke first, switching to Common. "Greetings, Aralyn, Gillon. We hope our peace will rest upon you and your home. I am Orandon of Aurellium in Eyndor, and this is my daughter, Elnala. You remember us, Aralyn?"

"Of course." Aralyn was quick with a nod.

Gillis wished she would wipe that gleeful expression off her face.

Orandon grinned. "Ah, good. With your permission, we would like to water our horses and to speak with both of you about a matter of grave concern."

"Take care of your animals. Then we'll see about this talk." Gillis opened the gate, and they dismounted. He led them to a water-filled trough near the stable.

"I will come to the point." Orandon patted his horse's neck while Elnala's expression of joy did not change.

"So will I. Call me Gillis while you're on my land. And then, Orandon, Elnala, state your business."

"All right." Orandon gave Gillis a small bow in acknowledgement and then lifted his gaze to Aralyn. "First of all, I'm delighted that you, Aralyn, remember Elnala and me."

"Yes, so am I." It was as if Elnala could no longer contain herself. She rushed forward and grasped Aralyn's hands. "You still have the gem wegaveyou? Haveyouseenwhatitdoes?"

Was she speaking in another Elvish dialect?

"I'm sorry." Elnala blinked, and her smile faded. "I tend to speak in a hurry when I'm excited. And I am excited to see—"

"Elnala. Remember what I said?" Orandon cleared his throat.

"Sorry, Father." She dropped Aralyn's hands and stepped back.

Orandon started again. "We need you both. The mistbows are dimmed, and we believe the ruffle birds have begun their attacks."

Gillis straightened.

"The ground itself seems to betray us," Orandon said. "And sometimes we can barely stand upon it. All of these are signs of—"

"The Age of Thunder," Gillis interrupted. "It's here or is coming. Is that what you're saying?"

"Yes, Gillis. Many don't remember the last one, but those who do tell tales of the destruction of our lands, invasion from enemies who see through defenses that keep us hidden. It hasn't fully arrived yet. These are only signs, but we need you before the borders fail. That could happen soon, and our enemies will not hesitate to take advantage. Even if the borders don't fail us, we need your help in fighting those with evil intent. We need your talents. And you, Aralyn ... we need you most of all."

"Why?" Aralyn tilted her head.

Elnala burst out before Orandon could answer. "You're our bowsinger! Surely you know that!"

"I didn't," Aralyn answered. "What does that mean?"

"I know you've heard the legend," Elnala said. "The one who sings to her bow? She never misses a target."

Aralyn opened her mouth and shut it. "Yes, that always happens."

Gillis ran a hand through his hair. So she was not only an Elf but someone valuable to them. He took Aralyn's elbow. "Come." He jerked his head toward the house, where they would be out of the duo's earshot.

"You knew you were the bowsinger?" He demanded.

"You didn't hear me," she said, her voice growing defensive. "I didn't know what that meant until they informed me just now."

He heard, but his emotions churned as memories descended on him.

"Why are you so angry with them? And with me?"

His hand dropped to his side. "You would never understand."

Aralyn pursed her lips. "Try me."

Gillis remembered well the day the fires roared and the smoke filled his lungs. He grabbed at his throat, knowing he had to quit thinking of this. "Not now."

"Gillis, we have to tell them." Aralyn's hands were on her hips.

"About?"

"The attack on you and the others."

"We'll see." He just wanted them gone.

Even though Orandon and Elnala hadn't contributed to the injustices he had once faced, they reminded him of that distant time when he had decided to flee Eyndor. He had vowed to embrace humanity, forsaking his Elvish heritage. He would blend in with the humans for as long as possible.

Aralyn made her way back to the Elves. "Perhaps you'd like some tea."

So she decided to play the hostess even if he disapproved.

"We don't require anything," Orandon said. "But that sounds nice."

"Well, come inside, why don't you?" Gillis folded his arms.

Aralyn apparently didn't catch the sarcasm, and she led them to the door. In the kitchen, Deonella brewed a minty tea and piled thin bread on a plate.

Aralyn was about to make the introductions when Deonella interrupted. "I know them, Aralyn. And they know me." Deonella gave each a nod and disappeared.

Orandon's gaze landed on Gillis. Orandon knew. Gillis was sure of it. Knew he was keeping something from them—the attacks from the ruffle birds. He clenched his jaw and pushed back mentally as he realized Orandon was trying to enter his mind. Orandon had no business doing that unless lives were at stake.

The pressure on Gillis' mind let up. But Orandon must have gleaned something.

"Lives *are* at stake, Gillis." His gaze switched to Aralyn.

"Gillis and his apprentice, who is part Elf, were attacked by ruffle birds," Aralyn stated calmly. "There were two Rangers with them, but they only received a few cuts." She swung toward him. "I had to let them know, Gillis."

Orandon rubbed his hand over his chin. "Gillis, it is urgent that you come with us. Mal'ev himself is on the move, and Elven lives are in danger, especially *pures*."

"Especially *pures*," Gillis repeated.

Orandon was silent for a beat. "Gillis, I understand you have your reasons for your bitterness toward us, but there is something you must know. If we do not return with Aralyn, our lands will be forever lost."

"I know the legends," Gillis replied. "And supposedly, you need the bowsinger to strengthen your borders? Somehow she,"—Gillis flicked his thumb at Aralyn— "will be the linchpin for that. Look, I've kept my identity as a part-Elf secret for quite some time. I've worked for humans and their king for over a decade and am quite content to continue. If Aralyn wishes it, she may go. Get permission from his mum, and I'll release Duncan to you. The king himself would be glad. He wants to maintain a good relationship with Eyndor."

Orandon's gaze landed on Gillis. "The only problem is...we have reason to think you and Aralyn are paired. We very likely need you both."

Chapter 17

Aralyn's chin dropped. "We're paired? What—"

"Yes, your talents work together," Orandon explained. "But it has nothing to do with your marriage or binding."

Aralyn blinked. "My talent is bowsinging? And Gillis' is ..."

Before Orandon could answer, Gillis said, "Paired or not, I have duties to the king. As I said, she can go."

Aralyn had few memories of the place where she had lived as a *nanio*—a young one. Much of what she knew came from books and an occasional Elven bard. She had dreamed of this moment, of going to Elven lands, and these Elves insisted she join them. The dream was within her grasp. She only had to say "yes."

"But, Gillis, the two of you will have to work together to find out how these talents operate," Orandon said. "We can confirm it as most paired have a distinct mark on their upper body. Perhaps you mistook it for a birthmark. It's usually raised, dark, and round with a sigil or symbol on it. Have you ever noticed such a mark?"

Gillis worked his jaw. "I have a mark below my left shoulder, but that—"

"It may mean nothing, Gillis." Orandon's tone was gentle. "What about you, Aralyn?"

"No, not that I've ever noticed." Her fingers touched her lips. "Are you saying that a *pure* and *non-pure* can be paired?"

Orandon nodded.

Elnala stood silently beside him, but a light danced in her eyes.

"Try this," Orandon told them. "Just stand together. It may show us something of your power and may help confirm that you are paired."

Aralyn positioned herself so that her shoulder brushed Gillis. A pulsing, warm sensation washed over her. She gasped. The pulsing slowed to a hum. Why had she not noticed this before?

Orandon's gaze pierced her. "What are you feeling, Aralyn?"

She had to tell him, but Gillis' eyes warned her not to. "I'm not sure. It feels like power building between us."

Gillis jerked away. "That's enough! I'll not let this continue. What exactly did you do?"

"You're paired," Orandon said with a satisfied nod. "We need you. For your protection and for ours." Orandon tapped the tip of his bow on the floor. "I think it would be best if we examined your marks." He nodded to Elnala.

"Where can we go?"

"Um, back here, I guess." Aralyn led Elnala to the room where she had washed up that first night.

Aralyn lifted her chemise before she remembered to warn Elnala.

Elnala gasped. "These scars! Where did you get them?"

"It's a long story, and I'd rather not discuss it."

"That's fine. I won't ask." There was a catch in Elnala's voice. "But I wish you would tell me."

"Maybe later, Elnala. Not now."

Elnala placed her finger over a spot on Aralyn's right shoulder blade. "Aralyn, this is enchanting. It's a dark blue circle with the symbol of a bow on it. But there's something else ... a water droplet, I think. I'm not sure what that means. We can ask the symbol master when we go to Eyndor."

"If I go," Aralyn retorted. But hadn't she made her decision? She chewed her bottom lip.

Elnala turned Aralyn to face her. "I pray you will."

"I want to see it." Aralyn turned her back to the small square mirror and looked over her shoulder at her reflection. The scars she saw made her cringe. That was what those lashes had done to her?

"Are you all right?"

"I've never looked at those scars before. Didn't know how bad they looked."

Elnala nodded, tears in her eyes. "But, Aralyn, look at this!" She placed her finger on the mark once more.

Aralyn stared, mouth agape. There—the size of Monpomme's eye—was an indigo-colored mark. How had she never noticed? Imprinted on it was the symbol of a bow just as Elnala had said. Next to it was a water droplet with a triangle around it, and yet a third symbol that looked like a series of circles. "It must be new." Aralyn placed her hand on it. "I know I would have noticed if it had been there before."

"We don't spend much time examining our own backs." Elnala chuckled.

"I know, but my mother or a healer, someone would have noticed it. Gillis would have seen it." Aralyn felt her cheeks redden at this.

"Let's see what Orandon says. He knows these marks better than I."

Aralyn and Elnala returned to the men as Gillis picked up his shirt.

"Never seen one quite like that," Orandon said to Gillis. "I'm not sure what to make of yours."

Gillis' voice was muffled when the shirt came over his head and mouth. "This ... sensation of ... whatever that was ..." His mouth came free. "We've been close enough to each other that we would have felt it before now. What you're saying makes no sense. You've worked your magic on us, haven't you? Made us think there could be something to this story of yours. Paired talents and so on."

Aralyn pondered his words. They had been closer than just touching shoulders when she'd ridden with Gillis and when he'd tended to her wounds. He had a point.

Elnala described Aralyn's mark, including the symbol that she couldn't decipher. She made a circle with her fingers to show him the size.

Orandon nodded. "His is a bit larger. You've noticed yours before, Gillis?"

"Been there all my life."

"Aralyn? What about you?"

"No," Elnala answered before Aralyn could. "She was completely surprised by it."

"And, Gillis, you've never seen Aralyn's."

"A few weeks ago, on her right shoulder blade, I saw what looked like a large freckle but didn't think anything of it."

Orandon reached out to Aralyn, took her hand, and closed his eyes. "Yours, Aralyn, has just recently arisen. It's new, not fully ... *emerled*? I believe that's the word. That's why you didn't notice the sensations before now—because your mark wasn't there, not completely." He opened his eyes. "But trust me, Gillis. I did nothing to create those sensations. There is a sure power flowing between you. You are paired, Gillis. I hope you both will see this as a good thing."

***

Conflicting feelings pulled at Aralyn as she glanced at Gillis' stoic face and the Elves' concerned yet hopeful expressions. The air felt heavy and seemed to weigh her down.

"Will you excuse me?" Without waiting for a reply, she turned her back and left the room. Upstairs, in a spare room, she found a full-length mirror. She stared at her reflection and thought of Gillis' words. "She can go." And an icy chill ran up her arms. Why did it hurt so much to hear him say that? Tears sought escape from a stony prison. Her memories of him caring for her when she was injured and of his protection made her recall the physical pain. Then the longing came and erupted in her heart.

The choice was simple—be with him here or not at all. She had to be strong and not allow these emotions to have total sway over her. And yet...

"Do I want him to love me?" She spoke to the reflection as it mouthed the words back to her. Did it matter if he loved her? Could she blame him if he didn't? And had she, or was she falling in love with him?

"I want him to fight for me. Not send me away." A lump formed in her throat, and her foggy image in the mirror smiled. *I'm not so hard to look at.* And she wanted to hear Gillis tell her the same thing. But he had. He had told her she was beautiful, or had he still been under the influence of the poison and fever?

"Be thankful you have Gillis. He is a fine male."

Aralyn swung around to see Elnala standing in the doorway. "How long have you been there?"

"You love him, don't you?"

Aralyn wasn't sure how to answer. But while she longed to go with the Elves, she ached for Gillis to join her.

"Oh, Aralyn, I won't pretend to be happy if you don't come with usIreallywantyoutobu—"

"Elnala, slow down. What are you saying?" Her irritation with Elnala's manner of speech flared up.

"Just that I want you to come with us. But you should also be with the one you love. Always." Elnala's eyes sparkled.

Aralyn turned back to the mirror. "I didn't say I loved him, and why is that so important to you?"

"You and he—they forced you to marry. The Elves, we knew that. The story of Brone's death reached us, and at first, we thought you were dead. When we found out you weren't, oh, the relief that flooded us! And then word traveled that you had married Gillis. I was giddy. Honestly, that is the best way to describe it. As I said, he is a fine male." Elnala's eyes grew distant, and the silence stretched. "The man I loved died in battle. We never married. I want others to appreciate those joys and never take a spouse for granted." Her voice trembled, and she bit her lip.

"I want to come with you." She watched Elnala's reflection in the mirror. "But not without Gillis. At least I know he respects me, even if he doesn't love me. And he wants us to be friends. That can be enough."

"I don't believe a word of it." Elnala shook her head. "You just said you wanted him to love—"

"I didn't say that. I was asking myself..." Ugh, that sounded pitiful.

"But you might as well have said it." She approached Aralyn and placed both hands on her shoulders. "It's all right to want someone to love you."

"What you say may be true, but respect is important too. If he doesn't respect me, how can he ever love me?"

Elnala frowned. "I have to admit, I'd never thought of it like that." Then her mischievous grin returned. "I can imagine what you'd sing to him. Not love songs, but respect songs." And Elnala clasped her hands to her cheek and burst into a melody. The song didn't make sense with the words rushed together to make them fit, and a melody that ended too high.

"Elnala, are you all right?"

"Oh yes..." Elnala straightened and smoothed her robes. "Some people say my grief has made me ..." She sighed. "That humor is my escape. People may not understand some of my ... quirky ways, but I'm not here to please everyone. Grief or no."

Aralyn could understand that—just as humans hadn't condoned her hunting abilities, claiming she needed to act "more like a young lady" or the ones who laughed at the dreams she'd once had—still had—of traveling through mountains and valleys, to Dwarven mines, and even Dragon lands.

Elnala tilted her head to the side. "Listen, I promise that if you come with us, it will be well worth it."

"It will?"

"Yes." Elnala quirked an eyebrow. "And besides, I think we'd be great friends."

Really? Aralyn's doubt must have shown on her face.

"Would you not like that? Judging by your expression, neither of us is good at hiding our emotions or our thoughts."

"Well, I suppose I could use ..." No, "use" wasn't the right word. "If we get to know each other, I'm sure I would enjoy being your friend."

Elnala clasped her hands together. "We could watch out for each other, Aralyn, and I could help you get to know our ways again."

Aralyn's mouth turned up, and Elnala hooked arms with her. They walked into the kitchen together and joined Gillis and Orandon.

"What have you two been up to?" Orandon asked, his tone playful, much more relaxed than before.

"Oh, talking about men," Elnala answered, her voice deadpan.

"I see. Did you come to any conclusions?" Orandon asked, a teasing lilt in his voice.

"We'd tell you, but then we'd have to kill you." Elnala laughed, and Aralyn couldn't help but join her.

Aralyn released Elnala and laid a hand on Gillis' arm. "The conclusion I came to is this—that if my man refuses to come, I will stay with him."

Gillis shook his head. "Aralyn, don't worry about 'your man.' In this case, I could have you released temporarily from your obligation to me."

Aralyn chewed on her lip. "No. I will not go without my ... without you."

Orandon's expression changed from amusement to concern to something darker—something Aralyn could not read. But it quickly passed, and he nodded. Orandon lifted his chin, and his gaze rested on Aralyn. "Very well. But you need to know something. We're not sure how quickly the Age of Thunder approaches. We only know we don't have a lot of time if the birds are attacking, even if they are not changing color."

Gillis folded his arms, and his eyes dropped to the floor.

Orandon's eyebrows came up. "The colors migrate from the mistbows around our waterfalls to their wings. It makes them nearly impossible to defeat, skews our borders, and, some believe, our laws of science. You know something about this, Gillis?"

"They are changing," Gillis muttered. "I've seen them."

Elnala closed her eyes. She turned to Aralyn, her eyes pleading.

"We'll leave for now," Orandon said, his face a mask. "We cannot force you to come with us."

"But we must. We,"—Elnala took a step toward Orandon— "can't just leave them."

"We can, child. And we will." Orandon's jaw tightened.

"You're not going to force us?" Gillis asked.

"No, as I said, we cannot, Gillis. The Council once compelled people to do as they commanded, but they are no more with us. Most of them died or became sickly after the plagues, and the Elders will not use such compulsions or force our will unless it is an infraction of laws."

Gillis' shoulders visibly relaxed.

"We will let you consider your decision, and then return in a month," Orandon continued. "You will still have a choice. We only ask you to choose wisely."

Chapter 18

"I'm not going back to them. Not returning to that land." Gillis reiterated.

They stood by the gate, watching the Elves retreat.

"But Gillis, they need us."

"Listen to me. You're all bloody excited because you didn't experience their cruelty."

Aralyn swallowed. "Maybe not, and I wish you would tell me ..." She cut herself short at Gillis' sharp glance. "Gillis," she began again, "my mother did experience it. She also has no desire to go back." What was it that Mother had said the night Aralyn returned from talking to Drehensil? *There's nothing but death there.*

"Then, blood of flames, why do you want to go back?"

She pinched her lips together. "I don't know, but I've dreamed of going. Maybe it's because I belong there."

Gillis grunted. He reached into his shirt pocket, pulled out his longpipe, lit it, and inhaled.

Aralyn watched the smoke curl into the sky.

"You like watching me smoke?" He cocked an eyebrow at her.

On a whim, she asked, "Can you make smoke rings?"

Gillis rolled his eyes.

Aralyn knew that was a silly thing to ask, and waved her hand to let it go.

Gillis held up a finger, worked his jaw, and made an O with his mouth.

Aralyn watched the rings rise in the air until they dissipated. "Too bad they don't last longer." She grabbed the top board on the gate, leaned back, and watched him make more. She felt more relaxed with this to distract her, even though her emotions were still churning.

Gillis pulled the pipe out of his mouth. "We've still got some daylight. Perhaps we can work on sharpening your arrowheads. And I know some of my knives need it. My sword as well."

Aralyn brightened.

Out in the stables, he had the tools and the oil that they needed. Aralyn took her time sharpening the arrowheads. She found her voice and sang.

Gillis joined with her, a wordless melody like her own. A soft echo of music rang softly, ending in harmony. Out beyond them, the forest grew still.

They both listened. Gradually, the sounds of streams and breezes and birds returned.

Strange.

"Would you like to try your new bow?" he asked.

"I'm not sure. But I think..." She shook her head. Secretly, she was afraid of what had been done to her muscles but wasn't willing to share that with him. Maybe when he was gone sometime.

"I'm hungry. I'll go fix us something."

"Without Deonella?"

"Yes, Gillis." She lifted her chin. "Without Deonella."

She could start a fire at least, and cooking on a stove was easier than cooking over a fire. Aralyn grabbed some wood from the stack behind the house and took it inside. She heard Gillis' footsteps a few moments later.

He brought more wood and dropped it in the rack. "Aralyn, another reason I cannot leave is that I don't know what I'd do with the servants."

"I see." She focused on preparing the meal, kitchen knife in hand.

"I'm glad you do." He sat at the table. "As I said, you can always go."

Aralyn slowed in her slicing of carrots and potatoes. "I understand your words, Gillis, but somehow ..." She cleared her throat. "It's like I told Elnala—it doesn't seem right for me to leave without you." The pot was waiting.

Gillis straightened in his chair and rubbed his hands on his trouser legs. "Whyever not?"

She spun around, still holding the knife. "Gillis, even if we are married in name only, I don't think you should be so eager to get rid of me." Why had she said that?

Gillis tilted his head at her. "Is that what you think? You think I want to send you off with a crew of Elves without some thought of your safety?"

There it was again. Her safety. "You don't trust them at all. Even the two who came? And what if they're right?" Aralyn finished scooping the vegetables into the pot. "About the Age of Thunder and how much we are needed for the survival of Elvish lands."

"Well, they'll have to work it out. I feel no obligation to help save their hides."

"What exactly makes you feel that way?" Aralyn laid the knife down harder than she meant to, but she had a right to know, didn't she? "Tell me about these injustices you—"

"I've said enough." His eyes flashed. "And I have no longing to speak of it. So stop asking."

Aralyn felt her jaw tighten. She wanted to feel more compassion for him, but he was hiding things from her. She went back to cooking, refusing to say more. She lifted a stove lid to add more wood and poked it down. When she did, a spark landed on her sleeve. It burned through to her arm. She cried out and clasped the spot with her hand. The wood popped. More sparks flew. Some landed on the floor. Others landed on her. Tiny flames burst upon her skirt.

Before she could swing a towel to put them out, Gillis was by her side, beating her skirt with his bare hands and shouting. "How in the world did you manage that?" He snatched the towel from her and kept beating at her skirts even though the flames were out. Stomped dying sparks on the floor. He went to the stove and replaced the lid with a loud clang.

"What do you think you're doing, woman? You're not a bloody child. Didn't anyone ever tell you to be careful with fire?"

Aralyn opened her mouth to answer, but Gillis was shouting. "Don't ever let that happen again." He swung around, boots stomping the floor, and he strode out.

Aralyn didn't know Gillis that well, and he seemed to be angry quite often, but she had never seen him like this. He was protective, yes, but this was something else—something deeper. She wanted to go after him and demand to know what was troubling him.

Instead, she went to the pump and ran water over the burn on her arm. The vegetables were boiling, and the meat sizzled. She would finish the meal, and perhaps by then, he would calm down and return to eat.

She waited, but saw no sign of him. Her feet took to pacing. The need to go to him overwhelmed her. She wiped her hands and straightened her skirt. Opening the door, Aralyn stepped out into the twilight.

By the time she found Gillis, the sky was more purple than blue. She stood, unsure of what to say. *Come to dinner. Please come home. Are you all right?* None of those words seemed adequate.

"The clouds are moving out. There will be lots of stars tonight." His gaze distant, Gillis' voice caught in his throat.

Aralyn waited. She had not come to talk about the sky, and he knew it.

Shadows drew across his face. "Are you all right, Aralyn? Did you get burned?"

She could barely hear him. "I'm fine, but you're not. Obviously."

He raised an eyebrow, almost invisible in the twilight, and inhaled with effort. "No, I suppose I am not." He sighed, faced her, and in the softened light, his tears fell. Tears. Except for Re'ah, she'd never seen a man cry. "I don't know what to say, Aralyn. But I ... I need to tell ye—even if our marriage is only in name as ye said—ye've still a right to know." His accent became stronger as his emotions rose.

But Aralyn breathed easier, knowing that whatever he said, it could not make things worse. "This has to do with your first wife, doesn't it?"

A sharp intake of air. "Yes ... Yes, it does."

Aralyn waited.

"She was pregnant. About to deliver." He swallowed hard. This was not going to be easy for him, but she needed to hear just as much as he needed to tell her.

"I had spoken with one of the mages. He was helping me with some stomach pain, horrible pain that kept me down for days at a time." More tears upon his cheeks. "He, for some reason, took it upon himself to start practicing his magic near our home. I told him not to. He told me not to worry. 'It's just water magic.' Problem was, he wasn't trained in water magic. I was outside one day, looking for Laella, not sure where she was." His voice wavered. "I heard an explosion. A fire had erupted in the kitchen. I ran to the house. Smoke poured from it. The mage was standing outside our home with his eyes wide and a half-smile on his blasted face.

"'Where is she?' I asked him, but I knew. The fire was blazing and ... that's when I heard her screams. And I saw her." His fist pounded the tree, causing pieces of bark to fall at his feet. "But I couldn't get to her! I tried. I tried, and that maggot-infested mage just stood there and did nothing! I thought I was close enough to reach her, but the flames...I felt them on my back. My clothes caught on fire. It was hot ... so hot."

With great effort, Aralyn remained silent and took a step closer to him.

"You ever feel flames licking you? Feel your flesh burning, blistering? Ever listen to someone you love screaming for help as they burned?"

She glanced at the hole in her sleeve. That one little spark had hurt, still hurt, but she knew it was nothing compared to what Gillis had suffered. And Laella...

"I could not get her out!" The anger, shame, and grief poured from him. "Someone grabbed me, threw me to the ground, and doused me with water. But she kept screaming. I let her die alone when I should have died with her."

Aralyn closed her eyes. A horrible way to die. And to watch someone die. That must have been where he'd gotten the scars she'd seen on his back.

But no, he should not have died.

She was hesitant to touch him, but it was time to think of Gillis. Aralyn took another step and placed her hand on his back.

He swung around and grabbed her hand, squeezing it tightly, tears streaming down his face. "Oh, how you scared me!" He sobbed. "You could have ..." He choked. "I'm sorry, lass." He tugged at a handkerchief in his pocket. "I am truly sorry for the way I treated you in there. I had no business speaking to you in that manner." He wiped roughly at his eyes.

"Gillis." Tenderness flooded her. "I'm here. Look at me. Touch me." She guided his hand to her face. "I believe Elyon has plans for us. And until he completes those plans, I will be here." Aralyn couldn't believe her own words. What was she saying? She wasn't truly devoted to Re'ah's god but had a profound sense that these words were from him. And at that moment, she felt surer than ever that she had to stay with Gillis. She knew he was hers.

Before she could think of anything else, he wrapped his arms around her, holding her close. So close. His grip on her possessive; it felt as though he would never let go. Her arms curled around his back and shoulders, and she let the feelings of warmth and yearning fill her.

"I'm glad you're all right. Believe me, I am." The words were gentle on her ear. "But I'm just not that certain of life anymore. For a long time, I wanted to give up."

Aralyn could only listen, feel the strength flowing between them. "There's something more, isn't there?" she asked as she held him.

"Yes." He nodded and released her. "The injustices I spoke of—I thought I could receive justice from the Elders, but the mage's father and mother were on the Council. They overruled the Elders. I wanted to build a fire for him and have him thrown in it. Perhaps a bit extreme." Gillis turned his eyes to the stars. "There was no punishment. The reason? I had asked him to come. Didn't bother them that he had used a magic he had no business using. *Untrained is untamed* is the maxim they use. I should have known better than to ask him for help. I packed up my belongings and went south to another part of Eyndor—where I thought the memories wouldn't reach me. I wanted to forget what they had done. Eventually, I came here."

Aralyn took his hand and squeezed it. He grasped hers, crushing her fingers together, and she sensed his anger, anger twisted with grief, and the need to blame, just as she had blamed herself for the tragedies in her own family. The pressure on her hand lessened, and Gillis ran his thumb over her knuckles, staring at the horizon.

The silence stretched until Aralyn spoke. "Remember when we were on the trail, and you said you hadn't laughed with a friend in a long time?"

Gillis nodded.

"Is this...is this why?"

"Yes, it is." His arms were around her again, and hers around him. He was the first to pull away, but he placed his hands on her forearms, and their eyes met. "I remember when I called you friend. I think we can give ourselves credit for that. We can at least be friends, don't you think?"

"Yes, Gillis." What else could she say? When in reality, she wanted him as more than a friend. But Laella still had a hold on him, crushing his heart, and Aralyn doubted that would ever change.

Chapter 19

Gillis left on the king's business in the early morning hours. Something about escorting an ambassador to the Montravian border, Deonella told her. Aralyn had just missed him. Deonella didn't make any cutting remarks—nothing about a wife needing to be up to see her husband off. Maybe Aralyn had won her respect. But she didn't count on it.

Aralyn decided it was time for her to try out her new bow. She lay aside the fear of punishment and the fear of weakness. With bow in hand, she saddled Monpomme and headed toward the stream. Aralyn kept her eyes out for deer sign but soon pulled Monpomme to a halt. Turned around, her sense of direction failing her, she had no idea which path would lead her back. How had that happened? She hadn't traveled that far from the house, had she? And yet nothing was familiar.

A hissing noise, much louder than any snake, and rhythmic clicks accompanied words in a strange language. The noises grew louder. Pressure built on her skull. The same horrible feeling of someone placing fingers into her mind, pushing open secrets, and exposing thoughts.

No! Leave me! She pushed back but to no avail. She imagined her *bar're*—the wall to protect her mind—building and grasped the dragon stone.

The attack did not stop. Her head spun, and she had to lean over Monpomme's neck. "Home," she whispered into her horse's ear, hoping someone had taught Monpomme the command. Monpomme trotted forward. "Good girl."

The house came into view. If this had been an attack by Mal'ev, her escape had been an easy one. The fear clung to her like an oily garment coating her skin. But the voice had stopped. Out in the forest, there was only the sound of birds and the rushing stream. Aralyn dismounted and leaned against Monpomme, trying to calm herself. But the pressure came again. She cried out, reached for her head, and fell to her knees. The fingers probed once more, this time playing on her deepest fears.

Her mother was dying. And so was Terrwynn. Sickness and pain washed over them. The plagues had reached them. Mother cried out for help, and Terrwynn struggled to rise. She had to get to them.

Monpomme nuzzled her. Aralyn gasped and shook off the vision. This wasn't right! She cried out for Gillis and remembered he was gone. He would never hear her. "Drehensil!" Could the dragon help her?

"Re'ah!" No answer came. What about Deonella? Monpomme nuzzled her again, more roughly this time, and Aralyn grabbed her bridle. The horse lifted her head, pulling Aralyn to her feet. She remounted. The horse took her back to the stable while Aralyn clenched the reins.

"Aralyn, girl, you all right?" It was Hermes, concern written on his face.

Aralyn slid off Monpomme's back, still in a daze. She managed a smile. "I'm fine." She handed the reins to Hermes and turned toward the house. "Put her up for me, will you?"

"Certainly, miss."

Aralyn hadn't expected Re'ah to answer her cry, but she needed to talk to him about this fear and about what had happened a few moments ago. Just as she'd made up her mind to find a messenger to locate him, a young boy appeared at the gate. "Hello, Aralyn and Gillis!" He cried out.

Aralyn returned his greeting and trudged toward him. The young man wore the armband of an official messenger and had a pouch tied around his waist.

"Hello, Mrs. Aralyn. Brought you a message from King's City." He held a rolled-up parchment in one hand. She took it from him and began to read, forgetting to thank the boy or offer payment. The words captured her, and by the time she looked up, the messenger had disappeared.

She read the words once more to make sure they were right. Re'ah would soon be on his way. Perhaps, somehow, he had heard her cry for help.

***

"You never shot your bow? Still haven't tried it out?" Gillis led Restless to the stables, Aralyn beside him, matching his stride. The orange from the sun's rays painted clouds in the distance, and long shadows angled eastward.

"No, I didn't want to go back into the forest. That's the second time it's happened—like someone probing my mind. I hate that feeling. I hate it."

"Well, I'm glad you're safe." This concerned him more than he could say. If it was Mal'ev attacking her mind again, Gillis needed to do something—and soon—or her sanity would be at stake. He removed Restless' saddle and brushed him down.

"I'll go start some tea," Aralyn said.

"Thank you, lass. We'll talk when I come in."

He finished caring for Restless and spoke to Hermes before heading to the house, deep in thought. He found her in the kitchen, sipping on tea. She pushed his cup toward him, and he sat. Her husband took her hand. "I'm sorry I wasn't here."

"You have a job. I was able to manage, but I thought you should know. I'll try again tomorrow." Aralyn glanced at his hand on hers and lifted her gaze to him.

"What is it?" he asked.

"Um ... you're holding my hand."

He released it and pulled away.

"I don't mind. Honestly. I kind of"—she pursed her lip, and he almost didn't catch her next words— "like it."

"Ah." His lips tugged up at one corner, and he reached for her hand again, giving it a small squeeze. No, he didn't mind either. His mind flitted back to the brief kiss he'd given her. An odd sort of longing came over him as he thought of it.

Aralyn ducked her head and changed the subject. "Re'ah is coming. I got a message from him. I think both of us could use his guidance."

"Concerning?"

"Concerning?" She repeated back. "The Elves. About everything that's happening."

Gillis shook his head. "Aralyn, don't you know he's busy? He has more important things to do?"

"I don't understand what could be more important than trying to save a whole race of people. Aren't we—the Elves—his people too? Don't many Elves follow him?"

"I wasn't sure you followed him, Aralyn. I hear you speak of the gods of the sky-haven."

Aralyn dropped her eyes. "I ... I try to follow Re'ah. I know he cares for me. But it's hard. In Sathria we had to pray to the others, pay homage at the temples at least once a month." She frowned. "It's odd...the Rogues never touched those temples."

Gillis nodded. "No, the cowards are too bloody superstitious even if they don't worship the same gods. I've heard of the worship you speak of." His voice was low, and he set his cup down, gazing at Aralyn. "Did they brand you?"

Aralyn swallowed. "Yes." She reddened, and Gillis wondered if it was anger or embarrassment she felt. She lifted her chin. "And I doubt those gods care anything about us. They just want us to worship them blindly."

Gillis tipped his head. "That branding doesn't mean you're theirs." He leaned toward her. "And, Aralyn, there is a God who cares for you."

"Perhaps your god is different, but the others—no, they just want us to bow down to them and follow rites and rules so they can hold us in their power."

"The old gods have no true power, Aralyn. You can't judge Re'ah's God by them. I hope you know that."

"I believe Elyon cares. I mean ... doesn't he? He also has a purpose for his people, right?"

What could he tell her? She was so adamant when she'd said nothing would happen to her because Elyon had a plan for them. "Aye, Aralyn. He cares, and we may not always understand his plans, but as you said earlier, he does have a purpose for us."

"Perhaps he's different. If Re'ah clings to him so, maybe he is different from the others." Aralyn changed the subject again. "At least Re'ah will be here soon. Maybe tomorrow."

"I'm sorry I snapped at you earlier, lass. It will be good to see him."

"You're forgiven. I know you're tired. Sure you don't want something to eat?"

"Maybe later. And being tired is no excuse for my sharp words."

Her eyes dropped, and she curled her fingers around his. "You know I've never been with a man."

Gillis choked and nearly spat out a mouthful of tea. His hand jerked back from hers, and he met her gaze.

"I shouldn't have said that." She glanced down again. "I don't know what made me. It just came out."

Gillis drew in a deep breath. "You might want to ease into that topic next time. Give a man some warning." He wiped his mouth and shoved his teacup away.

The quiet stretched on.

"Well, can we talk about it?"

"About you ... being ... having never ..." Gillis sputtered. He couldn't believe he was hearing this from Aralyn.

"Yes, and what we can do about it."

"What we can do about it? You and I?" He shook his head, unable to hide his surprise. "I didn't think that was an option."

"Who else, Gillis? And it's something I've been thinking about." Her face showed no hint of shame.

"That was an interesting way to bring up the subject." He folded his hands in front of his face and studied her. "Aralyn." Then, lowering his hands to the table, he said, "That's a big step." Good. State the obvious.

Aralyn's face lifted, and her eyelids fluttered. A tiny smile tugged at her lips. "I know. But we're married."

She was flirting, was she? Unashamedly trying to bed him.

"I don't know what to say, Aralyn." And that was the truth. "I'm sorry if I've made you think—"

"But you don't want me ... like that."

His hands flexed. "I could ..." No, he couldn't. Best to be honest with her. "I find you attractive and have discovered you have ..." What was the word?

"A good mind?"

"No, no. I mean, yes, you do, but you, your character. You're capable in ways I admire. You have a goodness about you that is just, well, good." He shrugged, hoping he hadn't offended her.

"I see." She grabbed her cup and saucer and came to her feet.

"Aralyn, I thought that, maybe it was a possibility. But ..."

"I know. You miss Laella. You can't because of her."

She'd remembered Laella's name. He rose, took the dishes from her hands, and set them down. He placed a hand on her face and brushed back her hair with the other. Before he knew it, her lips were on his. He returned the kiss, responding without question. He kissed her deeply, and she wrapped her arms around his neck. He tasted her lips. Sweetness. Utter delight. He could let this lead wherever it might. What would be wrong with that? As she had said, they were husband and wife. His heart quickened as she pressed against him.

But he didn't love her. He couldn't see taking her to his chamber and making her more than a bride. Taking what she had never given another man. He pulled away.

"It wouldn't be right, Aralyn."

"Why? What would make it wrong?" The confusion flashed from her eyes as she drew back.

"You said you've never been with a man. I want you to give yourself to someone who loves you the way you deserve to be loved." Their eyes locked. "And I'm not that man."

"Then it's not going to happen, Gillis. We're together. I'm not going to be unfaithful."

No, she would never do that. "I know, I know."

Her eyes filled. "I just made a fool of myself, didn't I?"

"No. No, lass. For a moment, I thought I could give you what you wanted, but I can't. And Aralyn, you're no fool." He meant every word.

She grabbed her cup and saucer again and turned to the sink. Water ran, and she scrubbed, kept scrubbing. She pumped more water and scrubbed some more.

Gillis should have let her go to begin with. To flames with tradition! He knew he should have taken her back to Sathria. Eventually, the magistrates would have caught up with him and arrested him, but she would have been where she belonged.

**

Aralyn wanted to hurl the cup and saucer across the room, to hear the satisfying crash of porcelain against the wall or shattering a window. She *had* made a fool of herself. And Gillis had encouraged her. She prayed Re'ah would be here soon. Even though she didn't always understand his god, she wanted him here.

It was almost evening the next day when she heard her name shouted in the wind.

"Aralyn!" It was him. Re'ah. He dismounted, and she opened the gate. "Where is your husband?"

"He went fishing. He's showing Duncan some 'survival skills.'" Aralyn knew Gillis wanted an excuse to catch some trout for their supper. "He'll be home shortly."

Re'ah headed toward the stable, and Hermes met him halfway. Re'ah handed the reins to him, and the two exchanged banter.

Aralyn made her way to the kitchen as the back door opened. Gillis' face lit up when Re'ah followed Aralyn in. "You came. Couldn't just send my wife a message, eh?"

Re'ah took a step toward him, and they gripped forearms. "No, I needed to see both of you."

Aralyn peered out the back door. "Where's Duncan?"

"Sent him home with his share of the fish."

Re'ah leaned back in his chair, put his feet up on another chair, and closed his eyes.

"Re'ah, are you all right?" Aralyn asked. Something seemed off. "Can I get you anything?"

"No, no. Just let me sit a moment. Get the sun out of my system."

What an odd way to put it. But Aralyn felt sure he was in pain. She would make tea and ask Deonella to cook some of the fish.

Re'ah opened his eyes when Gillis sat.

"Aralyn. Come sit," her husband said.

"I'm putting some tea on." Aralyn put water on to boil and joined them.

Re'ah's worn expression was from more than just the sun. "Both of you, please listen. The time for you to get to Eyndor safely is short. You need to go with the Elves when they return."

Gillis clenched a fist and tapped it on the table. He cleared his throat and spoke in a tightly controlled voice. "Re'ah, it's ... hard to forget what they did."

Aralyn read the compassion on Re'ah's face. "I know, Gillis."

"I get so bloody angry. And how do you know they're sincere? Is all they say true?"

"Gillis, you've been attacked by ruffle birds, right?" Re'ah knew he had. "I'm concerned for your safety. And Aralyn's. You don't have to wait for all the signs of the Age of Thunder. If you do, it may be too late."

Gillis leaned forward and splayed his hands on the table. "They say the Council is gone. Should I believe them?"

"The Council suffered more than almost anyone during the plagues." Re'ah's gaze grew distant. "As a ruling body, they are gone."

Gillis had another objection. "I'm answerable to the king. I can't just leave without his knowledge and permission."

"Gillis," Re'ah said. "Their borders are important, not just to the Elves but to the rest of the lands, so this is important to the king. If their borders fall, it will make it much easier for enemies to conquer Lahilla. Elven lands serve as a barrier to the enemies' power, keeping it from penetrating our lands. I know there are occasional Rogue attacks, but the full force of the Gehallion and Montravian armies has yet to attack the rest of Lahilla. I am surprised the Elves did not tell you this. I know you were mistreated and saw the cruelties of the Elves personally, but you and Aralyn—you could make a difference."

Aralyn's eyes lit up. "And maybe with people like Orandon and Elnala—"

"I don't know." Gillis interrupted. "What am I supposed to do with my home? My servants? And what about Duncan?"

Aralyn touched his hand. "Perhaps Duncan and Deonella could come with us?"

"I doubt that's what this bunch wants. I'm not a 'pure.' But those two—Deonella and Duncan have even less Elven blood. I can't just leave them."

Aralyn's gaze flicked to Re'ah. "You wouldn't advise us to go if this were not urgent, would you?"

"This is vital. If you and Gillis do not go with them, you may not survive. And Elven lands most assuredly will not."

Chapter 20

"Take care of Gillis, child." Re'ah's hug was warm and comforting as they stood outside by the gate.

"I'll watch out for him, Re'ah." She attempted a smile.

"Good, he needs that from you." Re'ah patted his horse's neck and combed his fingers through Fleece's mane.

"He does?"

"More than he would ever admit."

A bird twittered nearby, and bugs hummed on the breeze.

Aralyn looked back toward the house. "I think I love him."

"I think you do, too." Re'ah took her hand, his gentle eyes smiling.

"I mean, I think I am in love with him."

"I know."

"I kissed him, and he kissed me back. But"—Aralyn swallowed— "he doesn't want me, Re'ah. Not as a true wife."

"That makes it difficult for you, but keep on loving him." The tender, unembarrassed empathy in his face overwhelmed her.

"I'll miss you, Re'ah."

"I will miss you, too, Aralyn."

Gillis strolled toward them and spoke first to Aralyn. "I need to have a moment with Re'ah. Would you excuse us?"

"Of course." She returned to the house, rubbing her arms for warmth.

Gillis followed her shortly later, pulled a piece of parchment from his shirt pocket, and handed it to her. "I received this earlier and forgot about it. They let Lot'fe send a message, and she sent it to you."

"What have they done with her?" Aralyn took the message from Gillis' hand. She couldn't deny the concern she had for the herbalist, though she'd betrayed their friendship.

"She's in the prison. Locked up securely. Other than that, I don't know."

"What do you think will happen to her?" Aralyn unfolded the parchment.

Gillis scratched his chin. "Aralyn, our magistrate, judges, and anyone in authority up to our king show mercy as often as they can. But even though she turned herself in, things don't look good for her. She was involved in an attempt to kidnap you. The people she was with were on the king's land without his consent, and they trapped dragon lizards."

Aralyn understood, and she read the message. It was brief and to the point. *You are not safe here, little one. Do not worry about me. I didn't mean to harm you or your dragon lizards.*

That was it. No admission of guilt. Just a plea for Aralyn's safety, and almost an apology. Perhaps Lot'fe had not meant to betray her. Perhaps someone had coerced her.

***

Later that day, Aralyn joined Gillis on the front porch, where he sat whittling a wooden stick to a point. "I guess you read the message. It told me nothing."

"I am not in the habit of reading others' messages, but yes, in this case, I felt I needed to," Gillis admitted.

"I suppose it was right for you to read it under the circumstances." Aralyn folded her arms. "But please don't do it again."

Gillis raised an eyebrow and patted the seat next to him. Aralyn sat. He stopped whittling and set the stick down. "Aralyn, there are times I need to check communications, especially from prisoners. It's a privilege for them to send messages, and if she continues to write you, I will, or another official will check them."

Aralyn examined his profile and dropped her hands into her lap. She kept forgetting he was an official, like a magistrate or king's man. Aralyn's shoulders relaxed. "I understand."

"Good." Gillis squeezed her hand, and Aralyn took the liberty of resting her head on his shoulder. He didn't seem to mind. "You comfortable?"

"Yes, my husband-friend." Aralyn relaxed against him and closed her eyes.

"Your husband-friend." Gillis chuckled. "I'll take that."

"Yes, you are my friend even though you exhibit your anger in a great variety of ways," Aralyn went on.

"Ha! Is that right? But I'm still your friend?"

"Yes. And I'm perfect, right?"

Gillis let out a belly laugh at this. "Well, you're my friend."

Aralyn opened her eyes as he said this. "That was the wrong answer."

He laughed even harder, and Aralyn punched his arm.

"Ow!" He exclaimed, rubbing his "injury."

Aralyn was the one laughing now, knowing he was unhurt.

His shoulder bumped against hers. "You're all right, Aralyn."

"Just all right?"

"That's what I said. Not perfect, but all right. But I mean it in a good way."

"I'll take that," she said.

Strength and warmth flooded her as they sat together. This felt so right.

But almost immediately Gillis' attention was elsewhere, and she noticed he was staring at the wooden gate.

"You need to go with them, Aralyn." He was not commanding her, but seemed to express a wish. "I agree with Lot'fe that you will be safer somewhere else. Especially if Mal'ev is attacking you. If not for Drehensil, his forces probably would have returned."

"What about you, Gillis? He may be hunting you as well."

Gillis leaned forward and rubbed his hands together. "I'll have to see what I can do." His voice drifted off. "I'm going inside. Getting a chill."

Aralyn continued to watch the gate, as if the Elves would arrive at any minute. A familiar sound teased her ears—hoofbeats approaching. She had to be hearing things, but the noise continued to grow louder. Maybe it was the Elves. Her thoughts turned to Mal'ev's attacks, and the hoofbeats took on an ominous tone. She stood and backed toward the door.

"Gillis." Aralyn wanted him by her side. "Gillis!"

He stepped out on the porch, his eyes turned to the sounds Aralyn had heard. Banners flew and caught the breeze. These were Elves, most definitely. There had to be at least two dozen of them. An Elf in front of the group looked like an aged human. He had dark hair streaked with gray, and lines crinkled his eyes when he saw Gillis and Aralyn.

Gillis spoke, his voice almost reverential. "He's here. How in the world ..."

"The older one? Who is that?"

"Come." Gillis took Aralyn's arm, and they approached the Elves. He lifted the latch on the gate and let them in, inviting them to tend to their horses.

Gillis addressed the older Elf. "I'm surprised to see you—thought you were dead."

"Well, I couldn't let two of my favorite people get away from us." His voice was soothing and, once again, familiar. He dismounted. "And to answer you, I knew of the story concerning my demise. Those Montravians do like to tell tales. They underestimate old gaffers like me. We escaped—that is, I brought some of the younger Elven captives back—all sound and quite hale."

Aralyn watched the man's eyes. They gave her a sense of ancient wisdom as they reflected the sky and treetops. A light like the crescent moon shone from them.

The other Elves dismounted, and Aralyn spotted Elnala among them. Thinking hers and Elnala's greetings could wait, she led the group to water their horses. That was when Elnala almost tackled Aralyn. "I'm so glad to see you!"

"Uh, me too." She unlatched Elnala's arms from her waist. The woman was so undignified. "But take care of your horse, and we'll talk."

The older Elf chuckled at Elnala's reckless enthusiasm. He turned to Aralyn, gentle light in his gaze. "So ... this is our bowsinger. Aralyn, I'm glad to see you again. Always had my suspicions about you."

"You look familiar," Aralyn said. "But I'm not sure I know you."

He pulled on his whiskers. "I thought for certain you'd remember me. I am Guronde, the eldest of our Elders."

The word "Elder" triggered her memory, and explained why Guronde looked familiar. "You tried to help my mother." A wave of gratitude and terror rushed over her as the past slammed her like rapids upon rocks.

Guronde leaned on his staff. "Yes, it's a shame what they did to our Lethola."

"She goes by Deirdre now," Aralyn corrected.

"Ah, she wanted a human name." Guronde closed his eyes and shook his head. His kind gaze landed on Aralyn. "But you still have your Elvish name."

"Yes, but it's a human name as well."

"I understand you have a young sister now. How is she?"

"She is ..." Aralyn's voice faded. "She's not so good. She was taken. She fell into the river, and some Rogues found her, but my da—stepfather went after her. She came back, but he never did. And she was never the same."

Gillis' brow furrowed, but she noted the sympathy on his face. She had never told him any of this.

Guronde squeezed her hand. "It was not your fault, Aralyn."

How could he know that? Aralyn frowned, but Guronde's authority silenced her. The rest of the Elves turned their horses loose to eat, drink, and frolic, free of their saddles and bridles. They made the yard look tiny.

Elnala pulled Aralyn aside. "You'll come with us this time?"

Aralyn swallowed. "I ... perhaps. I want to. But, Elnala, who are these people, and why did you bring them?"

"They're friends of mine and Orandon's—archers, mages, melee fighters—some of our best. We want to assure you it's not only Orandon and me who want you to come. The Age of Thunder approaches, and we will do all we can to support and protect you both. Certain parties may realize what we are planning and try to stop us."

"Mal'ev." Aralyn recalled the body of Bek dead by her hands. Strange, she couldn't see his face. His body, yes, but his face was a blur.

Elnala hooked arms with Aralyn. "Come. Guronde wants to talk to you and Gillis."

"Where's your father?"

"He stayed behind. He's the second eldest of the Elders, and he stays in Eyndor when Guronde leaves. He has authority over us when the Eldest is gone."

"I did nothing to prepare," Gillis was saying to Guronde as Aralyn and Elnala joined them.

"I understand, Gillis, but ... Ah, Aralyn." Guronde's smile was gentle upon her. "We planned to leave in the morning."

"In the morning?" She had a decision to make and quickly.

"Yes, we brought our tents so we won't be invading your home. Now, Aralyn and Gillis, are you ready to come with us?" Guronde asked.

Aralyn shifted on her feet. "I've got my pack ready. Just have a few things to put in." But that didn't mean she was ready. Aralyn's gaze landed on Gillis.

She didn't want to beg him, but the words were out. "Gillis. Please. Won't you come with us?"

Before Gillis could say anything, Guronde spoke. "If you're worried about duties to the king, I've already spoken to him, asking him if we can have you in Eyndor for an indefinite time."

Gillis raised an eyebrow.

"He knows how important the lands of Eyndor are to the stability of Lahilla." Guronde was affirming what Re'ah had told them. "You should receive an official message from him any day now."

"I will have to wait on that dispatch from the king." His voice was firm. "I respect you, Guronde, but you have to understand."

"I do, and your loyalty is admirable," Guronde replied. "He also assured me your servants will be well cared for."

"Fine. Aralyn, you are free to go with them tomorrow. I want you to go. If it is as Guronde says, I'll be with you in a few days."

***

Gillis pulled out his knives and examined each one. They were fine. Nicely sharpened and honed. He balanced each one on his forefinger as he'd done many times before. He put them back in their sheaths and locked them away.

The Elves, Aralyn, his king, and his servants filled his mind. He had tried to sleep, but memories and questions sprinted across his imagination. He lay down and closed his eyes again. Useless. Shortly before sunrise, he tossed back the covers, arose, and paced. Not much later, he heard a shout from the gate. In the predawn light, someone dressed in the regalia of a king's man waited. His horse tossed its head and blustered. Hermes hobbled out to meet the man.

Gillis pulled his shirt on and trod downstairs. Hermes was gabbing away with the king's man as if they were old friends. When Gillis reached the gate, the king's man handed Gillis a rolled sheet of parchment secured with a golden seal.

The king's seal.

Gillis opened the gate, and Hermes turned toward the barn. "Stay. This may involve you."

Hermes tilted his head and raised his eyebrows. "Something from the king involvin' me?"

"Perhaps." Gillis put his finger up to silence him and read the message. Hermes came closer and looked over Gillis' shoulder. The man could not read, but letters seemed to fascinate him.

To Peacekeeper Gillis

Greetings from the sovereign of Lahilla

Your king, Maelin, of the city of Jeniva-Senallair in the Land of Lahilla

It has come to my attention that the Elves need your aid in their lands. Elder Guronde has informed me that you and your wife are key to defeating those who will take advantage of their now-weakening borders. I understand the hesitancy on your part but urge you to go with him and his entourage. Accompany them to Eyndor, and if need be, engage the enemy in battle. From what Guronde has said, an attack by a powerful mage is imminent. I have seen signs of the Age of Thunder, and I want their borders secured before the enemy attacks. I would send forces myself, but Guronde assures me that is not necessary.

On a more personal note, and as your friend, I want to know why the queen and I were not invited to your wedding. I understand you have remarried. I would have given you at least the requisite year off from your duties. I command you to take that year as soon as this business with the Elves is settled.

Perhaps you still miss your first wife just as I would miss my queen under the same circumstances. Therefore, I consider it most urgent that you take time with your new wife. She will be a fount of blessing to you. Of that, I am sure. This often takes time. I pray, my dear Gillis, that you will both find that most contented state where you and your mate are as one. I wish you well. Please send me word post-haste.

Blessings from the True Sovereign above and your earthly king.

Yours in service to our lands,

King Maelin

Postscript: Your servants will be brought to the castle to work if they wish. The Rangers in the area will use your home as a place to take shelter in your absence. Therefore, if they so choose, the servants can stay and continue to work for the Rangers and care for the property.

Gillis was free to go. Free to go with the Elves, and the king would give Aralyn and him a year to spend with each other. An entire year. Yes, that was the custom, but leaders seldom honored it. Who would release soldiers and Peacekeepers from their duties so they could be happy with their wives for an entire year? His king would.

Gillis examined the letter again for any irregularities. The seal was official. The words fit his king, who was also his friend.

"Will you be sending a reply?" The king's man was waiting. His cropped hair and scant stubble indicated he was quite young, and there was an enthusiastic, almost childlike demeanor about him.

"Yes, of course. Will you tell him I will do as he says, and about the wedding—"

"The king would have it in writing, sir."

"Of course."

"I'll git pen and paper fer ye," Hermes offered. "And is there really something in there concernin' me?"

"Yes, as a matter of fact. Involves you and Deonella."

Hermes nodded. "Let me fetch them writin' needs fer ye, and I'll be right back."

"I'll have to pack and get ready," Gillis muttered.

The poor fellow had probably ridden most of the night, and Gillis hadn't even offered refreshment for him or his horse. "Do you need to water your horse, lad?"

"No, sir, took care of that just before we arrived."

When Hermes returned, Gillis penned his reply. Yes, he would do as the king asked. Go with the Elves, spend time with his wife, patiently wait for love to grow. He also apologized for the lack of a wedding invitation and wrote that he would explain at another time. Gillis gave the message to the young man.

"Thank you, sir. I'll get this to the king by tomorrow."

Gillis raised an eyebrow and watched as the messenger rode off.

The Elves were stirring now. They would soon be up.

"Come with me, Hermes." Gillis strode toward the house. "I need to talk to you and Deonella."

They were all about to have their worlds turned upside down.

***

Deonella was fighting tears—her face red, mouth drooping in a frown. Hermes stood with arms folded across his chest, screwing up his face. "I don't see how they could use me at the castle."

Gillis was quick to respond. "Hermes, you're good with horses, and the king promised..." Gillis turned to the stairs as Aralyn came down them. "Ah, good morning."

Aralyn, fully dressed, had her bow in hand, a quiver over one shoulder, pack over the other. Aralyn placed her bow in the corner, and Gillis handed her the letter. Aralyn's eyes widened as she ran her finger over the now-broken king's seal. "What's this?"

"Just read it."

Aralyn scanned the letter. "It's settled then?"

"Aye. I'll be coming with you."

She handed the letter back to Gillis. No sign of joy, not even a smile? But Aralyn's attention was on something else. She looked from Hermes to Deonella. "They can't come with us, can they?"

Hermes' mouth turned up. "I'm no Elf, not a single one in my family, so I've no business goin' to Eye-yandoor."

"And apparently that's not an option." Gillis folded his arms and asked both servants. "What do you wish to do?"

Deonella's face relaxed, and she lifted her chin. "I want to stay here." Her voice was firm. "One day, you'll come back, and I want to be here when you do."

Maybe she was right. He might indeed return.

"Don't be worried about us," Hermes said with a wave of his hand. "We'll be fine. And we'll be here whenever ye get back."

Aralyn had a look Gillis could not decipher. "You're ready?"

"Aye, Gillis."

"Well, I need to get packing."

She nodded. "And I will get the horses ready." She spoke to the servants. "I want you both to know ..."

Their faces lifted to hers, and she put a hand to her chest. "I will keep you in my heart." Gillis stopped in his tracks, moved by her words. Tears sprang to Hermes's eyes, and Deonella's chin quivered.

Hermes nodded. "Thank ye, Aralyn." He cleared his throat. "I'll come help ye with those horses."

***

The path grew rocky and the winds colder—colder than they had ever been in Maizehollow. It made Aralyn's eyes water and forced her to gasp for air. The sky was a clear blue, no clouds threatened, and the ground was covered in snow. She had never been amid such wonder. Tall trees held the white stuff high in their branches, and every so often, they dropped their load. Sometimes the branch bounced back into place, while others broke and fell with their burden, and the crack of the limbs echoed over them.

"Ah, I love that sound," Elnala said. "Love being out here when that happens." Her smile reminded Aralyn of a river overflowing its banks.

Aralyn wasn't sure if she liked that sound or not. What if a tree let go of its load over their heads? But she had to admit, she had never before witnessed such beauty with everything blanketed in white. Flakes flew in her face from the trees, and she batted them away.

Aralyn enjoyed the peace of it all. The snow seemed to quiet her surroundings and her soul.

Elnala interrupted Aralyn's thoughts. "We will have so much to learn from each other when we get to Eyndor. I train with Guronde. But since you're an archeryou'lltrainwithOrandonandtheother—"

"Wait, Elnala. Could you please slow down?"

Elnala blinked. "Oh. Of course." She grew silent and kept riding.

Surely Aralyn hadn't hurt the girl's feelings.

"I keep doing that."

"Yes, you do," Aralyn agreed. "But it's all right. Really."

"I feel such excitement at the prospect of you coming with us. Fighting with us. You'll have to get used to Orandon, my father. He trains the archers and can be pretty tough on them. He wants the best out of everyone, and he expects alotbutheisfair ..." Elnala stopped midsentence. "I'm doing it again, aren't I?"

Aralyn leaned toward her. "Yes, you are."

Elnala shook her head and let out a small chuckle. That was all it took to free a laugh from Aralyn. "I hope you don't do that too often. We'll be in a mess in battle."

Elnala laughed outright this time. "Yes, can you imagine? I'd be telling my commander weneedtoattacktheirflank..."

"Or weneedtorideoverthatridge..." Aralyn giggled at her attempt to imitate Elnala.

Elnala continued to laugh and make conversation while Aralyn's mind drifted, and she heard it again. A soft voice in her head. *You will not make it to Eyndor. Your mother was right. Nothing but death there.*

Her head in a drumbeat of pain, the probing began again, nimbly touching memories and twisting them. She fought back, and she could see her *bar're* grow thicker at her command. The dragon stone flitted in her pocket, and she grabbed it. The crimson of the stone filled her vision and incorporated itself into her *bar're*. It was stronger now. The wall was like that of a castle with a vision of archers who stood ready to fight between crenellations. Murder holes with arrows protruding added to her defenses. But it wasn't enough. Everything she did only seemed to enrage the attacker. The pain struck—deep and merciless.

And another kind of vision danced before her. But it was not a vision. It was real. She could see her family, and they were in trouble.

Terrwynn. Her mother. Falling into the river, their bodies going under, swirling in the reddish-black water. Lot'fe standing on the bank, a long, curved blade in hand, their blood dripping from it, her mouth forming one word. "Death."

"No!" Aralyn was shouting. "Take me! Take me instead!"

Nausea gripped her just before the world spun, and her back hit something hard and cold.

"Aralyn, stay with me." Elnala's face was over hers.

How had she ended up on the ground?

Guronde spoke from atop his horse. "Elnala, help her. We have to move."

"Yes, Guronde. Aralyn, can you get up?"

"I think so."

Elnala reached out a hand and grabbed Aralyn's forearm. "What happened?"

"I have to go back." Her voice shook. She would ride hard and arrive in a few days, but she might be too late. The decision swung like a pendulum in her mind. It was impossible to decide. But she had to.

"What do you mean?"

"My mother and sister are in trouble. They need me. I have to go to them."

"You cannot go back, and we must move on," Guronde commanded.

Gillis joined them, brow furrowed. Aralyn glanced from one to another, and her gaze landed on Elnala. "I'm going back to Sathria."

Elnala's eyebrows lifted. "No, you cannot." She grabbed Aralyn's sleeve, but Aralyn snatched her arm away.

"I saw them, my mother and sister. They were ..." Aralyn didn't have time to explain. She mounted and choked at the memory that still lingered as she swayed in her saddle.

Guronde pulled his horse up next to hers and grabbed the reins. "Be still, Aralyn." He placed a hand on her neck, the other on her forehead. "Relax."

She was seeing it all again. No, gods, no. No! Elyon, help me.

Guronde withdrew, and the scene blurred.

"She's being attacked," Guronde declared, and he looked around at the Elves who were watching.

"Mal'ev." The color left Gillis' face.

"This has happened before?" Guronde didn't sound surprised.

"Yes, twice that I know of." Gillis shifted in his saddle and turned his gaze on her.

"Yes, Guronde. He's right," Aralyn said.

Guronde studied them both. "Aralyn, are you sure you can ride?"

"My mother and sister ... Lot'fe went after them with a blade, and she left them to die in the river. I ..." *need to go back*, she wanted to say. Even after Re'ah's attempts to help her build a *bar're*, she had believed what a powerful mage told her to.

Gillis continued to watch her, fear and concern both clear in his expression. "Aralyn, lass—"

"I know. The image was a lie." She turned to Guronde and clenched her jaw. "I will come with you. I cannot turn back now."

"We'll be riding hard for the next three days." Guronde watched her face. "I want you to keep up."

"Of course." Aralyn took Monpomme's reins. "I'm ready."

Chapter 21

As the sun went down, they continued to ride until Aralyn could scarcely see. Lights flitted in the trees as lantern birds appeared, radiant feathers on their breasts. Soon, a multitude shone through the branches above them. Perhaps the horses could keep going with this light.

When they stopped for water, Aralyn patted Monpomme's neck as she drank. "You'll show those old horses, won't you? You'll ride as hard as they do." But Aralyn's concern for the mare weighed on her. She was not an Elven horse.

Footsteps approached. She recognized them as Gillis', and her smile came easily.

"Are you all right?" he asked.

"Yes, I think so."

"Maybe you should ride with someone—Elnala or me."

"It might be a good idea. Monpomme could rest a bit then."

"That's what I was thinking, lass. She requires more rest than these other horses."

"Don't tell her that. She'll never speak to you again."

Gillis chuckled. "You really think that horse talks to you, eh?"

"All the time. In her way." Aralyn stroked her horse's flank. "Don't you, girl?"

Monpomme turned to gaze at Aralyn and tossed her head.

"See? She agrees. Are we going to stop for the night?"

Guronde must have overheard. "We need to get to Eyndor before the enemy attacks you again and before the ruffle birds completely change." Guronde leaned forward in his saddle. "It will mean, Aralyn, that the borders will soon fail and the decline of our land, even the death of it, could soon occur." He sighed. "But we do need to stop. At least for a few hours."

"Watch your boots for snakes when you get up. Not too many out, but those that are would love a bit of warmth." Gillis gave her a peck on the cheek and volunteered to stand watch.

Aralyn crawled into her bedroll under the bird-lit trees. No tents tonight to help stay the chill. No fires either. She slept close to Elnala, and someone she didn't know slept on her other side.

Aralyn didn't remember closing her eyes, didn't remember dreaming, but the stir of Elves forced her eyes open. How she longed for more sleep! She was sure others wanted their rest just as badly, but they were up, two of them handing out bread and dried meat. No tea. No coffee. Just water from her waterskin, which someone had filled for her.

They rode hard again that day and the next. Aralyn alternated between riding with Elnala and Gillis and felt ashamed of her head nodding while no one else had a chance to nap. With little to eat, Aralyn's stomach rumbled. She had lived on less before, but now realized how well Deonella had kept them fed. No one else complained, so neither did she.

On the dawn of the fourth day, the air pulsed. No one spoke of it until they came to their first rest. Elnala brought her horse to the riverbank, where Aralyn stood, allowing Monpomme to drink her fill.

"You feel it, don't you?"

Aralyn's face turned upward, and she took in the strangely familiar atmosphere. She tilted her head to Elnala. "It feels odd, even tastes odd, yet comforting. What does it mean?"

"I'm glad you sense it. It means the borders are not far, and the power of Eyndor is among us."

***

Gillis overheard the women. Yes, they were close to Eyndor. Very close. And he found himself asking again why he was accompanying another woman to this place. Ash filled his mouth as he thought of Laella. He needed to let it go. He had tried. Over and over, he had tried. But memories of her called to him. Invited him to find comfort in death, in joining her. He felt guilty for showing Aralyn even a bit of affection. Was he leading her to the cruel realization he could never care for her the way she deserved?

Grief could be vicious and cold. How could he make it let go of his heart? At least a little. He had prayed and continued to pray. Nothing seemed to help. Even the God he said he believed in had done little to silence death's call. And yet, somehow, Re'ah's presence always brought relief and encouraged him to keep on living. So he did.

And Aralyn.

She drew strength from him. He could sense it. Something was comforting in that.

"Mount up!" Guronde repeated the cry in both Common and Elvish.

The Elven horses chomped at the bit, sensing the change in the air. They would ride with no stops now. As soon as they all mounted, the horses took off, seeming to fly over the ground. The gates of Elven lands came into view, gates that reached the tops of trees, and the horses slowed, as if on command. The figures of heroes carved in the gates caused a certain reverence among Elf and beast alike. Gillis recognized his onetime mentor, Vaziel. His image reminded Gillis of who he was. No matter how he felt about the Elves, they were his people.

The gates opened. They entered, and a tremendous cheer arose. A chill ran through Gillis. Guronde motioned Aralyn and Gillis to the front. Gillis grasped the reins tighter and nudged Restless with his heels. The rhythmic sound of hooves against the stone pathway echoed, as if in a great chasm. He glanced at Aralyn. She held her head high as her horse trotted forward. Her gaze met his, and her eyes shone with joy and amazement.

But how long would her wonder last? Elnala had mentioned training for the inevitable conflict, and he could only think of the coming battle. He felt overwhelmed by his need to protect her. But what if he failed again? He reached out. Without thinking, he took her hand. She squeezed back. Yes, she was here. With him. And it was a good thing.

***

Orandon was waiting to greet them. Elnala dismounted, and father and daughter threw their arms around each other. A woman who must have been Elnala's mother gave her daughter a pat on her shoulder and a peck on the cheek.

Most of their traveling companions split off and headed to their respective homes. Gillis surveyed his surroundings as Elnala and Orandon joined Aralyn and him.

"This is the city of Aurellium. Do you remember?" Orandon gestured to their surroundings.

"Not much. I spent little time here." Gillis could tell Restless felt uneasy. Perhaps he sensed Gillis' discomfort.

"I do." Aralyn's face was bright. "At least some of it."

As Gillis, Orandon, Elnala, and Aralyn rode further into Aurellium, the sky hummed a quiet, soothing rhythm.

"The borders," Gillis whispered.

"Yes, the borders." Orandon clasped Gillis' shoulder. "You hear them strengthening?"

"Aye. Feel it, too."

Aralyn turned to Gillis with the wide-eyed marvel of a child. Yes, she knew what was happening. Finally, the small party came to a series of trees that seemed to reach up endlessly. Bluish-green needles covered them, and at their bases lay a bed of discarded foliage. The Oovel pines of Eyndor.

"Your home." Elnala led Gillis and Aralyn to a nearby hardwood tree. They dismounted, found a small pond nearby, and turned the horses loose to drink.

This tree differed from those surrounding it. A maple tree, if Gillis remembered correctly. Majestic branches reached taller than the trees outside Eyndor. Winged seeds fell from above them, twirling in flight. Stairs wound around the tree trunk, and Gillis and Aralyn followed Orandon and Elnala to the top. Thick material covered a doorway on the side of the dwelling. Elnala held it open for them to enter. They stood in a large room with rich tapestries hanging on the inner wall. Open windows made up the top half of the outer wall. A gentle breeze stirred. The ceiling arched overhead, with paintings of Elves and Dwarves fighting against a common enemy. Pillars of bronze with ivy etched into them stood at various intervals throughout the home. Floor pillows to sit upon, a small couch, and a simple wooden table with three chairs made up their furniture.

Gillis remembered now the richness of Aurellium. Nothing like his home in the northern part of Eyndor. He watched as Aralyn fairly danced into the next room, where she found the bed. He would have to decide what to do about that one bed. But not now. She ran her hand over the maroons and royal blues of thick blankets.

Aralyn's eyes widened as she regarded her surroundings. "It's beautiful." She took it all in. "I remember this. My uncle's home? Where is he?" Aralyn asked.

"He died in one of the plagues." Elnala's face saddened as she said it.

"I suppose my grandparents ... and my other relatives? There could be hundreds of them."

"I'm not sure, Aralyn. They might still be alive. We'll find out."

The plagues. Gillis had missed most of those. He had escaped before the sicknesses took down a third of Eyndor's population. He watched Aralyn's reaction to the news. He could tell nothing from her blank expression.

"We have taken care of your uncle's home. We knew you would return one day." Elnala grabbed Aralyn's sleeve, her grin back in place.

The house was immaculate. Gillis wandered into the kitchen, which was in the center of this treehouse. He found the stove and a sink, but no hand pump for water. The physics of pumping water to this height would be a problem. Streams flowed throughout all Eyndor, if he remembered his lessons correctly, and rainwater could fill the tank he spied on a small deck outside.

"... tomorrow," Elnala was saying.

He'd missed something. "Tomorrow what?"

"Aralyn starts training tomorrow. You'll be ready?" Elnala asked her.

"Yes, of course."

Orandon regarded Aralyn. "I'll be here in the morning. Early." He turned toward Gillis. "I know you can help us plan strategy, and you can aid us in working with our Rangers who are out scouting. But we also need to explore your other talents."

It sounded like an excellent assignment. Discussing strategy, helping with the Rangers? The two things he loved about being a Peacekeeper.

"I shall be ready," Gillis said with a quick nod.

"Good, I will send someone for you."

***

Gillis had a decision to make. Should he ask Aralyn where they would sleep? They were husband and wife now. They had slept together on their wedding night for warmth, hadn't they?

And the nights were chilly here. But that was no reason. He had often slept out in the open with nothing but a bedroll for warmth.

This was not a difficult decision. Or it shouldn't be.

Let her decide.

No, he would. He would be the gentleman and offer to sleep on the floor.

He stared at the bed and remembered her advances. And how he had almost given in to her. *Laella*—

"Gillis, is something wrong?"

"I'll sleep on the floor tonight," he said, barely turning his head.

She was silent, then finally, "All right."

"I say we get some rest. Morning will come soon enough."

"Yes."

Gillis could feel her eyes on his back, and he pivoted to face her. "What is it?"

"I wondered..."

He raised an eyebrow, waiting.

"Will you be warm enough?" Aralyn's words came in a rush.

He waved a hand at her. "Of course."

He pulled off his tunic, and Aralyn left the room, gently closing the door behind her.

***

Gillis was still sleeping when Aralyn left the bedroom the next morning and discovered the new clothes someone had brought her—Elvish clothes. The skirt was of the same material as her old cloak, but newer and the colors richer. Greens of the forest mixed with deep orange and browns. There was another outfit, more practical for training. It came with trousers?

"Time to break your fast," A feminine voice called from the kitchen. Another memory broke free, and Aralyn recognized the voice. Although the timbre had changed from when they were *nanios*, there was no doubt who it belonged to.

Aralyn flew to the kitchen. "Shenral?"

They embraced, and Shenral wiped moisture from her eyes. "It's been a long time, Aralyn."

"Yes, it has."

The girl, now a woman, gave Aralyn a tired smile. Her once-golden hair, now faded, was tied back in a tail. Her eyes were still the same green and gold, and she stood a bit taller than Aralyn.

"It smells wonderful," Aralyn said.

"Elvish bread and porridge always smell good in the morning." Shenral lifted a pot as it began to boil. "I'm making tea from a secret family recipe and added a bit of mint and cinnamon." Shenral waved her hand toward a pan of branch-water coffee. "And I made coffee for Gillis." She reached for a spoon, stirred the porridge, and scooped out a portion for Aralyn. "After all these years. I'm so glad you are in good health." Shenral's face puckered. "It has not been easy here. This is the work I do now. But you and Gillis needn't pay me. Not today."

Aralyn noticed the droop to her shoulders and was almost afraid to ask. "How are your parents? Your family?"

"Gone."

Aralyn blinked. "I'm sorry."

"The plagues took children, adults, babies...my babies. It didn't matter. We age more rapidly, too. Like Guronde has. The plagues seeped into us, into the very air. The diseases robbed us of the life expectancy we once had."

To live forever. Aralyn knew that was a myth. Elves could live for thousands of years, but it was unlikely they would last much longer than three, maybe four millennia.

"We took so much for granted, Aralyn. We took it for granted that we would live for an endless amount of time unless, of course, a battle or an all-out campaign was launched against us. Now, a few hundred years is all we seem to have. Such a short time to live."

Shenral's weary face no longer wore its former determination. The girlish smile and laughter—gone.

"I'm sorry," Aralyn said once more.

"Oh, and how is your family?" It was as though Shenral had to come back from some far-off place to ask.

Aralyn told Shenral about her mother and Terrwynn. "Sathria is not an easy place to live, but ... we live."

They set the food on the table. "I hate to wake him." Aralyn nodded toward the bedroom as she sat.

"You already did." He stood at the bedroom door and stretched. "But I need to be up anyway." His chair scraped across the floor as he joined Aralyn. Shenral sat at his invitation, and Gillis blessed the food.

He took a sip of his coffee, then seemed to realize what he was drinking. He blinked at the cup he held. "Where did you find this?"

"Travelers from Lianton, a village just east of here. They grow coffee, and we trade with them. I wanted to try it."

"Did you find it to your liking?" Gillis took another sip of his hot drink.

"Not really. I'll give you what I have left. I don't know of anyone living among men ... I mean humans, who don't like a good cup of coffee from time to time, and I am glad this is to your taste." Shenral gave him a hint of a smile.

"Yes, it is. Dark and smooth."

Aralyn swallowed a mouthful of porridge. "You're not training in any way, Shenral?"

"No, not presently. I do odd jobs. Cleaning and cooking, helping those who train every day. I make a living." She shrugged.

Orandon appeared at the door. "Good morning, Gillis. Aralyn. And Shenral—good to see you."

Aralyn would have to adjust to this—crossing a threshold without asking permission of the occupants. She had forgotten that Elves had little respect for privacy.

Aralyn stood and grabbed her bow and quiver. "I have to go. Thank you, Shenral."

"I'll be back soon, perhaps tomorrow, to help you out," she replied.

"We'll pay you in that case."

Shenral nodded.

"I'm waiting on Lemmon," Gillis said through a mouthful of bread.

"Lemmon? The man who rented us Monpomme? He's here?"

"Yes, he is. He sold his business and came back to Eyndor to train again. He's quite a talented swordsman."

"Really?" She couldn't believe he would trade his business for a sword. Lemmon seemed so content among his horses.

Orandon tapped the tip of his bow on the floor. "Time to go, Aralyn. Gillis, Lemmon can take you to the mage walk, where the Elders and some of our leaders are meeting."

Aralyn followed Orandon down the stairs, bow in hand, missing a few steps as she hurried after him.

"Lemmon! It's good to see you," Aralyn cried when she spotted him.

He looked brighter, happier than he had before. "It's good to see you as well, Aralyn. How have you been? How is Monpomme?"

Orandon tapped his bow on the ground again.

"We're fine, but I must go." She touched his arm.

"We shall talk later, Aralyn." He gave her a small bow.

In the early morning light, the trees glowed as Aralyn and Orandon trod a worn, broad path. Aralyn wanted to ask questions, but despite her long stride, she barely kept up with Orandon. The path branched off into an area of thinning trees, and dwelling places dwindled in number. Some of the grasses reached up to the lower branches of trees, dwarfing both her and Orandon. Others were only waist-high. A bird with pure white plumage swooped toward them, its long tail feathers swiping close to Aralyn's head. A bright-turquoise head popped above the shorter grasses to their left. A dark-eyed creature with long lashes and a tuft of white hair on top of its head narrowed its eyes at them.

"What is that?" She asked Orandon, pointing.

"A Grimswal has come to see you." Orandon chuckled. "They won't bother you unless you harm their families or, heaven help, their pets."

As soon as Orandon said "family," at least ten pairs of eyes appeared. None seemed threatening. One head stretched up farther than the others, exposing long forelegs. It stared at them and tilted its head.

"They have pets?"

"Oh yes, they might take a rabbit or even a snake as a pet, so watch what you kill in here."

Aralyn glanced back at the Grimswals, who now followed at a distance. A cacophonous whistling and flapping of wings caused Aralyn to jump. It must have startled the Grimswals as well, and they bounded toward the trees and out of sight.

Orandon chuckled. "Bolgrate birds. Rather brash and obnoxious," he said above the noise.

The birds grew silent, and a few turquoise heads reappeared.

"Listen!" Orandon put a finger to his lips. He slowed to a more even pace.

"I don't hear them anymore." Aralyn tilted her head.

Orandon grabbed her forearm and stopped. "No, not the birds. Just listen."

They were in a hurry. Why was he stopping?

Music—similar to her own wordless songs, but more like a breeze rushing through trees and shrubs and grasses came to her ears. Aralyn stood transfixed. "I hear it."

Orandon raised an eyebrow, grinning broadly.

The song was familiar somehow. Yes, she had heard this music before. Although the notes clashed at first, they eventually joined in harmony. Without thinking, she sang. Her voice grew in volume, and she knew Orandon watched. After a few strains, her voice faded, and her cheeks heated. She wasn't used to singing while someone stood by and listened.

"You were doing fine." Orandon's honest eyes matched his words, and Aralyn relaxed.

"These are the singing grasses, Aralyn." He showed her the pods on the top of one. "They sing melodies because the opening in the center of each pod varies in size. As the wind blows through them, they produce notes of differing pitches."

Aralyn bent to gain a closer look.

"Come—the others will think us late and irresponsible. They're probably practicing already." He took off at his former pace.

Another half a league passed rapidly, and Orandon stopped once more. "We're here."

That was good. But where was here?

"I neglected to explain. We're about to enter the Harp. His eyes shone. "This is where mages and archers have trained for tens of thousands of years."

Aralyn searched for a path, an opening, a gate, or something that would mark the entrance. But all that lay ahead was a carpet of grass, a dense forest, and swarming insects reflecting the sunlight.

Orandon produced a gem similar to her own. It emitted a hum that grew in pitch. He laid an arrow on top of it. A wind burrowed into the trees ahead and produced something like a rabbit trail.

"This way." Orandon beckoned her forward.

She followed him through a series of twists, turns, and numerous passages that seemed to double back on themselves. Darkness came upon them at one point, as if it were midnight. Crickets chirped. And just as quickly, the night turned into a brilliance that forced Aralyn to squint.

"Welcome to the Harp, Aralyn."

Chapter 22

When her eyes adjusted, the light proved it was still early morning. Her mouth dropped at the rich colors—jade, magenta, indigo, and bright orange—of plants and trees. Stone paths led to grassy hills and hillocks, and around mysterious bends, Aralyn couldn't wait to explore. Streams and small waterfalls swirled and splashed. The scents of honeysuckle, lavender, and cinnamon flooded her.

"It's amazing, Orandon." The place was worthy of reverence. The Harp. Refreshing, yes. Hard to believe it was where she would train to kill. The memory of other killings almost overcame her, and she thought how pleasant it would be to relax here and enjoy the quiet.

Orandon stood back, allowing Aralyn to take it all in.

They walked over a hillock, and she saw a group of archers practicing. The targets they aimed for shone brightly in the trees. They turned, and some of them darted out of sight just as the archer released an arrow. This led to groans of frustration.

"It's not fair. They move!" A youthful voice said in Elvish.

"And do you think your enemy will stand still, Greltey?" a trainer demanded.

Greltey lowered her eyes. "No, I don't suppose." She went back to practicing without another word.

Orandon approached the group. The leader held up a hand, and her group immediately stopped their training. The leader bowed to Orandon. Aralyn counted eleven young archers, but off in the distance was another group. She could hear still others but couldn't see them.

"Good morning," Orandon greeted them. "It's good to see all of you here so early. This is Aralyn. She came to us from Sathria, though she was born here in Aurellium. I'll start off working with her one-on-one before I assign her to a group. We invited her here because she is of utmost importance to our lands. Many of you have heard the stories about our bowsingers, who sing to their bows and shoot with amazing accuracy. Not only that, their presence in Elven lands is crucial as the Age of Thunder approaches." He paused for a moment as one of the archers looked at him expectantly. Orandon nodded to her.

"She's our bowsinger?" the one named Greltey asked.

Orandon nodded. "Yes, she is."

Excited voices murmured. "Our bowsinger!" "She's here!" Mouths fell open and eyes danced. "She'll really help protect us?" One asked.

"Yes, the Age of Thunder approaches, and she will—"

"That's just a legend, a story." Aralyn heard the voice but couldn't see where it had come from. So some thought her a fraud?

"Legends are often born of the truth. At any rate, part of that 'legend' was fulfilled. Perhaps you noticed yesterday. Something changed."

Silence.

"Some of you should have noticed," their leader put in.

Greltey gasped. "The borders. I could feel them growing stronger."

"Yes, and the time correlates with Aralyn's arrival," a tall boy said. "I remember seeing her ride in yesterday."

More excited chatter followed.

Orandon held up his hands. "Now, that's enough discussion. Continue as you were."

As a group, they went back to training, and Orandon motioned for Aralyn to follow him. "We'll start you out with something simple." He led her down a small hill into a damp, bog-like area where ferns grew thick.

Aralyn and Orandon stood before a row of large, round canvas targets. It would be impossible to miss them.

"Aralyn." Orandon indicated the nearest target. "Go ahead."

Aralyn glanced at him and hoped she hid the incredulous look on her face. This would be too easy. She nocked an arrow and drew back. Pain ripped through her shoulder and down her back, and she released the arrow before she was ready. It fell short of the target. She grabbed her back and let out a small moan. Aralyn hadn't expected this. She knew her back and shoulder muscles weren't the same since the beating but had never dreamed they would affect her like this. She could shake this off. A little pain would not stop her.

"Aralyn?" Orandon's voice held a fatherly concern.

Aralyn waved him off. "I'm all right." She blocked out everything else, determined to keep working. The sound of her draw was like thunder in her ears. More agony, but she held back the cry she wanted to let out. Again, she released the arrow too soon, but she heard stone tearing through cloth. Her shot was laughable. It barely hit the edge of her monstrous objective. If this had been prey, it might have been injured but not fatally. The target sat there, daring her to do more, and those horrid rings mocked her. Aralyn fought to stay upright. Someone giggled. Aralyn realized other archers were here, and at least one person was watching her.

Aralyn's voice was dead in her throat. "I can barely shoot."

Almost immediately, Orandon's hands were on her back. It made her uncomfortable to have him touching her, but the pain eased. Orandon murmured gentle words, odd words like none she had heard before. He placed a hand on the back of her head. It was all Aralyn could do to keep from jerking away. But his touch was light, and the tension traveling down her neck disappeared. "Breathe, Aralyn." His voice was calm, almost hypnotic.

What was he doing to her? Her shoulder and back muscles relaxed as if on his command. He removed his hands, but Aralyn still felt the healing warmth.

"What did you do?" She choked the words out.

"I helped you relax." Orandon's lips came up in a brief smile.

"I—but, you did more." Aralyn rotated her shoulders and reached for her back. They felt remarkably better.

"I want you to look at the target." Orandon pointed. "That, Aralyn, is your enemy. A Rogue. An evil mage. Whatever you see as the worst threat to you or your—"

"Are you a mage?" she interrupted.

Orandon threw his head back and laughed. "No, but I have some healing talent. That is all, Aralyn. I promise."

"I see." Her solemn tone clashed with his laughter.

Orandon's brow furrowed, and he gently squeezed Aralyn's arm. "I know about the lashing you suffered. It damaged muscles, and I don't know if they will ever heal completely, but I want you to try again." His voice was patient. "Did you not attempt to use your bow at all after that lashing occurred?"

"The lord confiscated my bow and my arrows as part of my punishment. Gillis bought me this one, but I never practiced with it." She'd been hesitant to try again after venturing into the forest where she had experienced the attack on her mind. But it was more than that. Fear of what might happen to her if she accidentally shot something she shouldn't and knowing her muscles had been damaged...it was too much. What if she'd lost her shooting ability? Her gaze met Orandon's, and she lifted her chin. "I'll ... do this." Her determination swelled.

He gave her a quick nod. "Good."

Aralyn tried again. And again. She ran out of arrows. Retrieved them. Even though she felt better, the pain was still with her. And her groupings ... there were none to speak of. For the first time in her life, giving up seemed a viable option. Give up on her archery—the very thing that had kept her family from starving. She had lost that part of her life. All of it.

"It's obvious I'm not meant to do this. I'm not the one you need." She gritted her teeth, dropping her bow at Orandon's feet.

She had taken two steps when Orandon's voice tackled her. "You're going to surrender your rightful birthright, Aralyn? You're going to let the enemy win? You are our bowsinger. I thought you could meet any challenge you faced. You have a place here. I have no doubt of that." He spoke gently, but it was plain he wasn't going to let her get away with self-pity.

Aralyn swung around to face him. She took a careful step toward him. The compassion on his face made her think twice about quitting. Not only that, she realized she did not want to disappoint this man. It was selfish to only think of herself and not of others. But the pain and the anticipation of pain made it difficult to do what he demanded. Perhaps there was no demand, only hope. She was the bowsinger. He said it with such confidence. Aralyn had no choice but to believe him, but it was up to her to take her place, to accept her position and purpose here. Aralyn returned to her spot beside him.

"You are right. I can't give up. Running from problems ..." Father's words played in her mind.

"It never helps, does it?" So Orandon knew that same advice. "May I touch your shoulder? Just for a moment?"

What did he want now? What was he going to do?

Orandon must have sensed her question. "Trust me? Can you do that?" Aralyn nodded.

Orandon placed his hand on her and closed his eyes. After a few seconds, he said, "Perhaps these injuries are too old. When I don't get to the damaged muscle soon enough, the muscle doesn't heal correctly." He took his hand away. "I'm sorry, Aralyn."

Aralyn didn't know what to say, but she had to keep trying. She was about to draw again when movement in a nearby tree caught her eye. Aralyn realized it was Elnala perched about twenty feet up, watching. Shouldn't she be with the mages? With staff in hand, Elnala dropped from branch to branch and shimmied the rest of the way down the tree, a huge grin on her face.

"Hello, Father." She bowed to him, and he returned the greeting.

"Aralyn, I think I know what will help. May I?" She reached for her father's bow.

"What do you know about shooting a bow?" Orandon winked at his daughter and pulled his weapon out of her reach.

"You might be surprised." She held her hand out and wiggled her fingers. "Just let me try."

Orandon rolled his eyes. "All right, Mage Elnala. Let's see what you know." He sighed, obviously exaggerating his reaction, and the two exchanged bow and staff. With the quiver on her back, Elnala took out three arrows and placed them in her left hand. She nocked one after the other in a blur and let them fly. Aralyn blinked as Elnala hit the target dead center each time.

Elnala lifted her gaze to Aralyn, barely containing her grin. "Not bad, eh?"

Orandon put a hand to his chest and gave a mock-gasp. "I had no idea, my daughter."

Aralyn shook her head at the pair, knowing father and daughter had just put on a performance for her. And now they were both laughing.

Aralyn stared at the target before speaking. "But, Orandon, she did something wrong. She ... she didn't pull back all the way, and she ..." What had she done that was so different?

"I did something wrong?" Elnala marched up to the target. Pointed. "Three arrows. Dead center. Although I do admit I am left-handed. That may have looked 'wrong' to you."

"That's not it. Orandon, she shouldn't have been able to ... to even hit the target like that," Aralyn objected.

"Ah, but she did." Orandon's grin spread from ear to ear, and again, Aralyn saw the family resemblance.

"I cheated." Elnala's face was serious now.

Aralyn knew the answer. "You used magic."

"No, I did not." Elnala folded her arms and lifted her chin. "When I was much younger, I wanted to learn how to shoot with a bow and arrow, but the instructors said I had to focus on my mage abilities. So I taught myself." She twirled an arrow over her fingers and back again.

"Aralyn." Orandon stepped in. "Watch her and then tell me exactly what she did 'wrong.'" He winked at Elnala again.

Aralyn narrowed her eyes as Elnala released three arrows in quick succession and then three more. Aralyn shook her head. "That's not right."

"Not right?" Elnala's smirk goaded Aralyn.

"No, it's not. But I see what she did, Orandon." She turned back to Elnala. "You didn't draw back far enough, and you flicked the bow forward as you released the arrows. That is not right."

"But I hit the target. Look. Six arrows. In a nice grouping, are they not?"

Aralyn stared at the target again. "But you can't shoot like that."

"Aralyn, listen." Elnala took her friend's shoulders. "I hit the target." She lowered her voice. "Hit the bull's-eye every time."

Orandon spoke up now. "Aralyn, I want you to try shooting like that."

Aralyn felt sick. "No, I can't—"

"It will probably take getting used to, but you can do this." Elnala held on to the bow. "I know you can."

"But shooting that way will cause me to develop bad habits."

"Bad habits?" Orandon asked. "You'd rather keep hurting yourself than try something that could make you a better archer? I'm going to leave the two of you to figure this out. I need to look in on the others again."

"You can do this," Elnala repeated. Her grin disappeared into a serious Orandon-like expression.

Aralyn bit her lip. She had nothing to lose. Elnala showed Aralyn the technique step-by-step, patiently adjusting her stance, correcting her draw. It felt like everything Aralyn had been taught had changed. Before Aralyn could release an arrow, she had to learn to pull back only partway. Without her full draw, Aralyn felt as though she were missing an arm or leg. It was just wrong. She also had to coordinate the release with the subtle flick of the bow forward. Time moved slowly, and Aralyn's progress was even slower. She shot one arrow at a time, not daring to try three as Elnala had done, and each fell short of the target. Elnala corrected and coached and criticized. After shooting what seemed like one hundred arrows, a few of them hit the lower left-hand portion of the target. One of them went through the target.

"You did it!" Elnala grinned so big, it looked like it would stretch her face out.

She'd hit the target. Just barely. Aralyn found it difficult to celebrate or even show a little joy, but the pain in her shoulder and back had almost disappeared. She would learn this. Aralyn exhausted her quiver, and she and Elnala retrieved the arrows.

"I just thought of something. Why aren't you singing? Don't you sing, bowsinger?" Elnala pulled an arrow out through the back of the target.

"I'm not sure. It's hard to focus on that too when I'm learning to shoot. It's like starting all over."

Aralyn practiced the song she'd heard in the grasses. The melody danced before her in colors of bright green and soft violet. Aralyn readied her bow, and the arrows seemed to settle themselves in her hand. Were they—here in Eyndor—becoming sentient?

The song repeated, and a strong smell of woods and grass and distant herbs struck her. She sang and released the arrows one at a time. The melody touched her in a way her songs had never done before. Tears stood in her eyes. She blinked them back.

Elnala cheered. "Look what you did!"

Aralyn crept to the target, afraid of what she would see, even though Elnala's excitement was obvious.

All of her arrows were in the bull's-eye. Every single one. A wonderful, tight grouping. Aralyn's chin quivered with emotion.

"See? I knew you could do this!" Elnala clapped her hands together but quieted when she read the emotion on Aralyn's face. "What is it?"

"Nothing." Aralyn cut her eyes away. "I knew it was right when I released the arrows, but I didn't realize it would be ... that I would feel ..." She turned to face Elnala. "I did it, but *you* showed me. I don't know what to say." Aralyn embraced her before she could stop herself, and Elnala returned the hug.

"I want to keep working on this." If she were to be proficient in battle, she would have to practice until she never missed. If the arrows continued to hit the center of the target, maybe she could return to her former level of skill, but she had a long way to go.

They both heard Orandon return. He stopped and stared at the target. He straightened his shoulders, and his smile radiated approval.

"Aralyn? You shot these arrows?"

"Yes, she did!" Elnala didn't wait for Aralyn to answer.

Orandon's gaze went from one to the other. "I am proud—proud of you both."

Elnala hugged her father. "I'm glad we made you proud. And she sang, Father!"

"Well, good." He released his daughter. "That's what she's supposed to do."

"I need to get back to my practice." Elnala exchanged Orandon's bow and arrows for her staff.

Aralyn looked from father to daughter. An odd feeling stirred in her. Something she was missing in her own life poured over her as she observed their relationship. Or was it jealousy when both her father and stepfather were dead? But this was no time for self-pity. She turned away from them.

"Goodbye, Aralyn. You were wonderful!"

"Thank you, Elnala." She was the one who had been wonderful, but Aralyn found it difficult to express the depth of her gratitude.

"Aralyn." Orandon came up behind her. "There is something else we need to work on."

Aralyn swung around. "Yes?"

"You need to learn more songs, but"—he pinched his lips together—"Re'ah informed me of Mal'ev's attacks. He's been attacking your mind?"

"Yes, he has. He makes me think I'm in a different place or I'm seeing things that are not re—"

Orandon held up his hand. "I know how it works. He makes you feel compelled to perform certain tasks or convinces you that someone you love is in danger. He confuses and confounds your instincts and abilities."

"Yes." He was describing exactly what had happened in her mind. "Can you help me? Re'ah said you can train—"

Orandon's attack came without warning and was not gentle.

Aralyn fought to keep her *bar're* in place, although she did not completely understand how it worked. Not to her surprise, it was falling. She had to show him she was stronger than this. Lights clouded her mind. The sun blinded her, and something swooped down on her. She drew her bow. The attack ended. Just like that, it stopped. And for some reason, she was on the ground again. Just as she remembered on the trail. Aralyn tried to rise, but Orandon held her down. What was he doing?

"Easy, Aralyn."

"Why did you stop the attack?" she asked from her prone position, although secretly, she was glad he had. "That was you, wasn't it?"

Orandon chuckled. "You were about to shoot me. And look at you. You fell, and here you are, opposite the sky. Are you all right?"

Everything felt fine. "I'm good. Let me up."

"If you insist." He grasped her hand and pulled her up to a sitting position. When she put a foot under her, he stopped her. "That's far enough." His face drew tight, and he sat across from her. He yanked on a blade of grass and lifted his eyes.

"What is it? Is something wrong, Orandon? Tell me."

Orandon only hesitated for a moment. "You are fighting me off, but your ability to do so is missing something."

"What do you mean?"

"Your innate ability is almost nonexistent. I see something in your *bar're* that looks promising, but it's as if a primary component...well, it's something I've never seen. Your *bar're* is flimsy. What did you use to construct it? "

"I think the dragon stone has something to do with it. But no one has shown me how to build one."

Orandon rose. "I'm sure I can find a way to help you with that. Perhaps we should practice some songs for now."

Aralyn was about to object when Orandon gave her a sharp look. "Until we can figure out a way to compensate for your lack of ability in this area, you will work on your songs."

Singing was one of her favorite things, but his firm hand made her want to throw something. But what was there to throw? A handful of grass or leaves?

Orandon strode away while Aralyn was thinking rebellious thoughts, and she had to run to catch up. He led her to a small waterfall, and she heard the music. She relaxed as it spread through her. Her heart listened, joined with her mind, and her voice sang of strength and power and victory. Orandon had her practice over and over until he was satisfied with her progress. They moved on to one of the quiet pools where runestones lay in the clear water. A melody she could barely hear drifted to her. Her voice struggled with this song.

That was when she felt it again—Orandon pushing on her *bar're*. This time, part of it crumbled, and she grabbed the dragon stone. It became warm in her hand again. Her *bar're* grew. Orandon was already inside it, though. He rifled through private thoughts, and she cringed. The small dragon from the dragon stone was inside the *bar're* fighting him with razored claws and fangs that pierced him. Her head filled with pain, but she persisted, working with the dragon, and they pushed him back. His thoughts were gone. Her mind was clear of him.

Aralyn lifted her chin and met his gaze.

"Hmm." He gave her a nod. "Not bad, Aralyn. Perhaps not as bad as I feared."

Chapter 23

A new sense of dread washed over her as she left the Harp. Even though she had defeated Orandon's second attack, her mind raced as she considered all the training she faced—a new way to shoot, more songs, and protecting her mind. They also needed to learn more about what her mark meant and how she and Gillis could work together. They were paired. There was nothing romantic about it, and it had nothing to do with their binding. But it brought added obligations and expectations from others.

Her thoughts turned to Drehensil. It frustrated her that she had no way of calling him. She needed him. Especially now.

"Aralyn."

She recognized the voice and smiled as the Elder Guronde fell in step with her.

"You've been practicing today?"

Aralyn managed a smile. Was she supposed to bow as she had seen others do? "Yes, I have."

"What's happened to your voice?"

"Singing. I've been practicing my songs." She pushed the words out around the raspy sounds accompanying them. She had exhausted her waterskin.

"You don't mind if I have a word with you, do you?" He stepped over a vine and pulled a branch back out of his way.

With this man's rank, did she have a choice? She was tired and needed to keep the sarcasm off her tongue. She replied with all the respect she could manage. "Of course not."

"You're sure?" He seemed to have read her thoughts.

Aralyn sighed. "I'm a bit worn, but I would like you to hear what you have to say."

"Some rumors are going about that you have placed us in danger, Aralyn. People talk. People get jealous and say unkind things when faced with something new or different. And others believe you should leave Eyndor altogether."

"Wait, how have I put us in danger?" And the answer came to her. "Because of Bek."

"Yes, Aralyn. Bek."

"Because I killed him, and now avengers want to kill me. Perhaps they should feel safer. I am on the Elves' side. I killed a legendary warrior."

Guronde chuckled. "I suppose. Others are having a difficult time believing you are truly the bowsinger."

Loweill birds sang in the trees, welcoming the sunset hours.

"But the borders are more secure now, aren't they?"

"Yes, they are."

"Isn't that enough evidence to prove that I am their bowsinger?"

The path became broader and the trees farther apart. Where was Guronde leading her?

"Some don't agree with that assessment. They claim to sense no difference, especially one young man who was formerly on the Council. He could cause trouble for us. Loves to stir the pot, and it makes him very nervous that you killed Mal'ev's brother." His voice seemed leagues away, and his gaze stared past the nearby hillocks. "Such a tragic story."

Aralyn stopped in her tracks. "What is tragic? That I killed Bek? He attacked my family—would have killed us."

"No, no. That's not it." He paused, rubbed his chin, and narrowed his eyes as if trying to remember something. Then his eyes lit up. "Oh yes, I've been meaning to tell you—your mother and Terrwynn are well. Doing quite well without you."

Before she could process this and ask how he knew, Guronde interrupted her thoughts. "Ah, here we are. I will leave you now. But we can get back to your questions sometime. For now, you must see our symbol master. He will examine your marks and see what he can discern. I bid you good eve, Aralyn. Gillis."

Aralyn blinked and realized Gillis stood before her.

"Hello, Gillis," she croaked. "Oh, and Lem. Hello. We're here to see you?" Both men had appeared without her hearing them approach. Was she going deaf *and* losing her voice? "Lem, it's good to see you," she managed. "You're the symbol master?"

He grinned. "Yes, I am, and it's good to see the two of you." Lem motioned them toward a narrow stone path leading to his home.

The cottage was small but cozy. It had only one room with a bed, a kitchen, and a small round table. Pillows piled on the floor invited them to sit. Windows with crisscrossed latticework peered out into the forest. Shelves held a small library of books neatly lined up.

"You seem out of place here, Lem." The words fell out of Aralyn's mouth before she could stop them.

"Where would you have me be?" Lem placed some ground leaves in a cup and poured hot water over them.

She dropped her gaze. "Forgive me, but I believe you are more suited to tending animals."

"And how do you know I don't?" His soft smile was infectious.

"I—"

"Come on, let's get this taken care of. Do what we came to do." Gillis' tone was flat, his face unreadable.

Lem placed his hand on a thick book lying on the table. "This is a volume of symbols passed down through the years. We attempted to keep the symbols and markings accurate and up to date. They reveal an individual's talent or ability. Some people call them gifts, believing they are from Elyon."

Gillis let out a long sigh. "Lem, could we move on? You need to look at our marks, don't you?"

"All right." Lemmon's voice was gentle, unruffled by Gillis' words. "Aralyn, let me have a look at yours first."

"Certainly." Aralyn hopped to her feet.

The Elvish clothes differed from the garments she'd worn in Sathria. The vest and a button-down shirt with long sleeves made removing them more difficult. She undressed as modestly as she could, pulling the shirt down to bare her shoulder blade.

Gillis stood, wandered to a window, and stared out.

Lemmon held the book of symbols, averting his eyes.

"I need to tell you something," Aralyn said. "I have some scars on my back, and they look pretty bad. I just wanted you to be prepared."

"I can handle scars." But a gasp escaped his mouth as he examined her back. "I'm sorry, Aralyn. For whatever happened." He swallowed but turned his attention to her mark.

"Just as I thought." Lem lay the book on the table and flipped to another page.

Aralyn was about to redress when Lem spoke. "Wait a minute, Aralyn. If you don't mind."

He opened a drawer. She looked over her shoulder as Lem pulled out a pad of paper and a pen. He glanced from her back to his paper as he recorded the symbols, pen scratching against the page.

"All right, Aralyn. You can dress." He laid the sketch pad down, tore off the sheet, and placed it on the table.

Aralyn stared at the drawing. One symbol resembled a bow. She'd seen that in the mirror, but not the others. Perhaps her mark was changing still, becoming fully *emereled*. Was that the word Orandon had used? Under the bow were concentric circles, the largest one not quite complete. Next to that was a drop of water with a triangle around it.

"Will you explain what these are, Lem?" Her curiosity made her impatient.

"Of course. But let me look at Gillis' mark."

"I thought they'd already decided we are paired," Aralyn said.

"Well, yes, but the symbols will confirm it and will help me determine the strength of your pairing." Lem tapped his pen on his notepad. "And in what area or talent you have the most strength together."

Gillis removed his shirt, and Aralyn could not keep her eyes off the scars on his shoulder and back. The story of the fire niggled in the back of her mind. His well-muscled arms caught her attention as well, and Aralyn wondered what it would be like to lay her hands on his bare chest while he held her in those arms. His gaze caught hers, and she lowered her eyes.

Lemmon finished the drawings and motioned to the chairs. "Orandon was correct. You two are definitely paired, and it is a powerful bond."

Aralyn glanced at her husband. "How can you tell, and what do these symbols mean?" She pointed to the sketches, comparing Gillis' and hers.

"Aralyn, you have a bow symbol, easily recognized. You also have a musical bond. It could give you more strength in battle if you sing together."

Gillis scoffed. "Sing? While I'm slicing someone's throat?"

Aralyn swallowed. He said it with so little concern for taking a life.

Lemmon shrugged. "People have done stranger things." He pointed to the series of circles common to both drawings. "This one outer circle that is not quite closed means your singing completes Aralyn's and vice versa. Now this one is rather unusual, and water mages have similar symbols, but the triangle—I'm not sure exactly what that means."

Gillis drummed his fingers on the table but stopped abruptly. "Wait a minute, Lem." He came to his feet. "Let me get this straight. You mean to say that we are mages and have some sort of power over water?" He took a deep breath as Lem nodded.

"It is a possibility," he said.

Gillis glowered at him. "Well, I will have no part of that."

Lemmon kept a steady gaze on Gillis. "I am the messenger, and I only tell you what the symbols say, my friend." Lemmon's voice remained steady, apparently unfazed by Gillis' statement..

Gillis' face relaxed, and his shoulders slumped. He sat back down. "All right, go on. I have been ..." He bowed his head. "I apologize."

"Apology accepted. But I have more to say, Gillis. Will you listen?"

Gillis nodded.

Aralyn wanted to stop Lem from saying more. Gillis was angry. Again. And some of that anger seemed aimed at her. Was it because their talents were similar to the power of a mage?

"This water symbol differs from the mage marks and"—he pointed to the symbol in the book that was most like theirs— "for another reason."

Aralyn saw it. "It is 'open' too, like the musical symbol." She had been paying attention, and now her eyes were keen on Lemmon and the sketches. "We're connected in that way, too?"

Lemmon's eyes danced. "Yes." He seemed delighted that Aralyn had caught it. His gaze flicked between Aralyn and Gillis.

Gillis leaned forward. "So what about this one?" He pointed to a symbol that was unique to his sketch.

"Ah, yes, the wolf or hound. It's another one that is uncommon and somewhat obscure. You see how its head turns back as if it is paying attention to something behind it?"

Gillis nodded.

"It's listening, Gillis. Listening to you. Do you communicate with animals?"

"Yes, many of them. There are exceptions, such as horses, herd animals, and cats. My father and his father have the same ability. We don't talk with them so much as get an impression of what they are telling us, and we do the same, give them an impression of what we need to communicate, or occasionally speak aloud. I hear distinct words with dragons but only because they have their own language."

Aralyn blinked, and Lem stared.

"What?" Gillis tilted his head. "Has neither of you ever heard of those who can communicate with animals? Aralyn, you speak with Drehensil, don't you?"

"Well, yes, but you could hear the dragon lizards ... and you told the gulley lizards to leave."

"I tried, but I mainly said that to shut you up."

"Really?" Aralyn raised an eyebrow.

Gillis placed his arms on the table, and a smirk curved his lips. "Worked, didn't it?"

"Yes, Gillis, you silenced me." It *had* worked. She hid a smile, glad his mood seemed to lighten.

Lemmon's gaze flicked between the pair, apparently amused. "To answer your question, Gillis, I have met very few people who can understand an animal's thoughts, let alone speak their language. It's rare."

"I wasn't aware," Gillis answered.

"The two of you will need to discover exactly how you can use your talents together," Lemmon said.

"This will give us something more to work with. Thank you, Lem." Aralyn stood. "What do we owe you?"

Lemmon laughed. "Not a thing, Aralyn. Only that, as you practice, you help me better understand how your talents respond to each other's. I sense the power flowing between you." He paused. "Be careful, and uh, watch your backs."

Aralyn chuckled. She caught the humor, and Gillis swiped at his mouth as his lips twitched.

What were they to learn together? And would Gillis truly work with her? Surely he would if it made the difference in life and death for them. And for Eyndor.

Chapter 24

Aralyn scrounged for food to break her fast and found some dried meat. Yesterday's bread was still edible. Aralyn dressed and gazed into the sky from the windows in her home. She wished to arrive at Lemmon's early without waking Gillis. She considered leaving a note just as he walked in.

"You ready to leave already?" Gillis rubbed his eyes.

"Yes, I wanted to get there early to talk to Lem for a bit. See if he's discovered any more about our marks."

Gillis nodded.

"Why were you so angry yesterday?" Aralyn asked. "Can you tell me?"

"I told you about Laella and how she died." He stared past her and out the window, then turned his gaze on her.

"I see." This was a life and death matter for the Elves. He needed to move on.

It was also life and death, perhaps for their marriage.

"You remember what I said, don't you?"

Lifting her head, she replied. "Yes. I do. I remember. You blame a mage for Laella's death. And you want nothing to do with that power." She swallowed. "Well, Gillis, I'm going."

"Fine." He hesitated, and his tone became gentler. "I'll be there, Aralyn."

Her face relaxed. "Good." She gave him a nod and grabbed her bow and quiver from the corner.

Her feet, of their own accord, flew down the stairs and to the path leading to Lemmon's home.

Once she arrived, she slowed and walked the stone path to his dwelling. She stopped just shy of the house. Maybe she was too early. Should she disturb him? It might be best to wait. A few seconds later, his door swung open.

"Hello, Aralyn." Lemmon greeted her. "Where's Gillis?"

"I wanted to come early. He'll be here soon."

"I'm going out to check on my horses. Care to join me?" He was already walking toward the stables.

Did he have to ask? "Of course, Lem."

Two horses greeted Lemmon and her with a whicker.

"Are these the horses you kept from your business?

"The mare on your right—yes, her—she has always been mine." He picked up a pitchfork and began mucking the stalls. "But the other is just old, and I wanted him to live out his years with me in peace."

"They're beautiful." Aralyn scratched the mare on her nose and patted the other one's neck. "It's good to see you with them. It just seems—"

"More suited to me?" He chuckled and grabbed a bag of oats. "They're not the only animals I tend."

"Really?"

"If you'd like, follow the path out here." He motioned to his left. "You'll come to a fork. Take the right fork, and you'll find a gate. It opens into a yard. Some of the forest animals come in the early morning. I have some more work to do here, but I'll join you shortly."

Aralyn followed the path as Lemmon instructed. Stepping through the gate, she discovered a small yard surrounded by shrubs and vines that probably flowered in the warmer seasons. A refreshing breeze blew across her face. The forest crowded in behind the shrubs. The trees seemed impatient, leaves rustling, as if demanding to come closer. Other than that, it was quiet. Aralyn waited, alert for signs of animals.

Shrubs rustled, and three rabbits hopped into the yard. Aralyn reached for her bow. An easy meal. But she couldn't, not if these were Lem's animals or at least the ones he tended. A moment later, she spotted a family of opossums rooting in the bushes. To her surprise, a Grimswal walking on three of its four legs leaped over the shrubs. Under its fourth leg, it held a creature that looked like a ball of fur with gigantic eyes. Oh yes, Grimswals had pets. The Grimswal approached her, holding the pet protectively.

The fluffy creature stared at Aralyn. She reached for it and felt a sharp sting on the back of her hand. The Grimswal had slapped her hand away, and a red mark was forming. Too late, she remembered what Orandon had said about Grimswals and their pets.

Lem came into the yard and noticed the Grimswal. "He's not bothering you, is he?"

"No. He's fine. He has a pet."

Lem approached, rolling up a length of rope. "A belfluff. Quite harmless, but I would leave it alone."

"Yes, I've been warned." She covered the red mark with her other hand.

Lem caught the motion and took her hands. "He stuck you?"

"It's all right, Lem. I've been warned about Grimswals and their pets."

He dropped Aralyn's hands and stomped his foot in the Grimswal's direction. "Go! Leave! You know better than to hurt my guests."

The Grimswal bounded toward the forest, the belfluff tightly in its grip. Before leaving the yard, he turned and hissed at them, showing his teeth.

"Leave!"

The Grimswal showed his teeth again and hopped into a nearby tree. The belfluff blinked at Aralyn.

"I don't know what is wrong with him." Lemmon shook his head.

One of the rabbits hopped toward Aralyn, showing no fear. Did it know how many of its kind she had killed? The brave creature had long rust-colored hair and shorter ears than most rabbits. A swag of fur fell over one eye.

"The hair on the top of his head looks as though it's been combed to one side," Aralyn observed.

"It's a lionhead rabbit, and it's a female."

"Does she have a name?"

"No, I don't name them. That would be like claiming them as mine when they belong to the forest."

"She seems very tame. I've seen wild rabbits, and ... Look! Does she want me to pick her up?" The rabbit stood on its hind legs, its forelegs resting on Aralyn's knee.

"You can if you like. I've never seen one act like that around anyone else."

"This is not a wild rabbit, Lem. It can't be. You've tamed her."

"No, honestly. She's curious about you for some reason."

Aralyn stroked the rabbit, its fur soft and warm against her hand. "You are so sweet. And soft." Was she talking to a rabbit that she had thought of as dinner a few minutes ago?

"I want you to know the Grimswals are usually pretty harmless, just mischievous," Lem said as the rabbit wriggled out of Aralyn's grasp. "One of them fed my flowers to his pet one day. I caught him out here with a handful of petals, and he ran from me. He knew not to do that. But I have learned to be patient with them." Lemmon finished winding up the rope and sat down with Aralyn.

"Is that how you are so patient? Like with Gillis?"

"What do you mean?" Lem tilted his head.

Aralyn hesitated. Perhaps she had spoken out of turn. "Lem, he was rude to you when we were here last. You didn't let him upset you. Is this part of the reason? Because you've learned to be patient with animals?"

To Aralyn's surprise, Mel frowned and would not look at her. His lips tightened. "The answer to that is something difficult for me to speak of."

Of course, he was not obliged to tell her.

Lem picked up the lionhead rabbit and held her close, snuggling his face into her fur. When he lifted his head, his eyes were moist. "After my father died, my grandfather came to live with us. He often raised his voice to Mother and me. Very often. And with no reason. It wasn't just the shouting and the things he said, although he threatened to kill us both. Several times. But it was also the way he spoke. Full of what we call *zyepth*. That's...similar to meanness but is more than that." Lem tapped his chin. "It's like saying the opposite of what you mean, but in an arrogant way."

"Sarcasm?" Aralyn offered.

"I believe so. I determined I would never speak to anyone like that. He was never violent, just threatening. I spent a lot of time with Guronde, hoping to learn from his calm nature. My mother has always been kind in her actions, but then her father's manner of speaking became part of her nature. She still struggles to overcome those habits even though he is gone."

"But she struggles." Aralyn lifted her face to him in the warmth of the early morning sun. "It means she's fighting. She doesn't want that nature to take over."

Lemmon's lips turned up a bit. "Yes, I suppose you're right. My mother—yes, she is not someone to quit easily. Always been a fighter."

Aralyn looked up into the trees. "You're not married, Lem?"

"No." Lem glanced at her and put the rabbit down. He stood and drew himself up to his full six and a half feet. "And don't get any ideas about suggesting one of your friends as a romantic interest."

"I would never do that. I promise." Aralyn laid a hand on her chest. Besides she didn't have that many friends. Perhaps Elnala. But she would never suggest the match to either of them.

"Good." His face relaxed. "Others have tried. People don't understand." He almost sounded harsh.

She had upset him somehow.

He swallowed, and a smile came to his lips. "They mean well." He shrugged. "I didn't mean to snap at you."

Aralyn waved him off. "If you can put up with Gillis, I can certainly let that go, my friend."

Lemmon chuckled and looked toward the gate. "Ah, there they are."

Aralyn had forgotten about the questions she had for him, and now it was too late. But perhaps she could ask later.

Gillis arrived and greeted Lem. Guronde followed behind him.

"Good morning!" Aralyn approached the pair and bowed to the Elder. "I didn't know you were coming, Guronde."

He bowed in return. "Good morning, Aralyn."

Guronde and Lem consulted for a minute and nodded in agreement.

The Elder clapped both Aralyn and Gillis on the shoulder. "This is indeed exciting—to work with a paired twosome." He lifted his staff, and small targets appeared in the trees, similar to those used for practice in the Harp. Aralyn watched the targets as they turned, disappeared, and danced between branches. All the while, the trees swayed in a brisk wind.

"Gillis, try to stay close to Aralyn while she shoots. I'd like to see what happens."

So Aralyn sang as she released an arrow. And missed a target altogether. She tried again while Gillis stood to the side, watching her. The strength she felt encouraged her, but when she tried again, she was nowhere near the target. Over and over, she missed. Something was terribly wrong.

Gillis grunted. "Seems I'm making her worse."

Aralyn swung around to face him. Was he gloating?

"And have any of you ever been in battle? I doubt I'll be standing around like this."

"Of course we have, Gillis." Lemmon didn't seem the least bit insulted or intimidated by Gillis' tone. "You both have a water symbol so perhaps—."

"Let's try something we do when first training the young mages," Guronde suggested.

Gillis stiffened.

"Do you have a bucket of water, Lemmon?"

"Yes, of course." He fetched a bucket from the stable and set it down between Aralyn and Gillis.

"I want you both to focus and attempt to make the water splash out of the bucket," Guronde instructed.

That seemed silly, but Aralyn was willing to try.

Aralyn focused on doing exactly as Guronde instructed, and Gillis seemed to do the same—both of them concentrating, working together. She looked down. Ice was forming on the top of the bucket.

But then Gillis' shoulders slumped, and he spoke evenly. "I just don't know if I can do this."

"Gillis..." Aralyn was pleading.

Guronde motioned for Aralyn to be silent and nodded to Gillis. "All right. But, Gillis, I'd like to know what—"

"It's me, Guronde." Aralyn tapped her chest, very aware she had just interrupted the Elder. "He doesn't want to work with me. Isn't that right? It's not just that you blame a water mage for...what happened, is it? It's me."

Gillis opened his mouth. Shut it and shook his head.

Aralyn knew there was a war going on inside him. He did not want this connection with her. Perhaps, once again, he simply wanted to be free of her.

***

Gillis didn't know how to answer her. He cared for her, didn't he? Hadn't he made that clear? And he cared about what would happen to Eyndor if he and Aralyn did not fight together. Then Aralyn's voice sounded out, crisp and clear in the morning air.

"May I be excused, Guronde?" It really was not a question.

Guronde raised his chin, and those kind, wise eyes met Gillis'. Not Aralyn's. His. But he answered Aralyn. "For now, yes, you may, but you will come back, won't you?"

Aralyn straightened. "I don't know."

Guronde raised his eyebrows. "Aralyn."

He waited for her to look at him. "You will return tomorrow morning at the latest."

Gillis caught her surprise, and she stammered. "I—yes if..." She lifted her chin. "Yes, I will."

He realized she didn't want to give up—she just needed to be away from him at least for a bit.

Aralyn trotted off into the forest. Lemmon cast a worried glance after her, and Gillis waited for Guronde to speak—to scold, correct, or perhaps discipline.

But Guronde surprised him. "Gillis, I think you could have handled that better, but you need to go after her, don't you agree?"

She was his wife. Perhaps he should go to her. "But she's right, Guronde. I want nothing more to do with magic or—"

"The only person you need to explain yourself to is Aralyn."

Gillis hesitated. "I—she wants time away from me. I know her well enough."

"Nonsense." Guronde's voice was kind.

If that was all Guronde required, he could agree. Gillis took off and soon found her trail. She hadn't left much of one, but he had tracked people and animals for decades. The footprints grew more distinct. She had slowed down here. And there she was, sitting at the base of a gnarled oak, knees drawn up, and head buried in her arms.

"Aralyn."

Her head came up. "Did Guronde tell you to come? Or Lem?"

He eased to her side. "May I join you?"

"Join me?" She scoffed. "Since when have you ever wanted to join me?"

"You know bloody well ..." He bit his lip before he could do any more damage. Maybe a part of him did want her out of his life, but that part of him seemed to shrivel away as he stood over his wife. She was a good person, perhaps better than he deserved. But not Laella. Laella was gone, and Aralyn only reminded him of that. He lowered himself to the ground.

Aralyn flinched when his arm brushed hers.

"I'm not here to cause you more pain or contend with you," he said, and his voice seemed to quiet her.

Aralyn closed her eyes, pressing her fingers against her forehead. "I can't continue like this."

"I know."

"You know?" Her eyes rested coolly on him. "You truly are a 'fine male,' as Elnala once told me. But I want more than that. You wanted us to be friends at one time, but you don't seem to want even that. Not anymore."

"I don't want to hurt you," he repeated.

"Then we need to live apart. I don't know where I will go, but I cannot live as husband, wife, and ghost."

"You won't go anywhere. I'll leave."

"Fine. But in reality, you have already left me for another woman." Aralyn chuffed. "No, that's not right. We have never been a couple. Paired or not, we have never been husband and wife. Why do we pretend?"

"Aralyn. I can't be what you want. I can't be the man you need."

"Can't or won't, Gillis? I think you're hiding from what you truly could be." Aralyn stood, and she loomed over him. "I am so tempted to return this bow to you. I'm thinking I don't need your gifts, but..." She glanced at the weapon in her hand. "Truth is, I do need it." Her voice held an unwilling humility.

He stood and faced her. "Listen. Aralyn..." He was about to reach for her hand when her words cut him short.

"We have something worth fighting for. But both of us have to fight for it. You're not willing to commit to loving your wife as you promised or to at least respect her. I know it was a promise made under duress, but I thought ... I hoped ..." Aralyn shook her head.

Gillis was quiet, knowing he should say something. There was so much he wanted to tell her—about how much he did care for her, about his admiration, how he was willing to try to at least work together for the good of their lands. But she wasn't about to listen. Not now. And she wanted more than that. What she referred to as something worth fighting for, she meant their marriage, and he knew she was right. He needed to talk to Re'ah.

***

Aralyn climbed the stairs leading to Orandon's home. The steps were taller and more numerous than her own, and she trudged up them. The curtain over the entrance swung back.

"Aralyn! It's so good to see you." Elnala was all smiles. "Please come in."

Orandon entered the room, and he turned to his wife. "Would you give us a minute, dear?" He kissed her forehead.

"Of course," she murmured, nodding at Aralyn.

"I need to tell you something, Orandon." Aralyn glanced at Elnala. "I suppose you need to hear this, too. Gillis doesn't wish to work with me, and not only will I oblige him, but I will not stay with him. I know we are paired, and I thought it only fair to let you know all this." Aralyn would not let Orandon convince her otherwise.

Orandon's hands dropped to his sides.

Elnala piped up. "What are you saying? You must keep training. You must stay with Gillis."

Orandon spoke. "Where else will you stay? Not here if that is what you are thinking."

"I had never considered staying here..." Her voice faded. "No, of course not."

Orandon lifted his face to his daughter. "I think Aralyn and I need to talk alone."

"Of course, Father. It's time for me to return home."

Elnala exited with a swish of the curtain, and her footsteps sounded on the steps.

"So, Aralyn." His eyes bored into her. "What do you plan to do with your joined talents, your gifts? Do you plan to abandon them? Have you thought of how that will affect you?"

He didn't sound at all concerned for the Elves and their well-being, but only for her.

"I can't do this if Gillis has to be involved. If he has to be part of my training."

"I see." He paced across the room and back. Faced her. "May I see your bow?"

Aralyn handed it over.

"Where did you get this weapon?"

What did that matter? He must have read her confused expression.

"Whoever chose it, chose well." He lifted an eyebrow.

"Gillis. He gave me the bow and the arrows." Aralyn swallowed, wondering what he was trying to say.

"And what was the occasion of this gift?"

"It was a wedding gift."

"If that is the case, he must put some value on you and your marriage."

Aralyn ducked her head. "I don't know, Orandon." Yes, maybe he did—at one time.

"You need to think about that and—"

"I have! He has shown me he cares, at least in some ways, but our pairing—it just seems to infuriate him. *I* seem to infuriate him."

He set his jaw. "I would strongly advise you and Gillis to consider the value of what you have."

Aralyn sensed his double meaning.

He handed the bow back to her. "All right, Elnala, you can come back in." Orandon barely raised his voice.

Elnala stepped through the doorway. "Sorry, Father." A smile played in her eyes, but she kept it off her lips.

Orandon wasn't through. "Another thing, Aralyn. Go home. I don't know of anywhere else you can live. And I won't have our bowsinger camping outside at the mercy of Grimswals, especially as restless as they are now. Go home. Get some rest. Gillis is a good person. He'll figure things out."

"Yes, Aralyn! He truly is a fine male." Elnala's smile exploded.

Aralyn wanted to scoff but held back. It was time to go home.

***

Aralyn entered, expecting to find Gillis, but instead, a note from him lay on the table.

Aralyn,
If you are reading this, I want you to know
I am presently training the archer guards .

I will return at sundown.

We will talk more then.

Gillis

So he would return, but not until evening. Very well. That gave her plenty of time to put her plan into action.

An ancient creature, one who remembered the last Age of Thunder, would know who Aralyn was and convince others, give testimony to the fact that she was indeed the bowsinger, and the Elves needed her. How else could she convince them? Not only that. She needed Drehensil's wisdom. But a teaching from long ago niggled in the back of her mind, and she knew this had to be done with discretion.

She pulled the dragon stone from her pocket, and it grew warm in her hand. Was it going to help her? Orandon had told her to use it only in the ways it revealed. Aralyn lifted the stone to eye level. "What have you revealed to me?" She spoke, she hoped, to the dragon that dwelled within.

Silence.

She hadn't really expected an answer but had to at least try. After a moment, she spoke again. "You helped me free the dragon lizards. You helped me call Drehensil before. Can you help me now when I need you most?"

Still no answer and no transformation. She placed the dragon stone back in her pocket. "What now?" She closed her eyes, shutting out the world. Aralyn needed wisdom, and she kept going over what Guronde had said about those who feared her and wanted her banned from Eyndor.

Drehensil had always been a source of wisdom. Using the dragonstone to find that wisdom—would that be wrong?

Something in the ancient manuscripts came to mind. Something about wisdom and where true wisdom came from. It came from above. So maybe if she sought the dragon as a source of wisdom...it might be a good thing? Or was that foolishness?

Her thoughts cut away from seeking for wisdom, and wandered to her days as a *nanio* and the lessons they'd learned about magic. Dragons held powerful magic, and if a dragon claimed someone, that was a powerful cord between them. Drehensil called her "my Aralyn."

He had claimed her.

A tiny gasp escaped as understanding dawned. They had deserted the Elves, the dragons had, and would not return unless...

Aralyn's eyes snapped open. She remembered. There were only a few places where her plan would work. Places along the border where alcoves of power lay obscured. She would need the dragon stone and...another item. Aralyn dug into her pack. From a hidden pocket, she pulled out a cloak that her father, her true Elven father, had given her. She had never used it, but now she knew it was necessary. No one need know of her plan, and the cloak would help her stay hidden. The lightweight material shimmered and gave an enticing call, an invitation to join in battle, to heed the call to danger. And a call from Drehensil himself.

It wasn't danger she sought, though. She desired wisdom and was determined to find it.

Chapter 25

Gillis was in the trees with the archer-guards, sword in hand. The air in this part of Eyndor refreshed him, as did working with this unique group of warriors. Here, he had discovered a new community. Shelters built in the trees, joined by rope walkways, provided homes for a number of the archers. Many of the guards stood on platforms, while others, both men and women, leaped from branch to branch. He admired their agility, balance, and silent movements.

The archer-guards had trained in the art of swordsmanship at one time, but it was so long ago that their leader was afraid they were ill-prepared for a hand-to-hand confrontation. It was unlikely that enemies would be able to climb into the trees where the archer-guards lay in wait. If they tried, they would probably receive an arrow through the chest or throat, but it was good to prepare these archers for the improbable.

Gillis eyed the weapon of the archer he was training today, a short-blade sword. Normally, a longer blade worked better against an adversary, but in the trees with limbs and branches in the way, the shorter blades might be an advantage. Eventually, he wanted to train them on the ground, but these archers were used to being in the trees, so that was where they would train for now. Gillis couldn't imagine teaching them footwork on branches that bounced with every step. He would have to adapt his style to this new environment.

A simple thrust and parry and a return to guard position came easily to the young boy-faced trainee. When they moved on to the more complex movements, he caught Gillis by surprise when he almost knocked his trainer's sword out of his hand. And something caught Gillis' eye. He motioned for his trainee to hold, and both men craned their necks to see a creature about the size of a large dog but with no distinct form creeping through the shrubs. It blended in so well, Gillis wasn't sure he could identify it. As it moved forward, an outline of its legs appeared, confirming there were four. But its hind legs looked longer than the forelegs and bent forward at the knees. Strange.

Gillis' eyes narrowed. "I'm not sure what that is, but it doesn't belong here."

His trainee nodded. "It's like no animal I've ever seen."

"I'm going to see what it is." Gillis climbed from the tree and dropped to the forest floor. He gripped his sword and crept toward the creature.

***

The archer-guards in the trees concerned Aralyn. If they spotted her, this plan might not work. Drehensil might not respond to her call. The cloak was supposed to help her blend in with the surroundings, but it couldn't hide her completely. She crouched as low as possible while moving forward. Occasionally, she pulled her hands off the ground and sat back on her knees to rest. Either position was uncomfortable, but if she stood, her feet peeked out from beneath the cloak. She crept farther away from the guards and deeper into the shrubs. At the edge of a clearing, she sensed him. A few bow shots away, Drehensil waited for her. Was it truly him? Had he been able to get inside the borders? Why didn't he speak to her?

A bright light shone from her pocket. The gem. She covered it with her hands, sure that it would call attention to her. But did this mean it was calling the dragon? Aralyn focused her thoughts on Drehensil, reaching out to him. The next moment, waves of grief came over her—the heartbreaking grief of Drehensil. It was him. He was here.

The gem squirmed in her hand, moving its wings, clawing her, and its crimson light grew brighter.

No! Stop. She couldn't hide the gem any longer.

Something hot seared her palm. Aralyn jerked her hand away and grunted. The gem flew from her pocket, but she grabbed it.

Someone spoke in an odd language. *"Sule mi las monas petros."*

The gem slipped from her grasp and tore through the cloak. She could see Drehensil's wings soaring above her. The dragon lizards fluttered around him as if they were upset, batting their wings in his face, crying out. Elouard spit tiny flames at him. She'd never seen them act like that. She crouched deeper in the grasses.

Without warning, an outside force ripped the cloak from her. It was Gillis. He yanked her to her feet. "What in the name of Elyon are ye doing?" He glanced up and saw the dragon. He lowered a fiery glare to her.

***

"Aralyn, do you realize what you've done?" Orandon paced, arms clasped behind him. Gillis stood by the table, arms folded. The tension in their home had never been so thick. "Why did you do this?"

"I needed his wisdom, and I hoped people would listen to Drehensil." And where was he now? Had he left her? The thought chilled her, but she went on. "I wanted everyone to hear what he had to say about me. About the Age of Thunder." That sounded so feeble, but Orandon didn't seem to hear her. Trying to gain his attention, she said, "Gillis hears him. He could tell—"

"I just don't understand." He continued to pace. "Do you realize what I'm going to have to do?" He didn't wait for her to answer. "You've endangered us all. All of Eyndor and especially those in Aurellium. You've possibly sent the enemy to our door. I imagine he is gathering his forces now. Do you think you are ready?" He muttered words in Elvish and Common, mixing the two, and threw in a few choice words. "Do you realize you've proven the point of those who would have you banned from Eyndor?"

"No! Yes, I mean, Drehensil could come back." Aralyn clasped her hands in front of her.

Orandon stopped pacing. Anger exuded from his very pores. "The dragon? Is that all you have to say?" His look was hard upon her. "You need to lower that chin and listen to me. Our borders were strengthened."

But not anymore? Her shoulders dropped.

"The Age of Thunder comes quickly now. We've been training hard, hoping to prepare in time for its full arrival. And meanwhile, you decide to call a dragon." He peered down at her. "There is a mage outside our borders now. Our weakened borders. Mal'ev may not know exactly where we are, but the dragon ..." Orandon closed his eyes. "He has left, but we are weaker. His powers interfered with the borders' strength." He inhaled and let out a slow breath. "That is why the dragons left us years ago. Not because of a sense of betrayal, as you may have heard, but because they knew their presence weakened our borders. And you may not have known the consequences, but what were you thinking?" Now he was quiet.

"I've been trying to tell you." Aralyn's words came in a fury. "But you won't listen to me. You don't want to under—"

He was upon her in two strides, his tone low and threatening. "You need to hear me, Aralyn, and hear me well. Your deeds give you no latitude for anything save answering my questions. You are not a child who needs to give excuses, and I am not some child you need to shout at. You will give me honest answers." His voice never rose, but the authority made her take a step back.

Aralyn swallowed. She waited for her husband to say something. Anything. He just stood there with an unreadable expression, arms folded.

Orandon's eyes followed her gaze. "Gillis, would you mind giving us a moment to talk?"

"Of course." He headed to the doorway. "I need some air anyway."

With his expression and tone now gentler, Orandon asked again. "Why?"

"Guronde said many people don't think I'm the bowsinger. He said a person or creature from ancient times would remember the last Age of Thunder, and they could see the signs, but he didn't know of anyone like that. I thought of Drehensil. He's lived for thousands of years. I wasn't sure about calling him at first, but people need to know who I am." *Didn't they?* "If I am to keep them safe, if my presence here is keeping the borders strong, they need to know, have the assurance that I am the bowsinger and to know if I left, what would hap—"

"I think I see now." He placed his hands behind his back. "Those reasons sound very altruistic. But, Aralyn, we are not totally dependent on you. And how was the dragon going to tell everyone? Do you think everyone can hear him?"

"But I can hear him, and Gillis can hear him. Surely there are others. We could tell them what he says." That seemed an inadequate explanation now that Aralyn thought about it.

Orandon shook his head. "Do you think the doubters would believe you? If they cannot hear him for themselves, they will not believe you or your spouse. And even if they could hear him, most of us choose to believe what we wish to believe. What you did was very foolish. You clearly did not think this through, and I think you knew it was wrong." He paused and straightened, and a harsh glare landed on her. "There's more to it, isn't there?"

Aralyn wanted to be honest, but she hesitated.

"Aralyn." His voice cut through her like an arrow.

"I wanted to seek his wisdom. I felt like I needed—"

"For what? For battle? For training?"

"Partially." Which was true. "I missed them—the dragon lizards. I missed spending time with Drehensil. And Gillis, he..."

"Gillis?" His brow furrowed. "What does he have to do with this?"

Aralyn swung away from him. She shouldn't have mentioned him.

"Ah, because of your problems with him?"

She found herself nodding.

"Look at me."

She turned, but her gaze remained on the floor.

He placed a knuckle under her chin and lifted her face to meet his. "You had some good reasons for calling Drehensil. Perhaps. But some selfish ones as well. And tell me what you hoped to gain from the dragon concerning your husband?"

Aralyn bit her lip. "I shouldn't have said anything about him. But I needed his wisdom..."

"I think I understand. But if you need to talk to someone about your marriage, there are others wiser in these matters, and this is important if you are paired. I told you before, you must be able to put your differences aside." Orandon paused and rested a hand on her shoulder. "Maybe you should talk to Re'ah."

She shook her head. "No."

"Why not?" He tilted his head toward her.

Aralyn couldn't think of a reason. It just felt wrong somehow. Just today, she had prayed to Sathria's goddess. And she remembered something else...her thoughts about where true wisdom came from, and all she had to do was ask. Consult Elyon's ancient manuscripts.

"Ah. You don't want to face him right now, do you?"

Aralyn's stomach was a solid knot. Her head bowed, she nodded.

"He arrives here in a day or two."

Her head snapped up. A day or two? "I'll talk to him," she managed to say.

Orandon's gaze was on the ceiling as if asking the sky for strength. "I'm going to have to discipline you for this. But first, I want to give you a chance to tell me of anything else I might need to know."

Aralyn considered his question. And it came to her. "I lost the gem."

"The gem?" Light dawned upon Orandon's face. "The gem Elnala gave you. How?" His voice was a jagged edge.

"It flew out of my hands when I used it to contact the dragon."

Orandon's eyes squeezed shut, and he muttered what Aralyn was sure was profanity.

"You told me to use it in the ways the gem revealed to me. The very day Elnala gave it to me, the dragon came to my home. And when I was on the trail, he came to me when I held it. I thought it would be all right to use it to call him."

"It was still foolish." Orandon pursed his lips. "Anything else?"

"I heard a voice, too."

Orandon lifted an eyebrow. "What voice?"

"I don't know...but it said something like '*Sulay mi lasas monas*,' I think."

"'*Sule mi las monas petros?*' Someone summoned the gem." Orandon's voice was devoid of emotion. "It was Mal'ev then. He had the ability in the past. With the gem in his power, he can find us. It could also help him develop a connection with Drehensil or another dragon, a dragon that is not as good as you seem to think Drehensil is."

Aralyn was spent, her legs incapable of holding her up. She grabbed a chair and bowed her head in surrender. "Please forgive me." Aralyn's mouth was dry, and beads of perspiration broke out on her neck and forehead.

Orandon pulled out a cloak from the deep folds of his robe. The one Gillis had yanked from her. "This is a dragonrider's cloak. Where did you find this? Answer me honestly."

Her tongue was thick, but she forced out the words. "Someone gave it to me."

"I'd like to know who. Or did they give it to your mother, and you took it from her?"

Aralyn hated the inferred accusation, and in her mind's eye, she could only see a rough hand reaching out to her, offering the cloak freely. But someone's blood was on it. Her father's?

"It takes some talent and training to use this properly." He put the cloak back into his robes. "I will keep this and perhaps give it to someone who can use it. Your father may have been a dragonrider, but you are not."

Aralyn froze in place. It was her father's? He had been a dragonrider? But Orandon was taking it. He couldn't. Was this her punishment? No, by the look on Orandon's face, there was still more.

"Good motives or bad, you should have known to talk to someone before you called the dragon. Do you not remember learning these things? No, I suppose you don't. You were young when you and your mother left." His gaze was a mixture of anger and sorrow. "This may not be the best time, but you will no longer train with the archers until you have studied the proper protocols of Eyndor. You will also learn the songs you need to know. Continue with the strengthening routines, and learn to build your *bar're*, but not in the Harp."

No.

She had to keep training. How could she be ready if the fight was imminent? Her eyes burned. She couldn't cry in front of Orandon. She turned her back on him again.

"Aralyn." Orandon's voice was gentler, but only a little. "Look at me."

She slowly pivoted to face him.

"Listen." He seemed to tower over her, though barely taller. "I will make sure you are ready. For now, you have an indefinite suspension to learn with the *nanios*."

"With the *nanios*?" Aralyn watched his face for some sign of humor. He was sentencing her to learn with the children? She tried to speak, but couldn't.

"You will also learn the songs. Memorize them. I'll draw up a list of the significant ones. The *nanios* pick up the songs faster than most, and they will be delighted to help you. You will also learn why we require certain behaviors, why it is so important to follow our protocols, and how to respect laws. Once Bielle assures me you are ready, you can return to training."

That was when a crack came to Aralyn's world. Like a barely perceived breach in a dam, the floodwaters of fear and abandonment threatened her.

Orandon was always nearby to consult as she led her group of archers. And now she would not see him or any of the archers for an indefinite period? She choked as unseen waters rose to her neck. Orandon giving up on her. She was a married woman, and yet his words made her feel like a little girl. No, she *was* a little girl. As in a nightmare, the memory's cold rush caught her in its grip.

Aralyn rode as fast as she could through a forest lit with glowing fireflies and lantern birds. She urged the horse on, letting him have free rein. Tree branches grabbed her. Whipped at her face. Ivy and thorns clung to her clothes. She heard something tear, but kept riding.

Father was gone. Nothing of her father was left. He would never return. An enormous, roiling wave of fear and grief threatened to crash down on her. It stood above her, suspended for a moment, then rushed to catch her in its grip. She was drowning. Her childhood, her heart, her laughter—all were drowning. And someone called her name. A frantic voice. "Aralyn! Ar-a-lyn!"

Aralyn's eyes snapped open. She gasped for air. Perspiration poured from her, and a chill seized her.

Orandon was staring down at her, his brow furrowed. "What are you doing? What are you thinking?"

"Nothing." She swallowed past the huge mass in her throat, and Orandon must have seen she was truly in distress.

"All right, all right. Take some deep breaths."

That was what she was trying to do!

He touched her elbow. "Deep breaths. Slowly."

She managed to do as he said. Whether a nightmare or memory—whatever it was—it was happening again. Someone she had grown to care for, perhaps too much, was leaving her. Maybe not forever, but still... "No, Orandon." Words she knew she shouldn't speak. But there was no stopping them now. "I need to keep training with you and the archers."

Orandon folded his arms across his chest. "Oh?"

"I can't stop training." A deep inhalation. She lifted her gaze to meet his hard one. "I won't, and how can you stop me? You can't keep me out of the Harp."

Orandon's arms relaxed, but his face was stone. "This is not entirely my choice. Guronde had a part in it, too. And yes, we can keep you out of the Harp."

Aralyn felt the blood draining from her face.

"Aralyn?"

She knew he sensed the questions she had. Perhaps knew more of her thoughts than she wanted him to know. "Why does this upset you so?" He waited. "I can understand that you want to keep training, but this reaction...what is going on?"

When she didn't answer, he tilted his head, and his mind probed hers so gently she almost didn't notice, and then her *bar're* went up.

The probing stopped.

Orandon nodded sharply. "Do you feel that we cannot do without you? Or..." And Aralyn knew he had seen something she would rather he had not just from that brief touch of their minds.

His head angled to one side. "Or is there someone you've made friends with, someone you will miss that badly? "

It was Aralyn's turn to acknowledge him with a nod.

He gave a soft chuckle, followed by an amused voice. "I'm not laughing at you. Well, maybe I am. But you gave a rather ambiguous answer."

"It's both."

"Can you tell me who it is?"

Confident and unafraid, Aralyn met his gaze. Orandon's eyes were gentle now. And a light came to his eyes. "It's someone you've developed *feelings* for? Is that it?"

Aralyn shook her head. But again, she needed to be truthful. "It's not romantic feelings. I love Gillis." That was a partial truth. She did love Gillis, but ...

"I see."

Panic twisted her gut. He did see. He saw right through her partial truth, her lie. "I would never ... I don't want or expect anything from them." And her next words came out in a rush. "When my father left, I wanted him to come back so badly. He left me, and I didn't know what to do, and I wanted to get away from all the pain, but I couldn't, and it was in here and"—she pointed to her chest, where right now her heart was breaking under the weight of the cloying memory—"and I cried to Mother, but Mother told me to stop, that crying wouldn't bring him back. I just remember riding fast and hard to get away from her, away from the pain, and didn't know, didn't care how I would get back."

Orandon took a step toward her, and she tried to continue. "And now you—"

"Hold. Aralyn." He dropped his hands. "You think I'm deserting you like your father did when he died?"

Her head shot up. "I don't, no. Yes. Please don't ... I didn't want these feelings." She stared at the floor.

"Go on."

Did he want to hear this? Aralyn wasn't sure she understood this well of emotion that crashed upon her. "I'm trying."

"I'm not deserting you." She sensed his hand moving toward her and then pulling back. "And I don't want to read more into this, but I sense something else. It would be best if you told me."

"Yes, there is more," she said barely above a whisper. But what she felt was wrong, and she knew it. He was Elnala's father.

Orandon touched her forearm.

"It's like I said before. Feelings I never wanted, never thought I'd ... Orandon." Her mouth moved with words she couldn't say. Feelings that needed to be forgotten, shoved into oblivion.

Orandon gave a slow nod as Aralyn's cheeks grew warm. He knew.

"It's all right, Aralyn, and I want you to know you're safe with me." His voice was gentle, understanding.

She should let him gather her in his arms. No! She couldn't.

"Have you told Gillis any of this?"

Aralyn shook her head, and her speech came in a rush once more. "I can barely admit it to myself, and I can't let this become more, and maybe I shouldn't have told you and IloveGillisand ..." She was running her words together. Like Elnala. Aralyn let her voice fade.

"You say you love Gillis." Orandon hesitated. "Perhaps this is not my concern as your trainer, but as a friend, I am asking, does he know?"

Aralyn's shoulders relaxed. They were talking about Gillis, still a tender topic but a safer one. "No, I haven't, and he does not feel the same."

To her surprise, she heard Orandon chuckle again. "I'm sorry." He sat and pulled her down to take a seat across from him. "I think Gillis is kidding himself. I think he does love you and loves you quite deeply."

Had she heard Orandon right? "Well, I wish someone would tell him so he could tell me."

Orandon laughed outright. "He's going to have to realize that himself, with Elyon's help."

"I should pray about this?" Pray to Elyon. She could do that. She had before, not sure if he had answered, but the peace he brought her was real.

"By all means." He grinned and patted her hand. His eyes showed clear concern, and he spoke slowly. "Would you mind if my wife and I came to visit you and Gillis, perhaps had a meal with you?"

Aralyn saw the kindest gaze, and she met it with what she hoped was equal kindness. "No, I don't mind." She allowed a smirk to play upon her lips. "And I promise I won't cook."

"Deal." He rose. He moved toward the door, hesitated, and turned back to her. "Aralyn, if you will work solely with the children for a week, learn the songs, perhaps you can start training again in the afternoons."

A flood of relief swept through her, but she tried not to let it show.

"I should go. It's late." He studied her face for a moment. "You take some time to rest tomorrow morning. Stay here, go for a walk, or perhaps go hunt. I need to get things set up with Bielle anyway. I'll have a messenger come when she is ready for you."

Bielle. She recognized the name as the teacher of the *nanios*. The little ones.

"And I am not doing this to humiliate you. You need to learn the things Bielle can teach you." He pinched his lips together, and Aralyn got the feeling he was having a tough time doling out discipline.

She would speak while he seemed to soften. "But the borders have grown weak, and the battle is coming."

"I understand, but it must be this way. You need to learn the songs. That is just as important, and so far, I have seen little progress in that area."

Aralyn could only swallow her pride. Once again, his voice left no room for discussion. He pulled back the curtain that led to the stairs and trotted partway down. While Orandon and Gillis exchanged quiet words, she headed to the bedroom and prayed silently. *Help me know what to do. If he loves me, help him to admit it.*

Elnala had said that sometimes the God above others spoke wisdom to her heart. "Just listen," she had said. So Aralyn did. She waited. And waited. Finally, Aralyn sighed and kicked off her boots.

At first, she thought it was a whisper of someone in the room, but it was even closer than that. In her thoughts, a quiet voice spoke to her aching heart. *I am with you, my child.*

Was that it? Had she heard Elyon speak to her? Such a simple message, but it was a wondrous thing to ponder. That this tremendous presence was with her. A god—perhaps the one true God—had called her "my child." And for the first time, she considered giving up on the old gods and ... and what? Worshipping only Elyon? That was scary. The goddess of Sathria's symbol had been burned into her flesh. What if Aralyn rejected her and the goddess punished her somehow?

"I talked to Orandon as he was leaving. He told me what you would do for now." Gillis spoke to her from the bedroom door.

Aralyn nodded. "Yes, not what I want, but I'm sure it will be fine." Not at all convinced it would be.

"It will." He sat on the bed and reached to take off his boots. He paused with one boot still gripped in his hand. His gaze fell on Aralyn, and he was still for a moment. "You know, I am exhausted."

"Yes, me too." Were they having an actual conversation?

"I'd like to sleep in the bed tonight. If that's all right with you."

Aralyn's head came up. "Of course, it's all right. I assume you mean I can sleep here, too?"

"Yes, of course. I would like for you to. I mean, we're both tired, and I didn't want to ... I mean, we're both tired."

Aralyn's lips tugged upward, but she forced her expression to remain serious. "I understand. It's just to sleep."

"Yes. To sleep."

"Sleep would be good right now." Aralyn laughed and knew she sounded awkward. Felt awkward. She continued to undress with her back to her husband. At one point, she was sure she felt his eyes upon her. Aralyn joined him in the bed, and whether or not he meant to, Gillis slipped his hand around her waist.

But as tired as she was, Aralyn could not sleep. It was Gillis. In the bed with her. This was the first time since their chaste wedding night. The light from a full moon shone in the window. She turned on her side and regarded his sharp features. Found herself wanting to trace a finger over them. His face was a handsome one, even with the scars. She truly did not see them anymore unless she looked for them.

She rolled to her other side and slid closer so her back was next to him. Gillis shifted, his arm still around her waist. Aralyn closed her eyes. Dare she encourage more? Last time he had rejected her, and it still stung. Maybe in his sleepy state...No, she wouldn't "take advantage" of him. For that is what it would be. But she wanted him closer. Much closer.

Just as she thought it, Gillis' arm tightened around her.

"Aralyn." Gillis sounded as though he was wide awake. Perhaps he was not sleeping either.

She pinched her lips together and faced him.

"Yes, Gillis." Her voice sounded different to her own ears. Deeper, gentler, filled with longing.

His breath trembled, and he kissed her forehead. "Do you mind?" He asked as he continued to kiss her cheek. Her throat. The neckline of her chemise.

Aralyn drew in a deep breath, let it out in a quiet sigh. "No, I don't mind." She was almost breathless now. "Gillis, are you...?"

"Yes, Aralyn. I am making moves on my wife."

"Are you sure?" She asked, pulling him closer.

"Do you doubt it?" He asked, his question muffled against her skin as he continued to place his lips on her shoulder and neck.

"No...I mean..." She stroked the back of his head. "What made you change your mind?"

Gillis let out a slow breath and propped his head on his hand, looked squarely at her. "Aralyn, I've been praying for us. Before you came home today, and even before that. What you said about us made a lot of sense. After that, I realized I had no excuses. So, my wife, it seems the only way to make our marriage right is to truly be husband and wife. And I know Elyon would approve."

"He would?"

"Oh, yes." He cleared his throat, hesitating. "I talked to Re'ah."

"About us? About this?"

"Yes."

"And what did he say?"

"Said I needed to complete my vows to you. Said he doubted you would mind."

She met his gaze and was surprised to see longing there. Longing for her.

"So…" Aralyn hesitated. "Elyon approves, and you really want…?"

Me, she was about to say. *You really want* me?

But Gillis cut her off with a kiss, the pressure of his mouth pushing her down yet somehow gentle at the same time. Her lips answered his, and she felt the yearning to share herself with him.

Together now. Fulfilling a promise they had made to each other.

And at last, at last, she would no longer be his bride.

Chapter 26

Aralyn listened as Gillis' footsteps faded. He would train today, and she had nowhere to go. From his gentle lovemaking last night to the discipline she faced, her disordered thoughts bounced between passion and guilt, love and shame over her actions. And it was real. All of it. Even if Gillis didn't love her in the way she desired, he had given himself to her. She would cling to that and look forward to more. But that didn't erase the sting of the discipline she faced.

For a moment, she considered taking her bow deep into the woods and not answering the message that would tell her when and where to meet with the *nanios*. Aralyn frowned. She knew that would not be right. Orandon had given her this morning, and perhaps, the whole day, off. That would have to be enough.

Orandon's words were haunting, and they spoke to her in the early morning light. He had said much that shook her to the core, but the one thing that stood out was an offhand comment. *"We are not totally dependent on you."*

No, she supposed, they weren't. They could practice without her. Life would go on. But if she weren't here in Eyndor ... Her thoughts came to an abrupt halt. The Elves did not depend on her for protection or safety from enemies. Not completely. Is that what she had thought? Calling the dragon was something she could do to help protect the Elves, to save them from their enemies, to let them know who and what she was. Was that for Eyndor's sake or her own? Obviously, it was partially for her sake. Aralyn felt sick at her selfishness.

Without her, Eyndor's survival was possible. It would be a much harder fight, but they could persevere. Hadn't they stayed alive for millennia?

She also recalled what Guronde said concerning Mother and Terrwynn. *Your mother and Terrwynn are well. Doing quite well without you.* The words stung just as Orandon's did. The family she'd left behind could survive without her. Nothing wrong with her ability to provide, but was it to prove something to them, especially Mother? Were her actions really about what Aralyn needed—to prove she was valuable and respectable? Even lovable?

And why had she tried to reach the dragon? To prove the same thing to the Elves? Not to build their confidence but to build her own? Because of her desire to prove she was respectable?

Aralyn blinked back tears. She had attempted to *use* Drehensil. If he sensed that, would he ever come back to her? She called him just yesterday, and as a result, there was now serious damage to their borders, but then he had left. Neither she nor Gillis had spoken with him. The dragon lizards had left as well. They were trying to convince Drehensil not to come here, she realized. They knew what Drehensil's presence would do. She needed to ask Orandon if the dragon lizards' presence had any effect on the borders.

A heaviness lay on her chest. It spread upward and pressed on her throat. Was this who she was? A needy woman? Not a leader of any sort? Not the brave warrior who'd killed Rogues and saved lives, but a woman who needed the approval and respect of others? Who felt she had to prove herself by protecting others, killing if necessary? That wasn't bravery—it was pride. Childish pride.

Aralyn wandered from the kitchen, went to one of the large open windows, and scanned the endless forest, brush, and grasses.

Even though the realization crushed her, it pushed her to a decision. She would do as Orandon said. She would go to Bielle's class, learn all she could, and gain whatever she needed to be a part of Eyndor. That perhaps was more important than fighting—to truly be part of the land of Elves by learning its songs, its ways, its customs. Those lessons would become a part of who she was as an Elf. Perhaps the real battle would come as she released the burden of saving Eyndor, realizing it was not hers alone to bear. Even the burden of protecting her family had never been hers alone.

Below her, two boyish figures in the near darkness practiced with blades, thrusting, parrying. A blur of movement. Why here? What were they doing out playing at this time of day? But she watched as their grunts and good-natured laughter rang out. One of them misstopped, and the other went in for the "kill." Their blades were still for a brief moment. Time slowed as the dim light reflected, bounced off the swords like tiny lanterns. And she felt the turmoil that longed to take her in its embrace once more, but she wouldn't let it. She knew what she had to do. First, talk to Re'ah. And when Bielle was ready for her, learn with the *nanios*.

***

Aralyn recognized Re'ah's footsteps on the stairs. He called her name, and she flung back the thick covering. "Come in, Re'ah." She wanted to rest in his arms, but his face was drawn, his clothes dusty.

"Sit. Please." She motioned to a chair at their table. "Would you like some refreshment?"

"How about some of that bankroot tea?" He closed his eyes, leaned his head back to interlocked hands.

Aralyn's shoulders dropped. "You have a headache?"

"Aye, that I do."

"Truth be told, I was about to make some for myself." She placed a pan of water on the stove.

Re'ah opened an eye. "You have a headache of your own?"

"Yes. We'll be good company for each other."

Re'ah's lips turned up. Just barely.

Aralyn sighed and shifted her feet as she waited for the water to boil. Re'ah rested his eyes, and Aralyn thought he had fallen asleep. The water came to a boil, and she placed the tea on the table along with a plate of bread and a bowl of berries.

Re'ah opened his eyes when he heard the clink of plate and cup. "You have read my mind, given me more than I asked."

"I don't know about reading your mind, but I thought you might like something to eat. Didn't know if you'd broken your fast."

He nodded, reached for some bread, and took a sip of his tea. "Would you sit with me?"

Aralyn took the chair facing him. "I suppose you want to talk."

"Aralyn, I always enjoy talking with you." He took another sip. "Is Gillis nearby?"

"He's training with the archer-guards. He could be right above us, I suppose." That wasn't likely, but it was fanciful to think so. "We don't have to talk if you'd rather rest."

"The tea is already helping." He took a large bite of the crust of bread and murmured his appreciation. "Did you make this?"

"Oh, no. A baker did. I buy it from him, or we trade."

"Ah, excellent choice in bakers." Re'ah nodded in approval.

"My cooking skills have improved little," Aralyn admitted. "All the magic in Eyndor couldn't do that."

Re'ah chuckled, put down his bread, and squeezed her fingers.

A silence rested between them as Aralyn drank her tea. The bankroot tea was bitter and strong, yet somehow smooth and settling. And it always eased a headache. Re'ah kept a hand on hers as he drank. "You seem to have conflicting feelings about something."

"Orandon banned me from training," she blurted. Should she let him know about last night?

"I see." He seemed to sense all that was going on in her mind.

But no, surely not.

"I heard it had to do with the dragon," he continued.

"Yes." Aralyn proceeded with the story—how she felt she needed Drehensil and why she thought it was right to call him—and Drehensil had come, and how she lost the gem. About Gillis discovering her under her father's cloak, and Orandon's punishment. "Now I have to learn with the children, but I know"—Aralyn squeezed her eyes shut—"I was in the wrong."

"Mm, so you're sure of that?" He took another slice of bread.

"Yes, I am. Of course." Could Re'ah tell she was sincere? "I felt at peace this morning," she said, thinking about the prayer she'd prayed and Elyon's response. but now... "I keep thinking about what I've done and why I did it."

"Go on." Re'ah brushed the crumbs from his fingers and reached for some berries.

"I don't like what I've found."

His eyebrows raised, a signal for her to continue.

She told him all she'd seen in herself this morning. "So being with the children is good, I suppose. I need to learn what I've forgotten or perhaps they never taught me."

"Good to hear." This time, a grin spread across his face. "I'm proud of you."

"Proud? How can you—"

"Because you realize you should have done things differently." He leaned toward her. "And because you're my friend. No other reason is necessary."

Aralyn opened her mouth, then closed it. She pinched her lips together. "Re'ah. I have some questions about following your god."

"All right."

"I prayed to him last night and only to him, not to the goddess of Sathria or any of the other gods of the sky-haven, and I think he told me something."

"What was it?" Re'ah leaned back again.

"Nothing big. I mean, maybe I shouldn't even mention it." Perhaps it had been her imagination, and Re'ah would laugh. Aralyn picked a few berries from the bowl. "He said, 'I am with you.'"

"Ah." He rubbed the back of his neck. "That is a good thing."

"Yes." It was a good thing. "After everything that happened yesterday, it was comforting. I slept better than I have in a long time." Well, that was partially thanks to Gillis. She touched her lips, feeling his warmth against them.

Re'ah smiled. Kept his gentle gaze on her. "Do you have something else to tell me?"

"Oh...no. It's just..." Aralyn shrugged.

"Something with you and Gillis?"

Aralyn looked at the table, then met his gaze. "Yes, something good."

His eyes lit up. Yes, he understood. Had it been anyone else, she would have been mortified, maybe even thought them overly curious about something so private, but with Re'ah, she felt none of that. Her cheeks warmed, and without meaning to, she let out a sigh and smiled, meeting his gaze. He gave her a wink and nodded.

Time to change the subject.

"Are you feeling better?" she asked.

"Yes, much better. And you?"

"Yes, it's good to talk."

"I need to leave if Gillis is not coming back soon." He came to his feet.

Yes, impropriety was a punishable offense in Aurellium.

Aralyn walked him to the door. "I'm still concerned about you. This isn't the first time I've heard you complain of a headache."

"I will be fine." His voice was reassuring. He must have seen more than concern on her face. "Now, do not worry. Perhaps I will see your healer while I am here."

"I just want you to be all right."

"I know. I will be. You keep up your good work. You are on the right track. And thank you for the tea and that delicious bread."

"Anytime, Re'ah."

He grabbed a handful of berries and bid her goodbye. She stared at the curtain as it swung closed, and his words sank in. He was proud of her. She was on the right track. Her heart felt lighter.

Chapter 27

A small wooden building sat in a clearing near the Harp. The outside walls had colorful artwork—rivers and streams, flowers, and trees full of life. This is where she was to meet with Bielle and the *nanios*. The school stood on short pillars with steps in the front. To the side of the building, under rustling trees, were pillows and blankets where the children would sit today. When the weather permitted, they held class outside.

Learning with the children was not as bad as Aralyn had feared. They seemed to delight in having her with them. One of the first things she noticed was that they never crowded her or tried to reach into her pockets the way children in Sathria did.

As Bielle taught, Aralyn made notes, unlike the children, who seemed to absorb it all. History lessons were not as boring as the human history she had learned. The Elvish stories of heroes, traitors, Dwarves, and epic battles kept her attention. When they learned of the dragons and their riders, Aralyn's heart pounded in anticipation. But the tragic stories made her blood grow cold. Dragonriders fell and died, the dragons unable to protect them from the enemies' weapons and opposing dragon forces. The dragons' desertion of Eyndor caused her to think of Drehensil. She shook the thought from her mind.

A memory rushed back. When the dragon returned years ago, her father had not. The crimson scales whirled before her. Drehensil.

Her father had ridden Drehensil, the dragon who returned with only a few snatches of clothes in his teeth. He had tried to keep her father from falling and had failed. It was Drehensil who let her down. Perhaps her father as well. Yet, for some reason, she had blamed herself.

"What's wrong, Aralyn?" Bielle must have noticed the look on her face.

She choked, tried to speak, but couldn't.

"Children." Bielle gave them a nod.

Aralyn felt hands on her head and her shoulders. From the youngest to the oldest of the *nanios*, they formed a circle around her. She didn't shrink from them. This touch was a kindness, but she felt exposed. Until at last, she didn't. All the embarrassment disappeared, along with the anger, fear, and grief that churned in her. Was this important to the Elves—this comfort and compassion for others? A thing they actively taught?

"It's all right, Aralyn," said one of the smallest. He patted her hand. "It's all right. Should we fix you a hot beverage?"

Aralyn laughed and shook her head. "No, I am all right, truly. Thank you, Chaon."

The rest of them lifted their hands, found their places, and sat back down while Chaon stayed next to her. She didn't mind him sitting so close. On the contrary, she found it comforting. This was part of the childhood she had missed. She needed this time to not only learn but to go back and be a child like these.

During the second day with the children, Aralyn realized she was learning their names. Bielle also started teaching the songs of Eyndor, a few of them from Orandon's list. Just as her trainer had said, the children caught on quickly, and Aralyn trailed behind. When they all sang together, the songs seemed to catch in the trees and rain back down on them. Sometimes the Loweill birds would join in even though it was early afternoon.

"Wow!" the one who had offered her a hot beverage cried. "We sound good with Aralyn. She helps us sing better."

A few of the children giggled at his interruption, and Bielle smiled.

"Well, she is our bowsinger," Bielle said when the children quieted.

Aralyn was secretly proud and beyond excited that someone believed in her.

"What is a bowsinger?" several *nanios* asked at once.

"You learned the history. Fielle, what is a bowsinger?"

Fielle's black hair swung about her shoulders as she pointed toward Aralyn. "She is."

The children laughed again.

"You're right, Fielle, but—"

"I know. Someone really good at archery because they sing, and that makes the arrows fly straight to the target every time," one of the younger children answered.

"Must be nice not to have to practice. And just sing," the one named Kalon muttered.

"Oh, she still has to practice, *megjilly,*" another replied.

Aralyn recognized the insult and wanted to giggle along with the children. In Common, it meant something like "big dumb one."

But Bielle clapped her hands. "Jurnal, you will not call names in this class." Her voice was calm, but she spoke with authority.

"Yes, my lady." Jurnal ducked her head.

Bielle stood with hands on her hips, and the class was silent again. "You are right, though. You do have to practice, don't you, Aralyn?"

"Yes, of course." Aralyn swallowed. "I also learn a lot from the others. I couldn't do it on my own."

***

Bielle excused Aralyn and Jurnal early one day. "Jurnal, I want you and Aralyn to go into the forest and learn these songs. You will hear them better away from the classroom." She handed Jurnal the list Orandon had given the teacher.

Jurnal took the list, looked it over, and handed it back.

Jurnal was taller than most of the other *nanios*, and older, Aralyn assumed. Long hair, the color of a fawn, framed a heart-shaped face. And smart. She had memorized the list in a matter of seconds.

"Come, Aralyn." She grabbed Aralyn's hand and led her to a part of the forest bathed in emerald green. The trees, the grasses, and vines were all of this unusual hue. Even the brook looked greener than any water she'd seen.

"Aralyn, listen," Jurnal told her.

Aralyn heard it—a song that made her gasp. The brook was singing to her. The song was similar to the river and stream, but with fewer changes in the melody. The song changed little in volume, and she found the rhythm simple yet engaging. Jurnal sang, and Aralyn listened. When the younger broke off, Aralyn wavered for a moment, but the notes flowed from her throat of their own volition. Her eyes closed, and the surrounding trees hummed. The whistling grasses caught the wind and joined with her.

The warrior's song seemed to be Jurnal's favorite. "It's very effective against most enemies."

"The song by itself?"

"Sometimes. It can be," Jurnal replied. "You know each bowsinger adds to the knowledge of bowsinging. We keep the stories of every bowsinger and pass them on to the next one."

Aralyn's heart thumped. She had learned nothing of these. Perhaps she needed to study them or ask Orandon. Another question niggled her mind. What would she add to their knowledge? What would be written of her in the bowsinger stories?

They continued to practice, and after an hour, headed back to class.

"You're doing well, bowsinger." Jurnal's silvery eyes shone, and her face dimpled.

"You think so?"

"Yes. Why aren't you training?"

Ah, she would ask that question.

When Aralyn hesitated, Jurnal continued. "I plan to train with the melee fighters soon."

This one dreamed of fighting, and Aralyn wondered if she had any idea what that was like.

"I don't want to kill." Jurnal pushed a branch aside, her expression solemn. "But I want to defend myself and fight if I have to."

"I understand." Aralyn shoved her memories away, thinking of her vow to never kill again. She hadn't wanted to kill, but to protect her home, it had been necessary. The land of Eyndor would soon require the same thing of her.

They rounded a bend in a path, and the clearing where the class met came into view.

"Is this right?" Aralyn turned to face Jurnal. "Where is everyone?"

They were gone.

Jurnal tilted her head. "They should still be here."

Aralyn shrugged. "Maybe Bielle let them go home ear—."

"Your borders have grown weak, Aralyn." A voice she recognized bled into her. The man standing in the clearing held a scimitar in hand. He slapped it on the ground, removing drops of blood. He sheathed the weapon and twirled a dagger through his fingers.

Mal'ev.

It was him. But why did he have a bloody blade? What had he done? She pushed Jurnal behind her and took a step back.

"You realize who I am, don't you?"

Aralyn nodded and swallowed. "I saw you with Siaon. Outside Maizehollow."

"Ah, yes. I'm flattered you remember. I was not in my best form. Uh, not in my form at all."

Aralyn's disturbing memory of Mal'ev possessing Siaon and his oppressive presence when his mind attacked her caused her stomach to churn.

"Aralyn, let's not dwell upon the past, but discuss your future." His voice joined with a smoky grayness streaming down on him.

"My future?"

"Yes, Aralyn. First, you've allowed me in, and you and these little ones have paid the price. But there will be more. Much—"

"You have no power here." Aralyn interrupted. She didn't want to hear his plans.

Mal'ev snarled. "Oh yes, I do. Some have already felt my power. And now ..."

Before Aralyn could blink, a knife flew toward Jurnal, who promptly snatched it from the air. She stepped in front of Aralyn. "She is right, Mal'ev. Your power is no good here."

"Oh. My." Mal'ev seemed entertained by Jurnal's ability. But then more daggers flew. Aralyn didn't have time to react. Jurnal did, however, and she knocked knives to the ground, grabbing one by the hilt.

Where had she learned this? And why was Mal'ev not using his magic? He was a powerful mage, wasn't he?

"Sing, Aralyn!" Jurnal cried, and she threw a blade, but Mal'ev dodged it.

Aralyn could not remember one song she had just learned, not one. A song from long ago came to mind, one she had used in Sathria. She sang it. Jurnal caught on and sang with her. The younger girl threw another blade. This time it hit Mal'ev's forearm.

Aralyn caught a glimpse of Mal'ev's confusion as he lost his balance and grabbed a tree limb. His face filled with fury, and he flicked another blade that grew in size as it flew toward them. This time, he did not miss.

Jurnal stumbled back, and crimson erupted from the wound in her chest. Aralyn grabbed her as the girl dropped to her knees, gasped and coughed.

She fell forward onto all fours and collapsed. More blood came from her mouth as she rolled onto her back.

Aralyn heard Mal'ev's steps behind her. "You see, Aralyn. I'm real. Not some apparition as you saw in Maizehollow." He placed a cold hand on Aralyn's cheek. It chilled her, probably as he intended, and he reeked of death.

Aralyn fell to her knees. She reached to pull the knife out. But she knew better. That would only make things worse.

Instead, she placed her hands on the wound in a feeble effort to slow the bleeding.

Mal'ev stood over them, casting a long shadow. Darker than what was natural. He could have killed Aralyn by now. Why didn't he?

A voice hissed behind her. "She's dead. Or soon will be. I promise." He reached down. Pulled the knife from Jurnal's chest before Aralyn could stop him. He wiped it clean. Blood spurted, and the last spark of life left Jurnal's eyes.

Aralyn pressed on the wound again, but Jurnal's color turned ashen. "No, no, no!" This couldn't be happening. Hoping against hope, Aralyn checked for a pulse. Nothing.

"Give up, Aralyn. Come with me." His voice snaked into her ears and down her throat. She choked.

Aralyn pulled her hands away and stood. No time to be sick, to feel grief, even though Jurnal's blood covered her hands, her sleeves. Only fury, a wave of wild anger such as she had never felt. And it rang through in her song. Into Mal'ev's face. The song of the warrior combined with passion emanating from her heart—her love for Eyndor, the love she had developed for this child. Even though tears fell, her song rang out—the song Jurnal had taught her. The trees hummed, leaves fluttering, and joined in harmony.

"This won't work." He reached for another blade.

Aralyn kept singing. Mal'ev covered his face, and the knife dropped from his hand. Was he really afraid of a song? Perhaps not, but he seemed immobilized by hers.

Mal'ev gagged. He stumbled, recovered, and almost fell. And over her song, his words rang out. "I hear you sleeping at night. I smell your very steps. I will meet with you soon. And you, girl, will need more than your songs!"

With that, he slithered into the forest as smooth as a snake. Someone was with him, and both mounted an animal like none she had ever seen. It was as tall as five horses, much thicker, and solid white. And much faster. The pair disappeared, heading toward the borders.

Aralyn swung back to Jurnal. She lay in the grass, and Aralyn knelt next to her. How had this happened? It was her fault. Hers. She closed Jurnal's eyes.

"Aralyn!" Gillis. How had he known? Their marks. He ran to her side and pulled Aralyn to her feet. "Are you all right? No, you're not, you're covered—"

"It's Jurnal's. Mal'ev was here. And she's"—Aralyn pointed to the slain child—"dead." A sob caught in her throat.

"What?" He brushed past Aralyn and crouched by Jurnal's side. He felt for a pulse. "She's alive, Aralyn. Barely. We need to get her to the healers."

Gillis bandaged her the best he could. He had few supplies with him. "Where is Mal'ev?"

"He left. He rode off." Aralyn pointed.

Gillis stood. "Take her to the healer, and hurry. Can you do that?"

Aralyn gathered Jurnal in her arms.

"Where are the others?" Gillis asked, alarm clear in his voice.

The other *nanios*. And Bielle. "I think they left for the day."

"They're over here," Elnala called.

Gillis ran toward her voice, and Aralyn made her way to the healers, picking up her pace. Jurnal lay pale and still in her arms. Aralyn found the strength to run, determined to help this one who had almost died at Mal'ev's hand.

***

Scattered bodies met Gillis, and he choked back the scream that struggled in his throat. They were lying in a shallow stream, clothes soaked in blood. Elnala knelt next to them, staff in hand, eyes filled with pain and horror.

Eight, nine. No, eleven bodies.

Gillis grabbed her arm. "You checked them?"

Elnala's tears spilled over. "Yes. They are dead."

There was too much blood for that to be untrue. "There might be others," he said.

A stirring in the brush on the other side of the stream, and Gillis drew his sword. Bielle stumbled out, fell to her knees, and sobbed. She beat her fists on the wet ground. Gillis sloshed through water that was turning a deeper red by the second. He helped her stand, murmuring to her. Bielle stared at the children's bodies. "He bound me somehow. He made me watch as he ... he butchered these children."

Elnala followed behind Gillis. "Are there more children?"

Bielle opened her mouth to speak but only bobbed her head.

"We have eleven here, Bielle," Gillis said as gently as he could. "And Aralyn took Jurnal to the healers. How many others?"

"Eleven?" She placed a hand over her mouth and paled. "You're sure?"

"Yes," Elnala replied.

"Seven more to find then," she whispered, pale from shock. "No, five. Two were with me." She pointed to the brush behind her.

"Are they alive? Hurt?" Elnala asked.

"No. Yes, they are alive. Not injured."

The two *nanios* appeared by the shrubs, staring at the bodies. Gillis strode toward them. They didn't need to see any more. He knelt beside them. "Come with me. Can you do that?"

The pair looked at Gillis with wide eyes and followed him. He found a place for them, away from the bodies and gave them his cloak to wrap up in. "Now, stay here for a moment. I'll be back for you." His voice cracked, and he turned his face away.

"I want to go home," the boy said.

Before Gillis could speak, the older one, a girl, took charge. "We have to wait here, and then they'll take us home." She put her arm around the boy, and he grew still.

When Gillis returned, Bielle was studying the faces of the dead *nanios* to determine who was missing. Elnala walked beside her. They brushed back hair and wiped blood from faces. Bielle choked out the names of the ones they needed to find, and they split up.

Gillis found two more bodies. He picked each one up and laid it by the stream. Gillis gazed on the children's faces—twisted and bruised. He couldn't look at the other wounds. A quiet weeping startled him.

Aralyn had returned. "This one ... I can't remember his name. He offered me a hot beverage." Her face crumpled. "Chaon."

"Aralyn, listen to me. We'll grieve later. We have one more to find." He laid his hands on her shoulders. "How is Jurnal?"

Aralyn nodded. "The healer says it will be a while before they know." She wiped her tears. "Let's find the other."

Hearing a cry from about ten feet away, they both ran toward the sound. Partially inside a hollow tree, they found a little one curled into a fetal position. He was alive. Aralyn coaxed him out and put her cloak around him.

Bielle and Elnala met them with two more—in shock but alive.

That meant, including Jurnal, six had survived. Six out of the nineteen. Gillis squeezed his eyes shut and braced his head with his hands.

They made their way back to the stream, where Aralyn's gaze fell on the bodies. "We have to tell their parents."

Bielle clenched her chin. "I will. I can do that much for them."

"I'll go with you," Aralyn volunteered.

"They're going to accuse me of all kinds of things." Bielle's eyes grew stony. "A teacher is supposed to keep her students safe." Her face lost all expression as her gaze met Aralyn's. "I will go to the parents. If you want to help, stay with the children." She bit her lips. "Line them up so the parents can identify them. Cover them with whatever you can, and make sure no more harm comes to them. Let the parents decide what to do. Elnala and I will take these home." Bielle hesitated. She surveyed her students—their bodies—and knelt by each one, speaking to them by name. She stood and addressed all of them in Elvish. *Domet sein, mi nanios.* Rest well, my children.

Gillis brought the two he had wrapped in his cloak to Bielle. She took their hands, and the other three surviving children followed Elnala. Without a backward glance, they faded into the forest.

***

"Gillis, we need to warn Guronde and the Elders."

"Let's take care of these little ones first. I have a feeling Guronde knows already."

Aralyn nodded.

It did not surprise her that Guronde somehow knew. Aralyn's mark came alive as she and Gillis toiled together. Their closeness brought a fleeting sensation of warmth, but it did nothing to calm her.

Finally, they had laid all the bodies side by side, some of them with mangled faces, arms, and legs.

They found a few thick blankets from the school and covered the children so only their faces showed. It gave the impression they were sleeping.

"He tortured them, Gillis."

"Yes."

"I was only gone an hour. How did he...?" She couldn't go on. The amount of time didn't matter. Only that he had done horrifying things to these young ones.

Aralyn remembered when she swore to never take the life of another person, whether human, Elf, or Dwarf. But Mal'ev wasn't a person. He was evil—a being who'd done horrific things. "Gillis, Mal'ev must be destroyed. And I must be the one to do it."

Gillis watched her with a critical gaze. "I want you to keep your head about you, no matter who or what we face next. You can't lose your head in battle."

Aralyn wasn't sure about that. She had heard of men going berserker, and filled with bloodlust, they fought with deadly determination. But she lowered her chin, and her eyes studied the forest floor. She faced him again and only hesitated a moment. "I must see him finished."

He glanced at the children's bodies. All thirteen of them. "Aye, I suppose you do."

A familiar voice caught their attention. "And all of Eyndor will stand with you."

Guronde stood before them, staring at the carnage. He bowed his head and leaned heavily on his staff. Aralyn could tell he was holding back some terrible rage.

"All these children ..." His head snapped in Aralyn's direction, his words precise and clear. "You must be ready to fight, child. I perceive Mal'ev's coming is imminent. This time, he shall have his forces, and you must prepare, Aralyn." His voice was calm, but Aralyn could sense anger and resolve as well as a deep concern for all of Eyndor. But it was as if he were giving her a special commission.

"You and Elnala will join the archers on the cliffs beyond the falls." His eyes dimmed, and he took note of Gillis. "You and I, Gillis, along with Orandon and the Elders, must finish working our strategy." His gaze flicked back and forth between them, seemingly at a loss for words. "But the two of you..." Guronde's voice faded.

"What is it?" Gillis took a step toward him. "Tell me what you're thinking."

"Ah, well. I seem to have lost my train of thought. But both of you must go, Gillis. Do what you can to prepare at once. We must be in position for the battle within two days. Right now, the parents of these poor children are coming."

Should she wait for them? Gillis shook his head when she asked and motioned her toward the track leading them home. They were almost out of earshot when a chilling sound met her ears—mothers and fathers crying out in grief for their dead children.

***

That evening the ever-present thoughts of the little ones weighed on Aralyn, but she had to practice. Orandon had not sent a message and invited her back to the Harp, so she found a place near her home. The forest seemed dead as she set up small targets to practice on. At some point, she felt her mark growing warm and turned to see Gillis watching her. She had missed a week of practice and knew her aim was not as sharp. Surely he noticed.

A mountain of emotions flooded her as he regarded her. The children, the dragon, Gillis himself—all were at the root of it, but she had to focus. Get through this.

"Gillis, he's coming, and I have to be ready." She retrieved an arrow from a target.

"You will be." He stood straighter, his gaze gentle on her.

"I panicked when Mal'ev came. I couldn't think of a single song except one I had used in Sathria, and then he attacked her—Jurnal—and I knew I had to sing, and so I did, and he couldn't stand it and—"

She was in Gillis' arms, wrapped in his warmth. How had that happened?

"Shh. Hush now." Gillis stroked her head. His other hand lay gently on her back.

Aralyn rested her ear against his chest, and his heartbeat was a steady, comforting rhythm.

"Let's do something." He hesitated.

"What?" Aralyn's head came up. Did he want more of last night? Now?

She fingered the neck of his tunic and ran her hand across his chest, giving him a coy smile.

He grabbed her hand. "Not that." He kissed her palm and placed his lips on her ear. "Later, I promise." He pulled back. "For now, I'd like to sing with you. Some of your songs. At least I can try."

Oh. "Fine. Yes. I'll teach you a few."

Gillis caught on to the simple tune of the stream and harmonized with her. The calming effect was powerful. They sang a few others, and Aralyn tried shooting again. It seemed easier now. She didn't feel the pressure to aim perfectly and to hit the targets every time. Aralyn wanted to keep practicing, but dusk was coming on.

In the near darkness, Gillis took her hand.

"I think we accomplished something worthwhile today," she said as they walked home.

His head dipped toward hers. "You do?"

"Yes, Gillis. We can sing together, and"—Aralyn cleared her throat. "I think I ... well, I know I feel better about my shooting when you sing."

"Ah. Glad I can help."

That was good. Maybe their new relationship would somehow help them when they fought together.

An interesting thought.

And Gillis seemed ready to put aside his feelings about the talent he possessed—the one that reminded him of the mage who had killed Laella. So he would be ready. And then she and Gillis and the Elven forces would drive evil from this land.

Chapter 28

Old maps and ancient tomes filled Guronde's study. The smell of aging paper reached Gillis' nose, and he sneezed. Gillis, Lemmon, and Orandon were meeting with Guronde, along with the other seven Elders and four Rangers.

The aged Elder unfolded one of the newer maps—a map of Eyndor and its surroundings. There were marks all over it, and they weren't only of mountains and streams and lakes. No, these were moving, moving toward Eyndor. He waited for Guronde to explain what it meant.

Guronde glanced at Gillis and turned his gaze to the others. He tapped on the map. "These lines and dots that are moving, as you may have surmised, are enemies. Each line is a detail of seven or more. Each dot is an individual. There are others, if you look closely, that represent mages. This detail—notice the mage symbols surrounding it."

A Ranger stepped forward. "That is Mal'ev's detail. We saw them at one point as we were scouting. They were on the move."

Guronde nodded. "That is your aim then—to eliminate his detail. Gillis, since you've been working with the archer-guards, I think you should lead a force here." Orandon tapped a finger on a cliff to the south of where they suspected the attack would come. "Judging by the way they are traveling, we suspect Mal'ev will make his way to this position and observe the battle, much like the king he fancies himself to be. But his habit is to join in the battle once they have thinned the enemies down."

Orandon made a circle with his finger. "Take ten of the archer-guards. Place them in the trees, of course. They will be key to ambushing Mal'ev."

"You think we can? With only a force of ten?" Gillis asked.

Orandon spoke this time. "One of our mages will be with them, so that's eleven. Add to that Lemmon, you, and I on the ground."

"And the mage you have is quite talented." Guronde tapped the tip of his staff with his fingers. The room grew brighter.

"Fourteen of us against Mal'ev and whatever forces he has." Gillis shook his head. "I know the archer-guards can move with barely a sound. That will help us with the element of surprise. But couldn't we take at least a few more? And more mages?"

Guronde answered him. "We need most of the archers on the cliffs or the main battlefield. We need the mages in both places as well. The archer-guards also need to continue their job of—"

"Guarding. I know." Gillis ran a hand through his hair.

"But there will be at least one mage with the archer-guards," Orandon repeated.

He was troubled. Gillis noticed his eyes, normally full of humor, were flat, expressionless.

"I need to place Aralyn with the archers on top of the cliff. Here." Orandon pointed to a field almost bare of trees. "Elnala will be with her. They should be safe."

"You can't be concerned with her safety," Gillis said more harshly than he meant. "This is a battle. Perhaps a war. You can't show my wife any special favor."

Orandon nodded, and he spoke gently. "I only say this for what I feel will serve us best strategically. Aralyn is key to this battle, and her safety is important." Orandon bit his lip. "I suppose I also speak from a father's heart. Perhaps I show Elnala favor by placing your wife with my daughter."

Despite Orandon's assurance, it wasn't "safe" anywhere in the vicinity of battle, not with enemy mages nearby. *Safer*, yes, and he had to admit that Aralyn's chances of survival would be much better upon the cliffs.

A cold rush of air came over him, and the thought that he needed to be with her while they engaged the enemy barged into his mind and refused to leave. That couldn't be right. How could he possibly stay with her while he fought?

***

"I've never faced battle before," Aralyn murmured. "And it's coming." She and Elnala walked with some of the other archers and mages toward the cliffs where Orandon had assigned them to stand and fight.

Aralyn caught Elnala gazing over the grasses and ravines and the trees in the distance. For once, she was quiet.

Aralyn felt her mark pulsing, and she halted. "Elnala, Gillis is preparing to fight. He's leaving for battle right now."

"You know this? How?"

"My mark. It's as if it's reaching for him. He is moving away from me, and I need to go with him." Aralyn attempted to quiet herself as a few archers turned to stare.

"Don't panic, Aralyn. We have to get to the cliffs. If your pairing works the way I think it does, you will be able to find him."

"No, Elnala." Aralyn tried to stay quiet so the others wouldn't know what she planned. "I'm going to him. I need to be at his side. Come with me?"

Elnala frowned and then nodded her approval. Aralyn grabbed her hand, and they took off, sprinting toward Guronde's home. Aralyn knew she would find Gillis in that direction. But before they arrived, Aralyn heard voices floating above her.

Aralyn realized they had run under a walkway made of evenly spaced boards about ten feet off the ground. She heard men's footsteps upon it. Through the openings in the bridge-like structure, she made out three pairs of boots.

"... with you on that." That was Gillis' voice. She had found him.

"Aye, we'll track him down." So Orandon was going with him.

Aralyn's mark throbbed. All her senses keyed on Gillis.

Lemmon's voice—he was with them as well—but she could not make out his words.

Aralyn and Elnala followed from just underneath them, listening to their conversation.

The men came to a set of steps and descended from the walkway. Aralyn hung back. Gillis split off from Orandon and Lemmon and headed toward their home.

"Go after him, Aralyn. I'll follow my father," Elnala whispered.

Elnala had only moved a few steps when Orandon swung around. He caught Elnala by the arm. They exchanged words, but Aralyn had no time to listen. Aralyn waited as Gillis ascended the stairs to their home. He soon returned with his sword and sheath. More blades lined his belt.

"Aralyn, what are you doing here? Aren't you supposed to be—"

"I know where I am supposed to be, and that's with you."

"Orandon said you were to be with the archers on the cliffs, lass."

"We need to be together—you and I." Aralyn wasn't about to give in.

Gillis' brow furrowed. "Orandon and I are leading a small party on what may be an impossible confrontation. I want you to do as Orandon has told you."

Aralyn huffed. "Just go with the other archers, the mages, and fight them from high ground while you risk your neck on—what did you say—'an impossible confrontation'?"

Gillis' mouth drew into a thin line. "Yes. Do as planned, Aralyn. I want you with me, but it's already settled."

Lem approached and nodded at Aralyn. "Are you ready to go?" he asked Gillis.

"Aye, we're going on foot for now."

"I'm sure Guronde wants to make sure Mal'ev doesn't hear our approach."

"Mal'ev? You're going after Mal'ev?" Aralyn folded her arms.

Gillis closed his eyes and took a deep breath.

Lem's face was grim. "Yes, we go to find Mal'ev."

Aralyn looked from one man to the other. "Then I am most definitely coming. I have reason to want him dead, and our pairing demands I stand with you, Gillis."

Gillis grunted. "Fated to be together, eh?" He wasn't smiling.

"My husband, you know, I want to be with the party—whomever it may be—when we bring Mal'ev down."

Gillis glanced at Lem, who shrugged and gave a small smile. Gillis spoke more firmly this time. "If you come with us, you must kill on sight, if necessary. And it will be more personal and perhaps scarier than being atop a cliff with hundreds of other archers, never knowing who you've hit, never seeing their faces."

"Gillis, he killed those children. I saw *their* faces. Children I should have saved. But I couldn't. I could not save them." She stomped her foot. "Do you know what that's like?" At the look on Gillis' face, she regretted those words. He'd said that very thing about his first wife. *He couldn't get to her. He couldn't save her.*

"That's enough." The pain in his eyes rested on her. "And yes, I understand."

Lem stood by, biting his lip. Was he trying to keep from laughing at them as he had before? But no, his expression was one of uneasiness with more than a trace of sadness.

"All right. Orandon may not like it, but blast it, woman, you're with us!"

"Gillis!" Guronde approached them, pushing himself forward with his staff. "Aralyn ... ah, Aralyn, in the nick of time." He paused, breathing hard. "She needs to go with you, Gillis. I sensed it before and couldn't quite work it out. The two of you,"—he pointed at Aralyn and Gillis—"need to be together."

Aralyn bit her lip to keep from smiling while Gillis fumed.

"All right." Gillis strode off without a backward glance.

"Where will you be, Guronde?" Aralyn asked.

"Wherever I'm needed. Perhaps with the archers on the cliff, but more likely on the battlefield. It depends on where I sense the greatest need. Tell Gillis that Elnala will be with you also."

Yes, she knew that.

"Now go catch up with him," Guronde said, his eyes smiling.

Aralyn ran, and she was soon by Gillis' side, Lemmon with him. "Elnala is coming too," she announced.

Gillis came to a halt. "What? Oh no, Aralyn. Where is she?"

"I only know she followed Orandon," Aralyn said. "And Gillis, she *is* coming with us. Guronde—"

"Rotted maggots! What have the two of you been planning?"

"Nothing. I'm trying—"

"Never mind. We'll see about this." He broke into a trot. Aralyn and Lem followed.

Aralyn knew she would hear about her disobedience from Orandon. But even Orandon's ire would not dissuade her, and besides, Guronde's orders outweighed her trainer's.

"I visited with Monpomme," Lemmon said as he jogged alongside her. "You've been treating her well."

"We make good companions, Lem."

"Yes, you knew you would be a good fit." He chuckled. "I remember that."

Gillis glanced back at them, his brow furrowed.

"I miss her, to tell the truth," Lem said. "Didn't want to sell her, but I know she's in good hands."

"Thank you, Lem." It meant a lot to hear his confidence in her.

The path narrowed, and Gillis came to a halt. "All right. Orandon said he would meet us here." Gillis eyed Aralyn as if he were sizing her up for the first time. "You've got plenty of arrows?"

He should know better than to ask. "Yes. And they're sharpened."

They only had to wait a few moments for Orandon to appear. He didn't look happy. Elnala was with him, and she winked at Aralyn, glanced at her father, and gave a little eye roll. Yes, she'd received a few choice words from Orandon.

Orandon's eyebrows formed a deep furrow. He blinked at Aralyn and swung to his daughter. "You didn't tell me Aralyn was coming."

"Father, she has to."

"She has—" His gaze fell on Aralyn and Gillis as well. "Gillis, did you approve this?"

"No, I—"

"Guronde did." Aralyn took a step forward.

"Why would he change our plans, Aralyn? Tell me that," Orandon demanded.

"He didn't say why. But I know you were the one who determined Gillis and I were paired—that our talents work together. It only stands to reason we need to be together in battle."

Orandon answered, his voice low. "But we still don't know *how* your talents work together."

Aralyn, just as determined, answered, "Perhaps not, but I need to be with my husband."

Orandon clenched his jaw and swung to face Gillis. "Is this right?"

"Yes, Guronde did say that. I didn't want her to come either. Felt she should be with the archers, but if we are to rid ourselves of Mal'ev, perhaps she and I do need to be together. At least for now."

Orandon scratched his head. "You believe, Gillis, that it will make a life and death difference?"

He'd addressed Gillis only, and it irritated her.

Gillis hesitated for only a beat. "I do."

"Very well. We need to go then. But not you, Elnala."

"Father! I thought we settled this already." Elnala's eyes flashed. "I will not go to the cliffs!"

Aralyn had never seen her so defiant. She didn't want to barge in and tell Orandon that Guronde had said she was going, so she let Elnala handle it.

"Father. You need me ..." Her voice trailed off, and she faced Aralyn. Something shone in her eyes. Tears? Surely not.

Whatever it was—an emotion only Orandon could read or perhaps a thought Elnala projected—made Orandon relent. His face relaxed. "All right. But you are to do exactly as you are told."

"Yes, Father."

"Aralyn?" Orandon raised an eyebrow.

"Oh. Yes, of course."

"And, Aralyn, there is a time for anger in battle, but do not let it interfere with the decisions I make." Orandon shook his head as if to clear it. He laid out a faded map on the ground, and they gathered close. Figures moved upon it, some with odd symbols next to them.

"Mages." Orandon pointed to various symbols. "And here, this is where the Rangers saw him." Orandon was whispering now, and he pointed to a figure with a mage symbol beside it—a flame and three straight lines. "This map has proven wrong before, but it should be accurate for our purposes. We will need to keep quiet from here on out. We will soon be almost upon him."

The narrow dirt path soon ended, and Orandon stopped. He motioned them forward through thick undergrowth. Aralyn watched the branches above her, knowing there were archer-guards in them. She could make out a few but did a double-take when she caught sight of a familiar shape. She stopped in her tracks and narrowed her eyes. There! That silhouette. It couldn't be. The distinctly female warrior paused and pulled something from her pocket. Aralyn's heart sank. What was she doing here?

Terrwynn was joining them in battle.

Chapter 29

One of the archer-guards signaled Gillis from high in a tree and pointed. The guard flashed five fingers three times. Fifteen of them. The archer caught Gillis' attention and pointed at his own chest with fingers forming a triangle. Gehallions. All of them. Another series of gestures revealed there were seven high-ranking mages. The rest were melee fighters with swords, knives, and armor. Two stood on guard.

Did the enemy truly think they could stay hidden from the Elves in their land? And was Mal'ev with them? Elnala pointed her staff to the ground, and the grasses flattened themselves. Sticks moved out of the way. Orandon followed the trail Elnala created and moved deeper into the brush. He motioned for Aralyn, Gillis, and Lemmon to follow.

Gillis had never seen Mal'ev, but Aralyn should know him on sight. His mark tingled, grew into an almost burning sensation. He looked into the trees again. One of the archer-guards gestured to him. *I see Mal'ev.* He seemed sure of himself.

The brush was still thick and provided cover, but Gillis could make out the movement of individuals within the camp. They spoke in Gehallion, and Gillis didn't understand a word of it. Three of them drew in the dirt, their heads close together. He could tell by the markings on their faces that they were mages. Others in the camp sharpened weapons. He caught sight of the guards, eyes darting through the shrubs.

One man stood in the middle of the camp, staring out into the forest beyond them, his eyes flickering back and forth.

Aralyn gasped before he could silence her. *That's him,* she mouthed. Gillis sensed her fear. At the same time, her anger and grief formed a toxic stew of emotions that almost overwhelmed him. He could feel her emotions? He prayed for both of them to stay calm.

Mal'ev turned to a silver-haired boy, not past his first decade. The boy spoke to Mal'ev and pointed upward. Mal'ev's gaze went to the spot the younger man indicated.

They knew about the archer-guards.

Gillis and his forces had lost the element of surprise. But before Gillis could signal them, arrows rained upon the enemies. At least six of the enemy fell before the others realized what was happening. Shouts of alarm went up. Several mages were still standing, including Mal'ev. The familiar zing of the sword leaving its sheath, the weight of it in his hand, and his instinct for battle overcame Gillis' last fragments of fear. He and Orandon led the way as enemies readied to fight.

Aralyn sang, and arrows whizzed past him. Intense determination—hers—washed over Gillis, and his confidence welled. His sword slashed across the shoulder of an unsuspecting mage who had aimed his staff up at the trees. Gillis had his attention now and ran towards him with a low growl, drawing his blade back as he did. The mage, caught off guard, held on to his staff in a defensive position. Instead of bringing the blade down, Gillis delivered a punch to the mage's belly. Again surprised, the mage doubled over, and Gillis drove his sword down into the mage's neck.

Another mage saw his mate fall and turned an outstretched hand to Gillis. But Gillis already held his sword with both hands above his head. The weapon came down in a killing blow that cut into the new challenger's skull. A young woman pointed three fingers and a thumb toward him. Opened her mouth to cast a charm. Her fingers were gone as his sword sliced through them. Blood spattered both of them. The mage wobbled on her feet. Disbelief crossed her face. Gillis took advantage and slid the sword upward into the woman's ribs. She fell. Aralyn's voice sang out, clear and strong.

The mage with the archer-guards had four enemy mages bound with threads. Elnala finished off three of them with a swing of her staff, forcing water down their throats. She was about to dispatch the fourth one when Orandon shouted, "Keep him alive!"

Gillis took note of the bodies lying around him—fourteen of them. Aralyn had fallen, but he resisted the urge to run to her as another archer knelt by her side. Gillis was sure they had cut off the head of the coming attack.

A crackling hiss interrupted his thoughts. The fireball flew over his head, and Gillis swung to its source. Mal'ev stood before him. Alive. Gillis' sword hit air as a conjured wind threw him backward.

Mal'ev grinned, cocked his head, and waited for Gillis' next move. What was he playing at? An arrow flew. Pierced Mal'ev's ear. The tip came out at the base of his skull. Aralyn. She stood with confidence, her bow still raised, another arrow nocked, and yet another in her hand. Mal'ev fell, and Gillis caught the surprise and confusion on his face. She had done it. He had to be dead this time.

Gillis ran to Mal'ev to make sure. The enemy moaned. Even as blood and clear fluid flowed from his wound, his hands formed an invisible sphere.

Gillis realized too late what the mage was doing.

Even as his head fell back, fire flew from Mal'ev's fingertip toward Aralyn.

"No!" It was Lemmon. He leaped in front of the fireball. It landed on his chest. And Gillis watched in horror as it sank into his friend's body. The fire burned away clothes and skin and flesh. Lemmon screamed.

"Lem!" Aralyn cried, and they both ran to him.

No, this can't be. No, no, no.

Lem was quiet now, gasping for air. He stared at the blaze on his chest and managed a small whimper. He gave Gillis and Aralyn a look of despair. Gillis removed his cloak to smother the flames, but the fire had gone out. Mage fire burned hot and fast and seldom lasted long.

Aralyn's knees hit the ground, and she pulled Lemmon's head into her lap. Gillis turned back to Mal'ev, who lay unmoving on the ground. With one long stride, he stood over the enemy. Gillis drew his sword and thrust him through to be sure this wickedness would never return. The only survivor of this group was the one Orandon wanted alive.

Gillis went to Aralyn's side and knelt next to her. Lem's chest made an effort to move, and he opened his mouth to pull in air, a short gasp that Gillis knew would mark his final moments.

Lem somehow lifted his head and exhaled his last words. "I'll be all ri ..." The corners of his lips turned up. That blasted smile of his! A hint of secret joy. His head fell back onto Aralyn's lap. He was dead. All was quiet as if the birds and insects had silenced in respect of Lem's passing. A rabbit came into the camp and hopped to Lem's side. It placed its front paws on Lem's shoulder and sniffed at his cheek as if waiting for its friend to awaken. A Grimswal appeared. He rose on his back legs and laid something on Lem's chest. His pet, his belfluff.

Aralyn gasped, a hand over her mouth, stifling a sob.

Gillis stood as shock rippled through him. Lemmon had taken a fireball to save Aralyn. The archers gathered around Lemmon. They all ignored Mal'ev except for Aralyn. She lowered Lemmon's head to the ground, rose, and approached Mal'ev's body. Gillis took notice and followed. Regarding the dead man, Gillis, for the first time, got a good look at the face of pure evil.

"That's not him." Aralyn's voice fell like blades of ice.

Even as she said it, the face contorted, nose and chin drooping like melting candle wax. Both hands curled in toward his chest. The face of a woman—no, a girl—appeared. Attractive and young. Too young to die like this.

"Body magic," Elnala whispered from behind him. "Mal'ev probably forced someone—a daughter perhaps—to do his bidding. Women are expendable to him."

The mage Orandon had told Elnala to keep alive, chuckled. Threw his head back and laughed. "I thought ... he ... she—Mal'ev. Real Mal'ev." His speech was in broken Common. He laughed again, belly shaking. "A girl! Ha!"

Gillis drew his sword and stepped toward the man. Put the sword to the man's throat.

"Gillis," Orandon warned. "We may need him yet."

"Fine. I just want him to tell me where Mal'ev is."

"How I know, should I?" He shrugged.

"What's yer name?" Gillis demanded.

"Grendalentin." The man puffed out his chest as if the name had special meaning.

Gillis couldn't stand it. Grendalentin had watched his companions die, and the man's pride was intact. "Very well, *Gwendolyn*. I still think you know something."

The mage snarled, and Gillis pushed his sword against the man's throat, causing a trickle of blood to form.

"Of truth, I thought that him." He pointed at the body where Aralyn stood transfixed.

"I don't believe you." Gillis grabbed the man's hair and pulled his head back.

"How say it, do you? Go ahead?" Grendalentin jeered. "Kill me, and that is all you have." He raised an eyebrow with a smirk. "Unless one of dead people tell."

So he did know something. Gillis' sword went deeper, pressed against a small vein. Blood flowed more readily. Not in spurts, just steady enough to let the man know his life was in danger. Grendalentin lifted his chin and, with his hands still tied behind him, muttered curious words. A wave of soil and rock spewed from the ground, shooting toward Gillis and the others. A geo-mage. Cries behind him and the sound of bodies hitting the ground let Gillis know the mage had hit several targets.

"Stop!" Gillis held onto the mage's clump of hair despite the attack, his sword at Grendalentin's throat. He spat out dirt and mud. Rocks pelted his face. But he refused to let go. An arrow shot through the mass of earth, barely missing Gillis, and Grendalentin grunted. The pelting of rocks and soil stopped.

The arrow had hit Grendalentin's shoulder and gone through his back. Gillis' face was within inches of the mage's now. He made sure the mage had a good feel of his blade's edge. Grendalentin gasped, and his eyes grew wide.

"Listen, *Gwen*. I can get that arrow out. Or I can leave it in. Let infection take you. Do you know how unpleasant that is?"

For the first time, Grendalentin looked frightened. "All's well," he said. "After Mal'ev kill learning children, he went home, but came back and hid from even Elder eldest man—Guronde. He gone to battle, to high hill in battlefield."

Apparently, the mage valued his life more than his loyalty. Coward.

"Aralyn, you saw Mal'ev ride away? What was he on?"

"I don't know. The creature he rode was white and huge—many hands high, with at least ten legs, and someone was with him."

"Creature is trogash. Mal'ev with his son. They riding the trogash." Grendalentin supplied.

Gillis was familiar with the animals. Not only capable of carrying great numbers of people, but they were also incredibly fast for their size.

"He went to the 'high hill'?" Orandon straightened. "Somewhere on the cliffs, I assume," he said to Gillis. "That must be what he means."

"Aye. We need to go then. Get there before—"

"He get bowsinger and capture her alive." Grendalentin interrupted. His eyes rolled to the back of his head. He had passed out, but he still lived.

"We need to go to the cliffs where the other archers are—I'm sure that's where Mal'ev thinks I am," Aralyn said.

Orandon nodded in agreement. "For whatever twisted reason, he wants to capture you alive."

Mal'ev wanted to take Aralyn. She had told him before. Not fight her, but kidnap her. Gillis glanced at his wife, her face covered in smudges of dirt and a bruise forming below her right eye. Glad she wasn't hurt any worse, he turned to Orandon. "Let's go."

"Wait!" Grendalentin cried, awakening from his stupor. "You say you help me."

"Aye, we'll help you." Gillis unsheathed his sword and, in one swift motion, drove his blade into the man's chest.

Elnala gasped. Placed a hand over her mouth. Orandon stepped toward Gillis and stopped. Aralyn stared at him, wide-eyed.

Gillis' gaze went from Orandon to Elnala and landed on Aralyn, where it lingered. "I helped him—put him out of his misery."

***

Aralyn didn't know Gillis was capable of such things. But he was angry. His friend had just died.

Gillis met each of their stunned looks and shouted. "We need to go! Now."

Aralyn lifted her head. "What about Lemmon?"

"We'll have to come back for him," he said.

Gillis and Orandon took off at a jog, and Elnala and Aralyn followed. After running for what seemed like an hour, they stopped for a drink. A nearby stream glistened in the afternoon sun, winking at Aralyn in the brightness. Her gaze followed the diamond shapes across the water, where she could see the ground coming to an abrupt end. Beyond that—the sounds of battle.

"I can hear them dying." Elnala stared into the distance.

Before Aralyn could comment, an archer-guard dropped to the ground.

"Regna, how do you fare?" Orandon's voice filled with concern.

"We lost one of our archers. But we will grieve later. Placing a mage with us has proven useful. She has healing abilities."

"How are you on arrows?"

Regna's mouth curved upward in a weary smile. "We're fine."

Aralyn glanced into the thick boughs. Terrwynn crouched on a branch, balanced in perfection just as Aralyn had seen her do at home. But she had no weapon. No bow. No dagger or sword. Nothing that Aralyn could see. She had seen Terrwynn work with a wounded rabbit. She had to be the healing mage Regna spoke of. Why else would she have no weapon?

"I have looked upon the battle." Regna's voice was solemn now. "Aralyn, they need you on the cliffs. I am sorry for my mistake concerning Mal'ev's identity. I am not sure where he is now. Our mage tried to tell us we were wrong."

Aralyn took a deep breath. Held it for a count of two. Let it out slowly. Someone placed a hand on her back. Elnala stood next to her.

"We split up now?" Aralyn looked from Orandon to Gillis to Elnala.

"We want you and Elnala together on the cliffs." Orandon placed the tip of his bow on the ground. "Gillis and I are going to join the battle. We'll find you later."

Aralyn swallowed. "I want to go with you."

Gillis glanced at Orandon. "Not right now. Later."

"But how will I find you?"

"You'll find me," Gillis said. "Just as you did before."

"But I need you—"

"That's enough. Go with Elnala." Orandon stood next to his daughter, his eyes full. "You two stay together."

"We will, Papa." Elnala never called Orandon "Papa." She stepped into her father's embrace.

"My daughter. Be brave." Orandon released her, and his hand brushed her face.

Gillis gave Aralyn a brief nod. He didn't offer a hug. It was probably better. She didn't need the tears she was sure would follow.

Aralyn and Elnala took off toward the other archers and mages. She could feel Gillis' gaze upon her back as she moved farther away. Aralyn glanced over her shoulder. He was indeed following her with his eyes. He lifted his hand and then marched in the opposite direction. She kept running and leaped a small stream that ran to a waterfall. And another. The ground became soft mud. About a half mile away, the archers were fighting, sending rounds of arrows to the battlefield below. But Aralyn knew their numbers had decreased, and a burst of energy came over her.

There was no weariness from fighting, and Elnala looked as energetic as Aralyn felt, refreshed even. They had killed. It had indeed been close and more personal as Gillis had warned, but it would be easier to do so again. There were no ill effects as she'd had before, no nausea or sickness or guilt feelings. She sped up as the ground grew more even.

Aralyn stopped in her tracks. Bodies—too many of them—lay scattered and broken, most of them with bows still in their grip, as if they would get up and start fighting again. Others, obviously mages, held staves. Worse than the dead and the smell of waste and tainted water were the sights of scattered arms, legs, and feet. Limbs that should be attached to bodies.

Elnala touched her arm. "Let's go. We'll do what we can, Aralyn."

At the edge of the cliff, a line of archers and mages still fought, firing upon the enemy. Aralyn could tell they were growing weary. Only a few dozen still stood. Aralyn and Elnala sprinted toward them.

Even as she ran, Aralyn sang. Two of the archers looked over their shoulders, and their faces lit in surprise. "She's here!" one shouted.

The archers shot randomly, and Aralyn knew she had to do something.

She corralled two and immediately recognized them. "Jonla, Erin, have you recovered any arrows?"

They examined their quivers and looked at her guiltily.

"Go. Look for more arrows—in the ground and in the bodies of the dead. Retrieve them."

The battle below was a mixture of sounds—cries of terror, slashing blades, and the snap of spells flying.

Even still, from here she could see the expressions of determination. Flashes of light, trails of flame sprouted from fingers.

And Gillis was there. Somewhere below her, nearby. Her mark felt alive. She couldn't stop a grim smile from forming.

The archers lined up again under Aralyn's command. Distinct lines of fighting had re-formed below as well. Marked chests, shiny with oil and sweat, told her who the enemy was. She spotted the gray cloaks of Montravian mages. Aralyn pointed them out to the archers. They knew. They had fought them most of the day. Instead of shooting as one, they would have to pick the enemy off individually. She gave the order to fire at will. To her delight, enemy mages and melee fighters below fell from their efforts.

Elnala seemed to know exactly where to aim her staff, protecting Elves with walls of water and drowning enemies.

Aralyn worked with different songs while shooting. To her surprise, Shenral arrived amid the battle, offering aid to the injured, bringing water, and directing a detail to move dead and injured bodies.

Something on the battlefield changed. It grew quiet as bodies fell. Too quiet. A line of enemy mages, at least one hundred, in grayish cloaks, focused on her archers and the mages around her. Their magic wasn't fire or water or earth but a series of threads that reached easily to the tops of the cliff. Her archers struggled against the constraints wrapping around them. Screams arose from mouths as the strings landed on faces and bodies. Some of the wires shone as copper, and others were dull as rusted iron. They twisted into barbs and embedded themselves in bodies. The screams became a wall of pain and turned into convulsions—archers and mages alike, but somehow she and Elnala stood unharmed. All around them, bodies fell. The whole scene became surreal, and Aralyn had no idea what to do next.

Mal'ev was below them somewhere. Yes, his mind was reaching out to hers, and she found him. His eyes glittered with desire, a sneer upon his face.

Behind her, a streak of red and gray formed, and Guronde stood with them, staff in hand. His powerful voice rang over the battlefield as the threads continued to fly.

"No!" Elnala cried. Then louder. "No! Guronde! No!"

Aralyn caught the full force of Elnala's scream as threads tore into her friend's arm. But she remained standing.

"I won't fail you, Aralyn."

The Elder mage glanced at Elnala, his face grave. He shouted again. Made broad motions with his staff over the battle below. The wiry threads stretched, snapped, and flew to their owners. Aralyn watched the enemies fall. Glad they suffered, dying in agony. But the wires still clung to their archers.

"We must help them, Elnala—before it returns." Guronde motioned to Elnala and the archers who still stood. Elnala and Guronde spoke incantations over those who were down. They drew the wiry threads from their bodies. Many of them writhed and screamed as the threads withdrew. Though covered in blood, with help from Elnala and Guronde, they were able to rise.

Aralyn looked over the battlefield. The chaos had returned.

"We must leave!" Guronde shouted.

Elnala grabbed Aralyn and strapped her staff on, grabbing another archer with her other hand.

Aralyn realized something was wrong. Very wrong. The words Guronde had spoken continued to echo through the plains, grew louder, and screamed through the air. They were coming back toward the cliff. Aralyn gasped at the force as they struggled to run. The echo hit, the entire cliff shook, and Aralyn's feet slipped. The soil grew hot even through her boots, and the ground crumbled and fell away. Steam rose and clouded her vision. Her lungs burned with the heat.

"He had to stop them, Guronde did. He had to stop the thread mages." Elnala shouted to Aralyn. "But this is the result."

Aralyn glanced behind her as the edge of the cliff came nearer her feet. The roar of an avalanche filled her ears. Aralyn had to move. More steam arose. Pressure built beneath her, and Aralyn knew what was coming. A geyser exploded, pushing rock and mud toward them. The ground continued to crumble. Archers and mages disappeared into the mass of dirt and stone as they fell to the field below.

Mud, hot mud scorched her, and she joined those who were tumbling down the face of the cliff. Dirt and rock and bodies pummeled her. The roar of boulders crashed around her. Smells of freshly turned soil, layered with death and blood, caught in her nostrils and on her tongue. Aralyn's jaw slammed together. Something hard and unyielding hit the back of her head. Her vision turned an odd shade of green, filled with stars.

Aralyn woke to wet grass against her cheek. A mist was falling, and she wiped at her face. Struggling to her feet, she took inventory of herself.

Her head pounded fiercely. And her ears rang. Throat parched, lips cracked. No waterskin. One boot was missing, and her toes were bloodied. Thick smoke surrounded her, and a horrible stench hung in the air. Aralyn stepped forward, testing her weight on each leg. One leg almost gave way. She grunted and stumbled, but still clutched her bow. Her quiver was on her back, and a few arrows remained. Amazing that she still had even that.

And where was the enemy? Had their forces been crushed by the falling cliff? Surely some still lurked nearby.

"Elnala." Aralyn spotted her friend sitting on the ground. She hobbled to the girl, the pain in her leg reminding her she couldn't run. Elnala's clothes were soaked in blood. Then Aralyn saw Elnala's arm—from the elbow down, it was gone. A steady stream of blood poured from the wound.

Aralyn removed her cloak and wrapped it around Elnala, ordered the girl to lie back, and knelt beside her. Aralyn pulled long strips of cloth from a pocket, tied one of them midway between Elnala's shoulder and elbow.

"My arm, Aralyn. There's something wrong with it." Elnala struggled to sit up.

"I know, I know."

"That's so tight." Elnala looked at her with huge eyes. "I know what's wrong." Her eyes rolled upward and closed for a moment. "I think ... my ... ugh! Maybe you can find it ..." Her voice faded.

"Stay with me."

Elnala's face grew whiter. Aralyn tore her skirt into wide strips, folded each, and pressed them against the wound. She added more. Eventually, the blood stopped soaking through. She whispered the song of the brook, keeping pressure on the wound. Elnala's face relaxed, and a smidgeon of color returned.

"Enemies," Elnala warned.

Yes, Aralyn needed to be quiet until she got her bearings.

Mal'ev's voice probed her mind. *Prepare to face me, Aralyn. I am coming.*

Chapter 30

No, she wasn't ready. All her training from both Orandon and Re'ah fled. The wall she had so carefully built with the help of the dragon stone sputtered and broke into pieces. She no longer had the dragon stone, and it would not help her now.

A familiar, unexpected voice spoke in the semidarkness.

"I will focus on healing Elnala." Terrwynn was here.

This was not the time for a greeting, so Aralyn stood. She would try to keep them in sight. Lifting one foot from the muddy ground, she glanced back. Terrwynn had Elnala sitting up again as she spoke healing words over Elnala.

A flash of orange light drew her attention, and she froze. Was that Mal'ev? She held her bow firmly in one hand and three arrows in the other. A picture of the children he had killed flashed before her. Her powers would be no match for his, but somehow she would defeat him.

Her ears rang in the silence. And that was when the attack came. In much the same way he had attacked before. A whisper set in a lyrical tone.

Aralyn.

With her name came a series of thoughts and feelings of horror, and her memories twisted again. Aralyn wanted to shrink away from this invasion.

The attack began in earnest as Mal'ev's determined fingers probed her mind. And there were others. Voices, not as strong, whispered in the background. Aralyn grabbed her head, her already throbbing head. He wanted to make her see things and think things that weren't real or true and push Aralyn to her limits of self-control.

"Don't fight him. Let him in." It was Elnala, her voice clear and coherent.

"I can't. I cannot do that." Her voice shook in response.

"Listen to me. Let him in, and let his thoughts flow with yours."

Flow with hers? The idea was ludicrous. "There are too many!" And Aralyn continued to fight with all her mental energy.

Nothing changed. It did no good.

"*Stop* fighting him. Focus on Mal'ev. If you let him in, the other voices will leave."

All right. Her efforts weren't working, so why not? Aralyn took a shaky breath and relaxed. The shadowy fingers probed deeper, seeing her secrets, feeling her weaknesses, strengths, things that embarrassed her, things she was proud of. Love. Hate. Indifference. Fear. But the other voices were gone.

As Mal'ev's probing continued, more thoughts, longings, desires that couldn't be hers joined in. He was taking her. Taking her mind, her emotions, everything she was. Replacing them with what he wanted her to feel and remember and love and hate. Even her body responded to desires she had never felt before. She stared unfeeling at those Mal'ev had hurt and delighted in his power. Such a heady feeling—to possess this strength. Laughter at lives destroyed. She stared at the destruction at her feet. The blood on her hands from a throat she had slit. Just a stray dog. Nothing else. No, this couldn't be right. She couldn't let this go on. Had to make it stop. She shook her head, fighting him. But the pain became greater.

Elnala's voice again. "Let him in ..."

All right, I'll do things your way. She relaxed again, and the emotions he had stirred in her all merged with his. She could not see where his began and hers ended. He pressed in. And something changed, for she saw his memories and felt his fears. His emotions formed rapids thick and white.

Still, she did not back away, and Mal'ev's images rushed in. Hundreds of them. Like small, noisy children, clamoring for attention until they slowed and filtered down to one image, one story.

Two young boys played in the dirt, making roads for imaginary chariots and tiny toy soldiers. Innocent boys, acting like children as children should. The older of the two boys was Mal'ev. Mal'ev as a child. The younger was Bek, the man she had killed.

Two women, both power hungry, sat nearby, their heads together, a scheme brewing. One of them was the boys' mother. The other was Mal'ev's instructor—an enchantress who taught him in the ways of magic.

How she knew all this, Aralyn wasn't sure. Whether he intended for her to or not, she peered into Mal'ev's mind and could feel the innocence of youth, the innocence of both Mal'ev and Bek.

His mother and instructor desired to use Mal'ev and his talents, not only to line their pockets but to gain power over others. And to see that power grow.

The enchantress tapped her fingers against her chin and nodded to his mother. "I will have to train him daily, and you must make sure he is ready for me. Convince him that he must do exactly as I say. If he doesn't, make sure the consequences will be severe.

We will make people pay when they need us to heal, to build, or even to kill. Once they allow us to help, we can use your son's power to gain control of their minds—to convince them they will continue to need us. While he will only have power over one of the elements, perhaps two, I sense his potential. Whether he controls wind, fire, water, or terrain, he will, with the proper training, be a great mage if we do this right. You need me, and I need you for this to work."

The mother nodded, and a sickening smile crept over her face.

The two brothers laughed and wrestled each other, the older careful not to hurt the younger.

The memory faded, and Aralyn had a sense of days passing. The scene changed.

They were inside Mal'ev's home, the mother preparing a meal.

Mal'ev sat at a simple wooden table, his feet dangling. "Where is Bek, Mother?"

"Bek is gone." She exhaled and closed her eyes.

Mother was sad, Mal'ev was thinking, but not really. Just pretending. He waited, watching her. He grew impatient. "Where is he?"

"Sold to the slavers."

Mal'ev's eyes widened, and Aralyn could feel his horror. "Why? Mother, who did this?"

His mother smirked. "I did."

Mal'ev's face grew pale.

"Maybe you'll learn not to disobey me or your instructor."

Mal'ev jumped from his seat. No, she couldn't take Bek from him. She couldn't sell his brother! Mal'ev left the room, looked all through their house for Bek, called for him, yelled at the empty fields. He must *be here. He couldn't just disappear.*

Mal'ev ran back to his mother, breathing hard, a look of despair on his face. She continued to prepare their meal as if nothing had happened and hummed a cheerful melody.

And he hated her. No. He couldn't hate his mother. But he did.

"*Do you believe me now?*" *She didn't even glance at Mal'ev.* "*Perhaps you will learn to do as you are told.*"

"*I couldn't do what she asked. Not to Bek. She wanted me to—*"

"*I know what she wanted you to do. It would not have hurt him.*"

"*He's my brother! He's only six!*" *Sorrow ran through him. His rage became an unquenchable fire.*

"*It was only a test.*" *Mother glared at her son.*

Mal'ev glared back and tried to reach into her thoughts.

"*All right,*" *she admitted.* "*It wouldn't have hurt him badly. The wounds would have healed in time.*"

"*But he'd be scared, too. It would have made him cry.*" *Mal'ev held back his anger.*

"*A bit of tears never hurt anyone.*" *Mother pointed at his chair and motioned for him to sit.*

"*But what if I didn't do it right? What if he died?*"

His mother's calm stoked the flames of hatred.

"*Your instructor would not let him. You know that.*" *She spoke in that faux sweet tone she only used when tormenting him.*

The memory turned into pitch darkness, and the terror of a young boy enveloped her.

Mal'ev lay on the ground, curled in a ball as the enchantress enunciated a spell, or was it a curse? Mal'ev shuddered, helpless under her power. The enchantress restrained his wrists with thick bands of dark leather, and he felt a strange draining sensation. What was happening to him? She next placed a thin chain about his waist and a thicker chain on his left thigh and locked them in place. The enchantress continued to invoke her power over him. These restraints would keep him from using his talents outside the village. Mal'ev would continue to train, but the enchantress could now suppress his powers. If he wanted to use his powers at all, he would remain in this village under his mother's "care" with the enchantress keeping tabs.

They cannot keep me here forever, the young Mal'ev determined, his jaw set. These two women will not keep me prisoner. He rose, and the enchantress frowned, stopped mid-chant. Her look of surprise delighted him, and he smirked. Her hand swung across his face, but he barely felt it.

Now the enchantress shouted and attempted to push him back to the ground with her chants. But Mal'ev stood. She dropped her hands and narrowed her eyes.

"Very well, Mal'ev. Go ahead. Defy me. But I promise you will never see your brother after this day, and Bek will die on foreign soil."

Rage rose from the young Mal'ev.

Prophecy. Set in stone. Somehow, he would keep it from happening and avenge those who dared lay a hand on his brother.

Mal'ev's memory fled from her consciousness. Aralyn fell, landing on her backside, and pain shot up her spine.

Mal'ev's brother, Bek—his mother had sold him. Aralyn had killed him and thereby fulfilled the words of the enchantress. Yet despite that, Mal'ev didn't want Aralyn dead. Their thoughts still mingled, and Aralyn longed to delve deeper. The fierce love he'd had for Bek had been transferred to his sons, along with his hatred for women and for girls who would grow up to be women.

Mal'ev's daughters lay dying in pools of blood or left on the rocks, plucked apart by birds of prey. The frigid memory from Mal'ev's mind brought her chills. The fierce love for her sister drew a parallel to Mal'ev's love for his brother. That meant she and Mal'ev—Aralyn swallowed—had this in common. As well as rage against the harm done to them.

Elnala's voice was weak, but it rang in Aralyn's ears. "Now think of anything but him or the battle."

Right now, she would not listen to her friend. Mal'ev's mind fascinated her. She wanted to remain in his thoughts more than anything. Learn his secrets and how to torment him as he had done to her. But more than that, to explore the depths of his pain.

But instead, her own pain ravaged her. Her memories returned, memories she had thought were gone.

Father, lifting her in the air, whispered sweet words meant only for her. "My Aralyn."

She laughed as they mounted his sturdy charger. Aralyn held a small bow. He was going to teach her to shoot from horseback. The arrow flew, and the song came naturally. She hit the target and never missed another one.

Father. Drehensil. The connection they had. Drehensil returning without her father. The horror she'd felt. Friends dying around her. Mother and her fleeing, not just from the plagues, but because of the Council placing restraints on Mother, afraid of her, taking her magic, draining her. Aralyn, as a nanio, *confused by all of it.*

Aralyn, caught in this web, her memories mingling with Mal'ev's, realized that he was forcing Aralyn's own thoughts on her. She gasped for air, but the horror clung to her.

"You need to force his thoughts out, or he will own your mind." Elnala somehow understood Aralyn's temptation to continue her journey into Mal'ev's mind.

"Push the stream you made of his thoughts and yours out of your mind. Now, Aralyn. Now!"

Aralyn no longer resisted Elnala's words. It was all too much. She must find her way through the darkness cluttering her mind. She fought. Pushed the thoughts out of her mind. The fingerlike probing left. And ...

He was gone. But the memories, her own memories, were back, completing something within her. As horrific as they were, she held out her hands to them. They were part of her, part of who she was.

Then the quieter memories came as a gentle rain. *Receiving Monpomme as a gift. Her father showing her how to shoot from horseback. Mother's once-gentle hands. She and Terrwynn laughing together.*

"It worked, Elnala."

"Yes," Elnala answered. "But now he knows precisely where to find you."

He would come to her. She knew it. With her mind still drunk on discovering Mal'ev's past, she felt something other than hate. But the evil he had done wiped away any trace of compassion.

Without warning, Vandel flew before her. Where had she come from?

Her mark grew warm. Gillis must be nearby. She tried to call out, but her tongue lay in her mouth like a huge slug.

"Aletha is with me, Aralyn," Elnala managed to say.

Vandel placed her claws on Aralyn's bow and back-winged, pulling so fiercely she almost forced Aralyn to drop her weapon. She followed the dragon lizard. Vandel pulled her to a copse of trees where thick ferns and vines spread over the ground.

As she peered through the trees, silhouetted figures appeared, their faces covered by birdlike masks, beaks long and black, staves glowing with sigils. Enemies.

Only four of them, but most likely they were mages. Bright lights behind them flashed and burned into Aralyn's eyes. A song rose in her mind. She wanted to sing, but she choked. Mal'ev appeared. Standing with his mages.

Aralyn froze.

With Vandel's soft thrumming in her ear, Aralyn pushed away from the panic.

"Aralyn!" Mal'ev cried out. "You know, don't you? You saw my brother and me." His manner seemed courageous, but she sensed his fear. He had revealed a secret kept close to his heart for decades.

Aralyn still didn't know if he had shared this accidentally or if he had a purpose in revealing his thoughts to her. But it didn't matter. She stepped forward, away from the shelter of trees. She must face him.

The other mages closed in. They formed a line before her.

Mal'ev's memories were seared in her mind, fresh and looming before her, but she quelled the thoughts of his love for a brother. Mal'ev was the enemy.

The line of mages drew closer. Aralyn willed herself to breathe evenly. One of them in a green-hooded robe, threw his arms forward, and something like a thousand stings penetrated her forehead. A burning sensation came over her as sweat mixed with blood. Warm liquid trickled to her eyebrows and down her cheek.

Two of the mages were down. How? Without thinking, she had responded. Sung, aimed, and buried arrows in their chests.

"I want her alive." Mal'ev cursed and signaled the other two to stand down. He strode forward, a look of deadly resolve, muttering an incantation. Light shone on Mal'ev, as if he were an angel from the sky-haven. He stopped in his tracks about a bowshot away. Was he waiting for her to attack?

Aralyn didn't hesitate. She sang and released an arrow, aiming at Mal'ev's chest. It flew true. A second. A third. Felt right. Had to be right.

Mal'ev held one arrow in his hand. The other two landed in the tree behind him. He grinned. "Now I better understand your capabilities, or rather lack of them. How do you—an archer—plan to defeat me?"

She fought to keep her expression neutral. Show no fear or surprise. She was the bowsinger, a warrior of Eyndor. He had killed defenseless children. She would destroy him.

But the pain from her leg and the throbbing in her head grew. Blood dripped from her forehead, made rivulets down her cheeks. Her left eye blurred, and sweat rolled through her eyebrows and eyelashes. She might be weak and injured, but Mal'ev wanted her to live. That was *his* weakness.

She would deny him that. One of them would die today.

Chapter 31

"You're determined to fight me? Very well." Mal'ev gestured to the two remaining mages. Their staves tapped the ground. Threads flew from their hands, and a body appeared at their feet.

Terrwynn.

No. Please. Elyon. Once again, she was tempted to pray to the gods of the sky-haven but resisted. Terrwynn lay on the ground, silent, her eyes wide. The third mage grabbed her sister and laid her at Mal'ev's feet.

"Now what will you do, bowsinger? I can save her if you like. Or would you let her die?" His eyes narrowed. "I will find your swordsman, as well. You do not want him to die at my hand. It would prove most unpleasant. But one way or the other, I will take you, and I'd rather entice you to come than force you."

He had Terrwynn. He would kill Gillis, too. Her perspiration grew cold.

"Ah, you need a moment?" Mal'ev's chuckle grated on her. He placed his foot on Terrwynn's chest. He signaled the mages, and they backed away.

Mal'ev's threads flew toward Aralyn. She sang, and the threads fell, and her bow was at the ready, ready to kill. Another flash of light burned her eyes. She released an arrow. Couldn't tell if it hit him or not. Dark spots from the light played havoc with her vision.

Before she could aim again, Mal'ev lifted his arms, brought his staff to the ground, and tapped out a strange rhythm. The air stirred, a mild breeze. He pushed the staff toward her, and a wind landed on her chest, forcing her backward. She stumbled, and a sharp pain lanced through her. She released another arrow. Mal'ev caught it. And now her arrows were gone. He pushed a tremendous blast of air toward her. This time, Aralyn lost her balance and fell to the ground. She tried to push herself up, but for some reason, that proved impossible. A chilling realization came over her. Mal'ev was coming to her. She envisioned him standing over her, and with his powers in full effect, picking her off the ground and forcing her to go with him. Perhaps he would manage to wrap her in the threads this time with barbs piercing her. But she would fight. Mal'ev would have to kill her. This was it. This was her time to prove her strength and either die for Eyndor or defeat the force of evil. That is what she had come to the Elves for, but here she was on the ground, feeling helpless.

Strong arms grabbed her, and helplessness overcame her. The arms pulled her deeper into the trees and lifted her, setting her on her feet.

"I've got you, lass."

Gillis!

He had found her.

"Where is Mal'ev?" Aralyn gasped. She had lost all sense of direction, but the weakness in her limbs was abating.

"Quiet. He can't see us now." Gillis placed his back against hers.

"I'm out of arrows," she whispered as the familiar warmth from his mark ran through her.

Gillis nodded. "I hear you, but we can do this. Now sing!"

She didn't question him, and songs from the forest rushed through her. Gillis blended his voice with hers, and the forest, the trees, and the distant sound of battle quieted.

"You are both fools, Aralyn. Both you and your swordsman! My strength grows here, bowsinger, and your songs will not affect me."

His arrogance grated on Aralyn. He would see the combined power of her mark and Gillis'. He was approaching, his staff tapping that strange rhythm that vibrated through the ground.

But they continued to sing, and Mal'ev stopped in his tracks. Aralyn watched, and Mal'ev stumbled back. His staff flew from his hands. He was on the ground. Aralyn wanted to run toward the downed enemy, but Gillis grabbed her arm. "Hold, Aralyn. We don't even know if he's injured."

"Then we must finish him off while he is weakened," Aralyn insisted.

Gillis' look of doubt changed to acceptance. "All right, let's go."

They advanced toward him. Mal'ev was on his back, staring into nothing. Aralyn knelt, cautious, reached to check his breathing.

Mal'ev's eyes blinked, and Aralyn jumped back.

"Look out!" Gillis was pulling her away.

Mal'ev angled his staff towards them, and a gale of air whipped at them. Her heart sinking, Aralyn realized the mage's power was indeed much greater than the last time she had faced him. Another blast of air pushed her away from Gillis. Mal'ev was on his feet, aiming his staff at Gillis.

Her husband cried out as barbed threads wrapped around his gut and chest, his arms and legs. Her mark was alive with her husband's pain, allowing her to experience his agony. Gillis pulled at the threads, and a few barbs came loose. Blood flowed from the wounds. He moaned in pain. Gillis' eyes fixed on her, Aralyn read something she had never seen on Gillis' face—horror. She attempted to go to him, but the wind held her back.

"Aralyn, you are determined to fight me to the death, and I want you alive—but I also want you to come willingly. So let me make this plain. Your life for Terrwynn's. And to be generous, I will spare your husband's as well." He waited, his words piercing the air. "This should make things easier for you. All I ask is *you* in exchange for the lives of your sister and husband."

But what would happen to Eyndor if she left with him? "Why do you want me alive?"

"Ah, she is curious." Mal'ev grinned, the light in his eyes piercing her. "I want you to be mine. Not my mate—no, no," he said to her sick expression. "But my son's."

He had to be kidding.

"My sons need to become men," he declared. "With you, at least one of them will have strong, talented children. And assure themselves of heirs."

One of his sons, who could only be as evil as he. She was not going with him. He was asking her to give him the next generation in his line. She wanted to gag but somehow kept her expression neutral even as Gillis continued to cry out in pain.

"It won't be so bad. Think of it. You, Aralyn, living where no one can harm you. Never having to struggle for food. And one day soon you will return to be the ruler of Eyndor." His voice took on the innocence of a lullaby. "Terrwynn will be safe. Elven lands will be safe. The lands of Lahilla—safe as well. All I want"—his eyes traced over her body—"is you. Come with me to Gehallia. Choose from my sons, be bound—yes, I will allow you to marry—and you will reign with him."

The proposal, or rather proposition, while sickening, intrigued her. Trust him. Make the deal. His offer made sense. She could rule Eyndor. Yes, one of his sons would be by her side. But as the bowsinger, she could counter whatever evil he might do. A living Eyndor was better than one overrun by death. Terrwynn could go back to Sathria in peace. And Gillis would live.

Not as hers, but at least alive. But if she made the agreement and left to be bound with one of his sons, Eyndor's borders would fall to him. To Mal'ev. But she, as their queen ... Confusion rocked her.

"How do you plan to keep other enemies away?"

"You underestimate me. My powers, as you have seen, grow stronger. My forces stand loyal with me. We will keep Eyndor alive and destroy all other enemies who attempt to enter." He paced before her. "Decide, Aralyn. Surrender your weapons." He licked his lips. "Or continue to fight. And they—" He pointed to Terrwynn and Gillis—"will be destroyed. Before your very eyes."

She couldn't let anything happen to Terrwynn. Not again. Her arms heavy, her gaze fell to her sister. "You'll let her go home?"

"Why, of course."

Mal'ev answered too quickly. Aralyn narrowed her eyes.

He must have seen her suspicion. "Do not worry. Your sister will be fine with the right healing."

Perspiration and blood still slid down Aralyn's face. The pain in her head grew to a new level. She glanced toward Gillis. He had stopped struggling. He was losing consciousness. Aralyn gestured toward him, unable to speak.

"Yes, yes, he will be fine as well." Mal'ev pronounced the words as if Gillis' suffering meant nothing.

She would make the deal—even if it meant mating with this man's son. Just as she thought it, another way cleared in her mind—snatch Terrwynn from the ground before Mal'ev had a chance to react. Forgetting the pain in her leg and her head, she lunged toward Terrwynn. Mal'ev put a hand up. Formed a wall of wind that turned to forged steel. Aralyn fell against it with a force that knocked the air from her lungs. She inhaled, only to realize her airway had closed.

Aralyn heard the barely controlled rage as Mal'ev spoke. "You must decide if you will give up your swordsman and your sister. It will only get worse." He lifted his hand to the mages. They threw more threads toward Gillis.

Aralyn managed to fill her lungs.

Gillis awoke, his body snapped into an awkward position, and he floated above the ground. His arms and legs spread apart as the thread mages pulled in opposite directions. Mal'ev's foot pressed down on Terrwynn's chest again, and Terrwynn moaned.

At least she was not fully conscious, but Gillis' screams were like none she had heard before. Terrwynn's chest still moved, but her coloring was wrong.

"All right, Mal'ev." Aralyn wiped uselessly at her bloody face with an equally bloody sleeve. She walked toward the mage, her chin lifted. She kept her distance. She would not lay her weapons at his feet. That might look as though she were pledging fealty to him. But wasn't this the same? She laid her bow down about ten paces from him. Everything in her cried out *no!* But she let go and placed the quiver on the ground as well.

"The knife too." He gestured to her waist.

The scabbard and knife came off.

A loud snap, and Gillis fell to the ground. He moaned once more, and his body jerked and twisted. He was not all right. How could she leave him like this and go with Mal'ev? Aletha was still with Elnala, and the dragon lizard could surely help Gillis. Or one of the healers would arrive as the battle ended.

Aralyn would go with Mal'ev. Her job here was over. She swallowed and took a step toward her enemy.

"Very good, Aralyn. Keep coming." He set his staff aside, pointed three fingers at Terrwynn, and muttered words Aralyn did not understand. With a gasp, Terrwynn awoke. She took in several deep breaths. The threads dropped from her, and the bleeding stopped. Mal'ev yanked the now fully conscious Terrwynn to her feet and kept a tight grip on her upper arm. Terrwynn didn't struggle but stood in a daze, her eyes unfocused.

"Let her go," Aralyn commanded.

"You must come to me willingly." He pointed the same three fingers at her injured leg, and she felt strength surge through it. The pain in her head was gone, too. And of all things, her nose began to run.

"See? You can trust me, Aralyn. Nothing to fear."

Aralyn placed her feet on the soggy ground, one after the other, feeling like a tortoise moving through sludge. She stood before Mal'ev and met his gaze. "I'm here. Now let her go."

He shoved Terrwynn to the ground where she did not move, and grabbed Aralyn around the waist. Pulled her close. "No." His mouth next to her ear. That one word fell like a blade cutting her heart. "I am keeping her to make sure you behave. Anytime you try to defy me, she suffers, and you will hear her cries for mercy." He handed Terrwynn off to one of the surviving mages.

Mal'ev had lied. Of course, he had. She knew better than to expect anything less. Disgust with herself overcame her. But she would do as Mal'ev wanted if it meant Terrwynn's safety. Yet where would the lies end? She had to take that chance. Do whatever she must. Even producing an heir with his son. Aralyn forced the bile back down her throat and gave herself to an enemy, unashamed.

***

Gillis lay on the ground as the cold air chilled him. Through muddled vision, he saw Aralyn lay her weapons down and trudge toward Mal'ev, favoring her right leg. What was she doing? Off in the distance, Elnala attempted to stand, Aletha still fluttering around her.

Gillis' twitching stopped. The threads were gone, and the pain diminished, but it was not through with him. He groaned and managed to push himself from the ground, but only made it to his knees. Vandel came to his side, clicking her teeth together, head bobbing.

What are you doing, little dragon?

Vandel had a stick in her mouth. The dragon lizard struck her teeth against it, and sparks flew. Not a stick, but flint? Gillis blinked, and a small flame came from her mouth. Vandel produced fire.

I am going to fight. Vandel lifted her head.

She was going to fight? Gillis raised an eyebrow, doubtful. He had to get Aralyn, but perhaps, just perhaps, Vandel could help him.

He struggled to stand and made it to his feet before his knees gave way. The pain in his shoulders and hips shot through him, but his mind fixed on Mal'ev and Aralyn. She had gone to him. Why? Vandel flew up into the trees, and Gillis crept through the thick night. His injuries forced him to stop. He grabbed a tree limb. Steadied himself. He was within twenty or so feet of Aralyn, Mal'ev still unaware of him

"Aralyn." Mal'ev had his staff in one hand, and with the other, he ran his hand through her hair. "You will indeed produce beautiful grandchildren. And who knows? Perhaps another son for *me.*"

Aralyn bent over at this, and Gillis heard her dry heaving. Mal'ev laughed.

Gillis kept moving. Fifteen feet. Ten. He wondered how close they had to be for their pairing to work. Aralyn stood, wiping her mouth. Gillis caught her eye and mouthed one word. *Sing.*

Aralyn gave him a bare nod. It was a song of sky and mountain, of flame and trees, sap flowing and popping. Gillis joined in, harmonizing as they had before. The forest grew silent once more. Maybe he was wrong, but even the smoke seemed to shrink away from them, and fires no longer crackled.

"No! Not this time. It will not work. You hear me?" Mal'ev dropped his staff, held on to her with one arm, and placed a hand over her mouth. But she sang.

"This nonsense you call a battle cry ..." He snatched his hand from Aralyn's mouth as though it had been burned. He grabbed his staff and pressed it into the ground. The engraved sigils lit like golden fires.

One of the remaining mages appeared, and the sigils on her staff glowed with blue, red, and brilliant white light. Fires flared out from each one and joined together, sigil to sigil.

The fires streamed to the ground and toward Gillis. He could only watch as a flame branched off and headed toward Aralyn.

No, Aralyn could not die like this. Gillis ran to her side. He must protect her. He refused to fail his wife this time. His first instinct was to wrap his arms around her and huddle over her, but instead, he placed his back against hers. The flames swarmed toward Aralyn and him, and Gillis prepared himself for the heat, the pain he would surely feel. But it never came. The fires arched over them and plunged into darkness.

He and Aralyn sang.

Mal'ev moaned, threw his head back, sweat covering his face. His staff shook in his hand, as did the staff of the female mage. Their eyes grew wide with fear, but flames still spewed and sputtered from the sigils. As both Gillis and Aralyn sang through the dying flames, Mal'ev's voice fell to a hush. The light of the sigils reduced to a glow. Two weary mages still stood, gazes fixed on Gillis and Aralyn, eyes wide.

Vandel appeared, her head swollen and eyes bulging. She breathed out. A stream of fire, much too big for her dragon lizard body, belched toward the mages. Mal'ev dove. Vandel's flame caught on the enemy's robe. The female mage plunged into the darkness, screaming in pain as the flames followed her.

"I will kill your sister!" Mal'ev screamed as he beat the flames on his clothes.

The fire might eventually go out, Gillis realized, but no magic would quench the fire of a dragon lizard. In the light of the flame, Aralyn found her bow. Gillis reached out, and she pressed her back against his once more.

Mal'ev pulled off his robes and stood, the fire still smoldering behind him. One of the remaining mages appeared, pulled Terrwynn to her feet, and placed a scimitar against Terrwynn's neck. It was time to end this.

A mist fell, and its moisture formed a film on Gillis. A blanket of warm water covered him. Strange. He could no longer force a song from his throat, and the water on his body migrated to his hands. Ice crystals formed on his palm and fingertips. He examined them curiously. Made a decision and flung the crystals toward Mal'ev. More pain in his arm, but he ignored it as the crystals grew in the air. They curved into sickles, flew into Mal'ev's body, and pinned him to the ground.

Mal'ev lay still, and Aralyn pulled away from Gillis. "I'm going to finish him off this time." She grabbed an arrow she found lodged in the ground. The arrow flew, but Gillis didn't see where it landed as a flash of light crossed its path.

Gillis hadn't counted on the female mage. Shining and golden, a thin sliver of metal flew from almost invisible hands and buried itself in Aralyn's side. She went down. He stepped into the mage's path as she made for Mal'ev. Gillis swung his blade, but she dodged it.

He could see Mal'ev clearly now. The sickles had sliced through his arms and legs, blood everywhere. Aralyn's arrow had landed in his chest, but he still breathed.

Gillis knelt next to Aralyn and examined her wound. He looked for something to use as a bandage and found some spider webs in a tree. As he applied them, he heard the downstroke of huge wings and a strong breeze to accompany it.

Aralyn turned her gaze upward. She coughed, grabbing his tunic. "Drehensil. He came. We're outside the borders, so it's good, right?"

Gillis' brow furrowed, and he glanced up. He had a bad feeling about this. He stood to determine Drehensil's intentions but kept an eye on Aralyn.

"Aralyn." Mal'ev's voice whispered, and Gillis heard the familiar death rattle. He would be dead within the hour. "It would have been a good life for you." He smiled and muttered an incantation. They were his last words.

Aralyn sat up, her eyes wide. "The pain's gone, Gillis. And the bleeding stopped."

Mal'ev had whispered a cure. He had healed her without reason.

Drehensil landed, standing before them, his wings lifted. His commanding presence made Gillis' heart beat in an unsteady rhythm. He could sense Drehensil's thoughts, but when he tried to communicate with the dragon, his words came back to him as a canyon's lonely echo.

Chapter 32

Aralyn had to get to her sister. The one remaining mage—she had to be with him. Through the mist, Terrwynn was running toward the dragon, the Gehallion mage with her. What were they doing? And why was Drehensil waiting for them? And not speaking to her?

"Dre?" Aralyn had to reach him. She got no answer.

With Terrwynn close enough to touch, Aralyn grabbed her sister's arm. Terrwynn swung around, a determined expression on her face. The mage loomed behind Terrwynn, staff lifted, his other hand in a threatening gesture. Terrwynn motioned to him, and he lowered his arms.

Terrwynn had authority over this mage?

"Aralyn." Terrwynn's voice was clear, unaffected by smoke or mist. "I must go."

The mage climbed onto Drehensil's back and reached a hand out to Terrwynn.

"No, Terrwynn. You don't."

Aralyn could feel the mage's eyes upon her. Terrwynn pulled back on the arm Aralyn held, but Aralyn's grip grew tighter.

"Perhaps you're right, but I have obligations, and I choose to fulfill them."

"What? No." Terrwynn believed she owed the enemy? Had obligations to them? Her sister had gained her voice but had lost her rationality. *Please come to your senses!*

"I'm coming with you." A fire in her gut told Aralyn she had to.

"No. You cannot." Terrwynn held up her hand, palm towards her sister.

Aralyn was aware of Gillis behind her, keeping his distance. She turned to him. "Gillis. Please ..."

Gillis took a step toward her and stopped, compassion in his eyes. Aralyn swung back to her sister. Something was wrong. Terrwynn's eyes stared into the distance, and Aralyn followed her gaze. Terrwynn was gazing at Eyndor and its borders. Then her eyes flicked to Gillis.

Aralyn understood the message that Terrwynn was trying to communicate. She must stay. For Eyndor and for Gillis. Her eyes filled. "Terrwynn?"

"You must let me go, my sister. Please," Terrwynn lifted her chin, a commanding look on her face, the sparks of determination in her eyes. "You know I will always love you."

Aralyn wavered. She could force this to go her way and leave with Terrwynn, but Terrwyn didn't want that. It really wasn't her decision to make, but it felt like it was. Just where did her loyalties ly? Elven lands and Gillis or her sister. Aralyn swallowed, a huge lump choking her. She backed away. Away from Terrwynn—the one she was determined always to protect.

Drehensil rose and flew to the heavens, her beloved sister, and an enemy mage securely on his back.

***

As grief overcame her, Aralyn's head spun. But she would have to process this later. Try to make some sense of it. Now was not the time. She raised her head and turned her eyes back to Elven lands. Her husband waited. She ran to him.

Gillis wrapped his arms around her in a brief hug, then pulled quickly away. "Mal'ev is dead, Aralyn. That's what matters."

"I know." It was time to move on to other things. Did he understand what she had just been through? "Where is Elnala?"

"We'll check on her." His voice was weak, but he invited her to lean on him.

Aralyn could tell he had a difficult time walking. Mal'ev had not completely healed him.

The adrenaline rush slowed, and her hands shook. Tears blurred her vision, threatening to spill over. Terrwynn had left. Lem was dead.

"Elnala!" Aralyn cried out. Elnala was lying down again, either sleeping or unconscious, with both Vandel and Aletha by her side.

Aralyn crouched by Elnala and checked her breathing. Great relief ran through her as she watched Elnala's chest rise and fall. And her arm. Where was it? They had to find it. But if it was here, it was buried in the muck and blood.

"Let me, lass. I'll take her." A firm hand on her arm told Aralyn that Gillis would not take no for an answer.

She ran ahead even as her bare foot and remaining boot sloshed through red puddles. A chill shot through her. She could only guess at the number who had spilled blood here.

Aralyn slowed and pressed a hand to her side.

"You all right?" Gillis caught up with her.

Aralyn nodded and kept walking. But pain burned her side—the same place where the blade had struck. Bodies lay all around them. Were any still alive? Gillis, trudging beside her, told her to keep going. As if he knew what she was thinking, he said, "We'll have to come back for them."

A figure dropped to the forest floor before them, and Aralyn raised her bow, forgetting her arrows were gone. It was one of the archer-guards.

"Regna. You're alive." Gillis croaked.

Aralyn exhaled with relief, her arms dropping.

"Yes. We've received messages from Orandon, Guronde, and the Rangers. All of them confirm that the enemy has fled—what was left of them." He glanced at Elnala and gasped. "Elnala ..." His voice caught in his throat.

"She's alive," Gillis said. "But injured severely."

They moved forward again.

"Her arm." Regna's concern was obvious.

"Yes, tended to, but she lost a lot of blood."

"The Age is almost here." Aralyn was gasping now as she held her side. "We must get to the borders."

The ruffle birds called out, drawing close. Her first instinct was to run. She remembered how Gillis had suffered under their attack. Then the pain in her side intensified. There would be no running.

Healers were on the field, coming to the aid of the wounded, bandaging, comforting, or offering a shoulder to lean on as they led them to safety. Carriages arrived, and Elves began to carry off the dead and injured. That was when she heard wings beating in her ears. The ruffle birds were close. Too close.

Vandel fluttered in her face. *"You are hurt."*

Aralyn could hear the dragon lizard speaking, but she felt no excitement. The fact barely registered.

"I'm..." *Fine,* Aralyn wanted to say, but the truth was the pain in her side was growing.

Vandel rose above Aralyn's head. *"I cannot help you with the pain. But I will spot enemies for you."*

"Yes. Good." Aralyn had to stop and grab her knees as Gillis kept walking. "But I think they are gone."

"I want to fight some more. I almost killed that man." As if to demonstrate, the dragon lizard's chest expanded, and she exhaled. A flame shot from her mouth, more extensive than before, and Aralyn felt the heat from it. This time, Vandel flipped backward and landed at Aralyn's feet. She shook her head and righted herself. Aletha landed next to Vandel and made a long series of clicking noises. Aralyn swore she was laughing.

"Where is Elouard?" Aralyn had not seen him at all this day.

"Gone. I cannot hear him." Vandel fluttered in front of Aralyn again.

"I cannot either," Aletha added.

Two figures came running toward them. Aralyn did not even think of her bow.

Re'ah called out, and Aralyn wondered where he had been. With the healers? Or had he been fighting? Guronde was at his side.

"I'll take her, Gillis." Re'ah reached for Elnala.

He was just in time. Gillis' arms gave out, and he almost dropped her.

"Be careful with her, Re'ah," Aralyn said. She glanced at Re'ah and read the concern on his face. The cut on Aralyn's head was oozing again.

"I'm all right."

Re'ah's face relaxed. "Do you think you can run now?" He nodded toward the borders. Aralyn looked at her feet. Could she run? She didn't know. But the ground was drier here. She could try. The problem was that her movements were slowing. The ground seemed to tilt, causing her to lean sideways. She was aware of Gillis behind her, his voice echoing. She swiveled around to see him more clearly. It didn't help. He grew fuzzy, face distorted. What had happened to him? Or was it her? She swayed on her feet.

"Something is wrong with you. I should have seen this." Aletha's voice filled Aralyn's head, causing it to pound.

Gillis stopped, his eyebrows drawn together as he studied Aralyn.

"I'm fine." But her voice was distant and hollow. If she—the bowsinger—weren't inside the borders in time, all this would be for naught, wouldn't it? The knowledge was a faint glimmer.

Lightning streaked across the sky. Violent. Furious. The Age of Thunder. Aralyn ticked off the signs on her mental list. The mist bows—gone. Lightning. Ruffle birds.

Sparks from the lightning clung to the trees. It lit the way home, yet at the same time promised death to Elven lands. Wasn't that what her mother had said? *Nothing but death there.*

The temperature rose, and sweat clung to her. The next minute, it plummeted and chilled Aralyn to the bone. That was the sign she'd forgotten—the air becoming unstable. Her breath crackled as moisture turned to ice. Ruffle birds dropped lower and circled. They were larger now, and brilliant rainbows covered them.

"The Age of Thunder. It is here." Guronde was beside them, pushing himself forward with his staff.

No. They had to reach the borders. Aralyn stumbled. Took two steps. Four. Six. Just a few more. Her legs gave out, and she fell toward the ground. It met her with a loud smack.

Gillis grabbed her. "Can you stand?"

"Yes, I'm sure I can."

Did it even matter? It was too late. The Age of Thunder had arrived. They were less than forty paces from her homeland. She would not give up. Her focus on Guronde, her voice echoed and faded as she spoke. "I've failed. And the borders will crumble, will they not?"

"Aralyn." Guronde's grip on his staff loosened, and he smiled. Amid the death and carnage, he smiled. "It will be all right."

Beside her, Gillis stared at the sky and pointed.

Guronde nodded. "Look."

Aralyn followed the direction he pointed and sensed the movement above her. An accompanying boom rang out.

"What was ..." But Aralyn knew.

Above and behind them, new walls had formed. They were inside the borders. Elves coming from the battlefield marched through them unhindered. The walls now obscured their lands from outsiders. The ruffle birds slammed impotently against them, their bodies dulling to a sickly gray.

"I don't understand. How did they form here?" She pointed. "I thought ..."

"Aralyn." Guronde chuckled. "We are safe. Don't worry."

Surely there was a story behind this, but Aralyn did not have the energy to ask. Besides, a dragon lizard lay at her feet, buried in leaves and debris. A surge of excitement ran through her.

Elouard. But was he alive?

Chapter 33

Vandel flew to Elouard's side, and he cried out with a tiny mewling.

Gillis crouched beside him, picked him up, and placed the lizard against his chest. Elouard snuggled down with a soft clicking noise. He hoped the little fella would be all right.

Aletha and Vandel hovered near Gillis' arms.

Gillis gave the dragon lizards a nod. "Yes, he's all right. Both of you girls, stop worrying."

Vandel flicked her tail, flew back to Aralyn, and landed on her shoulder. Aletha rode on Gillis' shoulder, dipping her head toward Elouard.

Gillis followed Re'ah as he headed toward the healer's tent with Elnala in his arms. Gillis wasn't sure where to take Elouard. He didn't have time for a damaged dragon lizard, but Elouard was different. He could not just leave him.

Vandel found the perfect place for him. Behind one of the tents, an unattended flame danced in a metal firepot. Gillis lay him down next to it while Vandel stood over him. Bobbed her head. *I'll stay with him. He just needs rest.*

Gillis gave her a nod.

Healers and their assistants brought waterskins to those who had fought. Aralyn took the proffered water, but when the healer tried to wash the dried blood from her face, she pulled away, refusing.

Gillis could tell Aralyn was still unsteady on her feet as she tried to catch up with Re'ah. He saw her hesitate, teeter, and then stop altogether. He strode toward her, and she collapsed against him.

"I hurt." She clung to his sleeve.

"Where?"

"My side."

"Let's get you to a healer." He ignored his own pain and led her to the area where healers and herbalists had set up tents and crude shelters.

"I thought I was all right. I started feeling better and—"

"Hush. You've done enough." Gillis took her to the nearest healer. The tent was crowded, to say the least, but he found a hay-stuffed mattress with a warm blanket and lay her on it.

"Let me take a look," Gillis said.

"No. Really, it's not so bad."

"You'll let me take a look." He wanted to swear. She could be so stubborn that it sometimes frightened him. Frightened him for her sake.

Aralyn sighed and grew still. His fingers fumbled to lift her tunic, and Gillis tried to show no emotion at what he saw. The wound on her side was closed, but infection had set in, swollen with angry red streaks radiating from it.

That bloody Mal'ev hadn't healed her. He'd poisoned her.

***

Aralyn managed to open her eyes, but the headache was back, blinding and pushing her into the blankets beneath her. It refused to loosen its grip. "Headache" was such a misnomer—this felt as though someone had placed razors in her skull. Her eyes fell shut of their own accord.

"Aralyn?" The voice sounded familiar. So familiar.

She couldn't answer. The words caught in her throat.

"Elyon, help her. I've done what I can. Please ..." A voice whispered and trailed off. "... lose her ... I can't ...not now."

She didn't know how long she slept before her eyes blinked open, fell closed, and opened again. She caught a glimpse of calloused hands clenched together. A blurred figure with lips moving and head bowed. Gillis? Had he come to pray for her? Pain and heat radiated from her side. Her entire body was ablaze. Her eyes closed again. She became oblivious to the pain.

***

"Where's my daughter?" Even in the haze of semiconsciousness, Aralyn recognized Orandon's voice. "They told me they moved her to this tent."

"She sleeps still." That was Gillis' voice.

"Do you know *where* she is?" Orandon's voice grew louder.

"Over—"

"Never mind. I see her."

Aralyn opened her eyes to see Orandon's back retreat as he limped to his daughter's bedside. Elnala was here in this tent. They had moved her here. *To be with me.* A nice thought, and Aralyn wanted to believe it.

Aralyn watched as Elnala stirred. She mouthed the words, *Daddy, Mother?* She tried to sit up but failed, and a look of horror came over Orandon's face. He gestured wildly at her partially missing arm and shouted at the nearest healer.

The healer stepped in front of Orandon and whispered a few gentle words, her mouth in a firm line as she motioned to his daughter and then at the door. He nodded and quieted. An assistant pushed a stool toward him, and Orandon sat, holding his daughter's remaining hand, his head bowed. Orandon's wife, Brehlena, walked in with quiet grace. A barely audible gasp came when she saw Elnala's missing arm.

Gillis had his eyes on Elnala and her parents, but he soon turned back to Aralyn.

"You're awake." Huge relief washed over Gillis' face.

"She's awake."

Re'ah and Gillis spoke at the same time.

"I need to go see her." Aralyn nodded in Elnala's direction and pushed herself up.

Gillis placed a hand on her shoulder. "Not now. You *need* to rest, and besides, her family is with her. There'll be plenty of time later."

A cool hand rested on her head—Re'ah's hand. "Her fever is gone, Gillis. You can sleep and eat now. I will stay with her."

"She may need help eating," Gillis objected.

"I will take care of that. Now go."

Aralyn closed her eyes and listened to the two men. It reminded her of the time they were on the trail when both had cared for her. But she didn't want help eating, and she didn't want Gillis to leave her side.

"I won't be gone long, lass." Gillis placed a kiss on her forehead and one on her cheek.

The food came, and she ate. Re'ah helped when her hand shook. At least he didn't have to spoon-feed her. She was hungrier than she realized, and she emptied the bowl of the thick soup. With her belly full, she felt refreshed. Re'ah remained with her, and Gillis would be back. She touched the place on her cheek where he had kissed her. Her gaze landed on Re'ah. He must have caught her lovestruck look, and he chuckled. Aralyn would have laughed if she didn't feel so weak.

***

Aralyn lost track of time, her body still insisting on much rest. She was aware of a hand on hers from time to time, prayers whispered. She finally woke for more than a few minutes. Someone else was here, not Re'ah or Gillis. She looked up into the kind eyes of her favorite Elder.

"Aralyn, you're doing well?" Guronde's smile seemed subdued, but his eyes still held a bit of that familiar light.

"My fever is gone." Aralyn hesitated. "Mal'ev caused this, didn't he? He made me think he was healing me."

Guronde tilted his head toward her. "Evidently, when Mal'ev realized he was dying, he decided to make sure you would not live either. I'm glad to see Gillis and Re'ah, with considerable help from Aletha, foiled those plans. Gillis and Re'ah came up with an antidote, and Aletha—as she does—enhanced the medicine's healing. She seems to have a calming effect on you as well."

"Mal'ev said he wanted to take me for one of his sons." She swallowed. "To mate with one of them." Nausea swept over her.

Guronde was silent for a beat. "He has a terrible habit of taking women for his or his sons' amusement. I imagine he wanted your powers to pass on to his progeny."

"Where is Lemmon?"

"That, child, I'm not sure of. Was he injured?"

"No...he..." She lowered her eyes, unable to continue.

"Ah." Guronde placed a hand on her arm. "I'm sorry."

Aralyn could feel his gaze upon her. "We can look for him, Aralyn. The death-takers are making a list of those missing."

Death-takers—the ones who took care of the dead, cataloged them, even prepared them for burial if no one claimed the body. She and Gillis could care for Lemmon if he had no one. He had mentioned his mother, but had he said she was still alive? She couldn't remember, and regret pierced her. He had died for her. Protecting her. And she didn't even know about his family.

"How long have I been here?"

"Three days. The battle is over. The enemy has left our borders and the lands outside them. We had to root a few of them out, but they are gone or held in our prison." His eyes dropped to Aralyn's one boot at the bedside. "Hmmm. We need to get you some new footwear."

"Or at least *a* new one." Aralyn chuckled at her little joke. She knew it wasn't that funny, but the laughter grew. Was she hysterical or just worn out?

Guronde wore a look of concern.

Her laughter fled, and she had to ask. "My mother. Do you know if she is all right? I know she's in Sathria, but Mal'ev's forces—"

"Have headed back to Gehallia and Montravia." He patted her arm. "Mercenaries and even those loyal to him decided not to attack Sathria or any of the municipalities south of here." He tilted his head toward her. "I sense a great fear among them. And Aralyn, your mother is not in Sathria."

The Elder's refusal to be direct caused her head to pound, and she demanded, "Where is she then?"

"Lethola, your mother, is in one of the healer's tents as well. She suffered several wounds but will be fine."

"She came to fight?" That actually made sense. If Terrwynn had come, her mother would follow. Of course.

"Yes, she did. Still has amazing strength as a mage."

"Does she know Terrwynn is gone?"

"No. Even I didn't realize she was. I am so sorry."

"She's not dead." He had misunderstood her again. "She left with one of the enemy mages, and"—Aralyn barely choked the words out— "Drehensil took them."

"I see." Guronde did not seem surprised at this, but then the Elder was unflappable. "Was the mage Gehallion? Did you notice?"

"I am almost certain he was. He was with Mal'ev."

"That makes sense." Guronde stroked his beard.

Aralyn didn't want to ponder this. "When do you think I can see my mother?" Aralyn had to be the one to let her know about Terrwynn.

"I'm not sure. She is not ready to see anyone."

"She's hurt that badly?"

"No." Guronde scratched his chin. "Perhaps I should say, she does not wish to see anyone right now."

Including me. Including her daughter. Aralyn had no energy for the anger and heartache that slammed against her. Her mother's rejection would not make her forget what had been accomplished—what Aralyn herself had done to save Eyndor.

***

Aralyn wished to be useful again. Numbness swallowed her as the healer decided her patient could help bury the dead—not carry bodies, but prepare them or perhaps throw dirt on the graves. And someone found Lem. To her horror, his body had begun to decay, birds had pecked at his eyes, and flies swarmed. She had to swallow her sick. But true to her word, she tended his body. A distant cousin came to help, and they placed him in a grave deep enough that the flies quit swarming, but the nuisances found others to haunt with their buzzing—more bodies in the same horrible shape.

"Go home, Aralyn," Re'ah insisted. "You need healing still."

She decided not to argue with this man who had cared for her. Aralyn didn't remember walking the path or climbing the stairs. But she was home. Without Gillis. He was probably helping one of the healers. Maybe she had just missed him.

Though they had cleaned her up at the healer's, Aralyn wanted another bath. She heated water—lots of it—and scrubbed, rinsed, and scrubbed some more. Her skin red and raw, she finally felt rid of death and flies and bloody water. She found clean clothes, put her feet up, and leaned her head back to stare at the ceiling. The portion of artwork above her told a story of Elves and Dwarves and peaceful times. Nothing like the last few days had been. Would she ever feel that kind of peace again? She stood, stumbled to their couch, and dozed.

"Aralyn." A quiet, feminine voice disrupted her sleep.

Shenral was here. She had a broom in her hand and had cooked, but it all seemed so distant. Even the aroma of baked bread, tea, and meat seemed far away.

"Aralyn, you need to eat."

Without objection, Aralyn took a chair at the table and lifted food to her mouth, but eating brought visions of crows feeding on bodies. She managed to take a few bites before giving up.

That night, she dreamed of a bloody hand grasping her ankle and a voice crying out for Aralyn's help. She awoke with a stifled scream.

"It's all right, Aralyn." Shenral was standing over her. "Go back to sleep. I'm here."

But sleep eluded her, and she paced the floor, trying to forget the battle, the carnage, the loss of Lemmon, and wondering what would become of her sister. She hoped Gillis rested and had found time to eat.

Daylight entered her home as she wandered to the living area. The pleasant feeling of welcoming a new day was absent, and as the bright morning pierced her eyes, she longed for the numbness to return, blessed numbness.

Shenral brought her some tea, and they sat facing the windows. The greens, blues, and magentas of the trees beyond appeared deeper and more vibrant now. Birds sang, calling, answering each other with small hoots, a series of chirps, or drawn-out whistles.

A swish of the curtain at their entrance, and an Elven voice called to her. *"Ousz li Gillon?"*

He wanted Gillis, and Gillis wasn't there. *"Aev les roles."* He's with the healers, she told him.

The messenger hesitated. *"De al uw. Al uw met art losa fe'ay."*

Aralyn came to her feet. *They're dying.* The wounded were dying.

Aralyn grabbed her cloak. It was clean. Shenral must have scrubbed the blood away.

Aralyn ran, and one thought filled her mind.

Elnala.

***

"Where is she?" Aralyn entered the healer's tent.

Re'ah caught her arm. "Aralyn ..."

Something in his expression made Aralyn fear the worst. "Where is she?"

"She was on the mend. But ..." Re'ah's eyes dropped.

Aralyn pulled away from him and made her way to Elnala's bed. Her friend wasn't there. Aralyn swung back to Re'ah. "Where is she?" she demanded again,

"She's ... Aralyn, Elnala didn't make it." The healer's eyes were red.

"You couldn't do anything?"

"I tried ... We tried." Tears fell from the healer's eyes.

Aralyn swung around to face Re'ah. "*You* couldn't do anything? Elyon couldn't do anything? *Your* god could do nothing?"

Re'ah's gaze met hers with such gentleness that Aralyn wanted to run to his arms, but she couldn't—the anger and terror gripped her. She clenched her fists and squeezed her eyes shut.

"She's over there." Re'ah nodded to where Elnala lay.

Someone had placed her in an area with other bodies and wrapped her in blankets. Aralyn barely heard Orandon and his wife enter. Orandon pushed past Aralyn and fell to his knees like a beggar, tears pouring down his cheeks. A quiet swish of fabric and Elnala's mother joined him, face stony. Her hand on Orandon's shoulder, he grasped it as someone clinging to a lifeline.

Any shred of numbness Aralyn had clung to fled, dropping like the last vestiges of armor from a long battle. Her heart shattered. Yet she knew Orandon and Brehlena were in far more pain.

She went to where Elnala lay, asked Orandon and Brehlana if she could join them.

Orandon looked up at her, tears streaking his face. He nodded, and she knelt on the floor next to him.

Aralyn sensed his brokenness, but Brehlana concerned her even more. Her face devoid of emotion, she knelt next to Orandon staring at her daughter's face.

"No," Aralyn argued when one of the death-takers came. She had to prepare the body.

The death-taker grew impatient, and he spoke harshly. "This job is hard enough. You'll let me take her."

Damnable vulture, was he?

"*I* will tend to her. Leave her." Aralyn focused on Elnala's face, unable to believe she was gone. "I tended to Lemmon. I can tend to my best friend."

Orandon stood and faced the man, pointed with his chin to Aralyn. "Let her."

The vulture glanced from Orandon to Aralyn, brow furrowed. He opened his mouth to argue and shook his head. "All right." He hesitated. Addressing Aralyn, he said, "I'm only trying to do my job, bowsinger."

Orandon's determined gaze met hers. "You take care of her, Aralyn."

"I will stay, too. I have oils." Brehlena's reserve was failing, and a tear fell as she drew oils from a leather bag.

Orandon knelt once more. He kissed his daughter's cheek and stood. "Thank you," He said roughly. He spoke a few words to his wife and left.

Aralyn thought she was ready for this, but listening to Brehlena's *faral'el*, she choked. The death song was familiar somehow and brought back memories of a long-ago time. But no matter her grief, she had to do this. How could she not? For Elnala—the one who had welcomed her in such a peculiar way and the only Elf she had truly befriended.

Aralyn anointed Elnala's head and neck, cleansing her from head to toe. Brehlena's song stopped. She nodded to Aralyn, directing her to sing. But it had been years. "I don't know it anymore." She felt helpless.

"You are her friend. *Be* her friend." Brehlena nodded tightly.

Instead of the *faral'el*, Aralyn spoke to Elnala of things she would always remember as though her friend were still in the land of the living and listening to their shared memories. She spoke blessings for the next life. Glancing at Brehlena, she sang her song of the brook.

"Her favorite." Brehlena nodded in approval.

If only Elnala's eyes would flutter open and surprise them. But that was not going to happen. So together she and Brehlena wrapped her up again and added the death blanket, the covering that would make her recognizable to the gods of the next world. Aralyn didn't believe that anymore, and neither did most of the Elves. They had long since abandoned the old gods, but traditions died hard.

"Is she ready?" The vulture had returned.

"I think so." Aralyn's chin quivered. "I will pull ..." She reconsidered her words. "May I pull the cart?"

The death-taker nodded. He knelt, picked Elnala up, and carried her outside. Elnala's body joined four others, crowded side by side in a wooden cart. Aralyn firmed her chin. She could do this—pull the cart to the grave site. She knew they would place these bodies in mass graves, and Elnala would be among the many warriors and innocents buried there. No ceremony except for one large memorial service, where they would pray and read a list of the newly fallen, casting stones of remembrance on the grave.

"Let me help you." It was Re'ah at her side once more.

Aralyn nodded, and the cart groaned as they pulled it forward. Orandon and his wife followed in silence.

Chapter 34

Gillis picked up Elouard, who was improving. Aletha and a healer had gathered herbs for him. Not a dragon's usual fare, but Elouard seemed to know this would help him and gobbled them down. Vandel stayed with him.

Gillis thanked the healer.

The healer bowed his head. "He should be fine. It always brings me joy to help animals when I can."

And just like that, he was thinking of Lemmon. Gillis choked, but he kept the grief at bay. No time for that. Not yet.

Gillis moved on to an herbalist's tent and then to another healer, but it seemed there was little more he could do. Those still alive who hadn't died in the wave of infection were stable or improving.

His mark pulsed as he caught sight of Aralyn. He no longer denied that they were paired, and their abilities joined. And the strange power that had come over him in battle had happened so quickly and proved he was something he did not want to be. If he was not a full-fledged mage, he was close.

Laella had been killed by a mage. Innocent Laella and the innocent life she'd carried. Both of them—gone because of a mage. His dreams of a family—gone with her. And now his feelings for Aralyn—they seemed to overwhelm him.

"Gillis." Re'ah stood next to him, his eyes full. "Are you—"

"I'm holding up just fine," he said before Re'ah could ask. He knew what Re'ah would say to his decision to leave, and Gillis was not ready to hear it. "Let's go to the grave site. I can help there perhaps."

Elves were gathered on a green hill, some sobbing, others stoic. This was one of the reasons Elves did not overpopulate the world—too many lost in the battles they had to fight over the same thing—power over Eyndor.

A quiet voice came to him. The words were soft and difficult to hear, but he tried to listen. Laella? A faint cry in fragmented Elvish. *Duneh ... Gillion. Ara ... tela ...* What was she saying? He shook it off. People did not speak from beyond the grave. But it sounded like her. Did he dare hope?

Aralyn was helping to unload a body. "No, don't ... Be more careful." She repeated the words several times, obviously upset by the death-takers' treatment of the dead. Orandon approached, and his Brehlana joined him, both laying hands on the blanket covering the body. They wore tired, troubled expressions. Orandon openly wept.

Elnala? She was dead? No.

"Re'ah. Excuse me." Gillis wove through mourners to Aralyn's side.

Aralyn's cries were quieter now. "Set her down easily. The blanket, keep it on her." Her voice shook with impatience and sorrow. Something fluttered by Aralyn's head. It was too small to be a dragon lizard or even a bird. Her gem? Was it returning in its living form? He could hear the thing humming. Humming a *faral'el*. Not the traditional death song but one with hope and, yes, joy. A song reserved for dragons. Aralyn jumped as it dove into her pocket. She reached for it, realized what it was, and her mouth fell open.

When Gillis approached her, she started. "Gillis." She dropped the gem back in her pocket, and her lips tugged upward despite her obvious grief.

"That's ... that's Elnala?" Gillis indicated the body Aralyn had been tending.

"Yes." Her voice was flat and weary.

His heart went out to Orandon and his wife, who stood nearby. He squeezed Aralyn's hand, and the wave of shock hit him. It was their marks responding to each other, and yet more than that. Aralyn was grieving and struggling with her thoughts. And he felt it.

He had to tell her he was leaving. Or should he tell her? His mark grew warm, and Aralyn's gaze met his.

No, her eyes told him. *I know what you plan to do. No, you cannot.* And her expression filled with fire. She wrenched away from him and grabbed the hands of Orandon and his wife.

He should say something. But nothing came to mind. He swung around, went back to work, side by side with Re'ah. Sweating, burying, praying. Until they finally laid the last warriors to rest.

***

Aralyn dropped the seemingly lifeless hands of Elnala's parents and stepped away from her friend's body. The afternoon sun was bright and springtime warm. Somewhere birds were singing. But that brought no comfort and no cheer to Eyndor. She found smooth grass to walk on as she moved away from the graves and the grief of so many. Her own grief caught her gut in a whirlwind, refusing to give way to the numbness she longed for.

Hands clasped before her, she wandered over the short grasses until she felt thorns stinging her bare feet. She had to stop and leap over the supine plants tormenting her. Wearing boots had caused the calluses of her once tough feet to soften. She wandered, directionless. The ground became bare of vines and grass and the trees farther apart. There were no paths to guide her, only the light from above.

Gillis. He was planning to leave her. Is that truly what she had sensed when he approached her earlier? Just as she thought their pairing and newfound intimacy, had brought them together, he was leaving. Just as she'd hoped that standing side by side in battle would complete the bond between them, he was leaving.

Her wanderings brought her home. To their home. To Gillis' and her home, but was he here? Would his presence leave this place empty and lonely? The endless stairs led her to the truth.

***

Gillis was gone, but Shenral greeted her, and Aralyn told her to go home. She would be all right, yes, really. As the other woman left, the loneliness and shock of his absence set in. Was he truly gone? She searched the hidden nooks where he stashed his knives, his sling, his sword. Nothing.

Outside, it began to rain. Lightning flashed through the sky. She ran to the shelter where they kept their horses. No sign of Restless, just as she had expected. But Monpomme nickered when Aralyn entered. Without thinking, Aralyn began brushing her and was rewarded with a gentle gaze from large dark eyes and a twitch of ears.

The chill returned. "Oh, Gillis. I wish you could have waited. At least one more day. Let me say goodbye," she whispered. "Why couldn't he wait,

Monpomme?" She didn't expect an answer, but the horse's eyes said she understood.

"Aralyn?"

"Re'ah." She had forgotten he was keeping his horse with theirs.

Re'ah smiled, but Aralyn detected sadness in his eyes as well. He too had seen people he truly cared for die in these last few days.

"You are not doing well, are you?" He approached her as if he did not want to spook a wild animal.

She put the brush down. Picked it back up.

"No, Re'ah, I'm not." Best be honest. "I didn't want Lem or Elnala or any of those children to die. I didn't want Terrwynn to leave. I understand there are reasons for all this, but I did not want Gillis to..." She stopped, unable to go on, and looked into Re'ah's patient face.

"Go on...you did not want Gillis to...?"

"To leave. That's all." She went back to brushing Monpomme's flank, aware she was brushing the same spot over and over.

"I did not want that for you either."

"Why then? Just as we were...learning more about each other." It hurt to talk. Everything seemed to hurt.

"Oh, child...Gillis needs to explain that."

"But why did you let him? He would have listened to you. He would have listened to Elyon." Surely, Gillis heard Elyon speak.

"Sometimes there is no reason that is easily understood. But sometimes the most loyal of Elyon's followers are unsure of what is right, or they do know but insist on doing things their way." Re'ah took a few steps closer. He didn't reach out for her or try to draw her close. That was probably a good thing. "I want you to do something for me."

Aralyn wondered what that would be. She was almost afraid to ask, and she was angry. Would she be one of those who refused to do as he asked? "I can try—yes, anything."

"I want you to keep Gillis in your heart."

Aralyn's eyebrows rose. What was he saying? No, that meant the hurt would always be there, always reminding her of him. So she recounted all the events that still stung. All of them.

"Re'ah, we had to get married under the law of *his* city. He didn't wish to, but he didn't have to be so angry with me. Even after I thought things were better, he was still angry. He didn't want to train with me. If we had trained more, maybe neither of us would have been injured when facing Mal'ev. And then...he leaves me." Aralyn stopped, resentment overwhelming her. She glanced up and caught the look on Re'ah's face. A mixture of sorrow, compassion, and tender rebuke met her. She opened her mouth, but the words caught in her throat.

"Can you trust me, Aralyn?" Re'ah asked. "Can you trust Elyon?"

The smell of horse and hay filled her nostrils, bringing back memories of the farm in Sathria and memories of Lemmon.

Aralyn bit her lip. She knew the right answer. "I try to follow you, Re'ah. I do."

Re'ah's face was troubled. "Aralyn." His voice was gentle, so gentle. "That's not what I asked." He waited.

When Aralyn remained silent, he took another step towards her and took her hand. Olive skin against fair. His gaze met hers. Brown eyes reflecting blue and back again.

"I'm sorry." Her voice broke. "I try to trust you and to do right."

His arms around her like a fortress of adamant, and he asked softly, "It is difficult, though, is it not?"

Next to her, Monpomme blustered. *Is everything all right?* The horse seemed to ask.

A thought occurred to Aralyn. She trusted Monpomme, didn't she? Trusted her horse's strong back to hold her up, to move in the right direction, to follow her instructions through the tug of reins or the kick of her heel. Maybe that was an oversimplified way to look at it, but ...

"Who is holding you, Aralyn?" Re'ah's words interrupted her musings.

"You are," she answered, wondering at the simplicity of his question.

"You trust me in this act, do you not?"

"Yes." Of course she did. His heartbeat was steady against her ear.

"If you trust me in this, can you stop carrying burdens that are not yours to bear?"

"Like saving Eyndor, keeping my sister safe? That wasn't completely up to me."

"No, it was not." When he spoke again, there was a catch in his throat. "Aralyn, I want to carry you on eagle's wings. I want you to see things that only come with trust in Elyon."

Aralyn pulled back. Tears rolled down Re'ah's cheeks and into his dark beard. She had only seen him weep over the sick, dying, and children too poor to have enough to eat. And now he shed tears for her?

"Aralyn." He released her. "I only ask that you trust me, give me your heart, and I will keep you in mine. Always." He placed a fist on his chest.

With her own eyes welling, she nodded. "All right." Something hard and brittle broke inside her, something that needed breaking. She needed to give up this hardness of heart.

"Aralyn, Elyon, can take that." Once again, Re'ah sensed the very thing she was thinking. "He doesn't mind taking the ugly, useless things that his children often cling to. You can admit anything to him, and he will carry that burden."

Aralyn considered her next words carefully. Maybe Gillis hadn't left her forever. After all, they had made vows. But he had left without telling her anything.

Without Re'ah prompting her, she thought of Gillis' goodness and recounted all that she remembered. "Re'ah, Gillis—he has learned to be a true husband. He can speak to dragons. He was growing more patient, and he did try to stop the lord from having me beaten. He even took a strike to the head. For me. I think he was going to appeal to the king."

"Did he not help you heal afterward?"

Aralyn swallowed. Re'ah knew the answer to that. "Yes, and he stayed up all night caring for me. He's capable in that way. He bought a bow for me and..." She stopped.

"So what will your answer be?"

"I really have no choice if that is what you want and what Elyon wants." But there was more. A realization dawned. "He is here already." She placed a hand on her chest.

Re'ah nodded. "And understand. I did not want him to leave, especially not without saying something to you."

Re'ah was looking beyond her. "Your mother is here. Hello, Deirdre."

Aralyn swung around. "Mother." It was all she could say.

Re'ah had a firm grip on her shoulders. "It will be all right. I'm going to leave you to talk." And he slipped out.

Mother's gaze swept over Aralyn. "You didn't receive any injuries?"

"Yes. I did. But, I'm fine, Moth—"

"Where is Terrwynn?"

Aralyn was not ready to answer that question, so she countered with one of her own. "Why are you here?" She knew, but wanted to hear it from her mother's lips.

"Terrwynn came, and I wanted to help when I realized the stakes. My hard feelings were doing me no good."

That wasn't exactly the response she had expected.

Mother placed her hands on her hips. "Now. Can you answer my question?"

Aralyn swallowed, trying not to let her voice break. "She's with a Gehallion mage. They left together on Drehensil."

Mother's mouth dropped, but just as quickly, her face relaxed, and she nodded. "Ah." Almost as if she had expected this.

That was all she had to say about Terrwynn's absence?

"You don't know, do you?" Mother asked, raising an eyebrow.

Aralyn could only stare. What was she supposed to know?

"Your stepfather, Terrwynn's father, was Gehallian. He fled Gehallia during a coup—a coup that killed all the royals." She paused. "Except for him. I am certain I told you this."

No, she had never heard Mother speak of Gehallia or royalty or a coup.

Mother continued. "He and I—we fell in love and married shortly after he fled. I truly thought you were smart enough to ..." Mother's gaze was almost apologetic.

And Aralyn grasped the truth. "That means Terrwynn is of royal blood."

Mother smoothed her hair. "Distantly related to the man who was king at the time. But yes, of royal Gehallian blood." Her voice grew gentler. "You didn't fail her. She had to go back. She will be treated as what she is. Royalty. No matter what Mal'ev thinks he can do." Mother shrugged. "He may even want the royals back in power."

"He is dead, Mother. They burned his body on the field of battle."

Mother frowned. "You saw him?"

"I killed him."

"I guess I should be proud of you."

Aralyn ignored Mother's caustic words. "Mal'ev wanted me to come with him. He wanted me alive." She didn't wait for Mother's response. "Did Mal'ev know she was royalty?"

Mother tapped her foot. "That I'm not sure of."

Aralyn closed her eyes, shoulders relaxing. Muscles let go of tension, and heartache eased. But she had to ask Mother one more thing. "What about before ... I failed her then, failed you, and failed Fa—my stepfather."

"In what? How did you fail?" Mother cocked her head.

"I went to the dragon, Drehensil, and I let her fall into the river, and she almost drowned, and she was captured, and Daniel went after her, and he was—"

"Yes, I know the rest." Mother stepped forward and took Aralyn's hand. "So what are you going to do? Try to make up for it as you did at home? Try to protect me and prove yourself so that ... what, Aralyn? I will care for you more?"

Mother had hit too close to home, and Aralyn winced. "I have nothing to prove. Not anymore. And even if I hadn't come here, fought, and killed Mal'ev—if you don't care for me then, you never will." The realization of truth in those last words crept into her mind and heart. "Even if Terrwynn is gone. And I wish it were me, and I wish I hadn't let her go, and Mal'ev had never found us, and—"

A smile tugged at Mother's lips. "Aralyn, you think so little of me—"

"No, Mother. I don't."

"Hmph. You thought that if you did enough, it would make a difference in my love for you."

Aralyn's throat closing, she squeaked out, "You were never happy with me, Mother. Never. Especially after my stepfather died, and Terrwynn was hurt. I just wanted to do something to make you proud again. But now I realize I can't, and I will no longer try."

"You never had to, child." Mother's expression softened, although still guarded. She tapped her fingers against the side of her leg. "But you were too blind to see that I still cared for you after what happened. Yes, I grieved. Grieved every day when I saw Terrwynn drifting from us. I still do. But I never stopped loving you. Why do you think I did all that sewing? Do you think I did it simply to have something to do? It was for you and for Terrwynn."

Mother's eyes filled, and Aralyn raised an eyebrow. Mother didn't cry.

"Aralyn, I sold those items to have money for seed and to pay the magistrate." This time, her tears fell.

"Money for what?"

"To keep men from claiming you."

To keep men from claiming her. Aralyn's mouth dropped, and she snapped it shut. "You paid the magistrate. You bought the claims from him."

"Yes, every time a man bartered or gave the magistrate coin to claim you, I'd pay him more so they couldn't. Worked out nicely for him. That's also why you had no dowry to marry someone better than Sathria's supply. Yes, I had to sell you—as you put it—to Brone."

Aralyn saw her mother with new eyes. It wasn't that Mother didn't love Aralyn—she just had a difficult time expressing it in a way Aralyn understood. "Will you go back now, or will you stay here?"

Mother tilted her head to the side. "Would you like me to stay?"

"Yes, please stay." Somehow, the words were sincere. She wanted her mother here.

Mother's shoulders relaxed, and the tightness in her face softened. "All right, I will. If the Elders and Council will have me."

"The Council is no more, Mother, and I'm sure Guronde and the other Elders will be happy to have you."

"The Council couldn't take all of my mage talent. If I live here and there is a need, I will help protect Eyndor again." A genuine spark lit her eyes. "And, Aralyn, Terrwynn will be fine. She is with her father's people. I'm sure she will experience some rigorous training, but soon she will be ready for her coronation. Who knows—one day Eyndor and Gehallia may be at peace."

They could hope, but Aralyn didn't like the scenario even though it was better than what she had imagined. She suspected Terrwynn had known all along. Aralyn thought of all those times when she challenged authority, lifted her chin, and walked with unexpected grace. "When did Terrwynn start speaking again?"

"Shortly after you left. The Rogues who captured her injured her vocal cords. It was only with pain that she could speak. Lot'fe discovered the problem and was able to create a remedy that allowed Terrwynn to speak again. But it still took her a while to think right." Mother tapped her head.

Aralyn stared at her feet. She didn't want to tell Mother about Siaon's betrayal and Lot'fe's imprisonment. She still wanted to find out what had happened with Lot'fe.

Aralyn gazed upward as she heard Vandel, Aletha, and Elouard's voices. They were somewhere nearby. Dragon lizards didn't interfere with Eyndor's magic, Orandon had told her.

"What about your husband?" Mother interrupted Aralyn's thoughts. "The man you were given to after Brone died—the escort Gillis?"

Aralyn shook her head. She didn't want to answer that question and changed the subject. "Mother, where will you stay?"

"Where I've been staying. With the Aunts."

"The Aunts?"

"Yes, you know, the women who take care of the children while mothers and fathers are training? Do you not—"

"I remember." Aralyn recalled the women from her childhood who had no obligation to family or training, most of them widows or childless. Two had helped care for her while her mother and father trained.

"Now." Mother tilted her head. "Your husband?"

"I'm not sure exactly where my husband is, but he should return before long." That was the truth—maybe not all of it, but she had to say it. Had to believe it. Gillis would return to her.

Chapter 35

Aralyn managed a few hours of sleep that night. The next morning, Shenral came again, but Aralyn had already finished breakfast when she arrived. "I had a feeling I would see you. I fixed some extra porridge and a few biscuits."

"No, thank you, Aralyn. I'm not hungry."

Aralyn shrugged. No one wanted her food, although it hadn't turned out half bad this time.

"Aralyn," Shenral began, and hesitated. "Are you going to be all right? You're here by yourself, and I'm concerned for you."

Aralyn waved her hand, dismissing Shenral's words. "Gillis will be back. I'm fine. I like being alone." *Liar. Not anymore.*

Shenral gave her a knowing glance. "Is there anything I can do today?"

"No, I'll take care of the horses and perhaps visit my mother and the Aunts. We won't be training for a while. I think it's foolish, but that is what Guronde decided."

"Your mother is here?" Shenral said it with mild interest. "I'm glad." She pinched her lips together. "Aralyn, I will continue to help you until you decide you don't need me."

"I suppose that would be nice for at least a few more days. I still tire easily. Thank you, Shenral. Let me know how much I owe you." When Shenral said nothing, Aralyn wondered if perhaps the girl wanted to help in order to stay busy and keep her mind off the past.

Two weeks later, Aralyn made up her mind to visit the Harp. She'd heard it was in disarray but had not expected the damage she found. What had happened here? Mud and debris choked the ponds and fountains and pools. Water flowed where it should not have been and flooded the lower areas. Oaks and wickless trees stood at odd angles, uprooted.

Orandon appeared next to her, regarding the damage. She had not heard him approach. "The magic that attacked our borders, including the damage from Drehensil's presence, did this." He took a deep breath and let it out slowly. "You will be responsible for getting it back in order."

That seemed like a huge task, but she didn't balk. He was talking about leading a team—not doing it by herself. "Yes, Orandon. I can do that."

"Good." He swung away from her and trudged toward a large fallen tree, examining its damaged branches.

Aralyn's heart swelled with compassion. Even in his grief, Orandon had come to check on the Harp. She wanted to tell him how brave Elnala had been, but instead she went to his side and stood with him, remaining silent. Perhaps he wanted to talk. If he didn't that was fine, but leaving him alone with his thoughts did not seem like a good idea

"I've discovered something, Aralyn." He was examining a patch of lichens with great intensity. "When I have a feeling about something, I should pay attention to it."

Aralyn didn't know what to say. She could sense his frustration and grief.

"I had a feeling something was going to happen to Elnala. When I let her go with you to the cliffs ..." His eyes welled with tears, but they didn't fall. "I had a feeling it would be bad. And when she was at the healer's, I knew those would be the last visits we had."

Aralyn's neck muscles tightened.

"I should have said goodbye before she left with you. I should have blessed her and wished her well. I should have told her a thousand things." He stared into the distance.

Aralyn parted her lips, ready to respond, to tell him it would be all right, but it might never be all right. Instead, she placed her hand on Orandon's arm.

His face relaxed, and his gaze landed on her. "You are wise, Aralyn. You've made mistakes, but now, right now, you say nothing about a grief you are unfamiliar with. You listen. You don't try to teach me, but instead let me teach you of regrets and grief that I hope you never have to face. That is a wise thing." His voice faded.

No one had ever said that of her. Wise. "May I ask you something?"

His head bowed, Aralyn barely heard his response. "Of course."

"Are you able to sleep, Orandon? Are you and your wife able to sleep?"

Orandon scoffed. "No, not I. I don't think Brehlena sleeps much either. She lies down at night, but she grows restless. She seldom shares what she feels during the best times, and now this ..." He was silent for several beats, wrestling with something. "Except she wants us to make things *normal* again. She wants us to have another child. I don't know if I can even think of it."

Aralyn wished she could tell him *I'll be your daughter.* But that was ludicrous, and she felt foolish for even thinking it. "You should know she kept her head when I faced Mal'ev. She was injured, and yet she helped me dispel his thoughts from my mind. The way she instructed me was different from the way you taught me, but I couldn't keep my *bar're* intact."

Orandon's gaze was intense, although Aralyn didn't know if he comprehended her words. He stared at the dying tree at his feet. "Yes, she always was quite capable. Even so, death took her."

***

As Aralyn entered her home that evening, she realized something was different. Moonlight poured in. A dark figure sat on the windowsill and turned to her. They stared at each other.

"You're back," she said. *Oh, brilliant.*

Gillis stood and set his coffee down. He lit the lamp on the table. "I had to leave. I needed the time to sort things out."

Was he back for good then? Or was he just back to visit?

Gillis reached out to her, his face in shadow. She didn't move.

"Aralyn, I wanted to come back. But I'm not sure you'll want me now." He dropped his hand, and his feet shifted.

He was here. She could feel his presence and hear his voice. Could she just take him back? That would depend on him. "May I ask what you had to sort out that would cause you to leave me? To leave Eyndor?"

Gillis rubbed his chin. "I left Aurellium. Never really left Eyndor, but yes, I left you. Went leagues and leagues away. To Laella's grave."

Aralyn nodded. "You wanted to tell her goodbye."

"Yes."

"And then you were going to leave for good,"—she cocked her head to the side— "without telling *me* goodbye."

"Aralyn." His voice was subdued. Not like Gillis at all.

"You can't, Gillis. You can't just leave ..." She choked. "Leave me like that. Without a word." Her father, her stepfather, Terrwynn—all had left—and now Gillis? Yes, he was back, at least for now. He was here. With her. But she needed to ask him a question. One that burned in her heart. "How can

I trust you again? If you stay, how do I know you won't leave me again? For her."

Gillis ran a hand through his hair. "I have no intention of leaving. Not now. Not ever. I'm speaking the truth."

Aralyn folded her arms. How could she believe him? She wanted to, but had he truly said goodbye to Laella?

"Aralyn, I will tell you this." Gillis moved closer and reached out to her again.

This time she took his hand.

He held hers with his palm open, lightly holding her fingertips. "I want you to know I'm scared too."

"You're scared? And you think I'm scared?" She pulled her hand from his.

"Yes. I do, Aralyn. I think you've been scared since before we met."

Aralyn shook her head. She was not afraid, not of much anyway. *Gully lizards.*

"I'm not talking about your fighting or the brave things you've done. You've proven yourself in battle."

"So what am I afraid of?"

"Of loving me."

Aralyn's brow furrowed, and her lips were a tight line. How could she be afraid of loving him? She did love him. He was just too blind to see it, but could he possibly see something she didn't? Or was it a fear that he would love her? But isn't that what she wanted?

"Perhaps you are right, Gillis. Perhaps I am afraid, but you are still in love—"

"*Was.*"

"Was?"

"I still love her, but I have let her go." His face came out of the shadows. "As you surmised, I went to her grave to say goodbye. But I came back. Had to."

"But why?"

"Why? I came back, Aralyn. Back to you. Isn't that all that matters?"

That wasn't what she needed to hear. "Why?"

"It should be—"

"Obvious? No, Gillis, it is not."

Gillis tapped his booted foot against the floor. "I have no doubt that I love you. Aralyn, I am in love with you. I love you as a husband should love a wife."

He was in love. With her. She wanted to take him at his word, but not a month ago, he had been in love with Laella.

Gillis spoke, breaking up the thoughts she was trying to gather. "I don't know what the future holds for us. I don't know how you will respond to my love, and yes, I wonder if you will be able to trust me the way paired individuals need to trust, but more importantly, as husband and wife need to trust each other. I know I can leave Laella behind. I will always miss her, but I can go on without her in my life. I promise you that. And maybe I'm afraid I'll lose you one day. At the same time, I can trust Elyon. Just as you told me to trust him when I got so angry at you for nearly setting yourself on fire."

Is that how he remembered it? Huh. A few sparks had flown, and he had gone into a rage because, according to him, she had almost set herself on fire? A smile crept across her face. He had been afraid then, afraid he would lose her as he had lost Laella. *Maybe he loved me even then.*

"Gillis." His name tasted sweet in her mouth. She flexed her hands at her sides. "This love I feel is like ..." What was it like? "When my father left, when he died, the feelings were so huge, so overwhelming." She swallowed and again saw that tidal wave chasing her down, trying to drown her as it pushed her to the ground.

Gillis' face was unreadable now. He was waiting.

She continued, carefully planning her words. "I'm afraid of going somewhere I've never been. What if I give my heart, my love to you? If I do, things will never be the same. And these feelings, they're ..." She felt a huge ocean wave rushing into her mouth, forcing its way down her throat. Feelings that were so much bigger than she, drowning her in an oncoming flood.

His face relaxed, and he seemed to read her thoughts. "This love won't drown you, lass. It won't leave you feeling helpless, and it won't shatter your life like the loss of your father. You were a little girl. Yes, it will change you. It will change everything. And I will tell you what to do with that love. Give it to me, lass. You can trust me with it. You can trust me with your heart. That I promise."

Aralyn's hands were trembling. She must do this. Quit keeping these emotions to herself and let him see what she felt. Trust him. Keep him in her heart as Re'ah had said. Hadn't Gillis proven himself trustworthy?

"All right." That was all she could manage, but it must have been enough.

Gillis closed the remaining gap between them, his lips on hers. He gathered her in his arms, drew the length of her body against his own. Her arms were around his neck. His mouth traversed hers, and she, hesitating at first, found tenderness and pleasure and hunger for more. His arms pulled her closer, and she didn't resist. Didn't know if she could. An enormous weakness raced through her. A quiet surrender to him.

When Gillis released her, she clung to him, eyes closed. Couldn't let go.

"Aralyn, listen to me." He grasped her upper arms.

She opened her eyes, saw he was serious, and drew back.

"I want us to marry again. To be married here in Aurellium."

Her eyebrows lifted. They were married, but he wanted more than an arranged marriage, or rather, a forced marriage.

"Aralyn of Sathria." Gillis knelt before her. Not on one knee in the way of humans, but on both. He cleared his throat and started again. "Aralyn of Aurellium." He let her name linger in the air. "Will you marry me?" A longing gaze awaited her answer.

"You're sure?" She couldn't believe this was truly happening.

"Look at me, woman. I'm on my flaming knees." His voice became gentler, and he squeezed her hands. "Will you answer me?"

Gillis was truly moving on and asking her to marry him. *Asking* her. Love, intense and pure and filling, washed over her.

"Gillis of Maizehollow—"

"Of Glenvine."

"Glenvine?"

"Yes, my home, where I was born and raised. Here in Eyndor."

Aralyn joined him on her knees. "Gillis of Glenvine." She liked the sound of that. "Yes, the answer is yes. I will marry you."

He pulled her close again. "I'm so proud," he murmured. "I love you, lass."

A tidal wave arose before her. She faced it, welcomed it, and, unafraid, she dove in.

Epilogue

Aralyn, her mother, and Gillis strolled near the falls. Droplets of water scattered the light to form mistbows once again. They were back in place. No more ruffle birds. At least not for a long, long while.

"I want the ceremony to be simple. Flowers would be nice, but not too many. Perhaps some candles ..." Aralyn knelt to pull a clover leaf from the ground.

"And a groom?" Gillis lifted an eyebrow.

"Now, why should I need one of those?" Aralyn teased back and reached for his hand.

"You'll want an attendant," Mother said.

Aralyn's face fell as she thought of Elnala. That would have been her first choice. Was there anyone else? Not that Aralyn could think of.

Mother sat on a nearby boulder. "When Drehensil came back to Eyndor, he felt he had failed his rider, your father," Mother said. "But he had not failed him. It was the enemy's fault."

Where was Mother going with this? She sometimes changed the subject for seemingly no reason.

"Just like with you, Aralyn. It was the enemy's fault that we lost your stepfather and that Terrwynn was different when she returned. It was never yours." Mother's voice held a gentleness Aralyn had not heard before.

"Neither was Elnala's nor Lemmon's death on your shoulders," Gillis added.

"But the children ... all those children."

"That was Mal'ev and only him." Gillis pulled her close.

"Do not blame yourself." Mother's words were a solid, immovable wall. Not harsh, but not gentle either.

"Aye, she's right, lass."

The three of them grew still, listening to the roar of the falls as they poured down the cliff. The ground shook with their tremendous power. Flashes of brilliant blues and reds where fish swam near the surface in water so clear it almost seemed it wasn't there. Aletha landed nearby and began bathing herself, splashing and making a great ruckus. Water, foamy and white, washed over her, and somehow, she kept herself from floating downstream. She stopped, tilted her head, and looked at Aralyn with one eye. She flew to Aralyn's shoulder, still dripping. Aralyn could feel the healing power as Aletha's wing brushed her. Healing for her sorrow over Terrwynn's absence, her grief for Elnala and Lemmon. And the children. Aletha jumped to Gillis' shoulder, bobbed her head, and made a trilling sound. Gillis closed his eyes. He was undoubtedly thinking of Lemmon. And perhaps Laella. But he was letting the small dragon heal him, too.

Vandel and Elouard glided above them on air currents from the falls. Vandel dove and floated before Aralyn while Elouard dropped to the ground. Aletha joined him. She stirred up insects and snatched them out of the air.

"They're beautiful," Mother remarked. "I had five dragon lizards that followed me when I was younger. They even came to my wedding."

Gillis chuckled. "They should be at ours then."

"That would be perfect." And Aralyn began to sing—a melody that soared through the trees, notes blending with the wind. Gillis joined her, and his harmony mingled with her song. Mother hit a third note that rose above theirs. Aletha and Vandel surprised them when they joined in a counter melody while Elouard snatched up a mouse in the grass. He held it by the tail and watched them all, tilting his head. The wordless music spoke to Aralyn, bringing her peace, healing, and understanding. Gillis held her in his arms. Mother placed her hand on Aralyn's back. The song ended, and she knew Re'ah was right.

She had found what she needed. She had found love. More than she could have imagined.

The End

Acknowledgements

Believe me when I say that writing a novel is far from a one-person job. Like many writers who spend hours on their laptops, I may sometimes feel that way. However, numerous people have contributed to this work as I learned how to put my story down on paper: beta readers, professionals who taught at conventions and online, and all those who cheered me on.

I especially want to acknowledge my husband, Mike, for your positive comments and proofreading.

To my editor, Dori Harrell, who "got" my story and gave me much encouragement and constructive criticism. (Can you believe that I am finally getting this published?)

Special thanks to those who have read past and present drafts of this novel. Your input and encouragement have meant so much to me: Wanda Bush, Donna Copeland, Katherine Briggs, Carole Lehr Johnson, Kim Vandel, and Bruce Hennigan. There are probably others whom I failed to mention, and I do regret that. I'll buy you a cup of coffee (or tea, if you prefer).

To Brookwood Baptist Church and The Well for providing a place to not only drink coffee but also an atmosphere perfect for studying and writing.

To my Heavenly Father for providing a Savior who not only promises life in heaven but an abundant life on this Earth as well. Thank You for showing me Your love every day. May my writing always give You glory.

ABOUT THE AUTHOR

Eileen Keir Copeland is wife to Mike, mother of two children, and grandmother to four. As a follower of Christ, she desires to teach others about the great depths of His love.

A certified road tripper, she enjoys traveling with her husband to various parts of the country. Sometimes they take off, unsure of where they will end up. She hopes to make it to all fifty states one day. Her favorite destination is anywhere there is a beach or snow-capped mountains. Not averse to traveling out of the country, she has been on mission trips to Mexico and Honduras, and visited Canada on vacation.

A retired clinical laboratory scientist, Eileen worked for over thirty years in a hospital lab. She now enjoys writing short stories, which have been published in anthologies.

Eileen is a member of American Christian Fiction Writers and various other writing groups. She enjoys time with friends, drinking coffee, and joining them in Bible Studies. She is active in Faith and Fostering, an organization that cares for young adults who have aged out of the foster care system.

Friend her on Facebook: https:www.facebook.com/
eileen.keircopeland
Also, check out **Eileen's Encouragement** on Facebook.
Instagram: @eileenkeircopeland
Visit:
eileenkeircopeland.com
eileenkeircopeland.wordpress.com

Author's Note

If you enjoyed The Bowsinger, please consider leaving a review wherever you purchased this book. You can also help by spreading the word on social media and by word of mouth. Thank you so much for reading my debut novel!

www.ingramcontent.com/pod-product-compliance
Lightning Source LLC
Chambersburg PA
CBHW060401260626
47160CB00006B/2396